THE PAST AND PRESENT COLLIDE IN THIS TALE OF ART THEFT, FORGERY, AND MURDER

THE PAST, AUGUST 1911: The *Mona Lisa* is stolen by museum worker Vincent Peruggia. During its two-year absence from the Louvre, replicas of the painting are created and sold as the original by a notorious duo of con artists. Several of these forgeries remain at large, prompting more than one art historian to speculate that the museum might well be displaying a fake.

THE PRESENT: Artist and art professor Luke Perrone hunts for the truth behind his most infamous ancestor, Peruggia. His search attracts a reckless INTERPOL detective with something to prove, a beautiful woman who may want more than Luke's affection, and a hornet's nest of the most unscrupulous art collectors and thieves.

A gripping novel exploring the secrets of the 1911 theft and the dark underbelly of today's art world, *The Last Mona Lisa* is a story of heart-stopping suspense as romantic and sexy as it is terrifying and thrilling, one that taps into our universal fascination with da Vinci, the authentic and the fake, and people so driven to acquire priceless works of art, they will stop at nothing to possess them—not even murder.

PRAISE FOR *THE LAST MONA LISA*

"Oh, what a web Jonathan Santlofer weaves in this unputdownable book! *The Last Mona Lisa* brings together past and present, seasons it with intriguing characters, and brushes it with plot twists that you don't see coming to create an unstoppable what-happens-next momentum. Santlofer has outdone himself this time."

—Michael Connelly, #1 *New York Times*
bestselling author of the Harry Bosch
and Lincoln Lawyer series

"Fabulous—instantly immersive, intriguing, and suspenseful, and expert and authentic too... Only a writer who is also an artist—or an artist who is also a writer—could have pulled it off. This feels like the thriller Santlofer was born to write."

—Lee Child, #1 *New York Times* bestselling
author of the Jack Reacher series

"From its seductive first pages, *The Last Mona Lisa* carries us along on an utterly irresistible time-jumping, continent-leaping tale of intrigue and family secrets, obsession, and the ineffable power of art itself. I could not put it down."

—Megan Abbott, bestselling and award-winning
author of *Dare Me* and *The Turnout*

"This is a terrific read—compelling, intelligent, fascinating, and deeply satisfying. It was a book I did not want to end."

—Peter James, UK #1 bestselling author
of the Detective Roy Grace series

"A riveting novel, weaving the real-life 1911 theft of Leonardo's masterpiece into a nail-biting contemporary drama where billionaire collectors, art historians, book collectors, and INTERPOL engage in so many double and triple crosses you're left wondering until the last page whom to trust and whom to fear. *The Last Mona Lisa* is like a master class in how to create a deep understanding of art history while making a seamless thriller."
—Sara Paretsky, *New York Times* bestselling author of the V.I. Warshawski series

"*The Last Mona Lisa* is a pacy, seductive international thriller of the first order. With its seamless blend of action, intriguing maze of family secrets, and the gripping, emotional journal entries of a long-dead art thief, this is a transporting novel, made all the more captivating because of the true story at its heart. Don't miss it!"
—Lisa Unger, *New York Times* bestselling author of *Confessions on the 7:45*

"Astonishingly, Jonathan Santlofer is a brilliant writer of fiction and nonfiction—and a superb visual artist as well. All his skills come together in *The Last Mona Lisa*, and the result is wholly satisfying."
—Lawrence Block, bestselling author of more than fifty novels, including *Eight Million Ways to Die* and *A Walk Among the Tombstones*

"It's hard to imagine another writer who could pull off a feat like *The Last Mona Lisa*, with its combination of thrills, history, and insider knowledge of the art world. A singular achievement by a terrific writer. Really stunning."
—Laura Lippman, *New York Times* bestselling author

"A deliciously tense read that mixes a present-day hunt for the truth with a real-life historical heist to page-turning effect!"

—Ruth Ware, #1 *New York Times* bestselling author of *One by One*

PRAISE FOR *THE DEATH ARTIST*

"A crime novel that is savage and erudite, layered in wit, satire, and psychosis—in short, a chilling read."

—*USA Today*

"Santlofer's insight into the passion at the heart of great art brings this evocative thriller to richly impastoed life."

—Page Turner of the Week, *People* magazine

"A rollercoaster...a sure sense of pace and engaging literary style."

—*Plain Dealer*

"Brisk...inventive...compelling."

—*Washington Post*

PRAISE FOR *COLOR BLIND*

"Smart, lurid, and fascinating, with layered prose and a wealth of detail...vivid and realistic characters who weave their way through the fast-moving plot."

—*Library Journal*

PRAISE FOR *THE KILLING ART*

"Entirely believable... Unsettling... Mr. Santlofer may become even far better known for his writing than for his paintings."
—*New York Times*

PRAISE FOR *ANATOMY OF FEAR*

"A riveting story of a serial killer, a police sketch artist who gets involved in the murders... A tense, psychologically nuanced story that is never less than compelling... The quality of Santlofer's art and the way it becomes a galvanizing force in his prose is stunning."
—*Pittsburgh Tribune*

"Santlofer sure knows how to tell a story! His writing is fluid and vivid, and the illustrations just add this whole other dimension to the suspense, especially toward the end, when things get really manic."
—*San Francisco Chronicle*

PRAISE FOR *THE WIDOWER'S NOTEBOOK*

"Wrenching, heartbreaking, intense, and emotional—but valuable too: we're all approaching the age where this will happen to us—or to others because of us—and understanding that it can be dealt with is consoling. I don't know how Santlofer found the fortitude to write this, but I'm deeply grateful he did. I think the world is a better place with this book in it."
—Lee Child, #1 *New York Times* bestselling author of the Jack Reacher series

"Jonathan Santlofer's stunning *The Widower's Notebook* raises all the blinds on immense and sudden loss, bringing light to all its dark corners. In so doing, he offers a deeply moving, often funny, always big-hearted portrait—not just of grief but of a long and rich marriage brought to vivid life and of a mighty father-and-daughter relationship both tested and enduring. A true gift."

—Megan Abbott, bestselling and award-winning author of *Dare Me* and *The Turnout*

"Deeply moving…beautifully written… It is such an achievement, like running uphill against a strong wind."

—Joyce Carol Oates, National Book Award–winning author

ALSO BY JONATHAN SANTLOFER

The Death Artist
Color Blind
The Killing Art
Anatomy of Fear
The Murder Notebook
The Widower's Notebook: A Memoir

Anthologies as Editor
The Dark End of the Street (with S. J. Rozan)
Inherit the Dead
The Marijuana Chronicles
It Occurs to Me That I Am America

THE
LAST
MONA
LISA

THE LAST MONA LISA

A NOVEL

JONATHAN SANTLOFER

sourcebooks
landmark

Published by Sourcebooks Landmark, an imprint of Sourcebooks
P.O. Box 4410, Naperville, Illinois 60567-4410
(630) 961-3900
sourcebooks.com

Library of Congress Cataloging-in-Publication Data

Names: Santlofer, Jonathan, author.
Title: The last Mona Lisa : a novel / Jonathan Santlofer.
Description: Naperville, Illinois : Sourcebooks, 2021.
Identifiers: LCCN 2020056377 (print) | LCCN 2020056378
(ebook) | (trade paperback) | (hardcover) | (epub)
Classification: LCC PS3619.A58 L37 2021 (print) | LCC PS3619.A58 (ebook)
| DDC 813/.6--dc23
LC record available at https://lccn.loc.gov/2020056377
LC ebook record available at https://lccn.loc.gov/2020056378

Printed and bound in the United States of America.
VP 10 9 8 7 6 5 4 3 2 1

*For Joy, who loved this book from the
beginning and with my deep regret that
she is not here to see it realized.*

BASED ON A TRUE STORY

"Imitation…is a double murder, for it deprives both copy and original of their primitive existence."
—Madame de Staël

"Nothing is original."
—Jim Jarmusch

August 21, 1911
Paris, France

He has spent the night huddled in the dark, mind burning with Bosch-like scenes from hell, hideous monsters, people writhing in flames. He stares into the gloom, knowing that he will spend the rest of his days in darkness.

We lose the things we do not cherish enough, his one thought, his only thought, as he slips into his workman's tunic, buttons it over his street clothes, and opens the closet door.

The museum is unlit, but he has no trouble making his way down the long hall. He knows the layout perfectly, his intention fueled by guilt. The Winged Victory casts a predatory shadow that causes him to shiver though it is stifling, airless.

Her face appears like a specter, beautiful lips cracked, flesh tinged gray. Somewhere, a baby cries. The crying swells to a sickening shriek. He covers his ears and lets out a sob, twisting one way then the other, searching in the dark for his lost love and his child, whispering their names, walls closing in, room tilting, that empty feeling in his gut expanding until that's all he is: a hollow man. Now he understands that the emptiness he has felt for so long has been a foreshadowing, a preview of the rest of his life, that he has been practicing to be a dead man.

Footsteps?

But it's too early, and a Monday, the museum closed to visitors.

He stops and peers into the dim hallway and sees nothing. He must have imagined it, no longer sure what is real and what is not. Gloved hand cupped around his ear, he listens, but it's quiet, only the sound of his own heavy breathing and the scudding of his heart.

A few more steps, through the arch and into the Cour Visconti Gallery, the high-ceilinged room large enough to hold mural-sized paintings. In the dark, the canvases appear as black rectangles though he can picture them: a landscape by Corot, a famous Delacroix battle scene, Jacques-Louis David's *Consecration of the Emperor Napoleon*, the dictator clad in outrageous finery, animal-skin cape, crown of ivy, a smug look of victory on his face.

It is then, as he pictures Napoleon, that his fevered brain comes up with the explanation he will give later, the one the newspapers will print: *I stole the painting to restore it to its rightful home.*

He will be a patriot, a hero, no longer the immigrant, the man without a home.

Steadier now, he heads down another narrower hallway, mind focused and filled with purpose. He will show them he is someone.

In the smaller Salon Carré Gallery, he can just make out the shapes of the paintings, Titian and Correggio and the prize shimmering between them—the lady of the rocks, the vampire who never sleeps, the most famous woman in the world: *Mona Lisa*.

Heart pounding, nerve endings tingling, a dozen thoughts in his brain as he unscrews the small wooden panel from its iron bolts. A man possessed, blind to the shadow of his face reflected, distorted in the glass he himself installed only last week.

It takes all of five minutes.

Then he is moving, the painting clutched to his chest, a shadowy figure darting out one doorway, through another, down a hallway and into a stairwell where he stops to remove the painting's heavy frame and plate glass and leave them behind. Moving again, through a narrow corridor lined with marble sculptures, faster now, panting, sweating, he cuts through an archway until he comes to the side door, the Porte des Arts, all of it exactly as planned, a perfect dream. Until the doorknob does not turn.

He tugs and twists, pulls and jerks, but the knob will not budge, his spinning mind the only thing that is moving.

A deep breath, then another until it comes to him: *the screwdriver, of course!* The same tool he has just used on the bolts he now uses to unscrew the hardware until the doorknob drops into his hand and he stashes it in the pocket of his workman's tunic, which he strips off, rolls up, and tucks firmly into the back of his belt.

He slides the panel under his shirt, aged canvas abrading his skin as he buttons his jacket over it, his heart beating against the mysterious four-hundred-year-old beauty who has witnessed her own abduction more than once, observed countless assignations from the wall of Napoleon's bedroom, and endured the gapes and stares of millions, and now, tired and world-weary, she yearns to rest—but her story is far from over.

1

December 2019
Florence, Italy

Carlo Bianchi dabbed the handkerchief to his dripping nose. His shop, on the Via Stracciatella, not far from the Ponte Vecchio, was small and cramped, books in shelves, on his desk, scattered around the floor in stacks like miniature Mayan villages, everything covered in dust, the place reeking of mold and damp.

Bianchi was looking for a book on rococo garden design, which he knew was here somewhere. He finally found it at the very bottom of a tall stack. Lying on his side, beard picking up lint, he was just inching the book out when he saw the man's thick-soled sneakers.

Bianchi twisted his neck for an angled view. "*Posso aiutarla?*"

The man peered down at him. "Do you speak English?"

"Yes," said Bianchi, getting to his feet, slapping dust from his pants and jacket. "One learns many languages in a lifetime of dealing with books."

"I am looking for a diary, a journal that you recently purchased from a French book dealer named Pelletier."

"Pelletier? Let me think. I should have a list of recent purchases." Bianchi made a show of sorting through a mass of receipts on his desk. He knew every book he sold or purchased, including those to and from the French dealer, Pelletier, though he never gave out a customer's personal information.

"This journal was written over a hundred years ago," the man said. Pelletier had sworn he'd sold the journal to Bianchi, and people rarely told lies when they had just lost a finger and there was the threat of losing another. "Surely, you would remember buying such a book." He laid his hand over Bianchi's, then pressed it against the wooden desktop.

"*Sì, sì*, I remember," Bianchi said. "It was handwritten and in Italian!"

The man eased up, and Bianchi slid his hand out, backing away, practically bowing. "I am sorry…but…the journal… I have already sold it."

"To who?"

"To an old man who collects such things, no one important."

"His name?"

"I don't re—"

The man grabbed Bianchi by the front of his jacket and lifted him off the floor. "The name. *Now.*"

Arms flapping, legs dangling a few inches above the floor, Bianchi gasped the name: "G-Guggliermo!"

The man let go, and Bianchi landed unsteadily, knocking over a tower of books.

"And where might I find this Guggliermo?"

"He…he is a"—Bianchi tried to catch his breath—"a *professore*, at the university—in Firenze—but, but I think he is retired." He stole a glance at the window to see if there was anyone outside, a passerby he might call for help, but the man shifted his body to obscure his view.

"His address."

"I–I am certain if you inquired at the university—"

The man gave him a dead-eyed stare, and Bianchi quickly thumbed through his Rolodex, fingers trembling. He found the card and began to read from it, but the man snatched it from his hand. "You did not read the journal, did you?"

"Me? No, no." Bianchi shook his head back and forth.

"And yet you knew it was handwritten and in Italian."

"Pelletier must have...told me...or...perhaps I glanced at a page, but that was all."

"I see," the man said, lips pulling back to reveal tobacco-stained teeth. He slipped the card into his pocket. "And you will not speak of my visit, not to this Guggliermo, not to anyone."

"No, signore. No. Not even to Pelletier. I would never say a word."

"Of course not," the man said.

Bianchi was still trying to recover his breath and balance when the man thrust a fist into his chest. Bianchi stumbled back, arms flailing, knocking over another stack of books before he fell.

The man lifted him up, hands around his neck, tightening and squeezing.

Bianchi tried to speak, to plead, but managed only a few strangled squawks, the room going in and out of focus.

"No. Not a word," the man said as he felt the bookseller's larynx snap.

2

Two Months Later

The email had arrived less than two weeks ago, and here I was, unable to think of anything else, bolting from my life on a possibility, a whim.

I tried to tamp down my anxiety, stopped to stretch the kinks out of my body, then wheeled my suitcase through one long corridor after another, a mix of exhaustion and adrenaline after an eight-hour flight from New York where I'd been too keyed up to sleep.

Leonardo da Vinci airport was like most: impersonal, crowded, harsh lighting. The fact that it was named for Leonardo struck me as prophetic, though clearly, they hadn't named it for me. I checked the time, 6:00 a.m. Then searched for the airport train and was proud of myself when I found it, slumped into a seat, and closed my eyes, a dozen thoughts buzzing in my brain like gnats.

Thirty-two minutes later, I was in Roma Termini, the train station huge, crowded, a throbbing nest of travelers, but with an element of romance, all those trains hovering just beyond the ticket stalls, belching white smoke into the winter air.

I cut through crowds of people—"*Scusami, scusami*"—thankful to my parents for speaking to me in their native tongue from the time I could crawl, moving from one train to another, clutching my ticket, eyes on the big board searching, for FIRENZE as minutes ticked away. I almost missed my train, listed only by its final destination, Venice, a place I would love to see, but not now when I was on a mission.

The train to Florence was clean and new-looking, the seats comfortable. I got my suitcase onto the rack above, took off my backpack, and twice nodded off to images of pages wafting through the air and me trying and failing to catch them.

I drank a Coke to stay awake and stared out the window, the landscape going from flat to hilly to distant medieval towns dotting the tops of even larger hills, all of it slightly unreal, as if I were in a movie and not on my way to discovering what I hoped would finally answer a hundred-year-old mystery and twenty years of research in pursuit of my family's most infamous criminal.

An hour and a half later, I was outside Florence's bustling train station, Santa Maria Novella, in the center of the city, lugging my suitcase over cobblestone streets, hazy sun dipping in and out of low clouds, the air crisp and cold. I replayed the events of the past two weeks: receiving the email, buying an open-ended ticket, going to the Italian consulate where I sweet-talked a young woman into giving me a cultural *permesso* and a letter stating I was a university art professor, which granted me access to Italian cultural institutions, then the call to my cousin in Santa Fe—a sculptor always eager to make the New York City art scene—who was more than happy to sublet my Bowery loft. A week later, I'd bubble-wrapped my paintings, left my college classes in the hands of my graduate TA, and taken off a week before intersession, a rash move for an assistant professor hoping to get tenure.

I crossed the wide street in front of the train station into a warren of smaller ones, trying to follow my cell phone's GPS that was constantly rerouting. I had to change directions twice but about ten minutes later came into a large rectangular plaza dominated by a sienna-colored chapel with a redbrick dome, the Piazza di Madonna, and there, spotted the hotel, PALAZZO SPLENDOUR, its name spelled out in old electric lettering.

The hotel's lobby was the size of a cramped Manhattan kitchen, the walls in need of a paint job, floors of badly cracked white-variegated marble, the only decoration a faded black-and-white photo of Michelangelo's *David*.

"Luke Perrone," I said to the guy behind the desk—youngish, ropy arms laced with badly inked tattoos, handsome in a drug-addicted sort of way, puffing on a cigarette, cell phone crooked between his ear and shoulder.

"*Passaporto*," he said without looking up. When I asked in my best Italian if I could leave my suitcase and come back later, he held up a finger as if I were disturbing his call, obviously personal unless he called all the hotel guests "*il mio amore*." I didn't wait for his answer, left my suitcase, and headed out.

Google Maps said San Lorenzo was five minutes away, which seemed easy enough, though I walked the wrong way before realizing I was reading the map upside down. I backtracked, rounded the domed chapel in Piazza di Madonna one more time, and followed the route, which led me alongside a series of stacked, ochre structures, then past a long expanse of ragged stone wall with stairs leading to blind arches, which ended at the corner. Piazza San Lorenzo was open and mostly empty, except for a few tourists and a couple of monks in long, brown smocks.

I tried to take it in, realizing what I had passed and where I stood were all part of one vast complex.

Directly ahead, the sand-colored basilica was rough and unfinished-looking, its three arched entrances with heavy wooden doors, all of them shut. To the left of the church was a smaller arch and a dark alleyway, which led me into the famous cloister of San Lorenzo, a place I had only seen in pictures.

A few steps in and it was as if I were entering a dream, the square garden with its hexagonal-shaped hedges and two-story loggia, classic and harmonious, all of it designed by my favorite Renaissance architect, Brunelleschi. For a moment, I tried to imagine I was an artist of the High Renaissance and not some struggling New York painter who taught art history to pay the bills.

I sighed, my breath a fog in the late-morning chill, everything in the courtyard covered in a silvery frost. Three monks in long, woolen smocks were wrapping plants with burlap while I shivered in my thin leather jacket. I hadn't thought it would be so cold in Florence. To be honest, I hadn't thought about much after receiving the email.

Dear Mr. Perrone,

One of Professor Antonio Guggliermo's last requests was that I get in touch with you regarding what may have been your great-grandfather's journal. The professor had planned some sort of publication about the journal, which he claimed would be a "revelation." Sadly, his sudden death prevented him from ever writing it.

The journal, along with the professor's books and papers, has been donated to the Laurentian Library in Florence, Italy. I was the one to catalog his works and placed the journal in a box labeled "High Renaissance Masters."

To see Professor Guggliermo's documents, you will need to obtain a cultural *permesso*, which should not be difficult.

If you request the papers, I suggest you do not mention

anything about the journal and would prefer that you kept my name out of the request.

Sincerely,
Luigi Quattrocchi
Quattrocchi@italia.university.org

I had contacted Quattrocchi right away, and he'd emailed back sounding serious and sane, assuring me of the journal's existence though he couldn't guarantee its authenticity.

For years, I'd been writing letters and emails for any information regarding my great-grandfather. Most went unanswered. The ones who did answer invariably demanded money, but none had ever panned out. This time, the information had come free of charge and with no ulterior motive—at least none I could see.

"*Scusi, signore,*" said one of the monks, young, with a russet-colored beard and startling blue eyes. "You wait for library to open?"

"Yes!" I practically bit his head off, then apologized. "You speak English."

"A little," the monk said.

I told him I spoke Italian.

"*Il bibliotecario e' spesso in ritardo,*" he said. The librarian is often late.

I checked my watch. It was exactly ten; the library was supposed to be open.

The monk asked where I was from and I said, "New York, but my people are from Ragusa," though I had never been to the Sicilian town and hadn't meant to say where my family had been from; I hadn't meant to say anything.

The monk extended his hand. "Brother Francesco."

"Luke Perrone," I said and glanced back at the door that led up to the library.

"It will open soon," he said. "*Pazienza*."

Patience, right. Never my strong suit, and clearly not now, when I'd bolted from my life on nothing more than a hunch.

I watched Brother Francesco rejoin the others in the garden, noted him whispering, then all three monks looking my way, their eyes narrowed in the cold winter light. I moved into the shadow of the arches to avoid their stares, leaned back against a pillar, pictured my Bowery loft and the haphazard collection I'd begun as a boy in my Bayonne, New Jersey, bedroom. It now filled an entire corner of my painting studio: copies of hundred-year-old newspaper stories, a floor plan of the museum with my great-grandfather's escape route mapped out in red marker, a metal file cabinet crammed with articles detailing the theft and various theories, one drawer devoted to the letters and emails I had begun writing as a teenager to anyone who might know anything about the crime or about my great-grandfather—and the answers, which were few and rarely, if ever, illuminating.

A cold wind whipped through the cloister, and I shivered. A tap on the arm, and I flinched.

The young monk again. "*Mi scusi, ma la biblioteca e' aperta.*"

I gave him a quick nod, then headed down the arched path to the wooden door, which now stood open.

3

John Washington Smith read the emails for a second time. Like everyone in INTERPOL's Art Theft Division, it was his job to watch all the obvious communiques and websites—antiquities dealers, art galleries, anyone suspected of smuggling or selling stolen art or artifacts—all of it continuously updated on one of his three computer screens. Of particular interest to him—something that had, over the years, become an obsession—was the 1911 theft of Leonardo's most famous painting, what went on during its two-year disappearance, and the idea that the *Mona Lisa* in the Louvre Museum today was not the original. For years, he'd heard the rumor that the thief, Vincenzo Peruggia, had kept a prison diary, something that had never been confirmed. But here was the thief's great-grandson, Luke Perrone, an American artist and art historian—someone he'd had under communication surveillance for years—emailing with an Italian professor about just such a diary.

Smith slipped off his glasses and pinched the bridge of his nose, a headache between his eyes. The result of too many hours staring at the pulsing light of the computer screens arranged in a wide U that filled most of his desk, a white Formica slab balanced on thin metal legs, jointed in such a way as to remind him of ET. The wireless keyboard and mouse were also white, as were the boxy file cabinets that formed the other end of the unit. White ceiling. White walls. Pale-gray tiles on the floor in a "nubby" pattern to give the illusion of being a rug. The tiles were slightly springy too, and Smith often wondered if that was for the benefit of the INTERPOL workers' feet or to create a virtually soundless space, though it hardly mattered since all the researchers wore some form of sneaker or walking shoe. Smith's were thick-soled white Nikes, which he kept clean with a soapy toothbrush.

Smith read the emails again, tamping down his excitement while taking stock of his options. He could notify the local authorities and have them watch Perrone and this Italian professor or issue one of the eight color notices INTERPOL used to designate the degree of a suspected crime—a red notice being the highest—but there was no evidence of a crime, not even any wrongdoing, not yet. No way could he get the general secretariat to issue such a notice.

Smith glanced at the computer screen on his left, the one reserved for data on international art objects currently missing or stolen and the date they had disappeared. Art theft and forgery were serious crimes, and the people involved—collectors, thieves, and middlemen—were not only unscrupulous but often danger-ous. According to INTERPOL's statistics, art theft alternated between the agency's number three and four spots in priority and importance, just below drug dealing, arms smuggling, and money laundering. Smith took it seriously, the way he did everything, like the daily calisthenics and weight lifting, which had added considerable muscle mass to his almost six-foot frame. The idea of being weak or perceived as such, something a black kid from Manhattan's Baruch Houses project had learned early he could not afford. Smith had never known his father, though he had taken the man's last name as his middle, a way to make the ordinary-sounding name more memorable.

He checked the time, nearly noon. Along with the headache, his back had started to ache after four hours of sitting since the drive from his one-bedroom apartment on the outskirts of Lyon, then fighting the city's traffic to get to the steel-and-glass monolith of INTERPOL's international headquarters, something he did every day, twice a day.

He needed a break, time to think, and a cigarette.

The cylindrical elevator took him down to the octagonally shaped courtyard in the center of the building. There were a few people here, though the cool minimal space made them appear unreal, like androids. Smith wondered if he looked robotic too, though he doubted robots smoked Marlboro Lights. He inhaled deeply while debating the pros and cons of what he was considering, knowing it was strictly against INTERPOL policy.

A look up at the courtyard's angled enclosures reminded him of the Baruch Houses' walls, both spaces a kind of prison, though these were graffiti-free and there was no one lurking in the shadows selling weed, meth, or H. Ironic, he thought, having traded one prison for another, though he had imagined this one would offer not only a way out but also success and glory. Was it too late for that? Another pull on his cigarette, a thought taking shape as if the smoke were skywriting in his lungs or on his brain: *If you are ever going to succeed, ever make a name for yourself, you need to do this*. Smith eyed the people across the space and wondered if they could read his thoughts. He had done things in his life he was not proud of; some he had never confessed to anyone. But could he do this?

He was still debating that when he finished his cigarette,

continued to debate it in the elevator, was still debating it and all that was at stake, as he made his way across the analysts' soundless floor. He passed researchers in open cubicles, others in what looked like small padded cells, three walls of tufted gray material to muffle conversation, used when one researcher needed to speak privately to another. He slowed down at a glassed-in conference room where an analysts' meeting was in progress, one he had not been invited to. He hurried past, fists balled at his side, neck muscles tightening, crossed the space, and sagged into the ergonomic chair behind his desk.

At forty-seven, he was still a criminal intelligence analyst, just one of many in INTERPOL's Art Theft Division. Every year, he saw other, less dedicated analysts ascend the ranks to join the General Assembly, INTERPOL's governing body, while he was passed over. Twenty years of logging data and research, twenty years since graduating from New York's John Jay College of Criminal Justice with a degree in data science and cryptography, and what did he have to show for it? A chair behind a computer ten hours a day.

Smith heaved a sigh, sat back, and stared up at the long, flat tubes of warm incandescent light. He needed to do something, something big, something unique, something that would be talked about, something to show the men and women at the top he was someone special.

He leaned forward and reread the emails between the two men, then routed them, along with their texts and calls, to his personal email and cell phone, something that would not be questioned—particularly as no one else would see it. He dragged his cursor down a column of documents and files he had been compiling for years, all of them pertaining to the notorious art theft, and opened one labeled PERRONE. His center computer screen filled with every known fact on the man: the almost twenty-year correspondence Luke Perrone had conducted with various people regarding his great-grandfather, his art exhibitions and teaching jobs, high school suspensions (there were four, one for smoking in the boys' room, two for classroom fistfights, one for gang affiliation), a list of women Perrone had dated for more than six months—there were many—with subdocuments on each, a DWI at sixteen, an arrest for breaking and entering, supposedly expunged as Perrone had been a minor, though working at INTERPOL had made it easy for Smith to tap into Bayonne's police records and obtain a copy, as well as documents on Perrone's parents and relatives.

Smith added the recent emails to the file. He found the number for the Carabinieri Comando Provinciale in Florence to inform the local Italian police, as was procedure, the way things were done at INTERPOL. He began to press it into his cell phone and stopped—a brief moment to consider the consequences—then called the Lyon airport and booked a flight to Florence.

4

Florence, Italy

At the end of the cloister, I headed through the open door, then an enclosed stairwell to the upper level of the loggia, all that pent-up energy propelling me forward. At the top, a faded fresco of the Annunciation caught my eye but didn't stop me. A guard, sitting at the library's entrance, a woman in plain clothes, went through my backpack, then waved me through.

The Laurentian Library's famous five-hundred-year-old vestibule was much smaller than I'd imagined, but it hardly mattered. All I could see was Michelangelo's grand freestanding staircase and the way it filled the room like a living, breathing thing. I imagined the stone in liquid form spilling forward like waves of lava, hardening and taking the shape of stairs, the movement trapped within.

The center staircase was cordoned off, so I took a smaller, flanking one and mounted the stairs slowly, one step, then another, as if I were not only walking up but into the past.

The library stretched out in front of me, long and rectangular, awesome and reverential. I was careful to stay on the rug that protected the delicate mosaic floor as I headed down the aisle, glanced up at the coffered wooden ceiling, then the stained glass windows that filled the room with warm natural light, which spilled over pew-like wooden benches. A childhood memory: crammed in a pew between my father and mother, the after-odor of beer, my father's breakfast chaser, loitering on his breath as he read responsively and I dreamed of getting out.

It was then it hit me that the benches were cordoned off and I was alone, not a single scholar nor visitor in the room. Then a moment of confusion followed by panic: would the journal really be here, in this mausoleum? Did *anyone* read in here? Had Quattrocchi made the whole thing up?

I reversed my steps, stopping by a young woman at a small desk hidden beside the entrance, and leaned over. "*Scusami...*" The word amplified, echoing in the space. "How do I...request books...papers?"

"In *here?*" Her face screwed up. "Is not possible. This is a monument. No longer a functioning library."

"*What?* Since *when?*"

"A long time. My mother studied here, but it has been thirty years."

"No, that can't be. I've come all this way—" I tried to think, got my backpack off, found the *permesso* and the letter. "But...I have this."

The young woman looked the papers over. "Is okay."

"Is it? *How?* If the library is closed—"

"*Devi calmati, signore.* Calm down." She reached out and patted my arm. "You want the research library. Next door. Just outside. Ask the guard in front."

I took a deep breath and a minute to process her words, then thanked her, turned, and headed down Michelangelo's grand staircase, this time practically running.

The guard out front perused my letter, then pointed to a heavy wooden door decorated with large nailheads like bullets, beside it a worn metal plaque, Medicea Laurenziana Studios, and a modern-looking box with buttons for a code and a bell, which I pressed, hard.

The woman who answered wore a cheery flowered dress though there was nothing cheery about her: midforties, cropped hair, tight-lipped, glasses hanging from a chain around her neck, which she raised to read my letter. She handed it back to me without a word. Inside, she took my backpack before ushering me through a full body scanner.

When the alarm sounded, I emptied my pockets, keys and change deposited into her waiting outstretched palm. Then I walked through again. When I set off the alarm for a second time, she put up a hand for me to wait, disappeared, and returned with a gray-bearded man in a baggy wool vest, who patted me down, torso and sides, up and down my legs and inner thighs, stopping just short of my crotch, the whole time avoiding eye contact.

The tight-lipped woman got my cell phone out of the backpack, held it up, and pointed to a sign on the wall: Niente Telefono. Niente Fotos. "I will hold," she said, "give back when you leave." She dropped the phone into a wire mesh basket on her desk, then continued to rustle around in the backpack and came up with a small box of hard candy, which she inspected as if it were a bomb.

"*Caramella,*" I said, "You know, candy."

"*Mangiare nella biblioteca e' vietato!*" she barked.

I promised not to eat any and made the sign of the cross, a vestigial tic from my strict Catholic upbringing. She looked me over, squinting. I smoothed my hair behind my ears, wished I'd gotten a haircut and taken the time to shave, the whole time feeling as if I were waiting for my high school principal to tell me I was suspended.

She took my laptop out of the backpack, set it aside, then

found the small bag of Jolly Ranchers. "*Mangiare vietato!*" she said again and tossed the bag into the wire basket. She slid the laptop back into my backpack, handed it to me, stared at me another moment while speaking in Italian to the man who had all but cavity-searched me, as if I could not understand. What she'd said was, "Show him into the research room but keep an eye on him."

The gray-bearded guy led me through a small room with a wall of card-catalog boxes, a glass-topped wooden table stacked with books, and a large hissing radiator. Then, into the actual research room, medium-sized and brightly lit, three walls lined with books, a long table that stretched from one end to the other. Two librarians, both women, seated at small desks, looked up when I came in. The bearded guy, who introduced himself as Riccardo, turned out to be a librarian as well and a lot nicer away from the commandant out front. In a hushed tone, he indicated that the long table was for scholars, like me, to read, that I would request any books or papers from the head librarian at the front of the room, then introduced me to her.

She raised her reading glasses and tilted her head with a look both shy and flirtatious before offering a hand with nails painted bright fuchsia. Perhaps fifty, attractive and voluptuous in a tight sweater, she asked where I was from in a throaty whisper and, when I said New York City, said she'd never been but wanted to go. In my best Italian, I said I would happily show her around if she did. She smiled, then cast a look toward the outer office and whispered an apology if "Mussolini" had given me a hard time. She said her name was Chiara, and she was there to assist me in any way, then angled her chin toward the desk beside hers, "Beatrice," she said, "*il mio assistente.*" The young woman, in her twenties, thick glasses and a loose sweater, looked up, ticked a nervous smile, then quickly returned to her work.

Chiara handed me a request form, which I filled out exactly as Quattrocchi had instructed: *Guggliermo, High Renaissance Masters*. She studied it a moment, then handed it to Riccardo, who gripped a metal book caddy beside her desk and disappeared into a back room while Chiara interviewed me: Had I been to Italy before? Did I have friends or family here? How long did I intend to stay? Then she told me to have a seat at the long table—anywhere I'd like—and watched me as I chose a spot facing her though on the far side and at the far end. I wasn't sure why, but I wanted as much privacy as possible.

I tried to get comfortable but could not relax, anxious to see if the journal actually existed.

Two men came in and took seats at the other end of the table, both in their midthirties, both wearing glasses, one with a close-cropped beard, the other with a mustache, a goatee, and a ponytail.

While I waited, I got my laptop out and plugged the charger into one of the outlets on the tabletop. I sat back, drummed my nails, and immediately stopped, the sound echoing, everyone in the room staring at me. I offered an apologetic smile, then closed my eyes and pictured the altar in my Bowery studio, the years of accumulated inquiry concerning my great-grandfather's theft, all the theories without conclusions, all the questions without answers.

I heard the book caddy's metal wheels and opened my eyes to see a long, flat white carton, Riccardo wheeling it toward me. He placed it on the desk, then wheeled the caddy away.

I stared at it a moment. Touched it as if to be sure it was real. Then raised the lid.

Inside, a stack of manila folders, each identified with neat hand-lettering: High Renaissance in Florence, Early Renaissance in Siena, Notes on Mannerism. It was clear Guggliermo was a very organized man. I plucked one out, then two, then three, then four, the stack growing. It was a few more before I saw it: a blue notebook wrapped and tied with coarse twine.

I sucked in a breath and cadged a look at the front desk: Chiara going through papers, Beatrice sorting index cards; then at the two men, both with open books, both typing on their laptops.

I placed the carton's lid on one of the wooden book holders the library provided, using it as a kind of shield, around that a few stacks of folders to create a little fort though I took pains to make it look unintentional. Then, I took the notebook out of the carton and untied the string. The cover looked worn, and I raised it carefully. The paper was unlined, slightly yellowed.

At the bottom of the first page, a signature, in pencil, small and neat: *Vincenzo Peruggia*.

I reached for my backpack to retrieve the sample I had xeroxed from the back of the mug shot and brought with me.

I held it beside the journal page and compared the writing. It was identical.

Below Peruggia's signature in the same tiny script was one line: *La mia storia*.

5

21 dicembre 1914
Murate Prison, Firenze, Italia

Non ho dormito in molte notti...
   I have not slept in many nights.

*The mattress is thin. With every turn I feel the stone floor below. The cell
is freezing. The plaster walls damp. The prison unheated. My blanket is
threadbare and scratchy. I pace to keep warm. I count my steps. One foot
in front of the other. Six steps one way. Nine the other.*
   *There is no sink. No toilet. Once a week we are permitted a cold
shower. There is one barred window. But not really a window at all. It
looks into a narrow corridor where the guards spy on us. The only relief
is our daily exercise in the courtyard. A place the sun dares not shine.*
   *I think of my trial and feel shame. I argued with the judge and
prosecutor and my own lawyer. I played the madman. The victim. The
so-called patriot. But I am no patriot.*
   My sentence was fair. One year and three months. I deserved worse.
   *Every day I receive gifts. Cigarettes. Wine. Food. Letters from
women who say they love me! But the only gift of value is the notepad
and pencils given to me by a guard who took pity on me. If Simone
could see me now would she think me a fool? In prison while those two*

scoundrels go free. I think of them day and night. Of getting what I am owed. Of getting even.

I try not to shiver as I write. To hold the pencil firm.

I close my eyes and imagine our apartment on rue Ramponneau. I see myself walking up the old wooden stairs and opening the front door. Simone greets me. I feel such sadness and such longing my eyes fill with tears.

But I need to think how to begin. How to explain how everything in my life went wrong.

I would say it began with good news.

6

December 1910
Paris

"Oh, Vincent, Vincent, I am so happy." Simone twirled around the bed, a mattress on the floor covered with two tattered woolen blankets on top of which lay three embroidered pillows she had bargained for at the sprawling marketplace of Les Halles. And she had done well, her eye sharp, always looking for inexpensive ways to brighten their dreary flat. Her thick blond hair whipped around her perfect oval face, her eyes glittering.

Vincent watched her spin, feeling something open up inside him, always surprised that this intelligent, delicate beauty had settled for him when she could have had any man in Paris. Her black smock-dress, the only concession she made to her current condition, billowed out, exposing an inch of white petticoat and tightly laced ankle boots, three years old, though on Simone, everything looked fashionable. Above them, coarse black leggings she wore both inside and out, their sixth-floor walk-up frigid, December in Paris as bleak and gray as some Siberian outpost.

Simone tugged at Vincent's jacket playfully. "I *insist* on your happiness!" she said, twirling again, then stopping to catch her breath.

Vincent got an arm around her waist, but she pressed her hand against his chest and took a step back as if to say, *You needn't hold on to me, I won't topple*, though he kept his hand in place.

"I am fine," she said.

"Rest, my darling, please."

"No," she said, her naturally red lips in a pout. "I am *fine*." Then, painting on a smile, she said, "This exhibition, it is what you have wanted, dreamed of."

"Yes," he said, trying hard to feel excited though there was a knot in his chest where there should have been release.

"Le Salon de la Nationale!" Simone's voice filled with pride. "The twentieth *anniversaire*, bigger and more important than ever, the best of Parisian art! I hear Rodin will be exhibiting. Imagine, Vincent, *your* paintings beside Rodin's masterful bronzes!"

He nodded, allowing himself to feel just a bit of pride.

"Oh, Vincent, this is so wonderful," she said, her breathing still a bit labored.

"Sit, Simone, please."

"It was just my silly twirling. I am perfectly fine."

Vincent kept an eye on her as he opened a tin of La Paz, shook some of the tobacco into a paper, and rolled it between his thumb and forefinger to create a thin cylinder. Looking at the cigarette reminded him of Paul Cézanne's words about seeing in nature the cone, sphere, and cylinder, words that Picasso and Braque, even his old friend Max Jacob, had taken to heart. Vincent frowned as he stuck the cigarette into his mouth. "The cubists—" he said, spitting the word.

"Oh, please, Vincent, not now." Simone gave him a severe look. "You *must* be happy. I insist upon it!"

He sighed, trying hard to take in the fact that two of his paintings would be included in the largest exhibition of the Paris season. "The fire, has it gone out?" he said, changing the subject, quickly heading into the only other room, one that Simone had transformed into another world, painting green vines and ivy from floor to ceiling in the style of a Chinese scroll. Miss Stein had called it droll and entertaining when she came for tea, though she had assumed it was Vincent's work; she rarely spoke to Simone, who, on their last visit to Miss Stein's 27 rue de Fleurus salon, had been relegated to her frightening, hook-nosed companion, Miss Toklas, the one who always talked to the *wives*. That visit had been almost a year ago. Their usual outings to galleries and ateliers had become less and less frequent as Vincent became more and more taciturn, even bitter, though Simone hoped this exhibition would change that.

She stopped Vincent from adding another log to the stove. "Do not waste the wood," she said. "Let's go out. We need to celebrate!" She threw her arms around his neck and kissed his cheek.

He wanted to say *And where will we get the money?* His meager salary was spent on books and art supplies, the rest tucked away in a small nest egg for the baby.

Simone stamped her foot. "We are celebrating and that is *that*! You will not argue with me today, Monsieur Peruggia!"

"I am not arguing," he said, and how could he? Simone, who never complained, not about the cold, nor the shared bathroom in the hall, nor the lack of money. He had not provided her with much. How could he deprive her of a small celebration?

He looked into her lovely face, fuller than usual from pregnancy, and managed a smile. He was to be a father, something he had never imagined. Still, he worried. Simone had a history of frailty and illness that attacked her lungs, persistent colds and coughs that lingered, a bout with pneumonia last winter. Though right now, she glowed.

"All right," he said, stepping in between stacks of books, many dog-eared and scribbled with notes, his life-long quest to overcome his lack of formal education. "I have something to tell you about what I was doing today at the Louvre."

"Tell me," she said.

"Not yet," he said, teasing. "At supper."

In minutes, Simone had pinned her hair up under a cloche hat, then tugged on a heavy sweater, the wool stretching over her newly expanded frame.

"Come," she said, extending her delicate hand.

Outside, Vincent wrapped his arm around Simone's shoulder, and she tucked herself into his side. He felt proud. And a little hopeful. Perhaps this exhibition would bring him the sales they so desperately needed. *Yes,* he said to himself, *things will get better.* He watched Simone slide her hands inside her sweater and rest them on her swollen belly. He could not believe they would soon be having a child.

They made their way across the Canal Saint-Martin. "Built by Napoleon," he said, his head crammed with the many facts he had read. Then, along the hilly rue de Belleville where they stopped for a view of the city below, the mix of gaslights and the new electric lights like incandescent fireflies.

"It is always so beautiful," Simone said, her breath generating white clouds as she spoke.

Vincent said nothing; Paris was neither his home nor his city. He had never felt welcomed here, always an outsider, except with Simone.

Once they left their poor, bohemian neighborhood, the smell of slightly soured goat's milk and garbage was exchanged for clean, cold air tinged with the aroma of chestnuts sold on corners in little paper bags that Vincent sometimes brought home, washed down with cold white wine, and called dinner.

When Simone grew tired, they took one of the new motorized omnibuses to the Place des Vosges, with its fine homes and mansions, which Vincent pointed out had once played host to Cardinal Richelieu, Victor Hugo, courtesans, and queens. One day, he thought, he would buy them a grand house like one of these. Simone deserved it, this woman whom he loved beyond description.

At the rue de Rivoli, there was traffic—the new motorcars and taxis overtaking the horse-drawn coaches—and they got off the omnibus to walk along the river where it was quieter. The trees were bare, gray trunks, spindly branches. A tugboat dragged a barge along the water, a swarm of seabirds above, squawking. The wind picked up, rustling Vincent's thick black hair and lifting Simone's wide skirt, which she struggled to keep down.

"Are you warm enough, my darling?" Vincent asked, always worried about her delicate health.

"Yes," she said. "I am wonderful!" Simone got her skirt in place and smiled up at him.

He knew she would not admit she was cold and ruin their time out together. He offered her one of his rare smiles and kissed her forehead.

They kept walking, debating where they might eat. Simone suggested one café; Vincent countered with another, cheaper one. Then suddenly he said, "We will eat at La Pêche Miraculeuse!"

"*What?*" Simone stopped walking and turned to face him. "Am I really with Vincenzo Peruggia, the man who complains of having no money from the moment he rises until the moment he sleeps?"

"I never sleep," he said, which was true, but he laughed, and Simone did too. "It is a celebration, a splurge, and we shall do it!"

With his arm wrapped more tightly around her, they passed the statue of Henri Quatre where the Île de la Cité came to a sharp point and into the small park at the river's edge. Just beyond, a tugboat blasted curls of smoke into the sky, everything gray, black, and white like a painting by Edouard Manet, whom Simone had come to admire and even emulate in her paintings.

Just beyond the park was the restaurant with its view over the Seine.

Inside, a din of chatter and clatter, the smell of seafood mixing with cigarettes.

"Oysters," Vincent proclaimed as soon as they'd been seated at a table beside a window, which he had insisted upon. "And a bottle of your finest Muscadet."

The waiter arched an eyebrow.

"Is there a problem?" Vincent asked, glowering and smoothing his threadbare jacket.

"No, monsieur," the waiter said and darted away.

"Did you see the way he looked at me? As if I did not belong here, as if I am an alien, a criminal!"

"Hush," Simone said. "Do not spoil this. It was nothing."

"*Nothing?* He looked at me as if I were some beggar come to rob his fancy restaurant."

"Vincent, *please*, not now."

Vincent lowered his head, humbled.

Simone lifted his chin with her delicate hand. "I am here with the smartest, handsomest man in the room."

"Smartest?"

"Who reads and studies more than you?" she asked. "Though I see you do not dispute handsomest!" she said. "And soon to be the most successful!"

Vincent could not help but smile.

When the oysters came, Vincent and Simone squeezed lemon on them and ate slowly, sipping salty water from the shells. They finished the bottle of wine and Vincent, possibly a little drunk, ordered a second bottle to drink with the *pommes de terre à l'huile*, potatoes cooked in oil with warm, crusty bread for dipping.

"What is it you wanted to tell me," Simone asked, "about your work today?"

"Well, you know Gaston Ticolat, that bastard who rules our conservation department like a tyrant, always calling me 'Immigrant,' bossing me around, ordering me to do this, do that—" He took a deep breath. "Never mind that. What I want to tell you is what he assigned me to do, to fit paintings with glass."

"Paintings under *glass*? But it will make them impossible to see, the glare—"

"Perhaps, but the museum has decided they must protect their masterpieces. Though again, that is not the point. The point is *which* paintings will now have glass, and *which* painting, just today, I was working on."

Simone leaned across the table, the candlelight reflecting in her eyes, turning them gold. "Which one?"

Vincent held the moment. He enjoyed the expectant look on his beloved's face. "Guess," he said, smiling broadly, such a rarity that Simone played along, tapping a finger against her lips.

"Courbet's *Allegory*."

"No, no, that painting is too large for any glass, and you know that," he said, the smile gone, his lazy right eye appearing even smaller when he frowned.

"Oh, don't look like that," Simone said.

It made him feel bad that he had so little patience with this extraordinary woman, but he wanted his story to match the thrill he had felt, and he wanted to impress her. "One more guess."

"That ghastly Titian in the Salon Carré?"

"No, but you are warm."

"*Tell me!*" Simone reached across the table and gave his arm a playful slap.

"None other than Leonardo's lady."

"*No!*" Simone's eyes widened "It cannot be!"

"*Yes!* I held her in my hands."

"The *Mona Lisa?* You are lying!"

"I had her *this* close to my face." Vincent indicated a fraction of an inch with his fingers. "I could see every detail—the mountains and paths, the fine brushwork of her hair, even the cracks in the glazed surface."

Simone's eyes widened further. "What was it *like*, Vincent? How did you *feel?*"

The question took him by surprise. What had he felt? *Thrilled?* Yes. *Excited?* Absolutely. Though months later, he would tell himself that at the moment what he had felt was envy—that Leonardo had created something he could never make, something perfect in every way—and that he wanted to remove it from the world forever.

"May I see her?" Simone asked.

"Of course. You can come to that wretched graveyard of art any day and gawk at the painting like everyone else."

"Oh, Vincent, what a thing to say. One day, your work, and perhaps even mine, will be in such a *graveyard*. But I meant, when you next get to hold the painting, may I come to see it in your hands?"

"Ticolat would never allow it."

"Well then, I have a better idea," she said. "Bring the painting home for me, and I will hang it over our bed!" Simone laughed and Vincent laughed too, though he thought he would bring it home for her if he could, that he would do anything for her, anything at all.

When they finished their food and were sipping sweet café crème, Simone said, "Oh, Vincent. This was perfect," and he agreed, though despite all the food and drink, he was aware of an emptiness inside him.

After dinner, they walked through the Tuileries Garden, past a fountain with its water turned off and rectangular flower beds where nothing was in bloom. Vincent kept his arm around Simone, and she pretended to be warm and he pretended he was full and content, though still he felt empty.

When he saw that Simone was shivering, he insisted they spend the money to take the omnibus once again, and later, even after they made love and he lay on the mattress with his hand on the rise of her belly and watched her sleep and gently tugged the wool blanket up to her chin, even then, as he marveled at the fine beauty of this woman who was his, he felt empty. And later, when he couldn't sleep and got up to pace in the room Simone had painted with green vines and ivy and to stare out the window at the half-built dome of the new Sacré-Coeur church illuminated in the moonlight, he felt it still.

From a stack of books, he picked up Baudelaire's poems *Les Fleurs du Mal* and read a stanza about death and decay. Hands shaking, he replaced the book quickly, though the poet's words echoed and lingered.

In the morning, Simone had a cold and did not feel well enough to go to her job at the drapery store. Vincent made a pot of tea and put enough wood in the stove so she would stay warm while he was at work at the museum. Before he left, he kissed her and felt it again, this time even stronger than before, though still he could not quite identify it, this feeling of emptiness.

It would be months before he figured out what it was, but by then, it would be too late.

7

The sound of footsteps broke my concentration, a blond with high-heeled boots click-clacking on the hard wooden floor. I watched as she made her way toward Chiara's desk, tugging off long leather gloves dramatically as if she were in a play. We locked eyes, and she seemed to be looking at me or through me or perhaps not at all before she turned away, leaning down to fill out a request form, her back to the room while she waited for her books, holding her gloves in one hand and thwacking them into her palm, a hypnotic gesture. Her shearling coat was ochre-colored, like so many of the buildings I'd seen in Florence, and I wondered if she'd bought it to blend in with the city, though it looked expensive, the kind of coat that gets noticed.

Riccardo returned with her books, and when she gave him a big smile, he blushed. Then she scooped the books up and held them against her chest like a schoolgirl and headed toward the table. I noticed the other men had stopped working too, watching her as she chose a spot at the far end of the table, away from everyone. She took her time getting settled, slipping out of her coat and arranging it on the back of her chair, more time looking at one book, then the other, the whole time playing with a few blond tendrils that had escaped the slapdash twist of her hair. I pretended to be reading but couldn't stop staring at her or the long curve of her neck. She glanced over at me, and I looked down at the journal, trying to remember why I was here, thinking again about what I had just read.

Over the years of collecting information about my great-grandfather, I'd never read anything about him being among the artists of the Salon de la Nationale and wondered if something had happened to bar him from the exhibition. But then, I'd never come across a mention of him being an artist at all. It was oddly comforting and made sense in a way—neither of my parents were artistic, nor my grandparents from what I knew—that at least one of my ancestors should be an artist. I tried to imagine what sort of paintings my great-grandfather had made and hoped I would find out. I jotted a note to look into the salon exhibition, then checked my watch. I was surprised to see I'd been reading for hours and that it was nearly one. I wanted to keep going and would have, but the library was closing for lunch, and I had a date with Luigi Quattrocchi, the man whose email had brought me here.

I placed the journal back into the carton, careful to cover it with Professor Guggliermo's folders before bringing it to the front desk. I already felt a kind of ownership—as if the journal had been waiting for me and me alone all these years.

I could have gone around my end of the table, which was shorter, but eased my way down the long end, where the blond was seated. She looked up as I passed, and we exchanged another glance. She was even prettier than I'd first thought, her face lit as if from within and with the kind of posture that suggested finishing school. *Out of my league*, I told myself, though it didn't stop me from another glance, our eyes meeting again, though she looked down quickly and buried her face in a book, as if I'd caught her doing something wrong.

In the outer office, "Mussolini" took my backpack, searched through it, then handed it back along with my phone. When I asked for my candy, she plucked it out of the wire basket and held it with the tips of her fingers as if it were some kind of poison and she did not want to touch it, then directed me through the body scanner with a less-than-gentle nudge.

Outside, I took a moment to look down at the garden below, its hexagon shape clearer from above, then across to the other side of the upper cloister where I thought I saw something or someone moving, not a monk, a man in plain clothes, though I couldn't be sure, the arcade cloaked in darkness.

8

The restaurant's cream-colored walls were dotted with framed stills from old black-and-white Italian movies. The clientele young, students I guessed. They looked the same the world over—here a bit more stylish, the boys with scarves coiled around their necks, the girls in V-neck pullovers and skintight jeans. A heavyset man, older by thirty or forty years, waved me over. I made my way through the tightly packed tables, generic techno-pop adding an electric throb to the din, everyone talking and smoking cigarettes, my eyes already stinging.

Quattrocchi nodded as I approached, and we shook hands, his soft and warm.

"How did you recognize me?"

"I Googled you," he said, "and there were pictures. If you don't mind me saying, you are a lot better-looking in person. Forgive me if I am embarrassing you," he said. "You just arrived. You must be tired."

"Actually, I'm great," I said, and it was true, that despite jet lag and hours hunched over the journal, I felt more energized than I had in years.

Quattrocchi looked like an Edwardian gentleman in his brocade vest and paisley ascot, out of place among the students, several of whom acknowledged him with an affectionate nod or smile as they passed our table.

"It's obvious they like you," I said.

"And I them—although teaching can be bloody hell at times."

"I'll second that," I said. "So you're English? Not Italian?"

"No, not English, but I went to Oxford. The accent and expressions were hard to give up, though honestly I did not try," Quattrocchi said. "I wager that you expected me to be wearing glasses."

"Why? Oh... Your name. Of course. Quattrocchi—'four eyes' in Italian. It hadn't occurred to me."

"It would if you had grown up with it!" Quattrocchi lifted a carafe. "Wine?"

I told him I'd stick to sparkling water and he frowned, insisting a glass of vino would make me feel good.

"*Too* good," I said, recalling blurred days and lost nights.

Quattrocchi signaled the waiter, asked if he could order for me, then did, minestrone soup and a bottle of Pellegrino. "Specialty of the house and best thing on the menu." He leaned forward, the buttons of his vest threatening to pop, and whispered, "Have you seen the journal?"

"Yes. It was at the very bottom of the carton, buried under folders."

"Was it? I thought I'd put it in on top. I must be getting old. Well, I *am* old." He dragged a hand over thinning hair he had combed forward in a failed attempt to hide his near baldness. "I must have forgotten. It was a difficult time, Tonio dying and... Is it interesting, the journal, I mean?"

It took me a moment to recognize that *Tonio* was a nickname for Antonio Guggliermo, the professor who had acquired the journal.

I told him it was very interesting and asked if he'd read it. He seemed appalled at the question.

"Not a word. I might have if Tonio had lived, but no... I am just getting used to the fact that I am...alone." Quattrocchi's voice cracked, and there were tears in his eyes.

"I'm sorry," I said, realizing that Quattrocchi had obviously been more than a cataloger of Guggliermo's papers.

"No need to be sorry," he said, swiping the tears away. "I was one of the lucky ones. I found love at a very young age. Tonio was my professor at university. I was twenty-one. He was forty-two. We were like Leonardo and Salaì."

"But you weren't *ten*!" I said. I knew all about Leonardo and his young lover, not just from my years of teaching art history but from my obsession with everything Leonardo.

"Nor a thief, nor conniver, nor beautiful—though I looked a lot better than I do now!"

"From what I've read, Leonardo was a beautiful young man who liked to parade through the streets of Florence in rose-colored tunics and purple stockings—but he grew old before his time."

"Don't we all." Quattrocchi dragged a multi-ringed hand across his comb-over. "You know that officially Salaì was Leonardo's adopted son."

"Didn't he forge some of Leonardo's paintings and try to sell them as originals?"

"Never proved, but possible. Though he must have cared for Leonardo—he stayed with him until his death." Quattrocchi looked away, eyes tearing up again. "Sorry. I am very nostalgic these days. It has only been a month since Tonio died, and on the day before his ninetieth birthday." He dabbed his eyes daintily, then pulled himself together and launched into a discussion of how gay artists dominated the Renaissance—"Michelangelo and Donatello among them—though only brave Leonardo was *out*, the others in the closet, and probably wise, as homosexuality was against the law in fifteenth-century Florence."

"Maybe *too* out for his time," I said. "He was arrested for sodomy with a male prostitute. And you must know his treatise on the male organ—'On the Penis'—where he claims the penis acts without the will of man and how it should be adorned rather than concealed? It's very popular with my students."

"Your art history class must be a lot more fun than mine!"

"I try." I smiled. "You said Professor Guggliermo asked you to contact me. How did he know to do that?"

"Oh, I imagine Tonio discovered you were Vincenzo Peruggia's great-grandson, and you are not difficult to find—Facebook, Twitter, your university profile. Tonio was a serious researcher and, despite his age, sharp as a tack." Quattrocchi signaled for the check and insisted upon paying when it came.

Outside, the air was chilly, the street wide, a mix of old tan and sienna-colored buildings. Quattrocchi was heading back to the university, and I walked with him, hoping for more answers to my questions.

"Do you know what he had intended to publish about the journal?"

"No. And he never got the chance. His dying was"—he took a deep breath—"such a shock. You must think that death at his age could not have been a surprise, but Tonio was not your typical ninety-year-old. He walked several miles a day and was the picture of health. Had it not been for the accident, I'm certain he would be sitting here right now."

"Accident?"

"Hit-and-run. Can you imagine, leaving an old man to die in the street?" Quattrocchi shook his head. "And then, on top of that, just a day after Tonio's death, some hooligans or drug addicts ransacked our apartment. It has taken me weeks to get it back to normal."

"What did they take?"

"That's the strange part: *nothing*. Perhaps they were looking for something, though the police speculated it was just a gang of malicious kids, or they'd have known enough to steal our antiques, several of which they broke!"

"But they didn't take the journal."

"No. It was in Tonio's office at the university."

The thought came to me buzzing and electric: if I had been searching for the journal and the answer to a hundred-year-old mystery for twenty years, others might be searching for it too. "How long did Antonio have the journal?"

"No more than a few weeks. Though it made an impression. He told me more than once that he was reading the most extraordinary thing—the diary of the man who stole the *Mona Lisa*!"

"Oh. So you know its contents."

"Only that much."

I asked if he had discussed the journal with anyone else, and he seemed insulted.

"No. Why would I?"

"Did Professor Guggliermo?"

"As he planned to publish something, I imagine he would have kept the discovery to himself."

"Do you know where he got it?"

"I assume a rare-book dealer. Antonio worked with many, mostly in Florence, a few in Paris and Germany."

"Did he have a list of those dealers, perhaps a receipt for his purchase of the journal?"

"I went through his papers, and I do not remember coming across it, and Tonio was a very orderly man." He paused as if picturing something. "Though I did not get to his desk until recently. That first week, I could not face it, you understand."

"Yes, of course. Did he have a phone book or an appointment book?"

"It was the only messy thing Tonio owned. He had it for years and refused to replace it. Come to think of it, I don't remember seeing that either."

"What about his cell phone?"

"Tonio despised them and did not own one."

Quattrocchi's pace was agonizingly slow. He'd opened his topcoat and was sweating, unlike me, freezing in my leather jacket. The streets kept changing—wide, then narrow, curved, then angular—until we came into a large open square lined with fancy shops and with an ornate old carousel in the center, though it didn't seem to be working.

"Piazza della Repubblica, once the site of the old Roman Forum," Quattrocchi said, pointing out the triumphal arch, which we cut under, then ambled along irregular streets, Quattrocchi's arm looped through mine. Every few minutes, he'd stop to catch his breath, then he'd take my arm again and we'd start down another narrow street of old ochre-colored buildings. Other than an occasional sigh or catching his breath, Quattrocchi had been mostly quiet, when he suddenly stopped and faced me.

"I just remembered something, a call I received from a collector of rare papers. That's what he called himself, a collector of *rare papers*. He said he'd heard about the journal from an old friend of Professor Guggliermo's, though he did not furnish a name, or if he did, it didn't mean anything to me. He asked if I knew of its whereabouts and offered a reward."

"What did you say?"

"That I had no idea what he was referring to. I had already carried out Tonio's request—that I contact *you* about the journal—and I had no interest in making money from it. Between Tonio's pension and my salary, I have more than enough."

"And he accepted that explanation?"

"I assume so. I have not heard from him since."

Wind whipped through the street, and I shivered, more from the idea that someone other than me had been looking for Peruggia's diary than the cold. I asked again if anyone else might have known about the journal, my mind still dwelling on the break-in and the collector of rare papers.

"The only person, other than myself, would be my secretary. She types up my lectures and emails, all my correspondence. But she is a lady of seventy-eight years old, has been at the university for almost fifty years, and is entirely trustworthy."

"Do you mind if I speak to her?" I asked.

"Signore Per-own-nay," he said, enunciating every syllable of my name. "Signora Moretti is the soul of discretion. But if you insist, it will be, as you Americans say, *your* funeral."

9

He has followed the two men from the restaurant, allowed plenty of space though there was no chance of losing them, the fat man's pace so slow he has had to stop, duck into alleyways, or hide behind parked cars. Not that they would recognize him. But he knows *them*, has viewed their pictures on his computer screen: Perrone, taller and more striking than he appeared in two dimensions, Quattrocchi fatter, leaning against a fence now and gulping for air like a fish out of water.

He sees them head toward the university, stops alongside a line of bicycles and motorbikes and lights a cigarette, watches college students coming and going, talking and laughing. He can't remember a time when he felt so carefree.

The smudge of a memory: his brother, falling. He drags the back of his hand across his eyes as if to erase it, though it lingers, an afterimage that carries with it an emotion he was certain he had disposed of years ago.

He squeezes his eyes shut, opens them when he hears the fat Italian laughing like a girl. He imagines he will scream like one too. He studies Perrone, strong and arrogant-looking, the kind of man he likes to bring down.

10

I found my way back to the Palazzo Splendour, got my key from the same guy behind the front desk, on the phone again or perhaps he had never gotten off. There was no elevator, my room two flights up, and he didn't offer to help with my bag.

I didn't expect much for a hundred and twenty euros a week, and I was right. My one room consisted of a tiny bathroom (sink, toilet, shower with no curtain) and kitchenette (half-sized refrigerator, hot plate, sink), a nonworking fireplace with a bare mantel above, a twin-sized bed with a worn chintz spread, a dresser topped by a wood-framed mirror, and an armoire so narrow that the three hangers only fit on an angle. The lone window had no shade, but it hardly mattered as it faced a dark alley.

Finally unpacking, suitcase opened across the bed, I felt the excitement of the long day starting to wear off. Thoughts of everything I had left behind—my job, my loft, my friends—came over me in a rush, along with a conversation I'd had with my Chelsea art dealer less than a week ago:

I have to close the gallery, Luke. I just can't afford it anymore.

What will you do?

Take a break, travel a little. The art world has worn me down these past dozen years.

You and me both.

Don't worry, Luke. You'll find another gallery.

I wasn't so sure. My last exhibition, four years ago, hadn't done well, the collectors not exactly lining up for my work, and I'd seen what happened to other artists when their galleries closed and they had no track record. They ended up in low-rent co-op galleries where the artists competed against one another, though no collectors or critics ever went to the shows, so it hardly mattered.

I arranged my underwear and socks in the top drawer of the dresser, trying not to think about my painting, though it had already triggered another conversation, the one I'd had with my department chair—an art historian with a specialty in eighteenth-century French rococo painting, his favorites Watteau and Fragonard, artists who made fluffy, pink pictures of girls on swings or couples swooning in gardens.

You're going to need an exhibition if you want to get tenure.

An exhibition? Without a gallery? Not so easy. Though I didn't tell him my gallery had closed.

I stopped unpacking, sagged onto the edge of the bed, and wondered if by coming here, I'd been running toward something or running away.

Exhausted, I closed my eyes, but while my body flagged, my mind continued to spark.

Lunch with Quattrocchi had provided more questions than answers. My visit to the university had been an exercise in frustration: Quattrocchi's secretary, a wizened old woman who looked as if she ate Americans like me for breakfast, had admitted to typing the email to me, but when I asked if anyone else might have read it, she cut me with a look and left the room without a word.

I lay back and stared at the ceiling's ornate plasterwork, the only beautiful part of the room. But a minute later, I was up, too jittery to sit still, unpacking the newspaper articles I'd brought with me, along with my only photo of Vincenzo Peruggia, a mug shot. The day I'd found it remained so vivid it could have happened hours earlier, not twenty years ago.

Dust and cobwebs. Dirt and mouse droppings. The low attic ceiling almost as oppressive as the heat beating through it: midsummer in Bayonne, New Jersey. Nothing worse, at least not to me, fourteen and trapped. Repeating ninth-grade algebra in summer school. *If X equals Y...* like I could give a shit. Exactly what I had told my teacher, who'd sent me to the principal, who'd sent me home. Ergo, the punishment, just one of many, this time, "Clean the attic!" An invented chore, since no one ever used it.

I'd spent the first hour sitting on my ass alternating cigarettes with a joint, then spied the old steamer trunk wedged into a corner. I didn't think it would amount to much, but when I swiped my hand through the dust, I saw the initials: SP. It took me a minute to figure out it must have belonged to my grandfather, Simon Perrone, who had lived in Italy and died before I was born.

I needed a screwdriver to pry it open. Inside, right on top, a rifle, which I lifted out and inspected: pockmarked wood, metal barrel, and rusty trigger. I pictured showing it off to my pals and later did.

Under the rifle, a photograph, a mug shot, full face and profile, and below them: *il carcerato 378.699.*

Prisoner. Signed on the back in a small, neat script, *Vincenzo Peruggia.*

My great-grandfather?

I no longer cared about the attic's heat or the flies buzzing around my head. I couldn't stop staring at the picture of this man, this *convict!*

That night, in the middle of dinner, I laid the photo on the table, watched as my father stopped eating midbite.

"It's your father's father, isn't it? My great-grandfather Vincenzo."

"It is...*no one*," my father said, already slurring his words, half-drunk. "You don't know what...you're saying."

I got up and bolted, not wanting the meat loaf or the canned peas anyway, my father shouting after me, "Get back here!" My mother looking like she was about to cry, which she did a lot—not her fault, she was no match for her bully husband or her delinquent son.

Later, I met my buddies at the Kill Van Kull, showed off the old rifle, and had a few beers. But I didn't show them the mug shot. That was for me—alone.

I brought him up to my parents for weeks, but it was always the same. They acted like he'd never existed, like they didn't know who I was talking about, like I was crazy. It didn't take much research to find out they had changed the family name, one more thing they'd never told me. That was the beginning of the late-night internet searches, letters, and emails, weeks and months, years of accruing information until it became my quest to find out anything and everything about Vincenzo Peruggia: the man who had stolen the *Mona Lisa*!

Holy shit! The idea that this guy, this criminal was my great-grandfather. I couldn't figure out why my parents were so ashamed when all I wanted was to tell the world. The idea of it was so exciting and dangerous I had to know everything about him.

And I had tried. Though after twenty years, the man remained a mystery. Until today.

After reading only a little of the journal, the mug shot was coming to life. And I'd been right: I had more in common with my great-grandfather than with my dull civil-servant father.

I put the mug shot aside to spread out the articles I had brought with me. First, a 1911 *New York Tribune* story I had long ago laminated under plastic and knew well.

DA VINCI PICTURE STOLEN IN PARIS

Paris, Aug. 22.—The art world was thrown into consternation today by the announcement that Leonardo's *Mona Lisa*, or as it is popularly known, *La Joconde*, had mysteriously disappeared from the Louvre Museum.

Not a vestige of a clue was left by the person or persons who took it. A search of every nook and cranny, from roof to cellar, brought to light only the valuable frame and glass that covered it, left on a back staircase.

The most remarkable feature of the case is that the picture was not missed for almost two days. It was assumed the painting had been removed for photography or cleaning.

I propped the article on the mantel, then looked at the others I'd brought as well. Perhaps here, in Florence, I'd see something in them I hadn't seen before. One suggested the *Mona Lisa* had been stolen by someone in a plan to blackmail the French government; another implied the theft was a German plot to embarrass the French; another, dated two weeks after the crime, maintained that no fewer than three witnesses had seen the *Mona Lisa* on a train headed for Holland, but the lead had never been followed and the witnesses' names never disclosed. Another suggested that a wealthy American, a "Westerner," had stolen the painting and taken it aboard the *Kaiser Wilhelm II*, but when the ship docked in New York, neither the Westerner nor the painting were anywhere to be seen, a true mystery.

Three more articles—one that blamed the Louvre for their lack of security, another that ridiculed the police for their botched investigation, and one that believed the theft was nothing but a prank. Of course the Louvre had been lax. Add to that the fact that the director of the Louvre had been traveling on the day the painting went missing, and the guard who should have been in the Salon Carré with the *Mona Lisa*, even though the museum was closed, had stayed home to take care of an ailing child, and there was plenty of reason to suspect an inside job or some sort of conspiracy.

There was one more clipping, to my mind always the most important. It had appeared in a small Parisian newspaper, *Le Cri de Paris*, exactly one year and one month *before* the 1911 theft.

MONA LISA SOLD TO AMERICAN

Paris, July 24.—Reliable sources have reported that the Mona Lisa was quietly stolen from the gallery of the Louvre one night in June through the complicity of an official of that museum, a copy substituted in the frame. The original, it is alleged, was ferreted away to New York and there sold to an American collector.

Though never proved, this story was the basis for more than one theory that suggested the *Mona Lisa* now residing in the Louvre Museum was a forgery, an idea that had plagued me since I'd first read it as a teenager and the reason I was here—hoping Peruggia's journal would provide the answer and I would finally learn the truth.

I tucked the mug shot into the wood-framed mirror above the dresser: prisoner number 378.699 in full face and profile, dark jacket, striped tie, and starched collar, thick black hair parted and combed neatly across a high forehead. With his broad cheekbones and full lower lip and despite a thickened nose that suggested street fights or barroom brawls, he was good-looking. I'd spent countless hours staring at the photo for the reason it had first entranced me, and it still did: if it were not for Peruggia's handlebar mustache and the drooping lid of his slightly smaller right eye, we could have been brothers. For years, I'd attempted to see beyond his guarded face. Now, after reading just a little of his diary, I thought I saw his need and desire, his hunger for recognition. Something I understood only too well.

"I won't let it slip away," I said, as much to the photo as to myself. I had managed to get away and become somebody, and no way I was going back. That lost Bayonne boy was going to stay lost, and I wasn't going to resurrect him. "I'll get the truth," I said, nodding at the mug shot, believing it for the first time. "No matter what!"

11

John Smith reviewed the dossiers he had transferred to his phone: one on the American and another on the Italian professors—the late Antonio Guggliermo and his younger lover, Luigi Quattrocchi, along with the emails between Quattrocchi and Perrone. He put the cell phone down and sat back, taking in the bedroom and small sitting room he would be using as his temporary base of operations. The hotel was far from deluxe, but he'd never cared for luxuries, always found them unnecessary, even frivolous. He pictured his Lyon apartment, sparsely furnished and spotlessly clean. As a kid, he'd imagined an exciting life beyond the projects, and though he'd made it out, enough of a feat, excitement had eluded him. Until now.

Tired but keyed up, he dropped to the floor and did a set of one-armed push-ups until he felt awake, determined. Breathing hard, he was up fast. Ignoring the SMOKE-FREE sign, he lit a cigarette, opened a window, and angled his muscular torso half outside.

You do your work well, Smith, but you do not go the extra yard, do not make the sacrifices.

A work review from his arrogant Danish supervisor, Andersen, only a week ago. A man who had been at the job less than three years, who enjoyed telling his subordinates and anyone who would listen that his name derived from the English *Andrew*, and that it meant manly and masculine. Not so Smith ever noticed.

Sacrifices? Apparently long nights and weekends didn't count. This job was his life; didn't Andersen know that?

He dragged hard on his cigarette, watched the smoke break up and disappear.

Of course he knew what his supervisor meant—that he had not been instrumental in *solving* cases. Unlike analysts who had not only tracked a missing artwork but whose data resulted in an actual arrest and return.

And you do not play well with others.

That really got to him. Smith imagined punching the guy, watching blood trickle over his pale-blond mustache and weak chin.

He would show his supervisor, the others too, would prove he could not only go the distance but a lot further, do whatever was necessary, whatever it took. After twenty years as a criminal intelligence analyst, he had an instinct for when he was onto something, and he had that feeling now.

Another deep drag, the smoke held in his lungs until they ached.

As far as INTERPOL knew, he was on sick leave (minor surgery, nothing serious, though he needed a week or so to recuperate), a surprise to his colleagues as he had never taken a sick day in his entire career. *No room for failure*, he thought. To fail now would be the end of his career, and that was not going to happen. He had made his decision, and there was no going back.

He flicked his cigarette out the window, watched it spark and fall. Looked across the darkened Piazza di Madonna at the gray-stone building and its electric sign, PALAZZO SPLENDOUR, blinking in the night like one of INTERPOL's damn red notices.

12

New York City

His wife had already stripped off her makeup and applied a coating of some absurdly expensive cream on surgically tightened skin that made her flesh look shiny and radioactive.

"Nice party—you did a good job," he said, although she had hired a caterer and waiters, so it was not exactly work or a job. Plus, he'd paid for it.

Without looking up or answering, she dropped her silk kimono onto the Empire couch where it slid to the floor in a heap. She made no attempt to pick it up, got into bed, switched on a lamp, and plucked a paperback off her night table, bloodred nails tapping the cover, something with *murder* in the title.

"Don't strain yourself with the heavy reading," he said.

"It's a *gangster* story," she said, "something *you* can relate to."

He took a step toward her, hands twitching at his sides while a series of old images skittered through his mind: the back of a bookie shop, smoke-filled and crowded; late-night rides with his father where not a word was spoken, other times a lecture he dared not interrupt; slaps across the face and worse, much worse.

"Go ahead," his wife said, angling her jaw, "hit me. I know you want to."

But no, he would not give her the pleasure of seeing him lose control or anything she could use against him in a courtroom, this once beautiful young girl he'd stolen away from a much younger man, her beauty now more memory than fact. He considered how he might kill her, arranging her body into some artful pose out of Goya or Velázquez. But he would never do such a thing, dirty his own hands, though at sixty-four, he saw no reason why he shouldn't have a third wife, one who would appreciate him.

"Are you going to read for long?" he asked.

"Why? Will it bother you all the way down the hall?"

They hadn't slept in the same room for years.

He turned away, thinking there had to be a way out of the marriage and the prenup. An accident? Not difficult to arrange, though he had more important things on his mind these days.

He headed down the carpeted hallway, then the winding staircase to the first floor of his townhouse. Did not stop to look at the painting on the landing, one of Renoir's fleshy pink nudes, too sweet for his taste, picked out by that thirty-nine-year-old gorgon upstairs. For a moment, he considered slashing it.

Another staircase took him into the finished basement and his home office. The only things on the desk, two books: a well-worn copy of Dostoyevsky's *Crime and Punishment*, his favorite novel— the first half, when the hero, Raskolnikov, commits murder and considers himself a superman and above the law, but not the second, with its dreary meanderings on guilt and repentance, something he could not comprehend. One simply went after what one wanted, the message of the second book on his desk: Machiavelli's *The Prince*.

Behind the desk, a tall wooden bookcase, a few art books, a row of auction catalogs, the rest of the shelves bare. He removed the remote device from the top drawer of the desk, hit a few buttons, and the bookcase slid on casters to expose the wall behind it.

Another code and the wall itself swung open. Behind it, a steel door. One more code, fingers tapping quickly, the door opened, and he stepped into the vault. He hit the remote one more time, and everything closed behind him—the wall, the bookcase all sliding back into place.

This was always his favorite moment, standing in the dark, waiting. He savored it until he could no longer wait, then flipped a switch, and the room was flooded with light.

Eighteen paintings. Eleven drawings. Thirteen prints. Each artwork with its own spotlight, accumulated over the past thirty years beginning legitimately with a small Blue Period Picasso. Beside the Picasso, the only other legitimate sale in the vault, a Rembrandt etching, currently worth a half million dollars—a pittance compared to the other artworks in the room. He often loaned these two pieces to museum exhibitions to show he was not only legit but generous.

He switched off the alarm and checked the thermostat to make sure it was at its constant sixty-eight degrees, then the dehumidifier, both backed up by a small generator, before perusing his collection. He paused in front of a Monet seascape, taking in the rich blues and purples of the sky and water. From there, to a small Van Gogh painting of a congregation leaving a church. He took his time, occasionally running his fingertips over paint, a sin—oily skin against delicate pigment—but he could do what he pleased, like flick his tongue over the painted nipple of a Gauguin nude, imagining the taste of sweat and salt, along with the history, the lives lived inside the painting, the artist Paul Gauguin in Tahiti with this unimportant though beautiful young woman he had immortalized.

He shuddered. Stood back, taking in his treasures, his children, relishing the idea that this art was his and his alone.

Selfish?

He didn't think so. After all, didn't he take better care of them than the careless museums and galleries they had been stolen from?

It was his calling, mystical and divine, almost religious, the way he would see an artwork in a museum or gallery, feel a palpable vibration, and know he *had* to have it, had to *rescue* it—the thought whispered into his mind as if from God.

He moved from Gauguin's Tahitian scene to a Madonna by the Norwegian artist Edvard Munch, surprisingly seductive, lips slightly open and dark red. He licked his own lips, then folded himself into the gold-plated Warren Platner chair, felt its curved back embrace his body as if he were floating. He skidded the chair a few inches closer to the painting, metal base scraping on the marble floor, the echo of a screech filling the room. He covered his ears, but too late; the ghosts were already here.

The chair screeched against the concrete floor of the garage where the man had been dragged from his bed in the middle of the night, eyes wide with fear, muffled pleading just barely audible through the duct tape across his mouth. The boy watched him, one eye on his father, who attached the silencer, then took it off and had him do it, hovering over him, wheezing from the beginning of emphysema that would have killed him had he lived long enough. The fourteen-year-old did it well, silencer on, off, hands moving deftly, trying to ignore the guttural sounds from the man in the chair.

"More tape on his mouth," his father said.

The boy tore off a strip, pressing it over the existing tape, felt the man's lips move under his fingers like worms. A smell too, heat and sweat and something sour, which he would only later come to identify as fear. He looked down, saw the wet stain spreading across the man's pajama bottoms.

"What if someone comes home?" the boy asked.

"No one's comin' home. Wife's away. Children—who knows where—and who cares? They don't tell me the guy's life story, just when and where."

"What if someone hears?"

"That's why the gun's got the suppressor, stupid. Won't make it silent, but not loud enough to wake the neighbors—and when the hell did I give you permission to ask questions?" His father pressed the gun into his hand. "Put these on," he said, handing him a pair of plastic glasses, at the same time pressing foam plugs into the boy's ears. "Don't want you going deaf or blind. What good would you be to me then?" He wheezed a laugh. "Closer," he said. "This ain't no shooting gallery."

The boy took a tentative step.

"I said *closer!*" He gripped the boy by the nape of the neck and pushed him forward.

The man jerked in the chair, head whipping from side to side.

"Do it," the father said, steering the boy's hand and gun toward the man's chest. "Pull the damn trigger already."

The man's eyes were blinking wildly, lips contorting below the tape.

"Now! Goddammit! *Now!*"

The boy fired, gun recoiling in his hand, the sound a muted *putt*.

"Goddammit! You hit his fuckin' shoulder." He grabbed hold of the boy's hand with his own, aimed the gun at the man's chest, and squeezed the boy's finger. Another *putt* and a spot of red appeared in the center of the man's T-shirt, expanding and blurring before he squeezed the boy's finger again, and another red spot appeared.

"Never take chances," his father said.

The boy watched as the man slumped to the side, taking the chair with him, crashing to the garage floor, everything about the scene, the moment, etched into his brain, though when he thought about it later, he realized he had felt nothing.

"Good boy," his father said, a rare moment of affection, patting him on the shoulder.

The wine-red lips of Munch's seductive *Madonna* came back into focus and he grew calm again, shifted his gaze to the prize, to *her* soft lips and enigmatic smile, the only painting in the vault to have its own wall. He leaned one way, then the other, her eyes following, then moved closer, fingertips grazing the cracked paint of her cheek, believing he felt flesh and warmth where none existed. He leaned in, his lips an inch from hers, painted features blurring, dizzy from the spell she cast. He took a step back, breath caught in his throat.

But is it really her?

He had to know.

He'd set the search for proof in motion, and there was no turning back.

"Whatever it takes, I have to know you," he whispered to her. "Whatever it takes."

13

Laurentian Library
Florence, Italy

"How did you know I'd be coming in?" I eyed the white carton already waiting on Riccardo's book caddy, careful to keep my smile in place, not to sound accusatory.

"I hear you with guard, in other room," Riccardo said.

I nodded, though I wasn't sure there'd been enough time for him to have gone into the back to retrieve the carton. But why be suspicious? Was I just being paranoid after so many years of looking for this elusive journal?

Chiara leaned toward us. "Is anything wrong, Signore Perrone?"

"Call me Luke," I said. "No, nothing at all." A thought: "I wonder, do you have anything on…" I stopped to think up a name. "Duccio?"

"There is much about the Sienese artist, Signore"—she smiled—"Luke. Rare books and more recent, how you say, scholarly papers."

"May I see them?"

"There are several boxes."

"The scholarly papers will do," I said and smiled back.

"*Uno momento*," she said, then spoke to Riccardo in Italian, while I thought about the break-in at Quattrocchi's apartment and the inquiry from a collector of rare papers. Chiara asked again if anything was wrong. I told her no, that I was just tired, and she said I was working too hard and patted my hand with her fuchsia nails. Riccardo returned with a carton labeled DUCCIO II, and I slipped my hand out from under Chiara's, balanced the Duccio carton on top of HIGH RENAISSANCE MASTERS, and headed across the room to the long table, where I took the same spot at the end.

The two scholars from the other day were there too, in the same spots, though none were assigned. The one with the ponytail looked up, seemed almost to be watching me, peering over his reading glasses. I stared at him until he looked away. Then I opened the Duccio carton, mostly folders and loose papers, and just what I needed. I set it aside, took a moment to create the makeshift fortress with Guggliermo's folders before I removed the journal, then found my place and began to read.

14

I did not want to go to Picasso's studio. But Simone insisted I spend more time with other artists. And it was difficult for me to say no to her.

I took the omnibus from Place de l'Odéon and got off at the top of the hill. Climbed another street lined with bakeries and restaurants where the air smelled of sweet pastry. My stomach felt hollow and empty. It had been hours since I had eaten. Only a slice of bread with strawberry jam Simone had made from berries she picked in the Bois de Boulogne.

I rolled a cigarette. Used the smoke to fill my lungs. Headed along rue Ravignan to the Ruche. A small wooden building. Several artists had studios here. Including Picasso.

I hesitated. There was still time to turn back. I had met the Little Spaniard before and did not like him. But Simone's words urged me on.

Picasso answered the door in paint-stained overalls. Told me to sit while he painted. Too busy to stop and be cordial.

The studio reeked of linseed oil and turpentine. And dog. An ugly old thing asleep at Picasso's feet. There were canvases everywhere. All in the new cubist style. Fragmented and ugly. I spied two small sculptures that looked familiar on a shelf. Iberian and primitive. All the rage in Paris. It took only a moment to remember where I had seen them last. At my job. At the Louvre Museum!

I kept my tone casual as I asked Picasso where he had gotten them.

When he told me from his friend the art critic Guillaume Apollinaire I felt a rush of anger. Apollinaire had singled out my paintings from a

*recent gallery exhibition. Had called them old-fashioned and dull. Words
that still burned in my gut.*

*Did Picasso know the sculptures were stolen? Perhaps he had even
been a party to it. I was not sure. But I made a note of them being here.
Picasso sang while he painted. A popular dance-hall ditty.*

*Oh Manon ma jolie
mon coeur te dit bonjour
ma jolie ma jolie ma jolie*

*He sang the silly verse over and over. Then he lectured me on art
and my responsibility as an artist. I listened without comment though his
lecture offended me. He talked of his friend the other cubist artist Georges
Braque. Referred to them as the Wilbur and Orville Wright of painting.
Such conceit! He talked on and on about old-fashioned artists and their
concern with beauty. I knew this was aimed at me. The same words
Apollinaire had used in criticizing my work.*

*Picasso put his brushes down. Faced me. Turned his painting around
so I could have a look. He explained at great length how he was reinvent-
ing three-dimensional form on a flat surface.*

All I could see was a fractured mess. But I did not say a word.

*He asked if I understood what he was saying. I felt anger rise up in
me. But I answered calmly. I told him I understood perfectly and asked
a question of my own. Why not paint the most beautiful picture possible?*

*Picasso spat his answer. Because it has been done before and better
than you or I could ever paint it again!*

*I told him that all I had ever wanted was to make the most beautiful
paintings possible.*

He looked at me as if I were an idiot. Said beauty was a thing of the past.

*We went back and forth like this. Neither one of us willing to concede
our point.*

Picasso finally offered me a cup of coffee. But it was too late. I had had enough of his lecturing. Enough of his insults.

I made an excuse and left.

Outside it was cold. Frost in the trees. I stopped in front of the Café des Abbesses and peered through the steamy window. Inside was my old friend Max Jacob. Drawing pictures in the air for a pretty young woman who stared at him captivated. I had not seen Max in months. Not since he had aligned himself with Picasso and Braque and that bastard Apollinaire.

I longed to sit with Max and the pretty girl. To drink coffee. To be part of their lively conversation. But no. I turned away and vowed never to come back to this place again. I was an outsider. Always would be.

I headed down the hill and walked swiftly to the Place de l'Odéon. I ignored the omnibus. I needed to keep moving. I headed up the hill and started to run as fast as I could. I know now that I was running away from the future into the safety of the past. But all the time I was running I thought about those sculptures in Picasso's studio. And how I might use them against him.

15

I stopped reading where Peruggia had drawn a heavy pencil line at the bottom of the page, noted that he had done this before, his personal demarcation to end a passage. I thought of him in Picasso's studio, how humiliated and furious he must have felt, and understood it too—the competition between artists. I got up and stretched, my back stiff from sitting for too many hours. The guy with the ponytail looked up and nodded and I did the same, noting with more interest that the blond was back at the end of the table. I'd been so absorbed in the journal that I'd missed her coming in.

Chiara had just left her post to follow Riccardo into the back room, Beatrice hunched over her desk as usual. The ponytailed scholar crossed the room to peruse a stack of books. I took advantage of the moment and did what I had planned to do earlier—emptied half the contents of the Duccio carton, placed the journal inside, then covered it with folders and papers. If someone was looking for the journal—and from what Quattrocchi had said, a collector of rare papers was—they would not think to look for it in here. It was a risk if the librarians checked. Would they think I stole it? Quattrocchi had said no one knew it existed, but had the library gone through Guggliermo's papers and seen it? I had no idea, but it was a risk worth taking.

I brought both cartons up to Chiara's desk. She asked if I'd found what I wanted among the Duccio papers, and I told her I had but needed to read more and would be requesting them again.

"*Certo*," she said, adding her usual flirty smile.

I went back to get my laptop and backpack, once again made a point of taking the long way around, smiling when I passed the blond, and this time when she returned it, I stopped and, in what I considered to be one of the boldest moves in my thirty-seven years, leaned down and asked in my best Italian if she would like to get a coffee.

"But I've got reading to do," she said.

"You're American," I said.

"Yes," she said. "So are you. I was sure you were Italian or Spanish."

I liked that she had imagined a backstory for me, even an incorrect one. I angled my head to read one of her book titles, *Painting in Florence and Siena after the Black Death*. "A real hoot. I've read it."

"You have not!"

"Swear to God." I made the sign of the cross. "Give me a good book about the bubonic plague, and I'm one happy guy."

She laughed, full lips parting over straight white teeth.

Chiara aimed a finger at us.

"You're going to get me in trouble," the blond whispered.

"Sorry," I whispered back. "But you know that book is in paperback and in English. You don't have to read it here."

"Oh, but I love it here."

"Me too. It's just that you can read about the aftereffects of the plague on artists anywhere," I said, showing off a little.

"Oh." She affected a pout. "Now you've spoiled the ending."

I laughed, and Chiara glared at us again.

"One coffee," I whispered, "before she throws us out."

With no windows in the research room, I'd had no sense of the weather since I'd arrived this morning when it had been cloudy and looked like rain. Now the sky over San Lorenzo was a pale watercolor blue with cotton-ball clouds, though the chill lingered.

"Is that real?" I asked, watching her wrap the fur scarf around her neck.

"If you consider rabbit real."

"I think most rabbits would."

"You're not going to report me to PETA, are you?"

I laughed as we headed down one of the streets that radiated off the square, this one narrow and angled and lined with shops—a fancy shoe store, a gelato stand, a trendy men's clothing shop, even a Foot Locker. Just beyond it, a small café, where I suggested we stop.

"But the weather has gotten so nice. Let's walk a bit."

"Sure," I said.

"You're easy," she said.

"I like to think so." I added a grin.

"Oh, you're worse than the Italian men. Have you been here long, or are you *always* like this?"

"Sorry," I said. "No, just a few days. By the way, I'm Luke Perrone."

"So you *are* Italian."

"Italian American. Does that count?"

Her answer was a raised eyebrow and half smile; one more time, I felt as if she were studying me or looking through me. "Does Luke ever have a nickname?"

"Nope," I said, though I thought back. My buddies in Bayonne had called me "Lucky," something I'd dropped the day I left, along with my Jersey accent and everything else I associated with the place.

"Luke then. It suits you," she said. She extended her hand without removing her glove. The leather felt soft and expensive. "Alexandra Greene," she said. "With an E."

"You ever Alex or Ali?"

"That depends."

"On?"

"Whether I like you or not." She looked me up and down. "I haven't decided yet."

We kept walking, the street mostly in shadow, buildings on either side so close they blocked much of the sky. I asked where she'd grown up and was not surprised when she said the Upper East Side of Manhattan. She had that combination of cool and sophistication Manhattan kids wore like a second skin. I was sure she'd gone to private school too.

"Friends," she said when I asked.

I would have guessed one of the tonier uptown schools like Nightingale or Brearley. "Is there a Friends School in Manhattan? I only know the one in Brooklyn."

"Brooklyn," she said.

"And your parents didn't mind you traveling all the way from the Upper East Side?"

"My parents are divorced," she said as if that explained it. "But aren't everyone's?"

"Not mine," I said. "They got a life sentence, no parole in sight."

"Not happy?"

"I don't think the word is in their vocabulary, plus they don't have the money to get divorced."

"Oh," she said, and for a minute, I thought she was looking at me differently, sizing me up as if searching for signs of poverty. She asked where I was from, and I admitted to New Jersey, then changed the subject, asked what had brought her to Florence.

"I'm finishing a doctorate...in...medieval history."

"Ergo the plague book."

"Just for fun," she said and smiled.

"Where are you studying?"

"Barnard. You know—the women's part of Columbia."

I was not surprised she was attending an Ivy League school. No way I'd be admitting to two years of community college where I'd worked my ass off to create the portfolio that got me into art school. "So you're a smart girl too."

"*Too?*"

"Smart and beautiful *too*."

"Your Italian heritage is showing," she said, "again."

"Sorry. Men are always in trouble, no matter what they say."

"It's not just *what* they say but *how* they say it. But you're not in trouble. Not yet." She added a half smile. "By the way, I know that book on the plague is available in the States. It's just part of an excuse to be here, but does one really need one?" She did a half turn on her boot heels. "I mean, it's so beautiful."

"Sure is," I said, watching her twirl gracefully, as if she had studied ballet, and she probably had. Obviously well-to-do, the kind of woman my younger self could not have imagined dating, let alone strolling with through the streets of Florence.

"Orsanmichele," she said, indicating a stone fortress-like building. "Let's go in, okay?"

Inside, it was like no other church, possibly square-shaped with an off-center altar, no tall windows to illuminate the space, which was dark. The few people milling around were lost in the shadows.

"It was once a granary," Alexandra said, and I remembered it now from my teaching, the grain market that became a church. I recognized the ornate tabernacle too, even more lavish in person, like a miniature Gothic church, white marble, inlaid with lapis and gold, built around a brightly colored painting of the Madonna.

"Andrea Orcagna," I said. "Another great Renaissance painter and sculptor." I moved closer to admire its intricacies while Alexandra wandered into the chapel just beside it, though she was out in a minute, clutching my arm.

"Let's go."

I asked about the sculpture gallery I knew was upstairs, but Alexandra said another time, anxious to leave.

"What's wrong?" I asked when we got outside.

"Some guy bumped into me—hard—and it seemed intentional."

I asked what he looked like, and she shrugged. "Hard to tell, it was so dark, but he was big, and he whispered *Watch out*, and not like *Be careful*—more like a warning."

I looked back at the church, offered to go back in, but Alexandra said no.

"So he spoke English?" I said.

Another shrug, she was no longer sure, then she took my arm and led me down a side street to a café she knew.

Inside, it was quiet, with red leather banquettes and gilded sconces above the tables.

Alexandra slid into a booth and shook off her coat. She had on a cream-colored V-neck sweater, cashmere I guessed. A thin gold chain around her long neck with an oval locket resting in the hollow between her collarbones. She ordered a caffè Americano. I ordered a double espresso.

She asked why I was spending time in the library, and I said I was doing a little research.

"On what?"

"I'm not entirely sure," I said, not ready to talk about the journal.

When she asked again, I changed the subject and told her I was an artist, a painter, something I immediately regretted, because she asked me where I showed, and I had to admit my gallery had just closed.

"You'll get another," she said.

"How do you know? Are you some sort of witch?"

"Could be," she said, "but I just have a feeling about you."

I had a feeling about her too.

We talked about New York—how it was hard but easy, the constant noise and dirt but the excitement too, like nowhere else—and school, her studies, my teaching—though she was constantly directing the conversation back to me, seemed genuinely interested. The time passed quickly and comfortably, as if I'd known her for a long time. I didn't want it to end, but then we finished our coffees, and her mood shifted.

She stood up abruptly and announced she had to go back to her apartment, that she'd barely unpacked, an urgency in her tone far beyond the task. I offered to help but she said no, and when I proposed walking her home, she refused. The consolation prize was a quick peck on my cheek and the lingering smell of her perfume as I watched her walk away, shearling coat billowing, the sound of her bootheels growing softer until the café door closed behind her.

16

He stares through the window at the American, as he has come to call him, a kind of code name and a way to keep it impersonal. Watches the way they smile, the American and the blond, and for a moment feels something he cannot place and does not want to; feelings have never brought him anything but trouble. He drags hard on his cigarette, stifles whatever it is he has begun to feel until he feels nothing.

His cell phone buzzes. He sees the number but does not answer. He will deal with his employers later. He continues to peer through the glass, has to fight the compulsion to walk into the café and insinuate himself between the couple, get a hand on the blond's thigh and one around the American's throat, though it is not part of the plan—not yet. His face pounds with blood.

The blond gets up and he watches her, eyes on her legs, the way she walks, like a racehorse or one of those runway models. He considers following her, mind rife with pornographic images so that he has missed the American paying the bill and has to do a quick about-face when the American comes out, just a foot away from him.

He waits a moment, then follows, stops when he sees the American head into the cloister, knows he is going into the library, then takes up his spot outside the alleyway on a convenient set of stone steps where he can be anonymous, where he can sit and smoke and savor the thoughts of what will come next.

17

È iniziato come qualsiasi altro giorno al museo.
It started like any other day at the museum.

I was busy building new frames and repairing old ones. I kept moving the painting from one end of my worktable to the other. I was trying to avoid the relentless gaze of Leonardo's lady. She seemed to be watching me. I finally covered her with a cloth and worked as fast as I could. I needed to be home early. Needed to buy honey for Simone's tea. Needed to relight the fire in our cold flat.

I had only a few francs left. Barely enough to get through the week. I knew Simone would not let me touch the money we had set aside for the baby. I swallowed my pride. I asked my boss for a small advance on my pay. He refused. I wanted to shout in his face. Wanted to strangle him. But I controlled myself for I needed the job. Now more than ever.

At lunchtime I went outside. It was cold but I needed the air. I ate the slice of bread and jam Simone had packed for me. But my stomach still felt empty.

It was then I noticed him. A man I had seen the day before. A flamboyant creature in cape and hat. An uomo effeminate.

I turned my back on him. Kept my head down. But could hear him coming closer. His silver cane tapping on the path. Until his shadow fell across me.

I looked up and scowled. Closed my smaller eye. A look I used to keep people away and it usually worked. But not this time.

He stopped in front of me. But I did not acknowledge him. He extended a hand with long spidery fingers. I ignored it.

He started to speak. I thought I detected an accent. Something cultivated and smooth like velvet. I had an ear for such things as I had worked hard to eliminate my own Italian accent. He said he was from Uruguay. In South America. Smiled exposing long yellowed teeth. His gums receding.

I looked away but it did not deter him.

He told me his name was Valfiero. The Marquis Eduardo de Valfiero. He repeated the name several times. Then sat down beside me. Opened a bag and took out an apple and a pain au chocolat and offered them to me saying he was not hungry.

I tried to resist but my stomach growled. I took them and ate hungrily. He prattled on about his noble birth and his friends. Said they were the most celebrated art dealers of the day. And that he had come to Paris to buy and sell art. I was interested but tried hard not to show it.

He asked if I worked in the museum. It was obvious. I was wearing my workman's tunic with the museum emblem. I nodded. But I did not tell him that it was a part-time job. Or that I worried I might be fired.

He asked if it was interesting work. I told him it was not his business. I stood and he dared to stop me with his spidery hand on my arm.

He said he had an offer for me. Something lucrative. I pulled out of his grip. Insisted I had to get back to work. But he continued to speak. Asked me if we could meet after work. I said no. All I could think of was Simone in our cold flat. Of the logs in the fire that would need replacing. I walked away fast. But he followed. The whole time he asked questions. What they paid me at the museum? Did I enjoy my work?

I did not answer.

He called after me. Offered a drink. More food. Insisted I hear his offer.

I stopped. Faced him.

He looked at me and smiled. Said he could offer me more money than I could earn at the museum in a lifetime.

I stared at him. Said nothing.

He reached inside his coat. Took out a small silver case. Handed me a card on heavy cream-colored stock. Then he turned and I watched him walk away. His cane ticking along the path. His cape swirling around him like a cloud of black ink.

I looked at the card. His name and address printed in an elaborate cursive script. I considered ripping it to shreds. But I slid it into my tunic pocket. I doubted I would ever see him again.

18

The restaurant was even noisier and smokier at dinner then it had been at lunch—and Quattrocchi was late. I scrolled through my emails. None from him. One from my university chair about meetings I'd be missing. I concocted an excuse: *In Florence seeing art I'm teaching next semester. Making notes that I hope will turn into a paper. Look forward to showing you for your expert eye.* A little ass-kissing never hurt.

I ordered the minestrone soup again and thought back to what I had just read. *Valfiero.* I knew the name well from my years of research—the mysterious con man who some believed had been the mastermind behind the theft of the *Mona Lisa*. I could picture him now, sharp-featured and with a limp, seducing my great-grandfather with the promise of gold. I wanted to know more, what he was offering, and would have kept reading had the library not closed.

I checked the time, almost eight thirty. Had I gotten it wrong, pushed Quattrocchi too hard last time with all my questions? I thought we'd ended on a cordial note, and it had been his idea to meet again.

I scanned the room. A girl at the next table, a student I recognized from the other day, returned my gaze.

"*Ma scusi, stavo qui l'altro giorno e...*"

"*Sì, sì.* I remember," she said.

"*Posso chiedere?*"

"I speak English," she said.

"Oh, great. The man I was with the other—"

"*Professore* Quattrocchi."

"Right. I was supposed to meet him tonight. Have you seen him?"

"No," she said, "but my class with him is not until tomorrow."

The boy beside her spoke up. "The *professore* missed class today."

"Do you know if he's ill?"

The boy shrugged.

I checked my emails again. None from Quattrocchi.

I finished the soup, ordered a slice of very good olive-oil cake, took my time eating it, then sipped an espresso, thinking of Alexandra Greene, how we'd hit it off so well, at least I'd thought so, then her sudden departure. Maybe it was true that she needed to unpack. Or maybe an excuse to break away because she'd felt us moving toward something too quickly? I liked that explanation better, and I was not ready to give up.

Outside, it was dark, lots of people strolling despite the chill, but I was tired, ready to call it a day. I tried calling Quattrocchi for the second time and once again got his voicemail. I was just putting my phone away when I bumped into a man, or had he bumped into me?

"Sorry," I said, seeing my own reflection in his dark sunglasses, the cigarette clamped between his lips. The guy turned away without a word. "Hey, you're excused," I called after him, but he was already disappearing into a crowd, his cigarette smoke mixing with the exhaust fumes that clouded the air.

19

Two long flights of stairs, then two shorter ones, Alexandra insisting we walk rather than take the elevator. I was a bit breathless, obviously missing my daily workouts. We reached the landing, and the Uffizi's second-floor hallway unfurled like a treasure chest—a long rectangle lined with figural sculpture, a wall of windows splashing the space with light, a carved wood ceiling ornately painted, the overall effect almost dizzying—or was it the four flights of stairs?

A half hour ago, I'd shown up at the library, psyched to read, but it had been closed by a strike—a handwritten sign on the research room door stating the hours, 9.00 to 16.00. Civilized but odd, a few scholars, including the usual two and me, standing around in various states of annoyance, until Alexandra showed up and suggested we hit the Uffizi, a surprise invitation but a good one.

"Uffizi," I said, "Italian for 'offices.'"

"I never realized that," she said.

"Designed by the artist Vasari to house the offices of the Medici family."

"I love how you have these facts at your fingertips," Alexandra said, then took the lead, heading into a gallery with two large paintings of the Madonna Enthroned. I knew them both from teaching, and Alexandra was impressed when I identified the artists from across the room.

"Cimabue and Duccio," I said, thoughts of hiding the journal in the box of Duccio notes in my mind, still worrying someone might find it.

"Something wrong?" she asked.

"Just overwhelmed by the art," I said, and I was. The medieval paintings had obviously been taken out of churches, some with ragged panel edges, others with frames that had clearly been part of something else. The word *theft* slipped into my mind, and I pictured my great-grandfather with the *Mona Lisa* hidden under his shirt.

Alexandra said she'd had enough of early Christianity and headed down the hall. I followed her to a room filled with paintings by the Renaissance master Sandro Botticelli.

"Amazing," I said, struck by a mural-sized painting that I was trying to see over the heads of a Japanese tour group, the leader wearing a headset, the group of at least thirty also with headsets, which sounded like a field of crickets.

I dipped in front, and Alexandra followed.

"*La Primavera*," I said.

"Spring," she said.

"Botticelli embracing a pagan subject from ancient Greek and Roman mythology—Venus inviting us into her garden."

"I'm in!" Alexandra said, and I thought she could easily slide into the painting, take her place beside the three Graces, and dance along with them. Her blond hair was down today, loose on her shoulders, an ideal subject for Botticelli.

"Is that Mars beside them?" she asked.

"No, that's Mercury, god of spring, clearing the winter clouds away."

Alexandra gave me a look, then headed into the next room— more Botticelli, his most famous painting, *The Birth of Venus*, the goddess on the half shell, as beguiling as any woman in the history of art, though I thought Alexandra could give her a run for her money.

It was hard to tear myself away, but I was glad I did when we came into the next room where the lights were dim and Leonardo's unfinished masterpiece, *The Adoration of the Magi*, hung on the center wall. I'd seen the painting in reproduction, but nothing had prepared me for this, half the painting just drawing on canvas, Leonardo's hand totally visible. The Madonna in the center was little more than a line drawing, a beautiful ghost, the figures around her in various stages of finish or not at all, the combination riveting. It was as if I could see Leonardo thinking, making decisions as he worked. In the background, a lone tree was completely painted while the landscape and action around it—walls, horses, and hills— were just sketched in.

"What do you think?" Alexandra asked.

"That it might be the most beautiful painting I've ever seen," I said, my eyes tracing charcoal and brushwork, feeling all the emotion packed into half-finished faces. It felt as if Leonardo were speaking to me across time, drawing me into his world and into the past.

"It's too bad he didn't finish it," Alexandra said.

"I'm glad he didn't," I said, a part of me thinking it was intentional, that Leonardo had been brilliant enough to stop painting at this incredible moment, when things were still coming together. The journal played in my mind, Vincent at his worktable in the Louvre, constructing a frame for the *Mona Lisa*, and for the first time, I could really imagine how it must have felt—the power Leonardo had to lure you in, to make you part of his living, breathing artworks. "I love seeing the artist's hand at work."

"The artist's hand," Alexandra repeated, taking hold of my mine impulsively or unconsciously, I didn't care which, a small jolt of electricity at her touch.

She led me down the stairs, but I would have followed her anywhere.

At the bottom, I felt something, stopped, and turned.

"What is it?" she asked.

For a moment, I'd felt as if someone was following me, but of course, there were people everywhere. "Nothing," I said and shook it off.

We cut through rooms of Mannerist painters—Pontormo and Bronzino—artists known for overstatement and embellishment, Parmigianino's wildly exaggerated *Madonna with the Long Neck*, where I might have lingered, but Alexandra was already heading into another room, where she finally stopped, and I joined her.

Two women held the general down. One of them drew a blade through his neck, blood spilling over the side of the bed.

"One of my favorite paintings," she said, "by one of my favorite artists."

"Artemisia Gentileschi, *Judith Beheading Holofernes*."

"Are you reading the label, or do you know it by sight?"

"It's a pretty famous painting," I said, though it was the first time I'd seen it outside a textbook. "I do an entire class on Artemisia."

"Really? My art history teachers hardly mentioned her. Amazing, isn't it, all the action, as if it could start moving, like a movie, and the look on the general's face—you can practically hear him screaming!"

"One of the few great women artists of the Renaissance," I said.

"That we *know* of," Alexandra said.

"It was her father who taught her to paint."

Alexandra turned to me then. "Are you giving *him* the credit— her *father*?"

"It's a fact, that's all."

"Either she had the talent, or she *didn't!*" Alexandra bit off the word. "She's as good as any of the Renaissance men!"

"No argument from me," I said, hands up in defense.

We stood there a moment, and I could sense her anger.

"Sorry," she said, but I could still feel it coming off her, heated and indignant; then she turned and faced another painting. "If I believed in God, this painting would make me question his existence."

It was Caravaggio's *The Sacrifice of Isaac*, Abraham about to sacrifice his only son, hand pressing the boy's head to a rock, knife raised, the boy's face distorted with fear.

"What kind of sadistic God asks a father to kill his only child?" she said. "What sort of *father* could do *that?*" She shook her head as if trying to dislodge the thought, and I felt it again, a kind of white-hot anger that was out of proportion to the art or the moment.

"Hardly anyone paints as well as Caravaggio," I said, trying to bring our conversation back to the painting, pointing out Caravaggio's dynamic composition, the way he swept your eye across the canvas, the combination of beauty and ugliness as well as something new and old, what artists had been trying to achieve for centuries, which had me thinking of Vincent in Picasso's studio.

Alexandra took hold of my arm and urged me forward though I didn't see the need to rush. We had plenty of time, and I said so.

"I don't want you blaming me if you don't get your research done—*whatever* it is," she said with a note of sarcasm, which I chose to ignore.

The next gallery had walls painted deep crimson and was the first to be packed with tourists.

"More Caravaggio. He always draws a crowd," Alexandra said.

We sidled through for a closer look at his portrait of *Bacchus*, everything about the picture sensuous, the boy in the painting both masculine and feminine.

"Ahead of his time," I said, adding the salient details of Caravaggio's tortured life—his bisexuality, the brawl that disfigured his face, the murder charge that forced him to flee Naples, the fact that when he died at thirty-eight, there was a question as to whether it was a fever that killed him or if he'd been murdered.

"Wow!" Alex said, "My art history professors always stuck to the facts. Your class sounds a lot more fun."

I suggested she take it when we got home, which had me worrying I might not be teaching at all by then. I was glad to be distracted by Caravaggio's painting of *Medusa*, decapitated, mouth open in a startled scream, eyes wide with horror, blood streaming from the neck, a thoroughly terrifying painting.

"It's a self-portrait, you know."

"Is it?" Alexandra looked surprised. "Why would he paint himself as Medusa—and with his head chopped off?"

"I don't know," I said. "Maybe it was his meditation on mortality." I moved in for a better look, but light reflected off the plexiglass box. "I hate these damn boxes," I said, thinking of Vincent building glass ones to protect the Louvre's most valuable artworks.

"It gives me chills," Alexandra said. "Those snakes look so real, as if they're actually writhing."

20

He stares at the metallic sheen of snakeskin, the decapitated head, red blood spewing from the severed neck, the glint of light in Medusa's dying eyes, everything about the painting so intense and real, his hand itching to touch it, and he might have if it were not inside a box—but he has been distracted for too long.

Where are they?

He scans the gallery, finally spots them at the other end, heading toward the exit, moves quickly though as if without purpose, keeping a few people in between for safety, follows them into the bookshop where they linger, checking out pads and pencils, picture puzzles and games, everything decorated with art from the museum. The American is considering a smartphone cover with a picture of that painting—the naked woman on the shell—which he shows to the blond, who gives him a look, eyebrow arched, then laughs.

Why is it that seeing them having a good time gets under his skin, an idea taking shape in his mind like a photograph being developed, fuzzy, as yet without details, though he is filling it in, as graphic and bloody as the *Medusa* reproduction he has just spied. He considers buying it, but too late; the American and the blond are already heading out of the shop.

21

The exit led us into a kind of nondescript courtyard, not really a courtyard at all, a semi-open space with a few afterthought wooden chaises that felt as if they belonged in a city housing-project playground, a couple of kids lounging on them while their parents consulted guidebooks.

"God, this is ugly," I said. "Couldn't someone have painted a wall or spray-painted graffiti so there'd be some sort of *art* here, some small segue from the Uffizi into real life?"

Alexandra looked at me with an unreadable smile, then leaned in and kissed me hard on the mouth, the tip of her tongue teasing mine before she pulled away.

I was pretty sure my face was registering surprise—and delight—but Alexandra looked guilty now, sucking her lower lip like a little girl. "I'm sorry..."

"I'm not."

"I shouldn't have done that... It was just all your talk about an entire class on Artemisia and having an art segue out here..." She shook her head. "Forget it."

Not likely, I thought but didn't say, though I could feel the smile on my lips.

"The library is open now," she said. "You should go."

"Trying to get rid of me?"

"No," she said and softened.

"Okay then, let's go back to the library together."

"I can't. I need to...take care of a few things..."

"Hey, if it's about the kiss—"

"I don't know what came over me. Can we pretend it didn't happen?"

"Maybe you can," I said and smiled.

"See you later," she said, already heading down the ramp so fast I didn't have time to ask *when*.

22

Alexandra hurried down the exit ramp. What was she thinking, kissing him like that?

Clearly, she wasn't thinking at all. Or was she?

She put a finger to her lips as if she could still feel it, the kiss lingering.

But it was ridiculous. Too much. Too fast. She should go back and say something. But what? That would only make it worse, make her look even more foolish and reckless, something she rarely was and could not afford to be now.

She dared a look back when she was a couple of blocks away, not because she expected Luke to be following but because she had the feeling someone was. Silly, of course, and no way to tell. There were people everywhere—another tour group, Italians toting shopping bags, vendors selling maps and trinkets. She made her way quickly across the piazza and kept going until she was on a narrow side street that ended in a small square with an old chapel. On impulse, she went in—she was all impulse today.

Inside, the church was whitewashed and austere, with a series of beautiful frescoes in arches. Alex stopped to read a plaque that identified the chapel as the Oratorio dei Buonomini di San Martino, the fifteenth-century frescoes as depicting good works performed by the voluntary order whose chapel this had been. The frescoes were high above her head, but she strained to see them.

In one, nuns tended to a woman in bed, the colors soft, the nuns' expressions kind, the patient's face pale and sickly.

Suddenly, she was crying, tears coming fast and hot. She told herself to get a grip, but she knew why she was crying and she could not stop.

She felt a hand on her shoulder and spun around so fast she almost lost her balance.

"*Scusi*," said an elderly nun all in white, face soft, expression kind, almost as if she had come to life from the painting. "*Stai bene?*"

"Oh, yes...fine..." Alex stuttered. She managed to thank the woman, then headed out of the chapel fast. Perhaps, she thought, this was an omen that she too needed to perform good works. But she was, in a way, wasn't she?

23

I opened the door to my hotel room and stopped, hit by an intense smell of tobacco, and saw the newspaper article I had propped on the mantel along with the mug shot of Peruggia, both lying on the floor. I didn't move for a moment, taking in the small space. There weren't many places to hide—the bathroom, under the bed? I checked both, then set the article back in place and wedged the photo deeper into the mirror's frame. I made sure the window was closed, which it was, so it hadn't been a breeze that sent those things to the floor.

Had someone been in here? The maid?

But the bed hadn't been made, and a towel still draped over the tub where I had left it in the morning. I went back to the window, opened it, and peered into the alley, dark and quiet. No one but Spider-Man could scale this wall. Even as a teenager who had scrambled over walls and chain-link fences, I'd never have been able to climb something this steep. I closed the window and locked it, tried to shrug off the queasy feeling of invasion, told myself things fell down all the time.

I finally relaxed enough to eat the slice of pizza I'd bought from a street vendor, washed it down with lukewarm Pellegrino, and thought about my three hours at the library. I got out the notes I'd made, fearing I would not remember as it had been hard to concentrate, Alexandra's kiss loitering in my mind and on my lips, my mind doing somersaults: she likes me, she likes me not. But she must like me, she kissed me! Then why the sudden need to leave? Again. Regrets? Embarrassment? I didn't know and had to stop thinking about her. I had not come to Florence looking for romance. In fact, I wanted a break from it. I thought about my last relationship, the ombudsman of my university, a supersmart redhead whom I'd met when I'd gone for advice about a difficult student. I came away with her phone number and six months of really great dinners, sex, overnights, and conversation. I ended it when she suggested we consider living together. Six months, then goodbye, my usual pattern.

I looked back at my notes, forced myself to forget about Kathy the ombudsman, Amanda the food writer, Terri the poet—and Alexandra! I needed to concentrate.

- Ticolat cuts Peruggia's hours.
- Simone's cold gets worse and she is unable to work.
- Funds getting low.
- Peruggia meets Valfiero.

I was trying to get a timeline that had led up to the theft, though how much actual time had passed between the events, I couldn't be sure.

I got up to wash the pizza grease from my fingers and caught a familiar glimpse of KILL VAN KULL etched in inky blue just below the sleeve of my T-shirt, a memento from my former life, the Bayonne Bridge etched above it. At the time none of us had any idea of Kill Van Kull's Dutch colonial roots, only that we liked the name because it sounded menacing and cool, like so many things do when you're fifteen. I remembered the day my five Kill Van Kull brothers and I got inked, too high on booze and weed and feeling even cockier than usual, the watch-out-world attitude we displayed indelibly engraved on our arms.

I made a muscle and watched the crisscross design of the bridge expand, something I had thought way cool back then, now glad I could hide it under long sleeves. The linked chain that circled the top of my other bicep was easier to conceal and did not require much explanation.

I could hardly remember who I was back then, the school suspensions, joy rides with my buddies in stolen cars, all those drunken nights. Not that my posse was all bad. We hid behind the idea that we were modern-day Robin Hoods, seeking revenge for those who deserved it—though we made the rules and decided who deserved what.

I read a few pages of a new biography of Leonardo I'd brought with me, the author going into detail about the fact of Leonardo being left-handed, and fell asleep thinking about how Leonardo drew from right to left so he wouldn't smudge his drawings, then dreamed of wrenching Peruggia's journal from the grip of an old man who lay in the street, bleeding, Alexandra watching from the curb, calling to me, then disappearing.

In the morning, I awoke shivering, the room freezing. I got up and tapped the radiator—it was stone cold. I played with the knob, twisting until the steam came on with a hiss. But when had I turned it off? I tugged on jeans, unable to shake the feeling that someone had been in my room yesterday. The stale smell of cigarette smoke still lingered.

The library was not yet open, so I checked my email, one from my TA saying the department chair had sat in on my class. He thought it had gone well and wanted to let me know. I pictured the chair, a sour look on his face, making notes about the class and the fact that I wasn't there or, worse, that my TA taught the class better than I did. I considered sending him another note saying that my research was going well, but was it? Would I really have anything to show for my time here? There was an email from my sculptor cousin too, the one living in my loft, saying he was having a great time in New York and had connected with a gallery in Chelsea that wanted to give him a show. I wrote back "great" and closed my laptop, trying hard not to feel envious that my cousin—who had spent less than a week in the city—was going to get an exhibition when I had just lost my gallery.

I buttoned my shirt, got my jacket, thought I should probably buy a sweater, maybe at that trendy store off San Lorenzo square, the place I'd passed with Alexandra. That was all I needed to start thinking about her again, not that I'd stopped replaying the kiss and the electric touch of her hand. I hoped she'd be at the library, in the way I'd hoped to see my junior-high-school crush, but it was a lot more than that: she'd gotten under my skin.

I stopped at the hotel front desk, asked if the maid had been in my room.

The same guy was there as always, puffing on a cigarette, the air around him a toxic nicotine cloud. He managed to tear himself from an Italian tabloid and raised his head in slow motion. "The maid?"

"*La domestica,*" I said.

"*Perche?* A problem?"

I told him no, I was just curious. He sighed as if the conversation were exhausting, then said the maid was ill and had not been in at all.

What about you? I thought, but the idea of him attempting to clean a room was ridiculous.

Still early, I forced myself to walk slowly from Piazza di Madonna along the side of San Lorenzo, stopped at the coffee bar

I had been to the other day, and was greeted like an old friend. I sipped espresso, chatting with the barman about the weather, colder than usual, politics, never a good idea, then Italian soccer, about which I knew nothing.

The combination of caffeine and conversation made me feel better, but as I reached the square, I sensed it again, that feeling of being followed. I looked over my shoulder: some obvious tourists, Italians with briefcases heading to work, no one on my tail that I could see, though I couldn't shake the feeling, my antenna well honed, something that had come in handy in my Bayonne days. I looked around again but didn't stop, anxious to get back to the journal as I cut into the dark alley that led into the cloister. Just beside me, a couple of monks, hoods pulled up against the cold, looked more ominous than righteous. We nodded hello, then they headed into the garden as I headed up the stairs to the library, the whole time feeling as if I were not alone.

24

He stares at his cell phone. The red dot that represents the American's movement from hotel to espresso bar has stopped, the red dot idling.

It had not been difficult to install the camera and sensor, only an eighth of an inch square, in a corner of the hotel room to gather information from the American's laptop and phone, good for a distance of up to three hundred feet, thanks to recent products from FFI Software Solutions, a spyware firm he has used before in his work, both activated from his cell phone. The American will have no idea that every one of his emails and texts are being read, his calls listened to, GPS following his every move.

That part of the job was accomplished with ease. The other part, not so successful. He had searched the room, every drawer, the narrow closet, under the bed, stopped to read articles the American had on top of the dresser, but what he had been searching for was not in the room. It must be in the library. He would have to go and see for himself. But how to break in? And how to remove it without getting caught and, if successful, without rousing suspicion? That is imperative, his mission.

The red dot begins to move again, and he follows, a block behind, but no need to rush; with the spyware installed, he will not lose the American or be surprised by any sudden movements. He enlarges the map on his cell with thumb and forefinger, sees the dot move along the street and enter the Laurentian Library. No surprise. He takes his time catching up, stops at an espresso bar, the same place the American had stopped, nice that they like the same establishment, even makes small talk with the owner, then continues on to his usual spot, where he sits on the stone steps and lights a cigarette. The square is quiet this morning, few tourists, the kiosks selling leather belts and shoes across from the church still closed. He peers into the dark alleyway to the cloister at the end, sees the same monk he has seen before loitering at the edge and gazing out. He does not look away. Why should he? He is just a man sitting in the square enjoying his morning coffee and a smoke. Nothing wrong with that.

25

The marquis told me to meet him at a small café.

The place was dimly lit but not so dark that I could miss the roaches on the floor or crawling up the walls. I did not think it was the sort of place a marquis would frequent. But he was there. He greeted me with a wolfish smile. Said we needed to celebrate.

I asked him why.

His answer was to remove a silk cloth from his pocket. Inside was a perforated silver spoon. He ordered a bottle of Pernod. Sugar cubes. A pitcher of water. Goblets.

He poured the Pernod. Placed a sugar cube onto the perforated spoon and carefully balanced it on the rim of each goblet. Then he slowly trickled water through the sugar until the emerald-green absinthe below turned a cloudy white.

He handed me a glass and told me to drink up. He talked and talked. Kept referring to me as DEAR BOY which I did not like. But I drank. The anise flavor was intense and sweet on my tongue. It burned my throat. But I didn't mind.

We had one drink. Then another. Valfiero kept refilling my glass. He talked of paintings he bought and sold for huge sums of money. How he had traveled the world. The important people he had met and knew.

I listened but did not speak. I had nothing to say. But after another drink my tongue loosened. I spoke of my artwork. How I longed to make something great and beautiful. I complained about my job and my boss

Ticolat. I even confessed my worry over Simone's health. The whole time Valfiero nodded sympathetically like an old friend. And continued to refill my glass. Then he leaned in and whispered. Said he had a way to reverse my fortune and laid out his plan.

He finished and I laughed. I was sure he must be joking.

Valfiero waited. Then he said it again and I could see he was serious.

I told him he was insane! I got up to leave. But the absinthe had gone to my head and I was unsteady on my feet.

Valfiero took hold of my arm with his spidery fingers and lowered me back into my chair. He explained how it could be done. Every detail. And how much money we would make.

I told him it was impossible.

We sat there a few minutes not speaking. I thought he must be crazy. His scheme the ravings of a madman.

It can be done was all he said. He patted my shoulder. My cheek. Telling me to trust him. Calling me DEAR BOY over and over. I wanted to spit in his face!

Then he offered me a few francs to help see me through Simone's cold. I did not want to take his money. But I did.

He told me there would be more. Much more.

And it is true I took his money. But I say now and before God that I had no intention of doing what he suggested.

And I would not have had things not changed.

26

I turned the page, expecting to read more about Valfiero's plan, but Vincent had switched topics, writing at length about the drawings he was carving into his prison walls with a stick he had picked up in the courtyard, smuggled into his cell, and sharpened on the stone floor—a partially nude woman, an homage to Simone, and Napoleon on horseback, the image based on a famous painting by the dictator's court painter, Jacques-Louis David, which Vincent had drawn from memory. When the bells of San Lorenzo basilica sounded closing time, I had still not learned how Valfiero had persuaded Peruggia to steal the world's most famous painting, and I wanted to know, wanted to keep reading. I reflexively went for my phone, as I had a half-dozen times before, to photograph the pages, then remembered I did not have it.

I closed the journal and looked up. Chiara was not at her desk, and Riccardo was nowhere to be seen. A minute to make the decision to do this. But how? I opened the top button of my jeans, and with my other hand still on the journal, I began to slide it off the desk.

27

From the outside, the café next door to my hotel looked drab, but inside, it was busy and crowded, wall sconces creating film-noir shadows. The bartender, a young guy with slicked-back hair, greeted me with a flashy smile and a complimentary glass of prosecco, which I wanted but knew better. I let it sit there and ordered a sparkling water while he described the three panini choices that constituted the bar menu.

"*Farmi una sorpresa*," I said. Surprise me.

A few minutes later, he brought me a panini of prosciutto di Parma and fontina cheese.

I had just taken a bite when a man eased onto the barstool beside me. "Chilly night," he said. "I didn't expect it to be so cold here."

I nodded, not in the mood to talk.

"American?" he asked.

I looked him over: cap pulled down just above thick, tinted glasses that were almost opaque in the bar's dramatic light.

I nodded again.

"Me too!" he said. "From Chicago. You?"

"New York," I said, not matching his enthusiasm.

"Greatest city in the world!"

"Sometimes," I said, then took a bite of my panini, head down, hoping he'd get the hint.

He lit a cigarette. "Thank God we can still smoke in Italy!" He offered me one. I hadn't smoked in years, another habit I'd given up and didn't want to start again.

The bartender poured him the complimentary glass of prosecco, which he chugged down and asked for another. He pointed to my panini and said, "*Anche per me*," then looked at me. "I hope I said 'Same for me.' I don't speak Italian, but it's in the guidebook."

I said, "You asked to sleep with his sister."

"What?" The guy's mouth dropped open.

"Kidding," I said. "You got it right."

"Good one," he said and punched my arm, like we were fraternity pals. "So what brings you to Florence?"

"Visiting," I said, still trying to keep my words to a minimum.

"I'm here on business," he said, though I hadn't asked. "To purchase some paintings and objects for my clients."

That got my attention. "So you're a dealer?"

"I don't care for the name, but yes, I buy and sell art."

"No shame in being an art dealer."

"No, but sometimes I think I should do something else, you know, something worthwhile."

"Buying and selling art isn't worthwhile?"

"Well, it doesn't do much for the betterment of mankind."

"Few things do," I said, wondering if that was what I was doing here—something for the betterment of mankind or just for myself?

"So what do you do?" He nudged my arm with his elbow.

I put my sandwich down, tried not to sigh. "Teach," I said, hoping that would end the conversation.

"Oh. What do you teach?"

I considered making something up, knew that my answer would spark further conversation, but couldn't come up with anything. "Art history."

"No kidding," he said. "Well, we have a lot to talk about."

And that was it, the beginning of his art historical discourse with an emphasis on Leonardo, his "favorite artist of all time," another thing that got my attention. Then it was everything, from Leonardo's remarkable oil style to his disappointing experimentation with a new fresco technique. "Hey, don't get me wrong," he said. "I love the guy, but if he'd applied traditional fresco rules, *The Last Supper* would not be in such terrible condition."

"Artists need to experiment," I said, not wanting to be drawn into the conversation, thinking of Vincent and what Picasso had said to him.

"I guess you're right, though I wish Leonardo had had more patience."

That was it. "Are you kidding? He worked on the *Mona Lisa* for like twelve years! Took it with him when he moved to France and kept working on it until he died. Come on. The guy had patience."

"I suppose you're right." He lit another cigarette. "But I wish he'd done more art or at least finished everything he'd started."

"Everything Leonardo made—whether he finished it or not—was great!" I pictured his *Adoration of the Magi* in the Uffizi, Alexandra beside me, and wished she were here now instead of this guy. "You're an art dealer, so what do you think about this new Leonardo, the *Salvator Mundi*?"

"You mean, *if* it's a Leonardo."

"You doubt its authenticity?"

"Doesn't everyone?" he said.

"I don't know, but it sold for like what—three hundred million?"

"Four hundred and fifty million to be exact," he said.

"Do they know who bought it?"

"Supposedly Saudi's crown prince, Mohammed bin Salman.

Now it's missing or in hiding. Not in the Louvre's big Leonardo exhibition, and the Abu Dhabi Museum has gotten cold feet about showing it—excuse me, the *Louvre* Abu Dhabi Museum. The power of a name. Stick the word 'Louvre' in front of a pile of steel and bricks, and you're suddenly a great museum with great art." He made a noise of disgust in the back of his nose. "Word is the Saudis might be holding the painting hostage as a bargaining chip in dealings with the French."

"How do you know *that*?"

"Heard it…somewhere," he said with a shrug. "You know that Napoleon took the *Mona Lisa* to hang in his bedroom, right?"

"Wouldn't you, if you could?"

"No way. I don't think great art should be removed from the world and hidden away!" His voice rose, cigarette smoke streaming from his nose like a dragon.

I told him to relax, that I was kidding.

"Sorry. Just a pet peeve of mine, the way some private collectors steal art from the rest of us." He paused. "You wouldn't do anything like that, would you?"

"*Me?* No. And I couldn't afford it, even if I wanted to."

"What if you could?"

"Again, I was kidding."

"Of course," he said, elbowing me, a big smile on his lips, the only part of his face I could see clearly in the dim light, the dark glasses totally hiding his eyes. "So how long are you staying in Florence?"

It was starting to feel like an interview, my old Kill Van Kull radar picking up a vibe I didn't like it, and I turned it around. "How long are *you* staying?"

"Depends on how well my business goes. What are you working on?"

I didn't remember saying I was working on anything, but either way, I'd had enough. "Time for me to turn in," I said.

"So early? The night is young."

I told him I was tired and wished him good night.

"Up early tomorrow?"

I hoped I would be, anxious to get back to the journal, but it was none of his business, so I didn't answer, slid off the barstool, and turned to go. He stopped me, a hand on my arm.

"Hold on. We never introduced ourselves."

"Right. I'm Luke Perrone."

He extended his hand. "John Smith. Really good to meet you," he said and punched my arm again.

I felt like punching him back, harder, something about him I didn't like or trust, those dark shades indoors, all the questions, but all I did was say, "Good night."

28

I have not been writing for days. I could not. The idea of putting this down on paper was too painful. Instead I made drawings on the walls of my cell. Anything to distract myself. But today I have decided I must write everything down. Exactly as it happened. Every word.

Days passed at the museum. When I finished my work on the glass box for the Mona Lisa Ticolat told me that my services were no longer needed. He used the excuse that I had taken days off. Which was true. But I had only stayed home to take care of Simone. Ticolat knew this but he had no sympathy.

I did not know what to do. How would I make money? How would we survive? I could not sleep. I could not eat. I tried to hide my worry from Simone. I pretended to go to work every day. I looked for carpentry jobs. But there were none. Our funds grew low. And I became desperate.

And so I met with Valfiero. I told him I would agree to his plan. I asked him for a few francs on deposit and he gave them to me. We shook hands. But I swear I had no intention of going through with the plan. Not until Simone's condition became worse.

For days she had been unwell. Now she was shivering. Her face flushed. Her breath constricted.

I wrapped another blanket around her. I told her we must go to the hospital. But she protested. Her voice was weak but her will like iron. She claimed the last time the hospital had almost killed her with neglect. She was confident she would get better. That it was just a silly cold.

But her cough worsened.

I implored her to let me take her to the hospital. Again she refused. She begged me. Told me how much she hated the place. That the baby would be here in a few days and she would be strong again. She said the medicine I had purchased from the chemist was all she needed.

It was impossible to fight her.

Another day passed and her cough persisted. And when I saw her handkerchief spotted with blood I would no longer listen to her protests. I lifted her into my arms. She was too sick to fight me and folded her frail body against mine. I felt her fevered breath against my cheek.

Down six flights of stairs I held her. The most precious object in my life. The whole time I prayed and whispered in her ear. Hang on my darling. You will be fine. I promise.

It was a frigid Paris night. No moon. No stars. With the little money I had from Valfiero I hired a taxi. A luxury I was unused to. It bumped over cobblestones and I shouted at the driver to slow down. A moment later I begged him to speed up! I clutched Simone to me. Her skin was burning. Despite the noise of the street I could hear a rattle in her chest. I cursed myself for waiting so long.

Over and over I told her we would be there soon and begged her to hold on. I smoothed back her damp hair. Kissed her eyelids. I saw by the light of a passing streetlamp that her skin had gone from flushed to ashen. I begged the driver to go faster. I held Simone tighter. Though I worried I would not be heard by the God I had long ago abandoned I prayed and prayed.

She clasped my hand and whispered my name. Told me I was a great painter. I must remember that. And to be happy.

I told her it was no time to speak of such things. That we were only minutes away from the hospital. But she would not stop. Said it was important that I remember.

I told her to be quiet. Lay a finger gently on her lips. Felt they had gone cold.

She asked me to promise to be happy when she was gone.

I could not bear to hear her say such things. Repeated there was no need. That she would be fine. But she would not stop. So I promised her. Promised I would remember. Promised I would be happy. Begged her to save her strength. Told her how much I needed her. Beside me. Her belief in me. That without her I was nothing. I made her promise she would always be with me.

And she promised. Whispered my name. Said she would always be with me. Told me to look for her in the shadows.

I begged her not to say such things! It was her fever talking. She would be fine. Healthy and happy and painting her own beautiful paintings. I pleaded with her to hang on. For me.

I kissed her cheeks. Her forehead. Her lips. I held her firmly as the taxi bumped along the Parisian streets.

She said she loved me. And I said I loved her.

I told her she was my world.

I felt tears in my eyes and on my cheeks. Simone closed her eyes and nestled her head against my neck. And I felt her tears too.

Then she asked me to sing to her.

Sing what? I asked. And why?

She said sing. Sing anything.

My mind was spinning. All I could think of was that silly ditty Picasso had sung and so I sang it.

"Oh Manon—ma jolie—mon coeur te dit—bonjour."

Simone started to laugh and coughed blood. On her blouse. On the blanket. And I tried to quiet her.

But she pleaded with me not to stop. To keep singing. She needed to hear my voice. Needed to know I was there beside her.

She clutched my hand tightly. And so with tears clouding my eyes I sang that silly song over and over as Simone's grip eased and the only woman I have ever loved died in my arms.

29

I splashed cold water on my face, the image of Simone dying in Vincent's arms still resonating in the back of my mind. I could not remember ever feeling like this, my usual MO to turn sadness into anger or simply bottle it up and pretend not to feel anything. More than one girlfriend had pointed that out. I had come here looking for facts, not feelings, but the journal was affecting me in ways I'd never imagined.

I was sorry I had not stolen it yesterday. And I would have if Riccardo and Chiara had not come back into the research room at precisely the moment I was sliding the journal off the desk and about to cram it into my jeans. I had to stop. Stealing from the Laurentian Library would surely carry a substantial fine and undoubtedly bar me from ever using the library again, maybe even get me arrested and prosecuted. I pictured myself in some crummy Italian prison, the futile calls to the American embassy where they'd look up my juvenile history and that would be that. I wasn't about to end up like my teenage posse, two of them dead, one in prison, the others, who knows?

Perhaps it was for the best, safer that the journal remained in the library where no one else could get it.

I looked into the restroom mirror and splashed more cold water into my red-rimmed eyes.

Back at the long table, I read how they had made it to the hospital in time where an emergency-room doctor slit open Simone's belly and saved her baby, Vincent conveying the scene in vivid detail over several pages. I was reading so intently that when someone tapped my arm, I practically jumped and closed the journal fast.

"Sorry. I didn't mean to startle you," Alexandra said, looking down at me, asking if I was okay.

"Sure," I said. "I'm fine."

"You don't look it."

Chiara shushed us.

"She hates me," Alexandra whispered.

"Really? I think she likes me."

"That's why she hates *me*."

I managed a smile, stopped myself from saying how much I had thought about her, how much I'd missed her. "How long have you been here?"

"An hour or so. You were so wrapped up in your reading, you didn't see me come in." She asked again if I was okay, and I told her I had a bit of a headache from too much reading, and she suggested I quit, it was almost seven, the library about to close. And when she proposed dinner, I gave her a cool "Sure, why not?" while my inner voice shouted *YES!*

The librarian in the front office waved Alexandra through the scanner but stopped me and called Riccardo. I raised my arms and spread my legs while he patted me down, red-faced and clearly more embarrassed than I was. While he did the pat-down, Mussolini went through my backpack, her face balled into a determined knot, though all she came up with were my pencils and notepads and candy, all of which she jammed back in with a huff. Why did she have it in for me? Could she read my thoughts? Like right now when I was looking at her, thinking *cow*. I went through the body scanner, turned back, and said "*Grazie,*" with the biggest, phoniest smile I could manufacture.

The sun was starting to set, San Lorenzo's facade catching late-day shards of light that made it look threatening.

"What was that all about?" Alexandra asked. "Does Griselda think you're going to steal something?"

"Is that her name? Wasn't Griselda one of Cinderella's evil stepsisters?"

"Drizella," Alex said.

"Close enough," I said. "So why would I steal something?" I said, doing my best innocent-boy impersonation. "I think Riccardo is tipping her so he can feel me up."

"Oh, you're awful," she said.

I told her she was not the first person to tell me that, fished the bag of Jolly Ranchers out of my pocket, popped one in my mouth, and offered them up.

"Seriously? What are you, like ten?"

"Sweet tooth," I said, and she made a face that made me feel exactly that: ten years old.

"You must be freezing in that jacket. Do you wear it to look cool?"

I told her I hadn't expected it to be so cold here, and she led me across the square to peruse the kiosks, but there were only handbags and belts. She suggested the trendy men's shop we'd passed the other day, so we headed down the same narrow street off the square.

The men's store window was all mannequins in skinny striped pants and matching vests, billowy shirts that looked out of *Lawrence of Arabia*, and definitely not my style, though

Alexandra thought one of the vests would look good on her, and I agreed.

I asked where she'd been the last two days, and she said, "Why? Did you miss me?"

"A little," I said.

"Liar," she said.

"Really," I said. "I did."

"I meant the part about *little*," she said and grinned.

Pretty sure of herself, I thought, but she was right.

She asked how my work was going, and I told her I didn't know, which was true. I still wasn't sure what I would learn from the journal or what I would do with it. She gave me a look like she didn't believe me, then asked what I'd been reading that had me looking so upset.

"A journal," I said, willing to tell her that much, "from a long time ago, a sad story."

"Whose?"

"If I told you, I'd have to kill you," I said and laughed. "I'll tell you about it when I know more. I promise." I made the sign of the cross.

"That's the second time I've seen you do that. Were you an altar boy?"

"No, much to my mother's disappointment. Among other things."

"You gave her trouble?"

"Like you can't imagine."

She tilted her head, appraising me. "Oh, I can imagine."

"And she didn't deserve it." Which was true. She'd always tried her best, and she loved me, I knew that. "I was afraid I wouldn't see you again," I said, a thought that I hadn't meant to say out loud.

"I didn't mean to disappear, I just—" She stopped, then

shrugged off whatever she was going to say. "There were a few things I needed to take care of…at home."

"Home here, or home in New York?"

"Both. Nothing serious," she said, but her brow was knit.

I wasn't sure I believed her, but when she looped her arm through mine, I no longer cared. Then she steered us toward a restaurant she knew, a place she said was popular with locals.

Inside, the restaurant was dimly lit, candles on the tables, no actual light fixtures that I could see.

"Are they being cool or saving on electricity?" I whispered as a waiter led us to a small table by the window. The restaurant was almost full, boisterous but in a good way, people enjoying themselves.

Alexandra slipped off her jacket. She was wearing a white blouse with pleats down the front like a man's formal shirt, half the buttons open, a lacy camisole underneath, the gold locket peeking out, a combination of proper and sexy.

"Nice locket."

"It's my mother's," she said, wrapping her fingers around it.

"Does it have one of your baby curls in it?"

"Please," she said and smiled, but her lips were tightly compressed.

"Something wrong? I'm sorry if I pried."

"No. It's…okay." She leaned forward toward the candle and opened the locket. Inside was a small photograph of a woman, undoubtedly her mother, the resemblance striking.

"She's pretty," I said. "You two close?"

"Yes" she said on a breath. "She's always been in my court, on my side."

"You're lucky."

"Yes," she said again, the locket trembling slightly in her hand. Then she closed it with a snap, signaled the waiter, and ordered a glass of red wine. When I ordered Pellegrino, she asked why.

"Don't drink," I said.

"Never?"

"Not anymore."

"When did you stop?"

"I'm about to celebrate my tenth anniversary sober. Ta-da!" I twirled my finger in the air and faked a smile. I watched for signs of judgment or disapproval, but her face remained still and unreadable.

"Good for you," she said. "What made you finally give it up?"

"Let's see…" I tapped my chin theatrically. "I'd have to say it was waking up in a dumpster."

"Seriously?"

"Yes. And I do not recommend it. Particularly as I had no idea how I got there."

"Blackouts?"

"Uh-huh. But that's all in the past, and I'm not ashamed of it. Well, actually, I am, a little."

"You shouldn't be. It's a disease, like measles or chicken pox. I have two friends in AA."

"Oh, I see. Some of my best friends are drunks, that it?"

"That's *not* what I meant," she said.

I apologized, said I'd tell her the whole sordid story when I got to know her better, then decided to tell her now, to get it over with and see if she'd run—just the highlights or lowlights—both my parents drinkers, how I'd started when I was twelve, the DWI at sixteen. "I've already scoped out an AA room, in a church, here in Florence. They're always in a church or school or community center basement, very glamorous."

"Have you gone?"

"No," I said, explaining it was purely backup, that I wouldn't go unless I had the urge to drink, and I hadn't wanted to in years. I felt better now that I'd told her, and she seemed totally unperturbed, already talking about her Florence sublet and how much she loved the city. She was either a good actress or really didn't care. I nibbled an olive and watched her speak, the natural curve of her lips, the way she swiped her hair behind her ears, ordinary things, but on her, nothing was ordinary. I tried to understand what it was about her that was special: her beauty, her poise, how easily we talked, how she hadn't seemed to judge me. There was something else too, an elusive quality, like a butterfly that only temporarily alighted, then flew away. I didn't say much, happy to listen to her, could feel myself becoming more and more entranced by this woman I hardly knew. Was it that she felt unattainable, a challenge, the way I'd too often felt about women in the past—as conquests? Or was it that she had already conquered me?

I ordered dinner for us, speaking to the waiter in my best Italian, and Alexandra seemed impressed. When the food came, I was starving, though Alexandra only picked at hers. She asked again about my research, and I said I didn't know.

"You mean you won't tell me."

"No, I would. I just haven't put it together yet." And it was true. I wasn't sure what mysteries the journal would reveal and what they might mean.

The conversation was interrupted by a commotion at a table across the room, one hidden in the shadows, the candle on the table creating an eerie underlight on the waiter's face, and he was speaking loudly.

"He's saying something about not smoking," I said, "and something about a cigar. It's odd."

"What is?"

"The guy is wearing a hat. Indoors. Oh, he's put it out."

"The hat?"

"No, the cigar." I could no longer see the red glow of its tip, and the waiter was clearing the table. Someone hurried past our table, a blur, then the front door opened and slammed shut with a blast of cold air.

Alexandra exaggerated a shiver and leaned across the table as if to warm herself on the candle. I got a whiff of her perfume, the scent familiar.

"Joy, right?"

"Wow," she said. "Is your research on women's scents?"

Now I was sorry I'd said it, because it demanded an explanation, and I didn't feel like saying that an ex had worn it, a woman I thought I'd loved who'd left me because she wanted to settle down and have babies and how I had let her go because no way I was giving up my fast-lane art career for some bourgeois white picket fence and kids. Though now, when my career had veered into the slow lane and I was dependent on my full-time teaching job, I had to wonder who had the more bourgeois life.

"I never wore perfume before," she said. "A friend gave it to me for my birthday, just a few weeks ago."

I wished her a happy birthday and asked which one.

"Twenty-nine," she said. "And you?"

"Thirty-seven. Thirty-eight in two months."

"Ever married?"

When I told her no, she narrowed her gaze. "You're not one of those toxic bachelors, are you?"

"No," I said, thinking of Kathy and Amanda and Terri. It was not the first time I'd had the phrase leveled at me. "I've had relationships." I tried not to sound defensive. "Just haven't met the right person—yet."

She gave me one of her evaluating looks but smiled. I asked for her number and handed her my cell phone to punch it in. She ignored it, wrote her number on a cocktail napkin, held it back, and dangled it like a matador. "I'll let you have it if you tell me how you knew my perfume."

"I'm an expert, world-renowned for my nose," I said and displayed my profile.

She laughed, then said, "A girlfriend wore it, am I right?"

"Guilty," I said, then quickly asked her a question—if she'd ever been married—and was surprised when she said yes.

"It's a sad, sad story—a starter marriage. It only lasted a year. I knew it was a mistake at the altar."

"Why'd you go through with it?"

"I was…running away," she said dramatically, as if making a joke, though I sensed something real underneath it. She forced a laugh, then asked how long I was staying in Florence. I told I wasn't sure, that I was on intersession.

"That means you could be here for what, a month?"

"Maybe. I don't know yet."

"You like playing the man of mystery, don't you?"

"Me? I'm an open book."

"In *Braille*!"

"Give me a break, Alexandra."

"Call me Alex," she said.

"Ah, so you *do* like me."

"Let's just say I don't *dis*like you."

When the check came, she made a move. I grabbed it though I couldn't really afford it. She offered to leave the tip, but I said

I'd settle for her number, and she dangled the napkin for a second time. I reached for it and got hold of her hand, and we stared at each other. Then I leaned in for a kiss. She let go of the napkin and my hand, sat back, and started to put on her coat as if she had to get away fast. I said I was sorry, but she waved a hand. A minute later, she was gone, the smell of Joy perfume loitering like a cloud of confusion.

Had I said something wrong? There was so much to choose from—my family, my drinking, my exes.

I watched her pass by the window, a blur, and just behind her, a shadow and the red glow of a cigarette tip. Or was it a cigar?

30

Back in my hotel room, I tried to replay it: what *I'd* said, what *she'd* said, what had gone wrong. Was it because I'd been about to kiss her? But she'd already kissed *me*. I was usually the one to play it cool, but not this time. I unfolded the napkin with her number, stared at it a moment, then called. After one ring, I hung up.

Seconds later, my cell phone rang.

"Did you just call me?"

"Sorry. I decided it was too late, so—"

"No, it's not. Is anything wrong?"

"That's what I was calling to ask *you*."

Silence.

Then: "I'm sorry I ran off."

"Did I say something to upset you?"

"No. I just…needed to get back."

I didn't believe her but didn't push. "Will I see you at the library tomorrow?"

"It depends."

On what? What sort of game was she playing? Whatever it was, it was working to keep me off-balance—and making me want her more.

"I'll try," she said, then "Good night."

I stared at my cell phone. Why had she bothered to call me

back? Then I threw it down on the bed. *Fine.* If that was how she was going to play it, forget it, forget *her.* I didn't need this. I crumpled the napkin with her number and tossed it into the trash can. A second later, I dug it out. Damn it. I didn't want to think about her, didn't want to think about anything except why I'd come to Florence. *Eyes on the prize*, I told myself.

It was after eleven, but I was wide awake now. I opened my laptop and started typing. Another list of what I knew, what I'd read, the various things that led up to the theft.

1. Peruggia meets with Valfiero.
2. Valfiero promises money but Peruggia turns him down.
3. Peruggia gets fired from the Louvre.
4. Simone dies.
5. Peruggia steals the painting.

But why steal the painting *after* Simone died? I didn't know.

6. What happened to the baby?

I couldn't answer that either, but it suddenly came to me that the baby was my grandfather. At least I thought so, unless Vincent had fathered another child.

7. How much money did Peruggia get from Valfiero?

From my years of research, I knew that Peruggia had been released from jail with nothing. Had he stashed the money he'd made from Valfiero and reclaimed it after prison? If so, where?

I got up and started to pace, the idea of waiting until tomorrow to read the journal almost unendurable. I wanted to read it *now*, to hold it in my hands, to take as long as I needed. And why shouldn't I have it? Why shouldn't I steal it?

One more time, I considered the question.

Because I liked going to the library. Because I liked being a scholar on a mission. Noble enough reasons, but in fact there was the practical one: how to get it past the commandant at the door, the inevitable body search, the scanner. Still, I was not ready to give up the idea. I'd gotten away with a lot more and done a lot worse, me and my buddies adept at getting in and out of a house with several pawnable items, and I'd only been caught once.

But I was thirty-seven now, not fifteen, a solid citizen with a master's degree and a full-time job at a prestigious university. Could I really do anything like that now? More importantly, could I get away with it?

31

I was early, nursing an espresso, had circled the cloister of San Lorenzo twice when the young monk came out to greet me. *"Signore Perrone, come va?"*

As always, Brother Francesco was smiling.

"Bene, e lei?" I said.

He lifted his hands toward the sky. *"Bello giornata. Niente da dire."*

"Sì, bellissimo," I said. "A very beautiful day." I had been too impatient to notice before.

"You are an artist?" he asked.

I couldn't remember ever telling him and gave him a half-hearted nod, though I didn't feel like one these days.

"You have seen the *Annunciation* by Fra Filippo Lippi in the north chapel?" He gestured toward the church on the other side of the cloister wall. I had never even gone in, always so intent on getting to the library. The opposite of the typical tourist who had to see everything, I had seen practically nothing. "It is very beautiful," he said, "but maybe I say this because it was painted by a monk."

"Monks make great painters," I said, "like Fra Angelico."

He asked if I had been to San Marco, and I shook my head, yet another place I had yet to see.

"One of the gems of Florence," he said.

I asked him how long he'd been part of the order, and he said for ten years, since he'd been eighteen.

"And you're happy?" I asked.

"I have never regretted it."

I said that we should all feel that way about our lives, and he asked me if I did not feel that way about mine. I wasn't sure how to answer him, wasn't sure how I felt about my life, which felt distant and precarious. I thought about where I'd come from, the things I'd overcome. I said, "I've changed my life a lot."

He looked at me with his big blue eyes, waiting.

"Let's just say I had my vices. I wasn't exactly a good kid. *Capisce?*"

"There are many examples of sinners who become saints."

"I didn't say I was *that* bad, but I don't think I qualify for sainthood either." I felt like I was at confession, but there was a kindness about the monk that made me want to open up. "When I was a teenager, I was part of a group, a gang—and we did some bad things. We stole and…"

"You know of Saint Dismas, the good thief? Another saint with a bad past. He was crucified beside Jesus."

"You mind if I hope for a better ending?"

The monk laughed. "You are funny, Signore Perrone. I am certain your life will turn out well. *Continua così. Avanti così.*"

"Stay on course?"

"*Sì.* My teacher, an older, wiser brother, always say that."

"Stay on course," I repeated and was about to say goodbye to Brother Francesco, when he stopped me.

"*Ha un amico a Firenze?*"

"Do I have a friend in Florence? You mean Alexandra, the America girl?"

"No. A man. He comes here, *ogni giorno.*"

"*Every day?* What do you mean?"

"*Lui aspetta.*"

"He *waits?*"

"*Sì.* I thought he waits for you."

"Why?"

"Because he is here when you arrive and gone when you leave."

"Where?"

The monk guided me out of the alley and pointed to a spot along the east wall of the square that led to the entrance.

"There," he said, indicating a low set of stone stairs leading to an old wooden doorway. "That is the entrance to—how you say—the dormitory, where the monks live. Where I live. But we do not use that entry. We go in through the cloister."

"What does he look like, this man who waits?"

"Tall," he said and made a move to show the guy was also weighty or muscled. But he could not describe his face because he "wears *un cappello*, a hat, and sunglasses—and he is always *fumando*." He mimed a smoker dragging on a cigarette.

I asked him to let me know if the guy showed up, and he said maybe it was a "*coincidenza.*"

"Maybe," I said. "But please let me know if you see him. I just want to meet him—see if I know him."

"I will, as you Americans say, keep an out eye," he said.

"An *eye out*," I said and had to smile.

32

The idea of a stranger watching had gotten to me. I knew I would not be able to sit still or read. I checked out the stairs Brother Francesco had indicated, did a three-sixty and scanned the piazza—people milling about, some tourists taking pictures, a few monks heading toward the cloister. I stayed there a few minutes, checking out men in hats—too many—anyone smoking a cigarette—even more. Then I gave up. But now, everything that had been bothering me was buzzing in my brain—the idea of stealing the journal, Alexandra's advance and retreat, Quattrocchi's odd disappearance. I had left him several messages and texts; now I tried his cell again, but it went immediately to voicemail. This time, I didn't bother to leave a message. Instead, I headed to the university.

Signora Moretti was in Quattrocchi's outer office.

"Professore Quattrocchi, is he in? I need to speak with him."

"No," she said and went back to her typing.

"No *what*? He's not in or I can't speak to him?"

She glanced up, then down, and started typing again.

"Professore Quattrocchi missed our dinner date, and he hasn't been answering my calls. I'm worried. Has he contacted the university?"

She shook her head no, but this time, I thought I detected some concern.

"I'm *worried*," I said again. "Does he usually stay away without calling, without contacting you?"

"The *professore* has been through much—with his loss. I do not wish to disturb him."

"But not to call, to drop his classes, just like that? I want to see him to make sure he's okay."

Signora Moretti hesitated, sighed, then nodded. "His home is near Santa Croce." She wrote the address on a piece of paper and handed it to me. "You will please to let me know the *professore* is fine."

I put Quattrocchi's address into Google Maps and followed the route, holding my phone out in front of me like a divining rod. It led me past the Bargello Museum, which I had been meaning to visit to see Donatello's young *David*, a sculpture that many art historians believed had kicked off the Renaissance, one more artwork I had taught and never seen. The crenellated building dominated a small square and blanketed the surrounding streets in shadow. If I was reading my GPS correctly, I was heading southeast, away from the historic part of the city into a less populated neighborhood, along one angled or curving street to another, buildings shifting from warm grays to tans to sienna and even rose. I could feel the presence of generations, the weight of it in the stone walls and peeling paint, could smell it in the air, almost taste it, not just the city's age but its history, and I was enjoying it.

My enjoyment stopped about the same time my GPS quit and I hit a dead-end street and had that feeling again, of being followed. I retraced my steps, wasn't sure if I was being paranoid, but my radar had saved my ass more than once, and I'd learned to trust it.

I found my way to a wider, busier street—the whole time looking over my shoulder—and my Google Maps came back to life.

I kept my eyes glued to the little blue ball on my phone's map so I missed the fact that the neighborhood had become rougher and grittier, ugly old buildings mixed with ugly new ones, more trash and graffiti than I had seen anywhere else in the city. I was glad when my GPS directed me onto a kind of neighborhood thoroughfare, one side lined with bicycles, the other with motorbikes, dozens of them all perfectly angled. Another block and I found Via dei Pepi, Quattrocchi's street, the sign high up on a drab tan wall showing serious symptoms of water damage.

Via dei Pepi looked too narrow for cars, which gave it a back-alley quality, though it still had charm, some of the houses with newly painted shutters on upper windows and lovely metal work covering the ones on street level, though I realized they also served as bars. Several houses had cracked stone surfaces and more water erosion, but others showed obvious signs of gentrification, freshly painted facades and shiny new doors, and number fifteen—Quattrocchi's home—was one of these. Three stories painted ochre bordering on yellow, shutters dark green, not a bit of peeling paint or water damage. The door looked new too, dark wood, and curved to fit into a stone arch, above it a half-moon transom of metal florets. In the center of the door, a dangling metal knocker. I lifted it and let it fall back against the wood, the noise sharp and hollow.

There was no answer.

Then I noticed the small but new-looking bronze plaque with a buzzer and an oval grating that appeared to be an intercom. I pressed it, waited, then tried again. Nothing.

I lifted the metal knocker and let it fall back.

Again nothing.

I tried calling Quattrocchi's number, thought I could hear a muted ring from inside the house before I got his voicemail, said it was me, and that I was just outside his door.

I crossed the narrow street and looked up, the shutters closed, everything about the place still and quiet. It didn't make sense, Quattrocchi disappearing without notifying the university or anyone, and it felt bad.

Without really thinking about it, I found the number of a nearby police station and called.

"*Persona scomparsa*," I said.

The cop asked how long the person had been missing.

"*Pochi giorni*," I said. "A few days."

"*Non abbastanza tempo*." Not enough time, he said and hung up.

I called back, got the same cop. "Can you at least check his house?"

The cop asked if I was a relation. When I said no, he hung up again. "Fuck you too!" I said to a silent phone.

Was I overreacting? It was possible Quattrocchi had gone away and wanted to be left alone. It was true he had been through a lot—though he had seemed okay at our lunch, friendly and eager to talk. So what had changed?

I looked back at his house, the shuttered windows, everything still. I'd always trusted my gut, and right now, it was telling me that something was wrong.

33

The gray-and-white marble room was square and austere, smaller than I had imagined from seeing it in photos, but taller and soaring, crowned by a perfect dome of circles and semicircles. I stared up as if looking into heaven, what I imagined Michelangelo had in mind when he had designed the Medici Chapel—the most famous tomb in the world, created for the Italian banking family who had ruled Florence for two hundred years and left their mark everywhere in the city.

After my futile search for Quattrocchi, I had come back to the library and read until the lunch break. I hadn't planned on coming to the chapel until Chiara mentioned it was just around the corner. It wasn't exactly—there were few actual corners in Florence—but all I had to do was follow the long wall of San Lorenzo back toward my hotel and there it was, in Piazza di Madonna, literally across the street from my hotel. How many times had I walked right by it, how many times had I noticed but not noticed the small modest plaque, CAPPELLE MEDICEE, and not given it a thought.

I stood practically alone in the center of the chapel—the only other person a guard seated in a far corner, typing away on a cell phone—and did a slow three-sixty, taking in the feeling of strength and monumentality Michelangelo had given the sculpture, the architecture, the blind windows that suggested there was no way out. There were no actual windows, a kind of glorious claustrophobia, and I had to wonder if Michelangelo wanted people to feel trapped here, as if in purgatory. I looked up at the more than life-size figure of Lorenzo de Medici, face hidden in shadow, a withdrawn and brooding quality that made me think of what I had just read—Vincent seeing his son for the first time in the hospital nursery, holding him and thinking he was all he had left of Simone, all he left in the world. Then Simone's mother, Marguerite, had shown up in a fury, accusing him of killing her daughter, a terrible scene to read, and Vincent had spared neither reader nor himself, accepting the blame and powerless to stop Marguerite from taking the baby and telling him he would never see the boy again.

It felt right that I should be thinking about that now, ruminating on birth and death in a funerary chapel.

I shivered, gazed back at the pensive Lorenzo de' Medici flanked by the allegorical figures of *Dawn* and *Dusk*, massive sculptures that only the great Michelangelo could have created, then did an about-face to take in Lorenzo Giuliano, equally massive but with a handsome idealized face and impossibly long neck, poised as if about to stand up, everything about him so alive, the two figures in stark contrast.

I thought of Vincent, who had contemplated his own death for days and weeks after Simone's death, the man riddled with guilt that made it impossible for him to sleep, and the nonstop drinking he had used as a temporary salve over his excruciating pain, something too familiar to me.

I regarded the allegorical figures flanking Giuliano, *Night* and *Day*, the former imagined as a woman, everything about her exaggerated, overlong arms and legs, more highly polished and finished than her male counterpart, *Day*, an almost brutish figure with a lionlike head half-hidden by his massive shoulder.

I moved in for a closer look at his roughly chiseled face, which looked unfinished, and remembered the entire tomb had never been completed, that Michelangelo had planned not only to be its architect and sculptor but to paint a fresco of the resurrection, but he never did.

I thought again of Vincent, contemplating suicide for weeks, until he realized he had a reason to live—his son! He'd written pages describing in detail how he had dressed and shaved and put on his best clothes and had gone to see Simone's mother in her Paris apartment, and though she had slammed the door in his face, he'd refused to leave, pounding on her door until she had no choice but to let him in. He pleaded to see his son, and she had relented that much. Vincent had lovingly depicted the baby, with soft blond hair and blue-gray eyes like his mother, then described how he'd held him and kissed him and begged Marguerite to let him take the child home or at least let him visit. She had refused, accusing him of having nothing, no money, no way to care for a child, and Vincent knew she was right. He'd left her apartment a beaten man, once again considering the ways he might take his own life, all of it written in such painstaking prose, I could hear his words and see him prowling the streets of Paris, dejected and suicidal, the great-grandfather I had never known, more alive to me than my own parents.

A glance back at Giuliano, so regal and alive, then across the room at Lorenzo, dark and brooding, and those allegorical figures surrounding them, and it came to me that the entire room was an allegory of transition—*Dawn* to *Dusk*, *Night* to *Day*, the passage of time, the days of our lives leading toward our eventual deaths.

But Vincent had not chosen death. Not yet. With the one thing, the only thing that mattered to him—his son—he knew what he must do to get him back.

The journal pages continued to echo in my mind as I made my way back to the library—why my great-grandfather had made the decision to contact Valfiero again, the answer to why he had gone ahead with the theft *after* Simone's death. It was simple: he needed the money to persuade Simone's mother that he could be a father to his son. And I knew something else: had he not been in the depths of despair, he would never have done it. The last pages I'd read were not only filled with Vincent's anguish over his decision but his plans—the tools he would need, which day would be best.

I took the stairs to the upper level of the cloister two at a time. I had to get to the library to see if I was right, to see if the next pages would tell me more about the theft itself.

34

Smith typed in his code, the email encrypted, as usual. The INTERPOL insignia filled the top half of his screen, the message from his supervisor, Andersen, below it.

> Interesting assignment for you. Suspicion of art theft ring based in Bahrain. Need analyst to coordinate with the National Central Bureaus. *On-site.* 12–18 months. Great opportunity. Full file and TBD when you return. Hope you are feeling better.

Bahrain? And for twelve to eighteen months *on-site?* No fucking way. This was no "great opportunity." It was punishment. Banishment. And for what? Taking sick leave? No, Andersen was trying to make him quit so he would not have to fire him, basically impossible after all the years he had put in. But Bahrain? He might as well have said Siberia.

Smith typed BAHRAIN into Google, scanned the data—*island in the Persian Gulf...gained independence from the UK in 1971... government protests and human rights violations*—then slammed the laptop cover shut. The nerve of that guy, who had been at INTERPOL what—three years? Smith knew about the latest INTERPOL directive too: pare down and cut waste. Was that what he'd become, *waste?*

Smith raised the window with such force it shook in its frame. He would show them. He was onto something a lot bigger than Andersen or any other art analyst had done, doing things none of them would dare to do.

He stared across the plaza at Perrone's hotel, decided that next time, he would throw a scare into him. In real life, Perrone had been quite different from the man Smith had known only from his file: cagier, smarter, perhaps not so easily duped or scared. But there were ways to frighten the toughest, smartest men; Smith knew that.

He nodded at the thought and felt calmer, pleased with himself, thinking how scared men made bad choices, mistakes. He straightened up and shivered, not just from the cold but from the notion that he too might be making bad choices.

35

Steam was rising off the Seine in the first light of dawn. I concentrated on slowing my pace and taking deep breaths. I passed early-morning fishermen and vendors setting up to sell souvenirs to the tourists. I kept my head down. The painting was under my jacket and I pressed it tightly to my chest. Tears burned my cheeks. But I had done it. Stolen the world's most famous painting for my son.

I got home and spoke to Simone. Told her I had brought her the painting as promised. Wrapped it in one of her scarves and placed it in a trunk I had specially built with a false bottom. Draped the trunk with a cloth and put a vase in the center so that it looked like nothing more than an ordinary table.

Then I waited.

A day passed. Then another. I scoured the newspapers. But there was no mention of the theft.

How was that possible?

More than once I opened the trunk to make sure the painting was still there. Afraid I had been dreaming.

Another day passed. Still no news.

I paced. I drank. I could not eat or sleep.

It was days later that the story finally appeared. Headlines on every newspaper. The famous Mona Lisa stolen!

I purchased all the papers and read every word. I had to see what they knew.

They did not have a clue.

The Louvre was closed for a week. Sixty policemen searched every inch of its forty-nine acres. They found nothing. Only the glass and frame I had left behind in the stairwell.

The French borders were closed. Every ship and train in and out of the country was searched.

I must admit it gave me pleasure to know the painting was in a trunk just a mile from where it had been hanging.

I read how Parisians grieved for the painting as if it were a loved one and I went to stand among these foolish mourners who left notes and flowers for a painting. I watched people cry. And I cried too. But not for the painting.

When the Louvre reopened thousands flocked to see the empty space on the wall where the painting had once hung.

Rewards were posted. The Louvre offered 25,000 francs. One newspaper offered 5,000. Another 40,000.

I was tempted to return the painting and collect the rewards myself!

Then I read how every worker at the Louvre would be interrogated. I knew they would eventually make their way to me. And they did. Four of them. An inspector by the name of Lapine. His fat assistant. And two gendarmes. They searched every inch of my apartment. Everywhere but the trunk.

Lapine sat me down at the table. The very trunk disguised as a table. He asked me why Ticolat had dismissed me.

I told him about Simone's illness. How I had stayed home to take care of her. How Ticolat had no pity. I cried. And it was not an act. I said Lapine could ask anyone at the Louvre if I did good work. Anyone but Ticolat.

Lapine asked what I had been doing for work since I had been fired. I told him I had been living on what I had saved from my wages. He gave me a suspicious look. But how could he prove otherwise?

He asked why had I come to France? And what I had done before? He asked about every facet of my duties at the Louvre. Especially my work with the Mona Lisa. I took my time to describe how I had constructed the wooden box piece by piece. How I cut the glass and fitted everything together. How I had prepared the walls for the bolts. I explained everything in minute detail. Over and over. His eyes began to glaze and droop. Just as I had hoped.

I knew Lapine was suspicious. But a calm had come over me.

Until he told me a fingerprint had been discovered on the frame left in the stairwell! Like every Louvre employee I knew my fingerprints were on record.

Lapine inked my hand and took new prints.

But luck was on my side. The museum had only printed each employee's right hand. And the print on the frame was from my left thumb and not a match!

Lapine had me sign a statement of innocence. He laid the document onto the very tablecloth that covered the trunk. I signed the paper picturing the painting only inches below.

The police were about to leave when I had a thought. I asked Lapine if he knew the poet Guillaume Apollinaire. I said how much I admired the man—the whole time thinking of the cruel things he had written about my artwork. I told Lapine how I had just read Apollinaire's column in L'Intransigeant. How he had called for the burning down of the Louvre. I quickly added I was sure he must be joking. I did not want Lapine to think I was trying to implicate the poet. Which of course I was. I added that Apollinaire might have sold some sculptures to the artist Pablo Picasso. And it was possible those sculptures might have come from the Louvre. I said this all in the most casual manner.

Lapine's eyes grew wide. He asked me how I had this information. I said I did not want to get anyone in trouble. I waited until Lapine *demanded I tell him. Then I said I had seen the objects in Picasso's studio. Lapine was immediately anxious to leave.*

It was soon after that I heard Apollinaire and Picasso had been arrested. I pictured the arrogant poet and the self-important Little Spaniard sweating while the police interrogated them. I took pleasure in it. And when I heard that Ticolat and the Louvre director had been fired I took pleasure in that too.

Days passed. And I waited. Waited to hear from Valfiero. And for the next part of the plan to begin.

36

I knew about Picasso's arrest and Apollinaire's humiliation. I had read lengthy descriptions—the artist and poet detained, stripped naked, interrogated for a full week, then tried. Now I knew it was Vincent's payback.

I took a moment to mull over all I had read and what I hoped to learn. I looked down at the journal, then up at Chiara and Beatrice. That thought again, my fingers practically itching, though I knew I could not get away with it. But could I possibly smuggle my cell phone in and photograph the remaining pages? But where would I hide it, and how would I take pictures without being seen?

I glanced over to the far end of the table, what I had to come to think of as *Alexandra's seat*: empty. I replayed the other night—missed our banter, her smile, the smell of her perfume, the way she held herself like a dancer—then her last-minute bolt from the restaurant. I still couldn't figure it. Maybe it was better that she wasn't here. I didn't need the game-playing, the disruption. A lie. I missed her and knew I'd sign up for more game playing if I got the chance.

I wrote her name on my pad and circled it. Jesus, I was like some moonstruck teenager. At least I hadn't drawn it inside a heart! I crossed her name out and wondered again about her sudden departure. Had she had seen through me? Underneath my facade of cool? What if she never came back to the library? What if I never saw her again?

I let out a sigh so loud the two other scholars on the opposite side of the table looked up. I smiled sheepishly and shrugged an apology. This was ridiculous. *I* was ridiculous, letting a woman I hardly knew get under my skin. Is this what I'd done to the women I had dated—drawn them in, played games, then disappeared once I had them on the line? Perhaps this was some karmic payback? Another sigh. It was nearly closing time, and I was tired. I closed my laptop and slid it into my backpack, along with my pencils and notepads.

I leaned over Chiara's desk, and she looked up, smiling, twirling a lock of hair around her finger. I asked her if she had seen Signora Greene, perhaps this morning when I'd been out?

Chiara's lips pursed. "No," she said, letting go of her hair. "I am the librarian, not *polizia*."

I cut through the cloister and alleyway, the guy beside me before I even noticed him.

"Hey, John Smith. Remember? From the other night—at the hotel bar?" He exhaled a plume of cigarette smoke, as if he'd been holding it in for too long.

I eyed him sideways, still wearing his shades and the baseball cap pulled down to his eyebrows. Though art dealers came in all shapes and sizes, he didn't fit any mold I knew, no Prada suit, no designer shoes or sneakers. I asked what he was doing in this part of town.

"I had business a few streets away, was just passing by, and here you are. What a coincidence."

I thought of my uncle Tommy, the retired cop, how he always said there was no such thing as coincidence.

"How about a drink?" Smith asked. "You look tired. Your research wearing you out?"

Had I told him I was doing research?

"A quick one—on me," he said, "at the café beside your hotel again?"

I took in his strong build, the hat, the cigarette clamped in the corner of his mouth: Brother Francesco's description.

We walked to the café, the sky growing dark, Smith whistling the whole time, which annoyed me. We found seats at the bar, and he asked what I'd like to drink, reminding me that he was paying, and frowned when I said "Pellegrino."

He ordered a beer, a Peroni, and made a big deal out of it being my name, joking that I was obviously the heir to an Italian brewery fortune. When I pointed out the different spelling, he waved it away, refusing to give up the joke, which he seemed to find funny and I found annoying.

When he asked again how my work was going, I turned it around and asked about his. He said it was going slowly, and I asked why, and he went into a thing about no one caring about old master art anymore and how it cost ten times more to buy an Andy Warhol than a Titian, and I pretended to commiserate because I wanted to keep him talking.

"Some people don't even *like* what they buy," he said. "It's all about the name, the prestige of owning something of *known* value."

I didn't think that was anything new, pictured my own paintings, bubble-wrapped and gathering dust in my studio.

"I hate the idea that art is traded like a commodity," he said.

"Isn't that what *you* do?"

He took off his cap for the first time and scratched his head, his hair buzzed a fraction of an inch, a shadow on his skull, but he kept the shades on, paused a moment as if considering what to say. "So what's worse, being an art dealer who has to buy and sell art he doesn't really like or being an artist who has to kiss up to collectors and critics?"

I told him I'd never been good at ass-kissing, and he said, "But you must make sacrifices to get what you want."

"Sometimes," I said, thinking more about the things I might have sacrificed by coming here—my teaching job, my art career—then turned the attention to him again. "How about your sacrifices?"

He paused as if composing an answer, then said, "It's an addiction, don't you think?"

I had no idea what that meant, though the word *addiction* was loaded for me. I wondered if he had picked up on my drinking problem and was giving me a dig. *But why?* "What do you mean by addiction?"

"Art, you know—making it, collecting it."

I told him I'd never thought of making art as an addiction.

"Collecting then," he said, "acquiring. Some people can't get enough."

"Then they have to pay for it. Simple as that."

"Not always so simple," he said, finishing his beer in one long pull, then ordering another. I was tempted to ask if *he* had a drinking addiction. "What if the art is not for sale?" he asked.

"Like art theft?"

"Sometimes people buy stolen art without knowing it's stolen."

Unless I was reading into it—and that was possible—the conversation was definitely taking a weird turn. Was it possible he was offering me stolen art?

I asked if he worked through other art dealers or if he had an office in Florence, trying to glean more information.

"Who needs an office these days?"

"So what then? You use a coffee shop or a library—maybe the Laurentian Library, like today?"

"I wasn't at the library, just passing by," he said. "I told you that."

"Oh, right. I forgot. Are you often in this part of town?"

"Not really," he said, taking his time to light another cigarette. "You know, sometimes people want something so much they stumble into dangerous situations without even knowing it."

Where did that come from? "Has that happened to you?" I asked, yet again trying to turn the question around. "Have *you* stumbled into a dangerous situation?"

"*Me?*" he said. "No, not *me*."

I didn't know what sort of cat-and-mouse game Smith was playing, but I was willing to play. For now. "Who then?" I asked.

He took a long pull on his beer, dragging out the moment. "When it comes to valuable objects, people can be ruthless," he said. "Believe me, I've seen it in my line of work."

I felt like we were at a tennis match, lobbing non sequiturs back and forth. "So how are you spending your days here? Exactly. I mean, without an office?"

"I go from dealer to dealer, client to client, like I said."

"Did you? I forgot."

"You have a poor memory, Luke Perrone."

"Actually, I have a very good memory, John Smith." I added a thin smile. "Like, didn't I see you hanging in front of San Lorenzo the other day?"

"What? No. You must be mistaken."

"One of the monks described you."

"So was it one of the monks or you who saw me?"

I didn't bother to answer, let my silence hang there, suspended between us.

A moment passed, then Smith asked, "*Which* monk?" He took a deep drag on his cigarette, let the smoke out slowly while I stared at the glowing tip of his cigarette.

"Just one of the brothers of San Lorenzo."

"I see," he said. "Well, I've been too busy to *hang out*."

"I thought you said your work was going slowly."

"Did I?"

"Yes. Perhaps it's *you* who has the bad memory."

He scoffed a laugh. "Not when it comes to something important. Then I remember everything. In detail."

"Good for you," I said, but I'd had enough of this—whatever *this* was. I said good night, and this time, he didn't try to stop me.

At the café door, I glanced back, caught Smith chugging the last of his beer. Then he raised the empty bottle like a toast, though there was nothing celebratory about it.

37

The morning was dark, the clouds low. As I headed out of Piazza di Madonna, there were sirens in the distance, a normal part of Manhattan's background music but here, in Florence, something I was unused to hearing. It was not until I came around the long, curved wall of San Lorenzo that I saw the cop cars, their lights flashing, and all the *polizia* and the crowd lining the perimeter of the piazza. Carabinieri were stationed at the alleyway and the cathedral and by the stairs that Brother Francesco had pointed out to me as the place the stranger had waited. The door behind the stairs was ajar, red-and-white diagonally striped police tape across it.

I asked one of the *polizia* what was going on, but he ignored me. Then I spotted Chiara, weeping theatrically, dabbing her eyes and cheeks with a lace handkerchief. I asked what happened, but she was crying too hard to answer. I put my arm around her, and she sagged against my chest, sobbing.

"*Cosa è successo?*" I asked.

"*Una tragedia!*" she said, lifting her head, tears tracking mascara down her cheeks before she fell back against my chest.

Beside us, an elderly monk with a face out of an old Rembrandt portrait wailed, "*È morto!*"

"What? Who?"

"Fra Francesco," he said.

Had I heard him correctly? "*Che cosa?*"

The monk looked up at the dark sky and said it again. *"Fra Francesco—È morto—È morto!"*

No way. Brother Francesco. Dead? Impossible.

Another monk joined him, the two of them crying in unison, crossing themselves over and over and repeating, "Fra Francesco."

Chiara looked up at me with swollen eyes. *"Nel sonno è suffocate,"* she said.

I couldn't believe it; the idea of such a young man suffocating in his sleep didn't seem possible. I asked about the door and the police tape. She shook her head. "An old door, *è rotto*, broken."

I patted her back, then looked past her to see the Italian equivalent of EMTs coming through the dark alleyway, a body covered with a sheet strapped to a gurney.

"I must pray," Chiara said.

I nodded, the idea of prayer something I had always loathed, but right now, it seemed like the absolutely right thing to do.

The alleyway to the cloister was closed, but the cathedral was open.

The interior was a surprise, expansive and impressive behind that plain, rough-hewn facade. Everything gray, white, and massive, the diamond-patterned floor leading me down a long, wide nave lined with tall columns that drew my eyes up to an ornate ceiling, hundreds of white squares lined with gold, each with a gilded floret in the center, a few with the Medici gold shield and small red balls. Nothing like any church I'd ever known, certainly not St. Mary Star of the Sea, the redbrick church my parents had dragged me to, always against my will—until I was twelve and refused to ever go again.

At the end of the nave was a sign for the Old Sacristy and a plaque that said it had been designed by Brunelleschi. It was a smallish room with a dome that looked like a large opened umbrella perfectly divided into twelve segments, and below it, on the back wall, a simple crucifix. The seating was cordoned off, and I knelt on instinct and made the sign of the cross, then headed back into the main church, which was practically empty. I found a seat in a pew and watched an old woman light a candle in the apse. Then I closed my eyes, and the young monk's words came back to me.

Continua così. Avanti così.

Stay on course.

I had wanted to ask him if what I had been doing here in Florence was the right course, but it was too late now.

Though I doubted that Brother Francesco needed my help, I recited a prayer, one I was surprised I remembered.

Eternal rest grant unto him, O Lord,
and let perpetual light shine upon him.
May the souls of all the faithful departed,
through the mercy of God, rest in peace.

According to my Sunday School teacher, the prayer would help those who had not yet reached heaven and would shorten their time in purgatory. I was pretty sure Brother Francesco was not stuck in purgatory—I didn't even believe in purgatory—but I said the prayer just the same.

Outside, Piazza San Lorenzo looked normal, a few people strolling, the kiosks open, a tour group taking pictures. How was it that life went on in the face of tragedy? The alleyway to the cloister was open again, everything back to business.

I headed through the alley and pictured Brother Francesco tending the cloister garden. It didn't seem right that he was not here. It didn't feel right to go back to the journal either, but what else was I supposed to do?

Continua così, avanti così, I said to myself. *Stay the course, go back to your reading.*

I started up the library stairs, then turned and looked through the alley to the low stone stairs and the old door to the dormitory, still cordoned off with police tape, and wondered if there had been a break-in. Was I the only one to put the two things together? A broken door. A dead monk.

38

Weeks passed. The night finally came.

I took the painting from the trunk. Wrapped it tightly in Simone's scarf. Hid it under my jacket. And set off.

It was late and had been raining for days. The sewers had overflowed. There were rats in the streets. Everywhere. Underfoot and foraging for food. Fat and disgusting. The Seine was a frightening sight. Yellow torrents flush with the banks. Threatening to spill. Already there was talk of flooded cellars. Building foundations weakened. Even those of the Eiffel Tower! I imagined the lower-level carpentry shop of the Louvre. Pictured artworks floating in dirty river water.

The meeting was on the far side of Père-Lachaise Cemetery. I tramped through the mud past graves and monuments. Everything covered in mist and fog. Pulled my jacket tighter to protect the painting.

I finally reached the other side and ducked under the remains of an old wall. Emerged on the other side of the cemetery. I was cold and shivering but relieved to be among the living.

It did not take long to find the art forger's building. The foyer reeked of damp and mold. The stairwell of turpentine. I trudged to the top floor. Knocked on the door four times. Paused. Knocked twice. Our prearranged signal.

Yves Chaudron opened the door. It was the first time I had met him. A man of middle age and middle height though his features were fine. Blue eyes enlarged by spectacles and rimmed red from strain.

The front room of the apartment was in total disarray. Books and clothes on chairs or dropped on the floor. Crumpled newspapers. The turpentine odor was stronger here but mixed with something rotten. Chaudron's shirt was dirty. His smock slick with paint. I glanced into his kitchen. Dishes stacked and encrusted with food. Roaches everywhere.

Chaudron was anxious to get his hands on the painting but I made him wait. We both waited. For Valfiero. Who was late.

Soon the art forger grew impatient. He said he could wait no longer. He was bursting to see the painting.

And I gave in.

He swept papers off a table. Propped the painting up. Stood gazing at it for a long time. Said it would be his greatest challenge and greatest achievement. Then he scooped the painting up and led the way into his studio.

On the walls were several paintings in progress. A small Corot landscape of a country scene with blue sky and gray clouds. I asked Chaudron how he had done it. He explained that like any good student he had simply set up his easel in the museum and made a copy!

There were two more paintings side by side. One was finished. The other in a half state of completion. I recognized the artist was Jean-Dominique Ingres. I looked from the original to the half-finished copy. It was remarkable. Chaudron said the collector intended to donate the original to a museum and wanted a copy for himself. Then he laughed. Said perhaps it was the other way around. But he did not care.

He boasted of his talent. I could feel his pride slip over me like unctuous slime. Knew he was waiting for a compliment. But I said nothing.

I listened to him talk of his artistic training and how he had dropped out of the art academy because his instructors could teach him nothing.

He said he had always been told he had a great hand. The greatest of any artist. And yet I detected some disappointment when he said it. Perhaps he felt that was all he possessed. He said he had once dreamed of becoming the greatest artist in Europe and I almost felt sorry for him. But then he claimed he was indeed the greatest artist in Europe!

I might have challenged him. But it was then that Valfiero arrived. Breathless from climbing the stairs and leaning on his cane. He stopped and stared at the Mona Lisa for a great while. His eyes hungry with greed. He rubbed his spidery fingers together and talked of his plan. Chaudron would makes copies. He would sell them. It was that simple. The paintings would fetch a fortune. And each one would be sold as the original! He said we would all become rich.

But all I wanted was enough money to get my son back.

I observed the greedy faces of these two men and knew I could not trust them. But I had done their bidding and was now part of their scheme. I had no choice but to go along. I had made a pact with the devil. And for that I would pay the devil's price.

39

New York City

The room felt warmer than usual, and for a moment, the collector worried. Changes in temperature could be dangerous to canvas and wood, which expanded and contracted, causing paint to crack. He checked the thermostat: sixty-eight degrees, as it should be. Maybe it was him; his body temperature seemed to be running high these days.

He had been drinking a rare Louis Latour Château Corton Grancey Grand Cru red while admiring his recent acquisition, a Matisse drawing removed from a small private museum on the French Riviera, a remarkable theft and a coup, for which he'd paid extra. His cell phone vibrated and he answered, irritated by interruption.

"What is it?"

"The American was tracked to the Italian's home."

"You have already told me that."

"Did you want me to follow up?"

"In what way?"

"Any way you would like."

The collector considered this. No, he did not want the American apprehended, not until he got the information he needed. Then he would be expendable. Right now, it was better to do nothing. See what the American discovered and let him lead them to the answer the collector was looking for.

"Continue to watch him," he said. "Anyone he meets. Anywhere he goes."

"Yes, of course. Don't worry."

This struck the collector as funny. He never worried. And he'd made up his mind: once this job was completed, he would have the American terminated.

He gazed at the small portrait, a Blue Period Picasso, a minor variation of the artist's more famous work, *The Old Guitarist*, something he should have given up long ago but had held on to for sentimental reasons. He pictured the painting in the Madison Avenue gallery where he had first seen it and how much he'd admired it. The timing was perfect, having just established his own fund and everyone telling him that a man of his stature should own serious art, about which he knew nothing, his taste adolescent, not yet honed.

It was a surprise though, his immediate love of art. The tug he had felt, this sudden need to own expensive things, the Picasso his first serious buy, just under a million, a lot of money at the time, but he wrote the check without hesitation.

It wasn't until later that he'd realized there were other, more interesting ways to acquire art.

"Are you there?" The man's voice a static whine through the cell phone. "Is something wrong?"

"*Wrong?*" the collector asked, thinking this man knew more than he should, that he too would have to go. "No," he said again, making his tone as breezy as possible. "Nothing at all."

40

When I finally saw Chaudron's Mona Lisa forgeries I had to admit that they were brilliant.

The man had a perverse genius for mimicry that was without equal. He had studied and replicated all the formulas. The ratio of sun-thickened linseed oil to Venice turpentine that Leonardo would have used back in 1503. He had purchased the same kind of wood Leonardo had used. Had cut each panel to size. Sanded and aged them with poppyseed oil. Cooked up rabbit-skin glue and coated the wood to protect it from rot. Then a layer of pure lead white. Then he covered them with damar varnish made from crystals he had purchased at auction from the workshop of a minor sixteenth-century artist. It was the technique used by all artists of the time.

Chaudron had gone so far as to purchase newly invented X-ray images from a dubious Louvre conservation worker. A man I knew and would never have suspected! These showed exactly what Leonardo had painted under the finished portrait. All the false starts. The ghosts. The pentimenti. Chaudron knew his forgeries would be examined under a microscope and the latest infrared X-ray. This hidden imagery would make it appear that each forgery was indeed authentic. He made certain his paintings would pass every scientific investigation.

He allowed these ghosts and false starts to dry. Then he painted in the thinnest possible layers. Used a feathering brush of the finest sable to smooth the paint. Layered glaze upon delicate glaze made up of just a *hint of pure ground pigment diluted with oil and varnish to produce the soft misty atmosphere that infused the master Leonardo's painting with the look of a dream.*

Chaudron proudly showed me the backs of the panels where he had duplicated every mark and every smudge. And for the pièce de résistance he had replicated the stamp of the Louvre Museum itself!

But that was not all. He had set the finished paintings in front of whirring fans and laid them near fires. He drew wicks of candles across their surfaces to age them. Added extra coats of varnish he knew would intentionally crack. All this had taken several months of his labor.

But I had been waiting nearly two years.

Now the six forgeries were ready.

It was Valfiero's turn to offer them for sale. He would do this on the black market. A network as convoluted and filthy as the sewers of Paris. A network Valfiero knew well as he was familiar with every unscrupulous art dealer and art collector in the city and beyond. He went about selling the paintings one by one. And each collector believed he was buying the actual Mona Lisa!

When Valfiero finished selling the forgeries he returned the original to me.

He told me it was my payment. Worth millions.

And I believed him.

41

For years, I had read about this elusive pair, but they were real now, exactly as some had theorized—Chaudron making copies, Valfiero selling them—but never proved. Vincent's words had brought them to life. But I needed to know if what he had written was true. Were there a half-dozen forged *Mona Lisa* paintings out there somewhere?

A year ago, I had discovered Yves Chaudron's only living relative, a nephew, Étienne Chaudron, who lived in Paris. I had done some digging, emailed him, and had gotten a terse reply: *I cannot tell you anything about my great-uncle because I never met him.*

Now I called.

"Étienne Chaudron?"

"*Qui est-ce?*"

"Luke Perrone," I said and reminded him of our previous exchange. "*Nous avons eu un échange de courier au sujet de votre grand-oncle, Yves.*"

"I speak English," he said, brusque, curt.

"I'm in Florence, but I have business in Paris," I lied. "I hoped we could meet."

"I told you before that I did not know my great-uncle."

"I understand, but there's something I'd like to discuss with you."

"There is nothing to discuss."

I was about to tell him how the forgeries made by his great-uncle Yves were chronicled in Vincent's journal, but he had already hung up.

"Are there other cartons of Professor Guggliermo's papers?" I asked Chiara when I arrived at the library later that day.

I had awakened with the thought that if Guggliermo had been planning to write something about the journal there could be notes about it.

"*Di che tipo?*" she asked.

"What kind? Oh, notes, papers, that's all." I strained for nonchalance.

"There is one box of…how you say…*note varie*, not yet put in category. I will find for you, after I finish this." She indicated a stack of index cards.

I wanted to shout *Do it now!* but smiled and said, "*Grazie,*" then went into the courtyard to walk off my impatience.

One of the monks was burning leaves, gray smoke coiling into low clouds as if creating them. I circled the courtyard, wondering if Brother Francesco had seen something or someone he shouldn't have. I peered through the dark alleyway. The police tape in front of the dormitory door was no longer there—and nobody was waiting by the stone stairs.

Chiara had Guggliermo's carton of *note varie* waiting, every-thing as neat and orderly as it had been in the other carton, each folder carefully labeled: ESSAYS AND NOTES FOR ESSAYS, SCHOOL ASSIGNMENTS, RECEIPTS AND SALES FOR BOOKS. In each folder were others, subdivided into more specific binders.

I started with ESSAYS AND NOTES FOR ESSAYS, all pertaining to art historical subjects and nothing about the journal. Nothing in

SCHOOL ASSIGNMENTS either. I doubted there would be anything in RECEIPTS AND SALES FOR BOOKS, but it was here I had another idea that had me going through bills and receipts for over an hour, compiling a list of about forty rare-book dealers that Antonio Guggliermo had dealt with on a regular basis. I then cross-checked the receipts to see who might have sold any kind of notebook, diary, or journal. There were nine possibilities.

Sitting at a nearby café, laptop open, an espresso for energy, I found the nine book dealers' websites and sent a general email to all of them. Within minutes, I received three responses from dealers who said they had never sold any kind of journal or diary that matched my description—though each offered to look for the kind of journal I'd described if I wanted to buy it. I politely declined and crossed them off the list. Two more responses, neither of which had sold the kind of journal I had described.

I ordered another espresso, and by the time I'd finished it, a book dealer in Berlin emailed to say he had sold Guggliermo an old journal. I called. Though the dealer confirmed the cover had been blue and the paper buff, it turned out to be a nineteenth-century notepad, never used and with no writing in it at all.

I was starting to lose faith, my brilliant idea not so brilliant. Only three of the nine booksellers had not yet replied. I couldn't wait for more emails, and called the first, Pelletier Editions, in Paris. There was no answer, no voicemail. The second, Scriptorium, in Mantua, sounded like something out of a horror movie and had a number no longer in service. The last, Libreria Antiquaria di Firenze, didn't answer, but I noted the Florence address, put it into my Google Maps, and saw that it was just on the other side of the Arno River.

It was heading into *riposo*, the midday break, and the store might be closed, but revved up on caffeine, I decided to take a chance. What did I have to lose?

42

The Ponte Vecchio, the aptly named old bridge, was not covered, though it felt like it with so many awnings from the stalls and shops, all selling jewelry, blocking out the light and river views. There were lots of tourists, the most I'd seen so far, people perusing necklaces and bracelets, couples staring into stall windows or haggling with owners, young women with their arms outstretched, trying on diamond rings. Everywhere I looked were couples. For the first time, I missed my friends back home, and not for the first time, I missed Alex. I still had no idea how she felt about me, about *us*, or where we were going—if anywhere. A young couple passed, locked in a kiss, and I had to stop myself from scowling.

The center of the bridge was open with beautiful views of the Arno, the river lined with houses in perfectly muted earth tones, but the sky had darkened, and by the time I headed off the bridge, it had started to rain. Oltrarno, as it was called, literally "other side of the Arno," was Florence's south bank and more bohemian, or so I'd been told. It was raining harder now, and I huddled under a store awning to check the bookseller's address in my GPS, then found a store selling cheap umbrellas. The streets felt different from the ones on the other side of the river, grittier and more working class, some wide, others narrow and medieval looking, and right now, mostly deserted. I moved fast, trying and failing to outrun the rain, and came to an open area just across from a huge, sprawling three-story stone building, red banners hanging from the second-floor announcing exhibitions: the Palazzo Pitti, better known as the Pitti Palace, famous for its eclectic art collection. Any other time, I'd have gone in, but I was on a mission.

The streets got smaller and narrower, and there did not appear to be any gentrification here, several buildings a mess of cracked stone and badly peeling paint, and no sidewalks at all, water rising from the steady rain and sloshing onto my ankle-high boots. The uneven cobblestones made the streets hard to navigate and slippery. I was relieved when the end of the street opened into a large though empty square.

The rain was coming down even harder now, my cheap umbrella not doing much. I ducked inside the nearest building, one with a nondescript stone facade, and shook myself off like a dog. It took a moment to see it was a church, Santa Maria del Carmine. The name rang a bell, but I wasn't sure why until I saw the sign for the Brancacci Chapel—a place that housed one of the most famous Renaissance painting cycles, one I had taught for years and loved. It had been high on the list of art I wanted to see in Florence, just one more place I had forgotten about.

I paid my ten-euro entrance fee, headed up a short flight of stairs, and emerged in what I would only describe as heaven. The fresco cycle filled the small chapel, dazzling even from a distance. A few steps up and through an open sculpted gate of gray-white marble and the cycle wrapped around me like old-time CinemaScope: two levels of paintings illustrating the life of Saint Peter, fully human figures with faces so expressively painted they appeared to be speaking, color that reflected the hues of Florence, shades of sienna and ochre, pale rose and lush Indian reds against emerald greens and soft blues, everything about the fresco cycle more beautiful and moving than I had imagined.

The artist was Masaccio, a Renaissance rock star dead at twenty-seven, that dangerous age for any great rock star. I knew he had only painted a few of the fresco scenes in the cycle, but the most famous ones, and they stood out from the others.

On the upper level to my left, *The Tribute Money* depicted Christ and the apostles confronted by a tax collector—the only guy among them without a halo! It got me thinking about taxes and the obvious losses I'd be deducting for my close-to-nonexistent art career. I thought about my great-grandfather's money troubles too and the fact that after he'd stolen the painting for Valfiero and Chaudron, who undoubtedly sold the forgeries for huge sums of money, they had little use for him. How, I wondered, could a man like Vincent, humble and without contacts, possibly sell such a famous painting? So much had already happened to him—Simone's death, losing his son, betrayed by Valfiero and Chaudron. And yet I had come to believe in him and believed he could do it.

I glanced up at the right side of Masaccio's painting. It showed Saint Peter pulling money out of the mouth of a fish, one of Christ's miracles. What my great-grandfather needed: a miracle. Perhaps what I was looking for too. The quiet was shattered by a German couple, chatting loudly and taking pictures.

I headed back down the few chapel stairs; I wanted a view of the fresco cycle from a distance. The rain must have stopped, because there was light streaking in from a window at the far end of the church. Other than that, the place was dark and cordoned off to visitors, though I saw something move, a man who quickly disappeared into a side room. I headed back up the stairs, waited for the Germans to get bored and leave, and was soon alone again, staring up at Masaccio's *Adam and Eve*. Adam nude, his face buried in his hands, Eve hiding her nakedness with her hands and howling with grief and shame, everything about the anguished pair conveying absolute despair. The way I had pictured Vincent, cast out and riddled with guilt at losing his beloved Simone and his son.

It was a moment before I felt it, turned, and spotted him again, the man I thought I'd seen at the far end of the church. He was maybe twenty feet away now, backlit by the light from the window, so I couldn't make him out clearly, only that he was big. I headed down the stairs for a better look, but he darted away, a shadow, a phantom.

I sucked in a breath, my radar still flashing. Something about the guy had felt not only threatening but familiar.

Outside, I began walking toward the bookseller's shop. The sun poked through the clouds the way it had through the church window, sharp and bright. I tried to shake off the uneasy feeling of that guy, but Brother Francesco's sudden death had left me feeling off-balance and suspicious about everything.

After a few blocks, I came into a lively square lined with restaurants and shops, Piazza Santo Spirito. The church was closed, but the cafés were open. I sat for a bit, sipped a coffee, and thought of my great-grandfather, a man who never quite fit in, a solitary man who had lost the one person who had truly loved and believed in him.

The area around Santo Spirito reminded me of Manhattan's NoHo or the East Village, with lots of restaurants and artisan shops of pottery and picture frames, handmade belts and shoes. My boots still wet, I was tempted by a pair of handmade wingtips until I saw the price tag.

Via Toscanella turned out to be only a few blocks away, the street lined with bookbinders and old bookshops, all of them closed, including the Libreria Antiquaria de Firenze. Most of the shops had signs noting they would reopen after riposo, but not Liberia Antiquaria de Firenze, its metal gate down and locked. I peered through the bars, but there was little to see. I was ready to give up when I noticed a blinking sign at the end of the road.

The Ristorante Americano had peanut shells on the floor, Dolly Parton on the jukebox, and Budweiser on tap—an Italian's idea of an American bar.

I ordered a Coke, and the bartender—masses of curly dark hair and bright-red lipstick—served it with a smile.

"American?" she asked.

"Italian American," I said. "Does it show?"

"You look like every good-looking Italian palooka I ever dated."

"Luke Perrone," I said.

"Like the beer?"

"Different spelling and nothing to do with my family."

"Too bad," she said. "Teresa Ferrara. Nothing to do with the bakery in Little Italy." She offered her hand, rings on every finger. "From Hackensack. That's in New Jersey."

"I know. I'm from Bayonne. How did you end up here?"

"Followed a boyfriend. Something I do not recommend."

"I'll remember that if I get a boyfriend."

Teresa laughed. "You hungry?" She didn't wait for an answer, disappeared into the kitchen, and reappeared a few minutes later with a plate she set down in front of me. "Homemade calzone. On the house. And no snide remarks because I made it."

I took a bite, told her it was great, and it was.

She thanked me and asked what had brought me to Florence. I told her I was doing some research and checked my watch.

"You in a hurry?"

I told her no, I had a half hour till the library reopened, though I was anxious to see what came next in the journal.

"Research," she asked, "in this part of town?"

"A bookstore," I said.

She nodded and asked which one.

"Libreria Antiquaria," I said, and her smile disappeared.

"You're not a cop, are you?"

"*Me?* No—why?"

"We had a lot of them when it happened."

"When what happened?"

"The owner of Libreria Antiquaria, hell of a sweet guy, Carlo Bianchi. He came in here all the time. Murdered in his shop."

"Jesus. When?"

"About two months ago."

"Robbery?"

"Unlikely. It's a little store filled with dusty old books. Who would kill an old man for a handful of euros? It made no sense then and still doesn't."

43

I should have known it would end badly. That those two scoundrels would betray me.

I hid outside Chaudron's building. Saw couriers come and go. Followed several of them and made notes as to where they went. But I had no idea what to do with this information.

I still had no money and no way to get it. Weeks passed and I was soon desperate. What would I do to survive?

Then I devised a plan. I would ransom the Mona Lisa!

I recalled the thought that had come to me at the Louvre on that August morning when I stood in front of the painting of Napoleon. I would offer the stolen painting to the Italian government. I would say that I was returning it to its country of origin. For a price.

I made plans to leave Paris and take the painting to Italy. I did not tell Valfiero or Chaudron what I planned to do. Or that I was leaving. But there was something they had not told me. Something I did not realize until I was in the Hotel Tripoli. With the two men I had contacted to sell the painting—the antique dealer Alfredo Geri and Giovanni Poggi the director of the Uffizi Gallery. I had just unveiled the painting. Both men stood before me with astonished looks on their faces.

It was then the first telltale sign made an appearance. The slightest smell of oil. Something I had not detected before. I thought it must be a residual odor from hanging around in Chaudron's studio for so many months. But it was too strong. I was certain the men would smell it too.

But they did not. They stood awestruck while I looked for some proof that the painting in front of me had been made by Chaudron's hand and not Leonardo's. Something I should have looked for when the painting was returned to me. Something Chaudron had pointed out to me months earlier. Something I had forgotten.

I searched the painting. Squinted to see if I could detect it. And I did!

Chaudron and Valfierio had played me for the ultimate fool. They had given me a forgery!

I said nothing. I knew the Mona Lisa I held in my hands looked exactly like the original in every way. Even the images buried beneath the surface would be identical if they were to X-ray the painting. But I knew for certain it was one of Chaudron's forgeries.

The smell had only been the first sign.

Now I had seen the proof.

What happened to the original? I did not yet know. I only knew that the painting I was offering to Geri and Poggi was not the painting I had stolen! And it was this painting that was finally returned to the museum.

If you doubt me go into the Louvre and bring with you a magnifying glass. Now slowly drag it over the surface of the painting and—

This was it, what I'd been waiting for, what scholars had been debating for over a hundred years. The question of whether or not the *Mona Lisa* in the Louvre, the one Vincent had stolen and returned, was a forgery—and if so, how to find out.

I turned the page.

Geri and Poggi notified the police, and I was arrested.

I flipped back.

Now slowly drag it over the surface of the painting and look very carefully at—

Forward again.

It didn't make sense.

Not until I saw the shredded edges of paper trapped in the binding.

Shit! No! I ran my finger over the torn remnants of paper, my mind whirring. I sat back, felt as if I'd been punched in the stomach. What I'd come to Italy to discover.

Gone.

44

Missing pages.

I tried to think it through and what, if anything, I could do about them. Who had torn them out—and when?

Had Guggliermo torn them out before donating the journal to the library? Or had it been Quattrocchi? Was that why he disappeared? Or had it been someone else entirely? But who? When?

I had to know, had to find out. I couldn't give up so easily. I'd risked too much. There had to be a way to find out what Chaudron had put into his forgeries. I forced myself to read what followed the missing pages—Vincent writing about his arrest. Interesting, but no clue to identifying the forgeries.

Had I missed something? Maybe there were enough clues here if I could study the page I had just read more carefully.

I looked up. Only one other scholar here today, and he was across the room going through a periodical. Chiara was heading into the back room. Beatrice sorting index cards as if her life depended on it. Riccardo nowhere to be seen. I reached down and opened my backpack. Only a few seconds to make the decision.

Do it.

A glance toward the front room. Again, how would I get the journal past Griselda?

I couldn't. It was too large.

But would she notice a missing page?

I shuffled papers, making just enough noise to cover the sound of tearing the page out, which wasn't difficult—it was already loose, the binding weak. Folded it quickly and stuffed it into my backpack, wedging it down behind my laptop. I slid my yellow legal pad on top and let out a breath. I looked up to see Chiara back at her post.

Had she seen me do it?

I glanced up at the ceiling, at the cameras in the corners of the room—I had completely forgotten about them. My back was toward them, but had they recorded my act of thievery?

I closed the journal as casually as possible, put it into the Duccio carton, covered it with folders and papers, and carried it to the front desk, along with Guggliermo's carton. I offered Chiara my practiced smile, then turned and headed out of the room, backpack under my arm, conscious to walk at a normal pace, but my heart was hammering.

At the door, evil stepsister Griselda stopped me as usual. I handed over the backpack, chatting about the weather and the newest strikes and anything else that came to my mind while she unzipped it and dipped her hand inside. I kept up a steady stream of talk, sweat inching its way down my back.

She seemed to be taking forever.

The other scholar joined the queue behind me, a stack of books in his arms, puffing and sighing with impatience until Griselda finally removed her hand from my backpack to check his books and waved us both through.

I could have kissed the guy. I closed my backpack, careful to steady my shaking hand, went through the X-ray machine and out the door.

There were a few monks in the courtyard, but I didn't stop to chat. Backpack securely in place, I headed across Piazza San Lorenzo, feeling too much like my teenage self after shoplifting, or worse. I reminded myself to slow down, to act normal.

On the east side of the piazza, I chose the shadowy less-traveled street that led away from the Duomo. Halfway down it, I had a thought, got my cell phone out, and made the call.

"Musée du Louvre," the operator said.

I asked for the curator of Renaissance painting.

When the curator got on the line, I listed my credentials— degrees, teaching, grants, awards, articles, more than a few embellished and exaggerated, but it worked. The curator agreed to let me into the museum on a day it was closed to tourists, the day after tomorrow. I immediately booked a flight to Paris.

I had done it, stolen the page to study it on my own. In another day, I'd be studying the painting itself. Maybe I'd see something in it that would connect to what I'd been reading. I leaned back against a building, my adrenaline starting to ebb, and had a thought I hadn't had in years: *I need a drink.*

I walked another half block, stopped to glance into a bar, then started walking again, faster. When I next stopped, it was a tabacchi shop where I looked in the window and spotted the green tin of La Paz tobacco, my great-grandfather's brand. I caught my reflection in the glass too, then another one coming up behind me.

45

"I hoped I'd catch you." Alex said, slightly out of breath as if she'd been running.

"Catch me?"

"Chiara said you'd just left." She studied me a moment. "Are you all right?"

I told her I was fine and asked if she wanted to get coffee or something to eat, had almost said a *drink*. If I continued to steal things, I would have to go to a meeting, and soon.

Alex said, "Sure," slipped her arm through mine, and we headed in the opposite direction while she talked about getting her sublet in order, the sun beginning to fade. We walked several blocks and ended up in the Piazza della Signoria, the large expansive square dominated by the fortress-like Palazzo Vecchio, people taking turns having their picture taken with Michelangelo's oversized statue of *David*.

"Don't they know it's a copy?" I said, the idea of forgery very much on my mind.

Alex shrugged like she didn't care and wandered over to the Fountain of Neptune, the marble sea god surrounded by cherubs and mermaids. Even in winter, the fountain was going strong. From my angle, it looked like Neptune was taking a leak—and I said so.

"Classy," Alex said but laughed, then tugged me away, spray

from the fountain getting us both wet. She stopped to read a small plaque, in Italian, and asked me to help translate. It was about the Renaissance monk Savonarola, who had preached repentance like some medieval Billy Graham. It explained how he'd been hanged and burned right there in the square. I suggested it was a fitting end for a guy who tried to control people's lives, burned books and anything else he considered blasphemous or vain, including a lot of great paintings—Botticelli and Michelangelo among them.

"He deserved worse!" Alex snapped.

"What's worse than being burned alive?"

"Some people just deserve to—" She stopped, wrapped her arms around her torso, and shivered.

I put my arm over her shoulder, but she shrugged me off as if I had just made it worse, whatever *it* was. I backed away, hands up, "Sorry," I said, a little surprised, a little hurt.

"No, I'm sorry," she said. "It was a chill, that's all—from the fountain's spray—and I didn't want to get you wet."

"I'm already wet," I said and told her it was okay. But what had set her off? What had I done that was so bad?

At the edge of the square, I got that feeling again. *Ha un amico a Firenze?* I glanced over my shoulder, but there was no one lurking nearby.

Alex, in a better mood now, took my hand, said she wanted to see the Duomo square at night, and I was happy to leave this piazza for another.

It wasn't far and was worth it, the buildings lit up against an inky-blue sky, the cathedral with its amazing dome, Giotto's bell tower, the medieval-looking baptistery. I couldn't believe I hadn't rushed over to see this the minute I got here, though I was enjoying it now with Alex, almost as excited as I was, by my side. I was surprised the area was almost empty, tried to picture it in its day, fifteenth-century men in tunics and leggings, women in tightly corseted gowns, hair elaborately braided, people strolling or heading to the cathedral obviously built to impress, which it did.

"It never disappoints, does it?" Alex said.

I agreed, as if I'd been here before, staring up at the church facade that rose up in front of us, pink and green marble, sculpted figures in niches, recessed rose windows, every inch of it decorated like an oversize wedding cake. Looming behind it, Brunelleschi's huge redbrick dome. All of it spectacular and beautiful but ominous too, the way the buildings seemed to lean forward, all the nooks and crannies and small pockets of darkness.

Alex pointed out a group of nearby soldiers in camo, heavy boots, and maroon berets, each holding an automatic rifle, pistols holstered at their waists. I thought they looked a little scary, but Alex proclaimed them "gorgeous," wondering aloud why every Italian man looked like a movie star.

I led her toward the baptistery—did not feel like competing with handsome soldiers—the low and octagonal building of green-and-white-striped marble, possibly the oldest building in Florence, if I remembered correctly. But it was Ghiberti's famous doors that I wanted to see. The Gates of Paradise, ten bronze and gold relief sculptures of Old Testament stories, Adam and Eve, Cain and Able, Abraham and Isaac.

An iron fence kept viewers a couple of feet away, but the reliefs were spotlighted, and we could see them perfectly, practically reach out and touch them. I knew the sculptor Ghiberti had won a competition to decorate a first set of doors at the age of twenty-four, then these, his second set, which took him the next twenty-five years of his life, and how Michelangelo had declared they were as beautiful as the gates to heaven, which gave them their name. I peered through the iron bars for a closer look at the artist's astonishing handiwork, some of the figures almost freestanding, along with the illusion of space, reality, and perspective that defined the early Renaissance.

I leaned over to tell Alex another fact and was surprised when she wasn't there; I had felt the presence of someone beside me. I found her a few yards away reading yet another plaque, this one about the flood of 1966 and how Ghiberti's reliefs had fallen off and almost washed away. I reassured her the actual reliefs were in the cathedral museum, that these were casts. But I had not shaken the feeling of being watched. I looked around, taking in the nearly deserted square, noted how the spotlights illuminated the buildings but left the streets in darkness.

"It's so empty," I said.

"Well, it is winter."

I said I was hungry, and Alex chose a restaurant in a small elegant hotel, dark wood, velvet-covered banquettes, and dim lighting. We settled into a booth, and Alex ordered wine. Me, sparkling water. I told her I'd been glad she caught me, and she said, "Did I…catch you at something?" I knew she was kidding but couldn't help thinking about the stolen page in my backpack.

She gave me an odd look, head tilted, assessing. "Are you growing a beard or mustache?"

"Mostly out of neglect." Rubbing a hand across my chin and cheeks, I added, "I'll shave if you don't like it," then said I had missed seeing her at the library.

"I missed it too," she said.

It? The library? Not me?

"How's your research going?" she asked.

I thought about the things I'd read and what I still didn't know. "Okay," I said.

"Is it so top secret that you can't talk about it?"

I told her it was nothing like that and admitted I was a little tense, worried about my teaching job, how I would have to come up with something to ensure my tenure.

"Publish or perish?" she asked.

"I guess—or get a show." Saying it aloud made my worry take shape and feel tangible. I switched the topic to the Brancacci Chapel and Masaccio's frescoes. Alex said she'd never seen them in person and wished she had.

"We could go together," I said, and she smiled without saying yes or no.

She switched from wine to grappa.

I stayed with sparkling water.

She seemed to relax, asked questions about my life, which I didn't mind. I was glad she wanted to know more about me. I told her how I'd been a terrible student but had "found myself" in art school, where I worked in the cafeteria to pay off my scholarship. "Nothing you ever had to do, I'm sure."

"What? You think I'm a spoiled rich kid with a perfect life?"

Before I could say I was sorry, she said, "You have no idea," pouted a moment, then stopped just as quickly and asked me more about art school.

I told her it was the first time I had ever really cared about anything, which got me thinking about all it had taken to become an artist—the studio visits and gallery hunting, all the rejections, how I'd balanced three adjunct teaching jobs while working as a studio assistant to a successful artist, everything I had put at risk by coming here.

We shared a bowl of pasta, most of which I ate.

When Alex finished her grappa, she said she had to go, but this time, I reached for her hand and held her there.

"It's late," she said, a mix of emotions I couldn't read traveling across her face like fast-moving clouds. "There's the library tomor-row, and my apartment still needs organizing and—"

I leaned across the table and silenced her with a kiss.

She pulled back, and I got ready for the protest, possibly a slap.

"Your mustache," she said, "it scratches."

"I'll shave it off tomorrow. I promise."

"No, it's okay," she said, then leaned in for another kiss.

46

The longest twenty minutes of my life, getting up from the table, finding the front desk, getting a room. But the moment that hotel-room door shut behind us, the two of us were locked in another kiss. I swept pillows and bedspread aside, stripped off my shirt, watched Alex shimmy out of her lace bra and panties, my lips on her breasts, the sound of breath catching in her throat. Rolling around on the bed, hands, fingers, lips slowly gliding over skin. Fumbling with a condom.

"Wait—" she said, pushing me back on the bed and getting on top, leaning down, her lips at my ear, whispering, "Tell me about your secret project or *else*." She laughed.

I didn't. The spell was broken, and I knew it showed on my face.

"I was *kidding*," she said, crushed, a little girl scolded.

"It's okay," I said, taking a moment to get back in the mood, and it didn't take long. I moved back in for a kiss.

"I'm sorry," she said. "I was just—"

"Shh, doesn't matter," I said, my tongue in her mouth to end the conversation.

Afterward, Alex's cheek against my chest, I took in the room for the first time, noticing the same old-world charm as the hotel's restaurant, flocked wallpaper, a cut-glass chandelier, our clothes strewn across the polished wooden floor.

"Oh God," she said. "Tell me this didn't happen."

"It didn't happen," I said and laughed.

"I don't do this, you know. Damn that grappa!" She tugged the sheet up to her neck. "I hardly know you."

Did she really feel that way? I had told her things about myself I rarely told anyone. Maybe it was that I didn't know *her*, though right now, I felt as if I knew enough; the rest I'd find out.

I put my arm around her, kissed her lips, her forehead. She traced the tattooed words on my arm, KILL VAN KULL. I tried to cover it, but she pried my hand off and asked what it meant. I explained it was something I had done when I was fifteen, "just one of the stupid things I did when I was young, going along with my friends, a group thing, all six of us getting the same tattoo."

"Were you a gang or something?"

I used the excuse that it was a long time ago, tried to change the subject, but Alex was now tracing the chain-link tattoo that circled my other bicep.

"Are you studying anatomy?"

"Just yours," she said, which I liked. "So you were a bad boy?"

I sighed. "We told ourselves we were doing good, regular Robin Hoods."

"Robbing from the rich to give to the poor?"

"Sometimes. Other times, we just sought *revenge*." I growled the word to make it funny.

"For *what*?"

"Anything or anyone we thought was wronged."

"A regular knight in shining armor."

"Not everyone would agree, definitely not my parents or teachers—or the police."

She asked if I'd ever been arrested and I admitted to once, omitting the times I'd come close.

"For what? It wasn't murder, was it?"

"God, no!"

"Did you go to prison?"

"No! Can we stop talking about this? It's embarrassing."

"Everyone has something they're embarrassed about."

"Do you?"

She hesitated, as if thinking it through. "The usual…you know, bad dates, wrong choices."

"At least they're not tattooed on your body."

"I think they're hot… Your tattoos, I mean."

"Are you kidding?"

"No. I was always such a…good girl. I'm impressed. Did your gang stick up gas stations and things like that?"

"Please. Stop. I *beg* you!" I tossed the sheet over her face.

She pulled it down, went back to my KILL VAN KULL tattoo. "What's this above it?"

"A bridge."

"I can see that. What bridge?"

I didn't want to talk about my background anymore, but she wouldn't let it go.

"The Bayonne Bridge," I said. "Happy?"

"I don't know. Should that make me happy?"

"You don't even know where it is."

"Bayonne, I imagine."

"Right," I said.

"Where you're from?"

"Uh-huh," I said. "You like the idea of slumming with a Bayonne boy?"

"What's that supposed to mean?" Alex propped herself up

on an elbow, narrowed a look at me. "Are you trying to pick a fight?"

"No. Sorry. I'd rather not talk about it, that's all."

"I'm just interested in knowing about you. Is that so bad?"

"No," I said and kissed her. "One day, I'll tell you the whole story of my misspent youth. It's right out of Dickens." Something about her made me want to open up, expose my well-defended vulnerability.

"How'd you get this?" Alex drew a finger through the scar that bisected my eyebrow.

"A fistfight," I said. "One I obviously lost. Are you finished with my physical exam, Doctor?"

"For now," she said.

I started to get up.

"You're not leaving, are you?"

"Just going to the bathroom." I leaned over to give her another quick kiss, took in her blue-gray eyes, the slight down just barely discernible on her cheeks. I held her face in my hands. "I'm not going anywhere. Anyway, I've already paid for the night, and this place is expensive! Sorry—that came out wrong."

"I'll say."

"I *want* to stay," I said. "Though how come we didn't go to your place?"

"It was *you* who got the room," she said. "You didn't ask to go to my apartment, though I'd have said no. It's a mess. Suitcases exploded, clothes everywhere. We'd never have found the bed!"

"I think I would have."

"I could ask you the same thing."

"You mean my place?" I pictured my tiny hotel room, the worn chintz bedspread, the shower without a curtain. No way I'd have brought a woman like Alex to my no-star hotel. "My place is even more of a mess, like a teenage boy's bedroom."

"God, I hope not." She made a face.

I dragged my hand slowly across her cheek before I headed to the bathroom. "Don't move. I'll be right back."

"Wait—" she said. "Stop. Your back... Let me see that!"

I'd almost forgotten, or tried to, another mistake that felt prescient at the moment. I kept trying to turn around, but Alex stopped me, her fingers already tracing the *Mona Lisa* tattoo that filled most of my back.

"When did you get *this*—and *why*?"

"I was eighteen, drinking at the time." The latter was true, the first part a lie. I'd been twenty-five and knee-deep in research about Vincent Peruggia and the painting. But I wasn't ready to talk about my obsession.

"It's so well done," she said.

"Is it? I don't see it very often. Guess I lucked out and got a good tattoo artist. Are you finished looking? I've got to pee." I made my way to the bathroom but got back to bed fast, suggested we stay in it for several days.

Alex pointed out that was going to get expensive. I said it was worth it, then remembered my appointment. "Oh, wait... I'm going to see...a friend in Paris, but that's not until the day after tomorrow."

"You're going away?"

"I won't disappear." *Not like you did*, I thought but didn't say. "I'll just be gone a couple of days."

She asked who I was going to see, and I made it up as I said it: "A French friend, an artist, someone I've known since art school." I put my arms around her, wanted to stay that way forever, and might have had I not already made the call and bought the ticket.

47

Alex listened to Luke's breathing grow deep and even. The sheet was down around his waist, and she watched the rise and fall of his chest, her eyes lingering a moment. She studied his face, the sharp angle of his cheekbones made stronger by the shadow of his beard, his slightly thickened nose and full mouth. She couldn't take her eyes off him. How long had it been since she'd felt so attracted to a man? She laid a hand, as gently as possible, on his chest, felt the warmth of his flesh and the beating of his heart. Luke stirred, a smile playing at the corners of his mouth. Then he rolled onto his side and she pulled her hand back; she hadn't meant to touch him but couldn't help it. She felt embarrassed, conflicted.

This was not the way it was supposed to be.

What was she doing, sleeping with this man she hardly knew? She couldn't lie to herself and pretend it was the first time, but she hadn't lied when she'd said *I don't do this*. She did not sleep around. Though that was only half of what she'd meant.

She waited a few minutes until Luke's breathing grew steady again, then slipped out of bed. She had the sudden urge to flee— the room, Florence. But it felt too late.

Bare feet on the carpet, she picked her clothes off the floor and folded them onto a chair. Then did the same with Luke's, a moment to check his jeans, then shirt. In the outer pockets of his leather jacket, she found his sunglasses and an old-fashioned-looking tin of tobacco. A surprise—she had never seen him smoke. In his wallet, a driver's license, credit card, Metro card, twenty-seven American dollars, thirty-two euros. She closed the wallet and slipped it back into his jacket, the whole time watching him, making sure he was asleep.

She noted his short black boots, one near the front door, the other upside down a few feet away. She was arranging them neatly at the edge of the bed when she spotted his backpack under it. A moment to slip it out, another moment to make sure Luke had not awakened. Backpack under her arm, she tiptoed to the bathroom and shut the door behind her.

Inside the backpack, a laptop and notepad. Crumpled between them, a slightly yellowed paper, which she eased out and unfolded.

Cool light filtered in through the window, just enough for her to read the handwritten page, her Italian rusty but good enough, the whole time her heart beating fast.

48

Alex was already out of bed, the sheet wrapped around her. "Checkout time is noon," she said. "Get up. You don't want to get charged for another day."

She headed for the shower, and I told her to hold on, that I'd join her.

Jets of hot water pounded against her forehead while I kneaded her neck. A hangover from that "damn grappa." She shampooed her hair, and I helped her rinse the suds. I could have stayed in the shower all day, but she was out quickly, toweling off, telling me not to look at her, that she must look awful, which wasn't true. With her hair wet and face clean of makeup, she looked eighteen and beautiful.

I leaned in to kiss her, and she handed me a towel, told me to cover up. I watched her drag a comb through her hair, dab her lips with gloss, tug on rumpled clothes, all in a hurry. I kept trying to stop her, slow her down or bring her back to bed, but every time I tried, she'd push me away. "Don't you need to get to the library, more of your secret mission?" she said, flashing her first smile of the day, a mischievous one.

"Oh sure, top secret stuff." I tried pulling her close for a kiss, and when she stopped me, I asked if she was sorry this had happened.

A moment of uncomfortable silence, Alex drawing her still-wet hair into a ponytail. "No," she finally said, "it was just…unexpected. I need to get…used to it."

"How about getting used to it tonight?"

Another hesitation, then looking away, she said, "Okay."

I took hold of her shoulders and turned her to face me. "You sure you're all right?"

The briefest eye contact and a nod. "The room charge, remember?"

I told her it didn't matter. I'd have been happy to pay triple if she'd stay or at least not appear like she was dying to escape. I asked what she was doing today, and she said she had things to take care, evasive as always, but I didn't pry. I had things to do I hadn't told her about either.

49

"I've been waiting for your call."

"I'm calling now."

"How is Florence? Are you enjoying yourself?"

"What do you mean?"

"It was an innocent question."

"Your questions are never innocent."

"I want you to have fun, darling, as long as you don't get too distracted."

"Florence is a distracting city," she said. "It has the best art in the world."

"Some of it," he said, glancing at a wall of his spotlighted paintings.

"I need more money."

"Fine," he said, examining the surface of a sixteenth-century oil on panel, *The Holy Family*, an elongated baby Jesus, the Madonna, Joseph behind her, the paint cracked badly over part of Joseph's face, something that would surely affect the $15 million value attached to the painting, which, a decade ago, had been taken off the wall of Santo Spirito Hospital in Rome during a Madonna concert, the irony not lost on him. He turned away from the damaged *Holy Family* to look at his prize. "Same account?"

"Yes."

"Same amount?"

"Yes."

He moved closer to the painting, ran a finger run over the half-smiling lips, wondered if they were the real lips.

"I've got to go," she said. "I'm meeting a friend."

"I didn't know you had friends in Florence."

"A woman...I went to school with."

"Really? How nice. Wait. You haven't told me if you've discovered anything."

Alex moved from bed to chair, glanced out at the balcony of her sublet apartment, checked the time, almost two hours since she had left Luke. She wondered what he was doing, wondered what the hell *she* was doing.

"Are you there?"

"Yes," she said, debating, delaying, knowing she would have to tell him—and then she did, describing the page she'd found in Luke's backpack and what it had said.

"Good work!" he said. "You are really earning your money."

Alex hung up without saying goodbye. She felt dirty despite the hotel shower, slipped out of her rumpled clothes and decided to take another. But no matter how long she stayed under the hot water, no matter how much soap she used, she still felt dirty, and it had nothing to do with having had sex with Luke. She pictured him asleep, his bare chest rising and falling, his handsome face, the tattoos.

Like a tattoo, he'd gotten under her skin, had touched something unexpected, things she did not want to feel, and it made everything worse, not better.

50

Nothing I had read added to the explanation or secret of the missing pages, other than the repeated fact that I would need a magnifying glass to find out. I made a note to buy one and headed to the library. I needed to go through the journal again.

One of the two scholars I saw almost every day, the one with the ponytail, was in the courtyard. I was about to head in when he stopped me. "You are an American artist and art historian, *sì?*"

I was not in the mood to strike up a conversation but was curious to find out how he knew.

"Chiara," he said in response to my question. "She make it her business to know everything about anyone in the library."

I hoped Chiara didn't know *everything* about me.

"Marco Pisano," he said, extending his hand. "I teach art history at Florence University of the Arts, contemporary Italian art, *transavanguàrdia* my specialty."

"The three C's—Cucci, Chia, and Clemente."

"So you know their artwork."

"Very well. I've taught the Italian trans-avant-garde, as we call it in America, in my art history class. I'm a big Francesco Clemente fan."

"It is too bad you were not here last month to see his exhibition at Le Murate Progetti Arte Contemporanea."

"Le Murate?" The name stopped me. "Isn't that the name of an old prison?"

"It *is* the old prison," he said, explaining that the lower part had been renovated by the arts organization but that much of the prison remained intact.

It had never dawned on me that the prison might still exist.

Less than an hour later, Marco and I were in an enclosed court-yard at a table of a hip restaurant, literally carved out of part of the prison, Caffè Letterario. When I'd told him that part of my research involved the prison, he'd called his friend, the director of the arts organization, and she'd invited me for a tour. Beside us, a table of young people eating pizza and drinking beer were talking and laughing loudly while I tried to imagine my great-grandfather imprisoned in these stone walls.

Valentina Gensini, the artistic director of Le Murate, dark-haired and olive-skinned, was as attractive as she was interesting. She asked about my project, and I told her half the truth: that my great-grandfather had been imprisoned in these walls and I was thinking of writing about his life. "A book, how wonderful! You must come back and read from it when you are finished," she said, a surprising offer.

I took in the high stone walls of the courtyard, which looked clean and scrubbed, while Valentina described how the place had been built in 1424 to house Benedictine nuns, who had chosen a walled-in life, "so the name, *Murate*, which means 'walled-in.'" It had not become a men's prison until the mid-1800s and remained so until 1985, when it was "crumbling and overcrowded," Valentina said, "and several prisoners drowned in the great Arno flood of sixty-six—and there were riots!" She was proud that the arts organization had fought to make the prison a landmark, "a testimony to inhumanity," and she had organized exhibitions around its dark history. Then she turned us over to a young man for a tour.

Stefano brought me and Marco inside to show off the art space, but I could barely look at it, anxious to see the prison, and when I said so, he directed us into a hallway where he unlocked a heavy chain, then led the way up a narrow staircase.

I had read about my great-grandfather's arrest and trial, his trip to the prison, stripped and searched, standing naked with other inmates under cold showers, shivering and humiliated, brought to his cell, door slammed shut, the sound of metal against metal as the locks were drawn, all of it written in excruciating detail. I could see it now as I took the steps slowly, the space tight and confining, already a prison, the only light from a window way above, casting everything else in darkness. Marco and Stefano were walking fast, disappearing ahead of me, and I could feel the years disappearing too.

The first-floor landing was a study in erosion: painted gray walls that had long ago started to peel revealed the stone below, fissured and water-stained, the floor a reddish-colored diagonal stone, scuffed and faded.

Stefano called out, and I was startled—I'd been lost in the past, picturing prisoners being led down this hall, my great-grandfather among them.

We headed up another flight of stairs.

Here, just off the landing, a round-ceilinged hallway maybe twenty feet long and eight feet wide and a series of heavy wooden doors. I stopped at one, stone molding with chunks of it missing, thick iron hinges top and bottom, a corroded iron bracket maybe ten by twelve inches with a bar that slid across and fit into another iron receptacle to lock it securely. In the center of the door, a small square window, hinged and locked. But at the next door, that same square window was open. I squinted, but it was too dark to see anything. Stefano signaled me down the hall to another cell, the door open.

But it was not a cell; it was a cage.

For a moment, I was unable to move, then I took a step in. Stood there. No toilet. No sink.

I recalled Vincent's description of the weekly gang shower under frigid water and the "shit sloppers," as they were called, the men tasked with the odious job of emptying the buckets.

The place was more a dungeon than prison, something out of *The Count of Monte Cristo*, so horribly real it seemed fictional, impossible.

I steadied myself, a hand to the wall. It was damp and cold. I shivered. Stefano pointed out that the prison had never been heated, though in fact it was warmer now due to the heat rising from the bottom-floor art space.

Stefano and Marco went into the hallway, but I stayed alone in the cell, Vincent's words echoing in my head: *I count my steps, one foot in front of the other, six steps one way, nine the other.* I placed one foot in front of the other, toe to heel, and it was exactly as he had said, six feet wide, nine feet long. I felt as if I were walking in his shoes, back and forth, back and forth. I thought how he had kept sane by plotting revenge against Valfiero and Chaudron, my mind, his mind.

I sat on the stone floor. Closed my eyes. Thought of the weeks and months my great-grandfather had spent in a cell like this one, recording his life. Opened my eyes, took in the one barred window that looked into a corridor. I stood up as if propelled and grabbed hold of the bars. My hands, Vincent's hands. How often had he gripped this same kind of bars?

Stefano offered to show me the corridor, a sort of tunnel, with corroded walls and floor. I remembered Vincent's words again: *There is one barred window—though not a window at all. It looks into a narrow corridor the guards use to spy on us.*

I pictured guards patrolling, thought of the guard who had given him the journal and pencils, one small kindness in this hellhole.

There was another open cell, identical to the others, only here there were drawings.

I dared to touch them, my fingers tingling.

One wall had a pencil drawing of a soldier in an old-time uniform, another a series of incised lines that took me a while to recognize as a crudely etched female figure. In the next cell, there were drawings too, the profile of a modern-looking woman just beside a small cropping of medieval-looking buildings, worn and faded, obviously very old but still legible, and I realized the graffiti had been created at different times, that it spanned decades, possibly centuries. It was next to impossible that any had been made by Vincent, but still I pictured him crouched by the wall, using the stick he had found and sharpened to carve the drawing as a way to stay connected to the real world, as a way to hold on.

I sat back and stared at the drawings, my hands on the cold stone floor, lost in thought about my great-grandfather, the months and months he'd spent in one of these cage-like cells, how he had managed to survive and to write his story. I not only needed to know what came next but wanted to know it all, everything about him, this man I had come to care about in ways I could never have imagined.

51

I met Alex for dinner, still a bit off-balance from my time at Le Murate, almost as if I had just served a prison sentence. The restaurant, Alex's choice, was family run, not chic nor expensive, and she seemed in a good mood. She asked if I was still going to Paris, and I said yes, thinking about my appointment at the Louvre and the other, unsolicited visit I was planning.

She said "good," though I wasn't sure she was happy about it. I told her I'd be back soon, and she said "good" again, then asked about my friend in Paris, and I made one up.

We skipped dessert and coffee. I was anxious to get going but didn't want to presume we would be leaving together, though I was relieved when she said, "My place or yours?"

"Yours," I said. "Mine's a dump."

She said she didn't mind. I said I did.

Alex's apartment was a third-floor walk-up in an old building not far from San Lorenzo, nice but not too nice, and I was glad. She gave me a tour of the living room, pointing out beautiful blue floor tiles in the kitchen and the little balcony with its wrought-iron railing. We went out on it for a few minutes to take in the view, the Duomo lit up against the dark sky, and I pulled her close. She surprised me with a kiss that felt urgent, almost desperate, and we stayed like that, hardly separating, Alex leading me to her bedroom.

The lovemaking felt urgent too. I kept trying to slow it down but couldn't, and it was over too soon. Afterward, we lay on her bed, not speaking. She got up to get a glass of wine, and I watched her walk away, afraid she might break into a run.

On the bedside table was a small framed photo of a young girl, obviously Alex, and her mother, whom I recognized from the locket.

"Nice picture of you and your mom," I said when she came back.

She nodded, half smiled. I could see she was struggling with something and asked.

"My mother's...not well. I'm mean, she's okay but..." She broke off, shook her head. "It's just... Never mind."

I told her it was okay, that she didn't have to talk about it.

After a while, she said, "I want to," took a swallow of wine, the glass shivering in her hand, then spoke quickly as if she needed to say it fast or she never would.

"She was always fragile, but wonderful and kind. At first, the doctors didn't know what was going on, depression or anxiety? Then they hit on a diagnosis—early onset dementia. The thing is she's not going to get better, only worse."

"I'm sorry. What about your father?"

"He's...out of the picture, divorced. I thought I told you." She expelled a short breath. "She's in a good place now. It's expensive, but there's no choice. She's only fifty-six—and it's bad...always worse. For a while, I tried to take care of her myself, moved her into my apartment, but even with an aide, it was too much. She was up half the night crying or confused—and me up with her, trying to comfort her, then slogging through the next day on no sleep." There were tears in her eyes.

I got my arm around her but didn't say anything, let her keep talking.

"It was after the second suicide attempt—the first with pills, the second with a razor blade..." Alex took a sharp breath, practically a gasp. "The doctors suggested it would be better if she were someplace where she could be watched. It's just..." Another deep breath. "I'm sorry..."

"There's no reason to be."

She swiped a tissue off the side table and dabbed at her eyes. "But I am. Why am I burdening you with this?"

I told her it was fine, that I wanted her to feel she could tell me anything.

"I'm not usually a crier," she said, sniffing back tears. "It's embarrassing."

"Hey, show me three minutes of *Bambi* and I'm blubbering like a baby."

"Oh sure," she said but managed a smile, then ran a finger along my tattoo. "Tough Mister Kill Van Kull."

"Not so tough," I said and meant it, drawing her into my arms, wanting to take care of her, to protect her. I was sorry to hear all she'd been through, sorry for her mother too. But it felt good that she had confided in me. I didn't know what love was supposed to feel like, but for the first time in my life, I thought I might be feeling it and did not want to lose the feeling, lose her. I wanted to say, *I'll help you with your mother when we get back to New York. I'll help you with anything* but I didn't want to scare her, so all I said was "It's okay."

That night, Alex slept in my arms, several times waking me with her violent twitching and mumbling, obviously bad dreams. "Shh," I'd say, stroking her forehead, and she'd settle back to sleep until the next bad dream.

In the morning, I slipped out of bed early, trying not to wake her, then stopped to kiss her when I was dressed and ready to go.

"Where are you going?" she asked, lifting her head from the pillow.

"Paris, remember? I'll be back in a couple of days."

"Oh…right." She tugged me back for another kiss, this one passionate but fraught, then pushed me away. "Go!" she said, pulling the blanket up to her neck and burying her face in the pillow.

52

Alex dressed quickly, started to make the bed, brought the pillow-case to her nose and inhaled Luke's scent. She was glad he'd gone, couldn't bear that he had. Jesus. She hadn't signed up for this. She exchanged the pillow for the framed photo, the one she always carried with her, she and her mother, the mother she preferred to remember, the mother who remembered her.

Why had she talked so much last night? Was she looking for sympathy, excuses, hoping to be rescued? Luke Perrone the white knight, she the damsel in distress? If anyone was going to need rescuing, it would probably be him, not her.

She set the photo back on the bedside table, thinking sometimes you did things for the people you loved, no matter how hard, how *wrong*, because you had to, because you saw no other way.

53

The morning sky over Paris was slate gray, though the city was as beautiful as I had imagined. I'd taken a cab from the airport and, eager to see as much of the city as possible, had dumped my bag and was now strolling in the Faubourg Saint-Germain, an historic district of whitewashed buildings with wrought-iron balconies, fancy boutiques, and high-end art galleries.

I found a cool-looking restaurant where I sat at a redwood bar, had an omelet, fries, and much needed coffee. My night of watching Alex toss and turn had left me tired and troubled. Was it talking about her mother's condition that had given her such bad dreams—or was there something deeper that had caused her such pain? I had to admit I liked the urgency of her goodbye kiss but not how she'd pushed me away just after. Was she still playing advance and retreat? If so, she didn't seem to be enjoying the game any more than I was.

My appointment at the Louvre was not for a couple of hours, so I took my time, soaking in the beauty of the city. Amped up on caffeine, I fast-walked around the grounds of Les Invalides, the complex of buildings dedicated to the French military, topped by a gold dome that managed to glitter despite the lack of sun. I strolled along tree-lined streets, stopped to admire a large tiered theater that turned out to be the famous Comédie-Française, and could have wandered along the streets of Paris all day if it were not getting close to the time of my appointment. I headed toward the Louvre with a mix of excitement and trepidation about finally seeing the *Mona Lisa*. Would I recognize what Chaudron had put into his forgeries, even if I saw it?

With his narrow face and angular features, dark hair and pointy goatee, the curator of Renaissance painting, Alain Gingembre, looked as he'd been painted by El Greco. He had bought my story: an art historian writing a paper on the work of Leonardo, though he seemed in a hurry, as if I were an annoyance taking him away from something more important. I followed him through the museum, his shoes echoing on the marble floors. The temperature-controlled air was cool and thin, a smell of something musty under lemony floor wax. I could see why Vincent had referred to the place as a graveyard.

We moved down one long hallway after another, ignoring works of art, and I couldn't help but think of my great-grandfather heading down these same halls to commit his notorious crime.

Every few yards, the curator looked over his shoulder and said "Come," as if to a dog. I was tempted to bark.

We finally reached the Salle des Ètats gallery, and there she was, Leonardo's lady, as Vincent had so often called her.

My first thought was *She's so small*. A moment later, her quiet intensity drew me in. Was it simply because the image was so famous or that I had been obsessed with the painting for so many years?

I moved closer. The shadowy face of a bearded man slid across the glass, and I shivered. It took me a minute to realize the reflection was my own. A deep breath and I stepped back.

"It's a shame to cover the painting with glass," I said as if Simone's words to Vincent had been whispered in my ear.

"But we *must!*" the curator said. "A deranged man once tossed acid in her face! Another threw a rock! Imagine, to do such vile things."

I nodded and inched closer. The woman before me seemed more than a painting, beautiful, pensive, practically breathing. If it was one of Chaudron's forgeries, it was a brilliant one.

I asked if he could turn on the lights, but Gingembre told me to wait until my eyes adjusted, that the natural light would be better, and he was right, even if his tone was condescending. After a minute, I began to see the subtleties in the painted flesh and the soft folds of the drapery more clearly.

Then we started bantering, or rather competing over who knew more facts about the painting—the sitter's name, the fact that the picture had likely been cut down, how the colors darkened and oxidized, that *Mona Lisa* once had eyebrows, which had faded over time, that Leonardo had worked on it for years and kept it with him until his death.

"Her smile is a kind of reference to her name, Giocondo, which means 'happy' in Italian," Gingembre said, his tight lips ticking a split-second smile. "And you know it was not such a famous painting until the mid-nineteenth century when the symbolist painters began to extol its virtue."

I could not resist adding, "And the 1911 theft helped to raise its status too. Let's not forget that."

The curator sniffed. "Perhaps, but to have the painting stolen, and have it gone for two years!"

"I'm sure the painting was greatly missed."

"No one is more aware of the painting's power to attract crowds than myself! The Louvre has the highest attendance of any museum in the world. Last year, we had over ten million visitors, and every one of them came to this very spot to gaze upon Leonardo's wondrous painting."

I said I was impressed, and I was.

He told me they'd just cleaned and painted the gallery for the five-hundred-year anniversary celebration of Leonardo's death. It gave me an opening, and I asked when the painting itself had last been cleaned.

"The painting is checked for signs of deterioration often," he said, "but when cleaning an old painting, there is always danger one may strip away the good with the bad, so it is kept to a minimum."

"Was there any repainting after the acid attack?" I asked.

He flinched. "Yes, but nothing one can detect with the naked eye."

"Where, exactly?"

"I have no idea. That would have been done long before my time at the Louvre."

I did not believe him. Surely, the curator of Renaissance painting would know exactly which parts of the museum's most famous painting had been retouched and where. I pushed further, asking whether there had been any repainting after the 1911 theft.

"Some scratches were filled in with watercolor," he said with an exasperated sigh. "But that too was a long time ago, so I could not tell you where."

Maybe not, but he had just told me something important: that the painting had been retouched with watercolor, which could be easily removed without any damage to the oil painting's surface. Plus, it could hide anything, including whatever Chaudron might have added to identify his forgeries.

"Is this what you are writing about, the condition of the painting?" he asked. "Every year, someone comes to the Louvre to try and disparage the condition, even the *validity* of the *Mona Lisa*. Absurd."

I told him no, that I just wanted to see it for teaching purposes, and he gave me a look, head tilted, and lips pursed, clearly trying to assess whether or not I was telling the truth. He was about to say something when a young woman entered the gallery.

"*Il y a un appel pour vous*, Monsieur Gingembre?"

He told her he would be there in a minute, then turned to me. "I must take this call. You have seen enough, yes?"

"No," I said. "I haven't even looked at the other paintings in the room."

Gingembre heaved a sigh and turned toward the young woman. "Marie, see if Gustave is awake and bring him here, and ask Bertrand as well."

A few minutes later, two guards appeared, one young and burly, the other old and gray.

"*Méfiez-vous de lui!*" Gingembre said to them.

"I'm sure they *will* watch me," I said.

The curator looked surprised and annoyed that I had understood.

"I can only spare the guards for a half hour," he said, lingering at the edge of the gallery, obviously torn about leaving me with the muscum's greatest work of art, then finally turned to go.

The guards assumed places on either side of the painting, and I took a step closer, my reflection in the glass so like my great-grandfather's it was startling. I leaned to the side to avoid the glare and study the misty mountains and lakes—the product of Leonardo's famous *sfumato*, literally "turned to vapor," which the artist had produced with thin glazes of linseed oil and pigment painted over and over until edges blurred and the picture took on its otherworldly haze.

What else was veiled? Could Chaudron's markings have turned to vapor over the years? I slid the magnifying glass from my pocket, and both guards practically pounced.

"Monsieur!"

"I'm not going to touch it," I said. "I just want to study the brushwork."

The guards moved in close as I brought the magnifier within a few inches of the painting's glass and slowly moved it across the surface—every crack and fissure enlarged, strands of Lisa del Giocondo's hair like rivers and gullies.

"*Que cherchez-vous?*" the older guard asked.

"Nothing special," I said, still moving the magnifier inch by inch. In fact, I had no idea what I was looking for—something covered by watercolor or something that had faded away?

The museum was hot and airless, and I felt flushed, the magnifying glass shaking in my hand. "Did you hear that?" I asked the guards.

"*Quoi?*"

"Nothing," I said, though I could have sworn I'd heard a baby cry, then the sound of a hammer or pliers wrenching something apart. "Are there carpenters working today?"

The guards said no.

I gazed at the painting. A flush of heat rippled my body. A moment later, my vision blurred, and the room began to spin.

"*Monsieur, ça va?*" the old guard asked, the younger one moving quickly, a hand at my back.

I wiped sweat off my brow and tried to find my balance as I began to sway and tip.

Outside, I gulped in air as if a gag had been pulled from my mouth. The guard had caught me before I fell but I was still feeling off-kilter. I needed a cup of coffee, something to settle my nerves. Though it wasn't coffee I wanted, I knew that. I fished the bag of Jolly Ranchers out of my pocket, only two left. Popped both of the sweet alcohol substitutes into my mouth. The candy helped my blood sugar but not my frustration.

Had I really expected to find a clue in the painting?

I glanced back at the Louvre, the *graveyard*, quiet and locked up with its great art and all the stories behind them.

Surely, over the years, dozens of conservators had inspected the famous painting after my great-grandfather had returned it. If there had been something off, wouldn't they have found it, reported it?

Or would they?

I considered the question. If someone had reported an irregularity in the painting, would the museum have divulged it? As the curator had just pointed out, the painting was the Louvre's star attraction. Could they afford to admit it was a forgery? Would millions of tourists line up to see a copy? It was all about authenticity, wasn't it? If the painting was a forgery, people might just as well stay home and check out the image on their computers.

54

He sees the red dot move out of the Louvre, but he is not ready to leave the café, moments of comfort and relaxation such a rarity. He takes a bite of croissant, a sip of coffee, and sits back. *Why rush?* He can watch where the American is going from here. He will catch up to him later, find out what he has learned at the museum, and hopefully get the answers they are both looking for.

55

I could not stop thinking about the *Mona Lisa*, the way it had drawn me in, overwhelmed me. It stayed in my mind as I walked through the Marais, stopped at the Place des Vosges, one of the oldest squares in Paris and considered one of the most beautiful with its large garden, central fountain, and buildings of redbrick inlaid with strips of stone. A place I'd like to live though could never afford. I had a momentary fantasy of me and Alex in one of these gorgeous homes, the idea that this woman who kept me almost as off-balance as I'd just felt in the Louvre would one day share a house with me improbable if not impossible, and yet I enjoyed the daydream.

Still feeling a bit shaky, I ducked into a tabac, perused the candy, chose something called Arlequin, in a garish multicolored bag. The hard candies were individually wrapped, which led me to believe they'd be more upscale than their artificial tutti-frutti supersweet flavor turned out to be.

I'd eaten three by the time I found 67 rue de Perche, an old three-story townhouse. I raised a bronze knocker in the shape of a lion's head and let it fall back.

The man who opened the door was wearing a blue satin robe, in his late forties, tall and striking. "*Qu'est-ce que c'est?*" he asked, his tone clipped and cool.

"Étienne Chaudron?" I asked.

He nodded.

"I'm Luke Perrone. We spoke on the phone—"

He took a minute to figure out who I was, and when he did, he didn't look happy. "I was perfectly clear that I have nothing to say to you."

"Yes, but I was in Paris and..." I quickly spoke the lines I'd rehearsed. "I've been reading Vincenzo Peruggia's diary, and your great-uncle, Yves, plays a major part in it. I have something important to discuss with you."

"And what could that possibly be?"

"May I come in? I promise not to take much of your time."

He opened the door reluctantly, and I followed him through a foyer with a decorative relief of unfurling ribbons just below the ceiling, obviously old, some of the plasterwork cracking, but still lovely. Several suitcases were lined up, and I asked if he was going away.

"A short vacation—the south of France," he said, leading me past a winding wooden staircase with a beautifully curved banister into a small sitting room with a marble fireplace, a crystal chandelier, built-in bookcases, and two comfy leather sofas. He indicated I should sit, though he remained standing, so I stood too.

"What is it you have to say that is so important?"

"I believe Yves Chaudron was in league with my great-grandfather, Vincenzo Peruggia, to steal the *Mona Lisa*."

"And?"

"That doesn't surprise you?"

"I have heard it before, many times."

"Peruggia's diary clearly states that your great-uncle painted several versions of the *Mona Lisa* during its two-year absence from the Louvre."

He sighed. "Every year, I hear another story about my infamous great-uncle and the forgeries he *supposedly* made, but there is never any proof they were made by my great-uncle's hand."

"That's exactly what I'm looking for—*proof*. A way to distinguish your great-uncle's forgeries."

Étienne Chaudron raked a hand through his hair and took a breath. "Even if the forgeries did exist, there would be no way to prove it."

"According to the journal, your great-uncle switched paintings on Peruggia, so it was one of his forgeries that was returned to the Louvre."

"Monsieur Perrone..." Chaudron shook his head and sighed again. "If that were true, it would be a marvelous hoax, but I have no idea about such a thing."

"Why would Peruggia make it up?"

"You seriously ask such a question about the man who stole the world's most famous painting? Have you not considered *qu'il était fou?*"

"That he was crazy? Yes, I have considered it, but I've found nothing in his journal to suggest that he was." I handed him the page I had torn out of the journal.

"A page from Peruggia's diary," he said. "You offer this as proof?"

A moment to realize I had not said where the page was from, and yet he had identified it.

"My Italian is quite poor," he said, though he skimmed the page before handing it back to me. "And?"

"And I was hoping you might know what the rest of it said, what it was your great-uncle put in his paintings to distinguish them from the original."

"I have no idea," he said, lips tightly compressed as if he were trying to hold words in. "Now, you will excuse me, but I have things I must attend to."

I folded the page back into my breast pocket. I felt he knew more than he let on and tried to think of what to say, to ask, something that would get him to cooperate. "I'm thinking of writing about this."

"About *what*?"

"The theft—and your great-uncle's involvement in making the forgeries."

"I would advise against that," he said, more cautionary than threat, then led me back to the foyer.

I stopped a moment to look through an archway into the living room, most of the furniture covered with sheets, not the sort of thing one did for a short vacation. Then I spotted a painting. "Is that a Vermeer?" I asked and moved in for a closer look before he could stop me. The painting depicted a woman playing piano, another woman holding a letter, a black-and-white-checkered floor like a series of diamonds, all suffused with the famous Vermeer light. "Is this your great-uncle's work?"

"I must ask you to leave," Chaudron said, his hand on my back.

Then it clicked. I *knew* the painting. It had once hung in Boston's Isabella Stewart Gardner Museum. A painting—along with twelve others—that had been stolen in 1990, an unsolved crime that still baffled the authorities. Was this an Yves Chaudron forgery, or could it possibly be the original?

"It's remarkable," I said.

"Yes, yes," Chaudron said impatiently. "It is my great-uncle's. You can see he had a meticulous hand."

I did. If it was a copy, I no longer had any doubt that Yves Chaudron was capable of producing a perfect forgery of just about anything. Then I realized Yves Chaudron had died long before the Gardner Museum theft, so when had he seen the painting to copy it so perfectly? I made a note to find out where the painting had been before it had made its way to the Gardner.

"How did you get it?" I asked.

A pause, another sigh. "It was among his things when he died. He had no children, so everything went to my older sister. Now I must ask you—"

"And your sister—"

"Is dead."

"I'm sorry. So your great-uncle's effects came to you?"

"Yes. This painting, some papers—" He stopped talking, sucking in his lower lip like a child who had accidentally said the wrong thing.

"Papers?" I asked.

Chaudron said nothing, again steering me toward the front door. His hand was at my back when someone called out, "Bonjour!" A pretty young woman at the top of the staircase, tugging the sash of her silky robe tighter. *"Je ne savais pas que nous avons de la compagnie."*

"He was just leaving," Chaudron said.

"Vous êtes américain?" she asked.

"Guilty," I said.

"You are not here about *that*, are you?" She tilted her chin toward the Vermeer. *"C'est un faux,* a fake, you know. Étienne's great-grandfather—"

"Great-*uncle*—" said Chaudron.

"Cela n'a pas d'importance," she said, then slid easily into the American idiom: *"Whatever."*

"Monsieur Perrone was just leaving," he said again, opening the door.

"Nice to meet you, Mrs. Chaudron."

"Mrs. Chaudron?" The young woman giggled. *"Pas de tout!"*

"Have a nice trip to the south of France," I said.

"*Quoi?*" the young woman looked perplexed. "No. *Mexique.*" She did a pirouette and disappeared down the upstairs hall. A moment later, there was music blasting.

"I thought you said the south of France."

"You were mistaken," Étienne Chaudron said and ushered me through the front door. It closed behind me with a thud.

56

A dark-haired young woman with a mournful face out of a Modigliani painting sat at a desk at Pelletier Editions. I introduced myself and asked if she knew my *friend* and fellow rare-book collector Antonio Guggliermo.

"I have not been here long," she said.

I showed her the receipt I had found for a journal Guggliermo had purchased at her store.

She studied it a moment, seemed to be fighting tears as she perused a drawer of folders. She plucked one out labeled GUGGLIERMO and handed it to me. "You may look through it yourself."

I skimmed through about a dozen receipts, all for books sold to Guggliermo, but nothing for a journal.

"There should be copies of everything," she said.

I told her I did not see a receipt for what I was looking for, and she said I could take the folder, that the shop would soon be closing, and she would no longer need the receipts.

"Closing?"

"Yes. For good. It belonged to my father, and I'm afraid he has…died."

I said I was sorry and asked when.

"About…two months ago."

"I hope you will forgive another question, but how did he die?"

She looked a bit shocked but answered. "It appears his heart gave out, though it is unclear. He was not very old and in good health. He was found here...in the shop"—she choked back a sob—"on the floor."

"So he died of natural causes."

"Yes, as I said—" She stopped, this time angling a suspicious look at me. "Are you police?"

"No, nothing like that."

"Then what? Is there something you are not telling me?"

"No," I said.

She swiped her tears away. "If there is no copy of the receipt, I cannot help you."

"I'm sorry for your loss," I said, thinking it was too damn coincidental, another of Guggliermo's booksellers dead.

57

"Pressing the buzzer is *inutile*—useless. She will never hear you..." A young French hipster with a man bun and paint-stained jeans. "But if you are looking for Colette, she is almost always home."

In fact, I had no idea who I was looking for, but the address in Belleville was right, so I nodded, and Man Bun let me in. I was amazed the old building was still standing and that I'd found it.

"Colette is at the top," he said, "*Faites attention!*"

I understood the warning as I started up the wooden stairs, eroded and treacherous, the hallway and landings permeated with the smell of turpentine. Clearly, Vincent and Simone's old building still played host to artists.

On the sixth floor, I stopped, caught my breath, and knocked on an apartment door, cracked paint exposing layers of a dozen previous colors.

Three inches of face appeared between door and chain lock, elderly, wrinkled, and heavily made up, wine-red lips and hennaed hair.

"*Qu'est-ce que vous voulez?*" she asked, her voice scratchy.

In my best French, I told her I had come all the way from New York, explaining that my great-grandfather had once lived in her apartment and how much I wanted to see it.

The old woman cupped a hand to her ear, made me repeat

everything twice, but finally invited me into the foyer where she spoke rapidly in a combination of French and English: *"J'adore les Américains!*—my name is Colette—*Ce n'est pas mon vrai nom* but I chose it, so Colette it is! I am a widow, *mon mari est mort* many years now—no children—but like Edith Piaf, *'Je ne regrette rien!'"*

I kept a smile glued on my face, trying to see beyond the small foyer into the apartment.

"Venez," she said, ushering me in.

I stopped, could not believe what I was seeing. Though the walls appeared to have been painted over many times, there were outlines of curling vines with touches of green leaves and pink blossoms— Simone's handiwork bleeding through layers of paint and time.

Colette followed my gaze. "It always comes through. What can I do?"

I moved in closer, fingertips against the painted ivy, a memento of the past refusing to give up. It not only brought the journal to life but it convinced me it was true.

Heat pipes clanged and Colette nattered on about the noise and the price of milk, almost chasing away the ghosts, while I desperately tried to hold on. I could not stop running my fingers over the pentimento of vines and leaves that bled through the old walls, my mind alive with images of Vincent and Simone.

I followed Colette into a bedroom with clothing draped over every surface—bed, dresser, a chair—but all I saw was the small painting, a still life of fruit arranged on a red cloth, everything outlined in dark blue-black. "That painting—"

"Ah, *oui*. It was here when I arrived, in the back of the little closet. I liked it, so I hung it up."

I looked at the signature and date in the lower left corner: *V. Peruggia, 1910.* "It belonged to my great-grandfather. I mean, he painted it."

"Vraiment?"

I studied the composition and technique, imagined Peruggia's hand and brush moving across the small canvas, saw how he had attempted to link everything together with his blue-black line. It was not revolutionary, but it had a simple beauty and integrity.

Colette lifted it off the wall with gnarled arthritic hands. "I have enjoyed it for many years, monsieur, but it belongs to you."

"No, I couldn't."

"You must."

I offered to pay for it, but she refused.

"Wait then." I took the stairs too fast, almost had a serious tumble, then slowed and managed to make it down to the vestibule and out the front door in one piece. Daylight was fading, a misty rain creating haze. The flower stand I had remembered seeing was still open. The old man, beginning to wrap up his stock, gave me a deal, two bouquets for the price of one, proudly identifying the various flowers in French. I thanked him and headed back, this time more cautiously up the six rickety flights.

I handed Colette the bouquets. She brought the flowers to her nose, closed her painted eyes, inhaled, and smiled.

The mist had turned to drizzle, and with nothing to protect the painting, I placed it under my jacket, the hundred-year-old canvas next to my heart.

When the rain got worse, I got a cab. I looked at the painting, noted the heavy paint, slightly cracked with age, but the colors remained vibrant and alive. When I finally stopped studying the painting, the Paris streets had gone dark. I got my cell phone out and saw I had missed two calls, both of them from Étienne Chaudron.

58

I let the lion's-head knocker fall back against the heavy wooden door, Étienne Chaudron's messages, both identical, playing in my mind:

I have something important I must show you, something in my great-uncle's meticulous hand… Please come.

His tone was urgent, almost pleading, so much so I had asked the taxicab driver to take me directly to his home.

I jammed Peruggia's painting into the waistband of my jeans and tried the knocker again. When there was no response, I used my cell, but the call went straight to Chaudron's voicemail for the third time.

"It's Luke Perrone," I said. "I'm at your front door. It's…"—I checked my phone—"almost nine o'clock."

Why, after being so insistent that I come, was he not home? I slid the phone into my breast pocket just behind the stolen journal page and tried the knocker one more time.

I have something important to show you, something in my great-uncle's meticulous hand…

I backtracked down the townhouse stairs and looked up. Several windows were lit like bright rectangles of yellow against the dark night.

Back up the stairs, I tried the knocker again and called out, "Étienne!"

Was that music? Maybe that was it... They couldn't hear me over the music. I leaned against the door to listen, and it creaked opened.

"Étienne?" I said, quieter now. "It's Luke Perrone." No one could possibly hear me over the music, which was blasting, the same pop song the girlfriend had been playing when I had been here earlier.

I took a step in.

A ceramic lamp cast everything in shadow: wallpaper, rugs, an antique side table—on it several cigarettes crushed in an ashtray. The suitcases were still lined up in the hallway.

Another step in, I called louder, "Étienne!"

The song ended, but a moment later, it started again, as if on repeat. It was coming from upstairs.

I'd taken only a few more steps when I saw her, Chaudron's girlfriend, on the staircase, her head on the bottom step, one leg stretched above, the other bent at an impossible angle, her eyes open and fixed.

Breath caught in my throat, frozen for a minute, then I moved on automatic, searching for a pulse in her neck, her wrist, though there was little doubt she was dead: her nightgown was soaked with blood.

Hands trembling, I fumbled the cell phone from my pocket, smearing it with the girl's blood, not sure who to call. Did the French use 911?

That damn pop song was playing over and over. Steam hissed from a radiator. The smell of tobacco gone sour in the air. I fought nausea as I followed bloodstains trailing up the stairs.

Étienne Chaudron lay on the floor just outside his bedroom, face beaten, blue robe gone purple with blood.

The music was blaring, sending shock waves through my body,

the bedroom door half-open, and I dared look in—the room trashed, drawers dumped, pillows slashed, feathers everywhere, several doing a slow dance in the air. *Had this just happened?*

From the look of Chaudron's face, or what was left of it, I guessed he had not given up whatever it was the killer had been searching for.

Something important to show you, something in my great-uncle's meticulous hand...

My pulse was racing. Had Chaudron's call been interrupted—or had there been a gun to his head when he'd called? Had someone else wanted me here?

An alarm—intuitive and raw—sounded inside my head: *Get out—now!*

I moved backward down the stairs, almost stumbling over the girl's body, the cell phone in my hand covered in her blood, and could not stop the thought: *What else have I touched: the doorknob, the lion's-head knocker, the banister—the girl!—my name and number on Chaudron's cell phone, along with my messages!*

Head pounding, mouth dry, I made it to the bottom landing, stood there a moment, looking one way, then the other, alarm still sounding in my brain, body tingling. In the living room, the sheets had been pulled off the furniture, cushions slit, foam bubbling out of them as if they had erupted, a shattered vase, shards of pottery on the floor, an armoire with its drawers open, a table upended.

I tried to think over the music and the sound of my own blood pulsing in my ears. I looked up and saw the Vermeer painting.

Something important to show you, in my great-uncle's meticulous hand...

The same words Chaudron had used earlier when speaking of the Vermeer painting.

I wrestled the painting off the wall and turned it around. There was a wad of folded pages wedged into the wooden stretcher bars. I got them out, unfolded them... No question they were from Peruggia's journal, the handwriting, the buff paper, the torn edges.

Everything of my great-uncle's went to my older sister...this painting...some papers...

I tried to read, but my mind was spinning, impossible. I'd read them later. *Now, get out of here!*

I stuffed them into my jacket pocket. A moment later, I felt the stirring of air and heard the intake of breath.

"Just what I have been looking for."

The man came around to face me, gun in his hand. "I will take that."

A split second to think, a move toward my breast pocket. He slapped my hand away and reached in. He came out with a folded, blood-streaked page. Then he pressed the gun against my temple and cocked the trigger.

59

New York City

The collector replaced the burned-out spotlight, then moved from one artwork to another. He took in the skillful brushwork of a Monet seascape, the brilliant color in a Matisse still life, lingered in front of a piece he'd acquired only a few days ago, a Toulouse-Lautrec gouache on cardboard, a woman pulling up her stockings, simple and sexy. He admired the way the artist had created a figure out of a few quickly sketched lines, the use of white paint on the shoulders and breasts to give them volume and bring them forward, the stark red-orange of her hair. He did not need the piece, nor had he commissioned the theft. He had almost said no, but the opportunity was too good, the artwork first-rate and an excellent addition to his collection.

From Lautrec to Leonardo, the two artists worlds apart, yet both fascinated by feminine beauty, Lautrec's woman earthy and real, Leonardo's lady ethereal and bewitching, beyond mortal man. But not beyond him.

It had been twenty years since he had acquired the Leonardo, the fence who'd sold it to him a Frenchman who claimed to represent an upper-class French family whose great-grandmother had owned many well-known artworks of dubious provenance. The family, afraid to have such a famous painting in their possession, were willing to part with it for a mere five million dollars, though he had bargained them down to three, a pittance if indeed it were real, but he still did not have proof.

How many trips had he made to Paris and the Louvre to stand in front of the painting to study it for similarities or differences, none of which he could ever see? He knew about good forgeries, and it was possible that was all he had. He raised his magnifying glass and drew it slowly across the painting's surface. But what was he looking for? Was there something here that would prove the painting's authenticity? He had no idea. Not yet. But soon.

60

At the sound of the cocked trigger, I reacted, elbowed the man in the ribs, and he faltered but fired, the gun going off so close to my head I felt the bullet whiz by, my ears ringing. But the gun popped out of his grip, zipped through the air, and hit the floor with a clunk, both of us now lunging for it, falling together, the big guy landing on top of me. Air exploded out of me, a sharp pain in my ribs, but I still scrambled, straining to reach the gun.

He got there first.

His hand on the grip, other arm around my neck, cold steel against my temple, the trigger cocked again. No time to pray.

A flash. Not a shot. Another man sprinting across the room, knocking the gun from the big guy's hand, a kick to his gut, the guy rolling off me as the second man dove, the two of them rolling on the floor just beside me, and I joined the fight—all of us punching, kicking, cursing, staggering forward to get hold of the gun, one massive six-armed, six-legged creature. I wasn't sure who got it, just knew it wasn't me, heard it fire, and a yowling cry, a man up, holding his side, tearing down the hall and out the front door.

I managed to get up, the other man still on the floor.

"Perrone!" he shouted.

I tried to get my bearings, to make sense of it—make sense of him. "What the... What are you doing here?"

"How about saying"—he struggled for a breath—"thank you for saving…my life?"

"Fuck that," I said. "Maybe I…just saved *yours!*"

61

I was led from the townhouse to a police station and into an interrogation room where I was left alone. Cold fluorescent light. One mirrored wall. No doubt someone watching from the other side. I rapped on it, asked "Anyone there?" then stared at my reflection—disheveled hair and sleep-deprived eyes, one swollen and twitching, a purple bruise already forming on my jaw. An hour passed. I knocked on the mirror again and called, "Hello...hello?" then asked to see a lawyer. I might as well have been talking to myself.

Another hour passed, then the door opened, and the guy strode in, deep scratches on his cheek and the beginning of a black eye. He handed me a Styrofoam cup of black coffee.

I stared into his face. "Who *are* you?"

He dragged a chair up to the table, lit a cigarette, then laid his ID on the table—blue, laminated, his picture on it, the word *INTERPOL* at the top. He took out a second card, said, "This has my personal cell-phone number," and jammed it into my shirt pocket. "You're going to need it."

"What's this about, Smith, if that's even your name. John Smith... You couldn't think of anything better than *that*?"

"I never gave you a false name, no reason to..." He raised his glasses, met my eyes. "The Paris police have lent me this room for my investigation."

"*Investigation?*"

"I've been following you, Perrone, and it is a good thing for you that I have, or you would be dead."

"Like I said before, it's debatable who saved who."

"The man had his gun to *your* head, Perrone."

"And then at *yours*," I said.

"What did you stuff into your pants after the fight?"

I tugged the small painting out of my waistband and placed it on the table. "I always keep a spare in my pants."

Smith didn't laugh, stared at it a moment. "Whose painting is it?"

I considered telling him it was mine but told the truth. "Peruggia's."

"I'll just hold onto that," he said, "for evidence."

"Evidence of *what*?"

He didn't answer, instead told me he had already searched my Florence hotel room, had been through my laptop too, then slapped the journal onto the table.

"How did you get that?"

"INTERPOL credentials open doors. I asked the librarian what you'd been reading and might have implied you were under arrest, so she was particularly cooperative. I don't think you'll be welcomed back there. I thought it was a good idea to get the journal when I saw you were leaving Florence. A lot safer with me."

"Yeah. I feel safer already."

"I could have gone to the library anytime, you know, but I wanted to watch you, see what you were up to. You could have died tonight." Smith sat back, locked his hands behind his head, said he knew I had come to Florence to read Vincenzo Peruggia's journal, that he'd seen my correspondence with Luigi Quattrocchi.

I cut him off to say that Quattrocchi had been avoiding me, that he was missing.

"Quattrocchi is dead."

"*What?*" I had known something was wrong, but still it was a shock.

"You don't realize who you are dealing with, Perrone. There's a network of art thieves and collectors out there who will stop at nothing to protect themselves and get what they want. That man tonight, he'll be back. If not him, someone else."

"Why?"

"I would venture to say that he—or the people he's working for—think you know something important."

"I don't know anything."

He leaned across the table, face close to mine, prickling with expectation. "You speak to Quattrocchi and he's dead. You visit Étienne Chaudron and *he's* dead—"

"I don't know anything about that!" I bolted up, knocking my chair to the floor.

"Sit down," Smith said.

I wavered a moment, then righted the chair and sat.

"What did Étienne Chaudron tell you about the Vermeer painting, the one in his living room?"

"That his great-uncle painted it."

"Why did you take it off the wall?"

"It was already off when I got there. I stopped to look at it, that's all."

Smith eyed me coolly. "There are two dead bodies on the floor, but you take your time to look at a painting?"

I told him yeah, that I liked art, and his eyes went dark, almost black.

"You understand you are in serious trouble."

I didn't answer, slipped off my jacket, pushed my shirt sleeves up, wanted him to see my muscles and tattoos—my version of a big-dick contest.

Smith rolled up his sleeves. No tats, but his muscles were bigger than mine.

He told me that the Vermeer was on its way to a lab for testing to see if Yves Chaudron had painted it or if it was, in fact, the original. If the paints and solvents dated earlier than Chaudron, then the painting would go to the Gardner Museum for further tests. Then he asked again why I had taken it off the wall. When I didn't answer, he slammed his hands down on the table so hard, it rocked.

I kept my cool, repeated the painting was already on the floor, or maybe it had fallen off when that thug attacked.

He glared at me, a muscle in his jaw twitching, asked why I'd gone to see Étienne Chaudron, and I told him the truth—that I'd been reading about his great-uncle, Yves, the art forger, so I wanted to meet him. "If you have the journal," I said, "then you know what Peruggia wrote."

Smith sucked in a breath, something behind those dark eyes I couldn't read. "Truth for truth, Perrone?"

I waited; a flickering overhead light added a kinetic throb to the moment.

"A deal of sorts. I have the journal but haven't read it, because I don't read Italian. For that, I'll need an interpreter."

"I'm sure you have plenty at INTERPOL."

"True." Smith paused. "But I want someone discreet. I want *you*."

I saw it in his face: Smith had no intention of turning the journal over to INTERPOL. I didn't know why, but now I had something he wanted. "Why should I help you?"

"Because the games are over, Perrone, and you're in trouble. I may be the only friend you have, your only chance."

I laughed, and that did it. Smith reached out and grabbed me by my shirt, a vein in his temple pulsing. "Luigi Quattrocchi is dead! Étienne Chaudron and his girlfriend are dead! The girl's blood on *your* phone, *your* shirt, *your* hands!"

"You trying to pin that on *me?*" I wrenched free. "You know I had nothing to do with that. Fuck you, Smith!"

"What I know and what I will tell the French police are two different things. You get my drift, buddy?"

"I'm not your *buddy*."

"You got that right," Smith said. "You will be arrested and found guilty when an INTERPOL agent testifies against you."

"Fuck you," I said again, but much of the fight had gone out of my words. I could see it, my arrest and trial spooling out in front of me, the obvious verdict.

"You play ball with me, or that's it—you're a guilty man. And believe me, the French prisons are not nearly as nice as the ones in the States, and from what I know, those aren't very nice at all."

I fought the urge to throw a punch, took a deep breath, tried to think. Smith would learn what he needed from the journal anyway, no reason not to tell him. I asked him what he wanted to know, and he said, "Everything."

"What do I get in return?"

"My protection, INTERPOL's protection—and you're going to need it."

He had a point. If he hadn't come along, that thug would have blown my brains out. I took a moment, then said okay. Smith lit another cigarette and sat back. I told him how Valfiero had lured my great-grandfather into stealing the painting, how Chaudron had made copies, and how the pair had schemed to make forgeries and sell them as the original. When I stopped, he asked again why I'd come to Paris to see Étienne Chaudron.

"I wanted to see if he could add anything to what I'd read."

"There's something else you're not telling me."

I told him he was wrong, that there was nothing else.

He stared at me, said he knew all about me: my past, my present, the school suspensions, the arrests for breaking and entering.

"Ancient history," I said. "Who cares?"

"I think a judge and jury will. Your delinquent past isn't going to play well in your murder case." He added a mean grin. "Your prints all over the townhouse, the girl's blood on your phone—"

"What's my motive?" I folded my arms across my chest, trying to hide my anxiety.

"How about art theft? It runs in your family. You were in Chaudron's home earlier, saw the Vermeer, wanted it, and went back to steal it. But you know, Perrone, that hardly matters. Your DNA alone will convict you."

I kept my mask of cool in place best I could, but I knew he was right.

"I want your full cooperation, and I want it *now*. Starting with *why* you went to see Étienne Chaudron and *what* you learned from him."

"I already told you."

"There's more. *You* know it and *I* know it!"

I was pretty sure he was bluffing. The way he kept threatening, then backing down, my Kill Van Kull radar reading him like it would any punk on the street. Something was off. Smith had a secret, same as me.

62

I walked fast, shoulders hunched, head down, no direction in mind. I just had to keep moving. The rain was coming down hard now. It soaked my hair and streaked my face. I didn't think Smith was following me or having me followed, but I couldn't be sure and wanted to put as much distance between us as possible. He'd let me go with a threat to turn me in for the murders of Étienne Chaudron and his girlfriend. I knew he was bluffing, or he'd have already done it. Letting me go had been the proof.

I crossed streets, turned corners, and cut through alleyways, always checking over my shoulder, consumed by one thought—reading the pages I had found in the back of the Vermeer painting. I kept my hand flat against them, wedged in my pocket to keep them dry, to make sure they were there. I replayed the way I had tricked the man with the gun into taking the wrong page—the intentional feint toward my breast pocket, a decision made in a split second, directing him to the page I'd torn out of the journal and brought with me to Paris, not the ones I had just found hidden behind the Vermeer. It still amazed me that I had pulled it off, and I was pretty damn proud of myself.

After an hour of walking, wet and shivering but fairly certain I had not been followed, I looked for a place to stop. I peered through the window of a bar, too crowded. Another block, a courtyard with a small graveyard, tombstones tilted and worn. I circled the periphery, superstitious about walking over the dead. Then came to a back street where I spotted a shabby-looking café. Under its tattered awning, I took a minute to shake off the rain and smooth my hair.

Only two people at the bar, both huddled over drinks. Neither one looked up when I came in.

The bartender offered me a table, but I asked first for the men's room.

A bare bulb dangling from a chain illuminated a toilet, pitted sink, grimy black and white floor tiles. I blotted my face with a paper towel, tried hard to ignore the smell of urine and ammonia, got the pages out of my side pocket, and unfolded them. The first page stopped me. This was it, what I'd been looking for. The sentence continuing exactly from the last one I'd read…

…look very carefully at the shadow cast by Lisa del Giocondo's left hand. Where the hand meets the book. You will see two tiny marks. They will look like nothing more than that. Because you need to turn the painting upside down and look again. Now use the magnifying glass and you will see exactly what the forger Yves Chaudron has painted into every one of his copies.

Two marks. The letters Y and C. For Yves Chaudron. The forger has dared to sign his work!

This is all the proof you need to identify the forgeries. When you find the one without Chaudron's initials you will have found Leonardo's original!

I stared at the words, the paper trembling in my hand, could hardly believe I'd found it. I would have to go back to the Louvre and see the painting again, but this time, I'd know what to look for. I skimmed the remaining pages quickly. They appeared to be written after Peruggia had gotten out of prison. I put them back into my pocket, would read them later. The first page, the important page, I folded into a small square, found the tiny tear in my pocket, and forced it through until it lodged inside the lining.

I caught my reflection in the mirror above the sink, dark shadows of my beard and mustache, hair slick with rain, one eye swollen from the fight, a crack in the mirror bisecting my other eye and making it appear smaller. I stared at my face, but it was my great-grandfather who stared back.

63

The rain was no more than a drizzle now, everything cloaked in heavy fog as I made my way down the street, trash floating in puddles, half the lights burned out, shops closed, homes dark—not a desirable neighborhood for this time of night.

A man, hulking and ragged, appeared out of the mist, and I flinched.

"*Pardonnez-moi*," he said, apologizing for startling me. "*Je ne voulais pas vous effrayer*." A homeless guy with a surprisingly young face half-hidden under a scraggly beard and matted hair.

I dug around in my pocket, came up with a handful of damp, crumpled euros, and handed them to him.

He thanked me and wished me "*bonne chance*."

I wished him good luck as well. I felt like we both needed it. I was tired, my body aching and heavy, the day finally catching up to me. And I was lost.

I huddled under a bus stop, got my cell phone out, and ordered an Uber. I felt for the paper in my jacket lining again, my mind churning with thoughts and images—Yves Chaudron's initials in the paintings, the dead girl on the staircase, Smith's threats—so I didn't see anything until the blow came against my back. Stunned and stumbling, I turned but was hit again, and this time, I went down, knees against concrete, filthy water splashing into my face, my mouth. I looked up to see the man who had been fighting with

me and Smith, the recognition processed in split seconds before
he hauled me to my feet, knife at my neck, a hiss in my ear. "You
have other papers."

"I already gave them to you," I said, trying to breathe, to think.

"Time to kill you."

"No—wait. You're right. There are other pages, but they're—in
my hotel room."

"Perhaps your life means nothing to you," he said, his flat,
colorless eyes on mine as he drew the knife around to the back of
my neck, slid it across my skin. "It is up to you."

I didn't think, thrust my arm into his gut, heard the air go out of
him, saw him stagger and hold his side, then fall. I sprinted down
the street, saw the Uber turning onto it, waved my arms, shouted
for it to stop, pulled the door open, "*Allez! Allez!* Go! Go!" I said,
collapsing into the back seat, winded, in shock.

I looked back to see the man on the ground getting to his feet
and staring after the car as we drove away.

The driver asked what I'd been doing in such a bad neighborhood, but I didn't answer, intently checking the lining of my jacket
to make sure the paper was still there. I touched the back of my
neck, and my hand came away stained with blood. Then I noticed
my knuckles and palms were scraped, the knees of my jeans torn
and bloodied.

I fumbled the card from my shirt pocket, hands shaking. Not
feeling very tough anymore, I got the cell phone to my ear and
made the call.

64

I slammed the palm of my hand against the hotel room door, knuckles too bruised to make a fist.

Smith opened it. He was in boxer shorts and a tee, eyes puffy from sleep.

"Attacked—" I said before my knees gave out.

He got an arm around me, led me to the bathroom, knocked the toilet seat down, and told me to sit. Helped me out of my jacket, then my shirt, ran a washcloth under cold water, dabbed at the back of my neck. "It's nothing, just a flesh wound," he said, opened the medicine cabinet, came out with a bottle of alcohol, swabbed the back of my neck, then helped me up again.

I washed my hands, watched the water go from red to pink.

Smith doused them with alcohol too, told me not to a baby when I winced.

"Now tell me what happened."

I tried to explain it, seeing the guy, the fight, in fragments, how he'd come out of nowhere.

"Did you recognize him?"

"Yeah, the same guy we fought with earlier."

"Did you kill him?"

"No."

"How you'd get away?"

"I'm a tough guy, remember? You know my history."

"Yeah, real tough," he said. "Take your pants off."

"Excuse me?"

Smith indicated my knees, the torn fabric, the bloodstains. I eased my pants down, sat on the toilet seat again.

"So what was he after? The *truth* this time, Perrone."

"Might be time you called me Luke. I mean, with my pants down and all."

Smith almost laughed, handed me the washcloth to clean my knees, asked if I had other pants, another shirt, which I did, back in my hotel room.

"Good," he said. "So the man you fought with... Was he injured from the shot fired earlier?"

"He was holding his side, so probably, or I wouldn't have gotten away."

Smith led me out of the bathroom, offered me the only comfy chair. I took in the room for the first time, utilitarian and bland, a charmless businessman's hotel. He got a couple of tiny liquor bottles out of the mini fridge, held them up. "Scotch or vodka?"

I told him I didn't drink.

"Right. I forgot." He handed me a glass of water. "Here you go, *Lucky*."

I scoffed a laugh. "Is John Smith really your name?"

"John Washington Smith."

"Has a ring to it," I said.

"Now tell me what you didn't tell me before."

I drank the water. It did little to calm me. I wanted the scotch, could practically taste it. I needed a moment, closed my eyes, and silently recited words I knew by heart: *Honesty—Hope—Faith—Courage—Integrity—Willingness—Humility—Brotherly Love—Justice—Perseverance—Spirituality—Service*. More than their meaning, it was the act of saying them that helped. Then I told Smith I was ready.

I described how I'd found the pages in the back of the Vermeer and how I'd switched them on the guy who'd attacked me. I looked down at my bloodied knees and raw palms, admitted I'd been in over my head. Smith didn't take the opportunity to gloat, which I appreciated.

I asked him what was next.

"Now that we know what to look for, we go see the painting."

"No way that Louvre curator is going to give me another private viewing."

"An INTERPOL employee can make certain demands," he said, a look sliding across his face, what I'd seen before, something he wasn't saying.

"Tell me," I said.

"Tell you *what?*"

"Whatever you're not telling me. I just came clean. How about you?"

Smith went to the window, pulled the curtains back, and peered out. "Nothing to tell," he said. "You were the one holding things back, not me."

"And I said I regretted it."

He said he was sorry I had to get hurt to feel that way, but he needed my honesty from now on, and not just because my life depended on it.

"That is a factor," I said, then gave him my word: no more heroics, no more secrecy. I reached out and we shook hands, still waiting for him to say what it was he wasn't telling me.

"Kill Van Kull," he said, reading the tattoo on my arm.

"Name of my teenage crew—but you already know that, right?"

"There are pictures in your file."

"Of my *tattoos?*"

"No. Of you with your buddies, your *crew.*" He shook another cigarette out of a pack. "So the initials in the painting… We've got to be certain Peruggia is telling the truth."

"I'm sure he is," I said.

"Maybe. For now, we proceed with skepticism and caution."

"Caution for sure," I said and asked if he had any idea who the guy was who'd attacked me twice.

"Who knows? A thug. Hired help to do someone else's dirty work, to protect their interests." He shrugged. "It continues to amaze me what people will do to own a piece of canvas covered with paint."

"Not just *any* canvas and paint."

Smith nodded, then laid out what he needed from me. If Peruggia was telling the truth, Smith wanted to be the guy, the INTERPOL agent who after a hundred years revealed that the *Mona Lisa* in the Louvre Museum was a fake.

I said fine, then told him what I wanted: the right to tell my great-grandfather's story because it was *my* story too.

Smith paused. "All right. Once I break the case, the story is yours. But we work together. No secrets."

"None," I said.

He handed me my leather jacket and bloodstained shirt, checked his watch, told me to go to my hotel and get a few hours of sleep. "It's late, and we've got a lot to do."

I asked for a day off. There was something I needed to do.

"We don't have time to waste."

"There's someone I need to see," I said, "in Florence. You can go with me if you don't trust me."

"We have to stay in Paris, go to the Louvre. We could be here for a while."

"This won't take long," I said. "I can fly to Florence and be back the next morning. I'm asking for twenty-four hours, that's all."

Smith asked who I was seeing, and I said a friend and that it had nothing to do with any of this.

"The blond?"

"So you were watching me—*us*—in Florence."

"Yes. And no doubt the other man was too. Possibly others."

"I need to see her," I said. "You going to make me beg?"

"You're not going to run, are you?"

I promised him I wouldn't.

He hesitated a moment, seemed to be mulling it over.

I told him he could trust me, and I meant it.

"Okay," he finally said. "You have one day."

He watched me over my shoulder as I made the reservations online.

"You understand," he said, "I *will* come after you. *INTERPOL* will come after you, if you're not back tomorrow."

65

Smith paced. He hadn't been able to get back to sleep or relax since Perrone had left for the airport at dawn. Had it been a mistake to let him go, to follow his heart of all things? Jesus, he was getting soft. But he needed to trust the guy, and if Perrone failed to return, he *would* go after him.

He drummed his nails along the bottom of his laptop, felt like he was on the edge of a cliff about to jump. But he'd already jumped. The question was, would he fly or fall? A deep breath. Too late to worry about falling. Go back a hero or don't go back at all. And not to Bahrain!

In the bathroom, he washed his face, looked in the mirror, saw himself on the pitted concrete court of the Baruch housing project, smallest kid on the ad hoc basketball team, though he knew what to do when he got the ball: head down and move toward the goal. Like now.

A minute to sign into his INTERPOL email, several messages in regard to pending art investigations, nothing new or conclusive, none that needed his immediate attention. He sat back, lit a cigarette, took a drag that burned his throat, and squashed the cigarette out. One thing Perrone was right about—he smoked too much.

Enough. He closed the laptop, needed to go out, get some fresh air, see some life.

The streets around the hotel were bustling, the rue du Faubourg-Montmartre twisty and crooked. For a man who'd spent half his life in France, Smith hardly knew Paris, and he felt like a rube. He guessed he'd feel the same way if went back to Manhattan's Lower East Side where he'd grown up. From what he heard, the neighborhood was gentrified now, boutiques and hip restaurants, nothing like he'd ever known. He pictured his mom in their cramped kitchen, heating up dinner, a bowl of Campbell's soup, and worrying, always worrying, about bills, about her boy. *Get out of here and do better.* Her mantra.

He passed half a dozen cheap hotels and even more snack bars, then a handful of costume shops, one with a garish neon clown over the entrance, red nose blinking. Was that what he was, a clown, a fool for giving up his secure job? *Get out of here and do better.* What he had done and was doing again, only this time, it was getting out of a secure job for a fantasy of glory. What would his mom think about that? A decade now since her premature death, too late to ask and probably for the best.

The flashing sign of the Restaurant Chartier reminded him that he was hungry. He checked the menu, then made his way past the entrance into a back courtyard where he was shown to a table by a bored-looking waiter. He took his time eating an uninspired terrine de campagne smeared onto crusty or possibly stale bread, washed it down with an acidic white wine, the whole time thinking about what he was doing—the risks, the stakes, the possible rewards of success, the humiliation if he failed. The waiter stood over him while he drank his coffee, impatient to have the bill paid and the table filled with the next customer.

For a while, Smith meandered along the boulevard, worrying about Perrone. Had he really put his trust in a former alcoholic and juvenile delinquent? The guy may have grown up, but did anyone ever really change? He wondered if Perrone was telling him the whole truth and doubted it. Of course he was not telling the whole truth either.

66

I'd managed three, maybe four hours of sleep, then caught a flight from Paris to Florence. Now I waited in the café where Alex and I had had our first coffee, rehearsing what I'd say when she walked in, cheeks pink from the cold.

"Your eye—" she said. "What *happened?*"

"Just a clumsy accident."

"But you're okay?" She gave me a strange look, then pecked my cheek and unbuttoned her coat. Her cream-colored sweater made her skin appear ivory. I told her she looked beautiful, and she told me I looked terrible.

"I thought you were staying in Paris for a few days."

"I am," I said. "I mean, I was. My friend got called away, but I'm going back."

"Oh. When?"

"Soon. But I wanted to see you first." I reached for her hand.

"Your knuckles!"

"Part of the same clumsiness. It's embarrassing. I tripped over a sidewalk grating."

"Seriously?"

"I swear I'd had nothing to drink."

"I never thought that for a minute. How's your friend? In better shape than you, I hope."

"He's"—Étienne Chaudron's battered face flared in his mind—"fine."

She asked if he was an old art-school friend, and I couldn't remember what I'd said before, except that he was French. I fought the urge to tell her what was really going on, wanted to tell the truth so she would understand, but knew I couldn't. We were both quiet a moment, light through the café blinds painting us with stripes, like prisoners.

"Something *is* wrong," Alex said. "I can see it. Are you sure you aren't hurt?"

I told her I was fine, asked what she'd been up to, anything to delay what I had to say.

She thought a minute, then said she had finished reading the plague book and was reading *The Decameron*, in Italian. I told her I was impressed, surprised too. "I didn't think you spoke Italian."

"Oh, I can't speak it, not really. But I can read a little—and it's a way to learn." She touched my hand again, said it looked like I had punched someone.

"Oh, sure," I said, forced a laugh, then took a deep breath. It was time. I had to tell her. Couldn't put it off any longer. "Listen, I'm going to be busy for a while and—"

"Busy?"

"I mean away."

"Which is it, busy or away?" Her expression shifted from concern to wary.

"Both," I said, just as the waitress delivered our coffees. We both waited for her to leave. "I wanted to let you know so you wouldn't think there something was wrong if I wasn't able to get in touch with you."

"*Why?* Are you going into hiding? You're not some sort of spy, are you?"

"Obviously, it's nothing like that."

"Wait…" Alex sat back, sliding her hand out of mine. "Are you breaking up with me? Not that we're really—"

"No. Of course not." *You don't understand. I'm trying to keep you safe!* "I'm just going back to Paris for a while—to see my friend—and do some business."

She asked what sort of business, and when I said it was too soon to say, she accused me of being mysterious again, her tone gone cold. So I told her we were thinking of opening a gallery together, could almost taste the lie, acidic and bitter. I hated pushing her away when all I wanted was to hold her close.

"When," she asked, "and where?"

I compounded the lie, said my friend had a place in the south, so probably there where it would be cheaper. "I'll be going back and forth for a while. That's why—"

"Oh," she said. "I see."

No, she didn't see. How could she? I sounded suspicious even to myself. "I'll be back at some point."

"Some *point?*"

I wanted to explain it, to tell her everything, but knowing could put her in danger. I watched her fold into herself, retreating, pulling away. I wanted to shout, *No, you don't understand—I think I love you!* Instead I said, "I don't want to lose you," quietly, though I meant it.

A montage of emotions played across her face—resentment, sadness, and something else I couldn't read.

"Fine," she said with calculated indifference. "We hardly know each other. What happened between us just…happened."

"I'm not sorry it happened."

"No, I suppose you're not," she said, "now that you're leaving." Angry now, followed by another look I couldn't read, something roiling beneath the placid surface, but then she sighed and it sounded almost like relief. *Relief? That I was going away, leaving her?* "Something is obviously going on that you won't tell me," she said, "and that's *fine*. When you're ready, *if* you're ready, call me"—she stood, buttoning her coat—"or don't."

I got hold of her arm, fumbled for the right words. "I'll call you when I get back."

"You mean at *some point*?" She tugged free, and I saw it again, anger traded for a kind of acceptance. But *why?* And which emotion was real?

She stared at me a moment longer as if deciding whether or not to say something, then turned and without another word headed out the door.

67

Alex refilled her wineglass and took a sip, the taste bitter, or was it all the lies she had told that had left the bad taste in her mouth? She looked around her "charming" apartment but hated it, hated everything about being here, but most of all hated herself. She dumped the wine in the sink, disgusted with everything she had done, thought about the conversation with Luke: *busy…away… opening an art gallery with my friend.*

She was pretty sure he was lying, knew when she was being dumped. And she deserved it, didn't she?

I don't want to lose you.

Was that a lie too?

The expression on his face when he'd said it had looked authentic, earnest and pained and something else she couldn't read. But how could she expect the truth from him when everything she had said had been a lie?

No, not everything. Not in bed with his lips on hers. That hadn't been a lie. Not part of the plan either. She pictured him naked, beside her, on top of her, below her, his hands on her body, squeezed her eyes shut trying not to see him, because maybe that was all this was to him, sex, and now that he'd gotten it, he was moving on.

She wandered out to her balcony, took in the view, ochre and rose-colored buildings, terra-cotta rooftops, a slice of the Duomo.

Like a storybook, she thought, make-believe, like the romance between them.

She gripped the terrace handrail, stared down at the small courtyard below, leaned so far over she felt dizzy. Whipped her head back and caught her breath. For a brief moment, she had considered letting go, pictured her body careening to the ground, but she could never do that, the idea of leaving her mother alone unthinkable.

Still dizzy, she lay down on the sofa, stared up at the ceiling, then closed her eyes and pictured Luke, his arm around her while she had told him about her mother.

That was real, wasn't it? One of the few times she'd been honest.

The phone's ring startled her, the number lighting up her cell phone.

"Yes," she snapped.

"What sort of greeting is that?"

"The best I can do."

"Oh, we're in a mood, aren't we?"

"Not *we*."

"Have you seen him?"

"Yes."

"And?"

"He broke up with me."

"I don't believe you."

"It's the truth."

"What did he say?"

"That he was going away."

"Where?"

"Back to Paris or…somewhere. He wasn't clear."

"Either he's lying, or you are."

"I'm not."

A pause. "You have to see him again."

"I told you, he doesn't want to see me."

"But you must."

"It's over. I'm through."

"No," he said, calm but determined. "It is not over. You are obligated, remember?"

Alex sucked in a breath and let it out slowly. "But he doesn't want me."

"Oh, darling, that can't possibly be true. He's playing hard to get, that's all. Find a way."

"How?"

"Use your feminine intuition."

"I hate you," she said.

"That isn't very nice, and you know it's not true."

Alex thought it was the only true thing she'd said in weeks. She stared at the phone, thought about her obligations, what she had promised and why. Then thought about Luke and how she would get him back—with more lies? More seduction? The idea of it, of continuing to lie to this man she thought she might love, made her feel empty and sick.

68

I still had my room at the Palazzo Splendour and headed over there, replaying our conversation the entire way, thinking of a dozen things I should have said but didn't, couldn't. The guy at the front desk was surprised to see me and told me what I already knew, that a man from INTERPOL had searched my room. He seemed excited, interested in me for the first time. I told him it was a misunderstanding, that I would clean out the rest of my stuff, but asked to spend the night.

It was clear that Smith had been through my room, dresser drawers open, newspaper articles I'd brought from home missing, though the mug shot was still wedged into the mirror's frame. Tired but restless, I went next door to the café where I'd first met Smith. I took a seat at the bar, the place crowded and smoky.

The bartender recognized me with a nod and a smile, asked if I wanted my usual Pellegrino. I told him no, ordered a scotch neat. Lifted it to my lips, smelled the musky aroma. Put it down. I wanted it bad. I eyed the glass for another full minute, lifted it again, a dozen images playing in my mind: stumbling drunk along the Kill Van Kull, fights where I'd been too numb to feel the pain, blackouts.

I tilted the glass, the taste of warm liquor on my lips, my mind doing flip-flops... *Yes—No—Yes—No!* Then I thought about Alex and the way I'd held her in my arms while she had bad dreams and

how she'd told me about her mother, and I'd told her about my
drinking, and she didn't seem to care. I thought about my teaching
job, now on the line, how hard it had been to work my way up and
how I might lose it. I thought about past relationships with really
good women who I'd left or had walked out on me because of my
drinking, thought about my last big drunk and crawling out of that
dumpster.

I put the glass down. Asked the bartender to take it away,
ordered a panini, even though I wasn't hungry. Knew I was not
past the danger, so I ate the panini quickly and got the hell out of
there.

Outside, I found a cab. I didn't know St. James Church or
where Via Bernardo Rucelli was, but the driver did.

The room was in the church basement. They were always in a
basement, this one with a blackboard and wooden chairs with half
desks attached, the kind you have in elementary school. It turned
out the room was used for Sunday school, though the meeting
could have been anywhere: New York, Boise, Florence. Every
AA meeting felt the same, the only difference being that this one
was in Italian. About a dozen people, old and young. I sat, my
heart beating fast as one after another gave testimony, thinking
what I could say, *should* say—how close I'd come to drinking—
but I couldn't move, couldn't speak. It was like watching some
bad Hollywood movie: guy at a bar having a second, third, and
fourth drink, staggering along the street going nowhere, waking
up disoriented, hung over and hating himself—and the star of the
movie was me. I shivered. Listened to a woman say how she'd been
demoted year after year until she was finally fired from her job
for good, another talking about her broken marriage and crying,
familiar stories.

I gripped the seat of my chair like my life depended on it

because I wanted to bolt, to get the hell out of that church, to find a bar and have a drink. I locked eyes with a woman who nodded at me and smiled sweetly, as if to say *You can do it, you'll be okay*. I wasn't so sure, but the brief human exchange helped bring me back to the moment, the room, the reasons I was here. Next up, a guy, reed thin with sunken cheeks, looked fifty though he said he was thirty-eight, only a year older than me. He talked about two decades of drinking and drug addiction and how he'd been clean now for two years and everyone applauded, and I did too, clapped so hard my hands hurt.

After that, a man read from the Big Book, which at one time I'd known by heart though I was clearly in need of a refresher, even in Italian. After the meeting, there was coffee, and I talked to a sexy Italian woman in her fifties, divorced twice she said. I told her I'd never taken the plunge, and she told me not to, then invited me home. Another time, I would have said yes, but not anymore. I was clearly committed to a woman I had just pushed away, possibly forever.

69

I brushed past Smith and collapsed into the one comfy chair in his hotel room.

"Hello to you too," he said.

"Don't start. I've been back and forth to Paris in less than twenty-four hours and hardly slept."

"It's an hour flight," he said, "and it was *your* choice, not mine."

"An hour and *forty minutes*," I said, yesterday's conversation with Alex still playing in my mind like an old record stuck on repeat. "Let's get to work."

"Have something to eat. I got some rolls and cheese and coffee."

I was starving and tired, emotionally drained, touched that Smith had thought of getting food though I couldn't bring myself to say so. I ate a roll and drank some coffee, Smith smoking a cigarette, waiting.

"You know, I may have given up the love of my life for this," I said, a thought I hadn't meant to say aloud.

"We all make concessions," Smith said. "I've made plenty."

I didn't want to get into a pissing contest but pointed out that his concessions were part of his job, a rung up the INTERPOL ladder; my concessions were personal.

Smith shook his head and stabbed his cigarette into an ashtray so hard the thing almost toppled. "This isn't part of my job."

"What do you mean?"

Smith eyed me, looked away, then back. "I'm a criminal intelligence analyst, a researcher," he said, then paused, "not a police officer of any kind. There's no such position at INTERPOL. Our job is to gather information about a crime and turn it over to police in the countries that subscribe to INTERPOL."

"Wait... So you have no authority here?"

He nodded slowly, the secret he'd been hiding, the one I had glimpsed.

"Does INTERPOL know what you're up to?"

Smith shook his head.

"So why are you doing it, taking such a risk?"

"Because I'm as interested in solving this mystery as you are."

"And if you solve it, you'll be a hero at INTERPOL?"

Smith scoffed a laugh. "Let's just say if we figure this thing out, make a major discovery, it will make it difficult for them to fire me."

"I knew you were lying to me about something."

"Yeah, and you lied to me about *everything*. So we're even." He sighed. "You think it's easy for a man like me to move up the ladder at a place like INTERPOL?"

"No idea," I said.

"I dedicated twenty years to this job. Man, did I ever have dreams. I was going to be the next James Bond." He snorted a laugh. "When I joined INTERPOL, I thought I'd arrived, that I was finally somebody, no longer a fatherless kid from the projects." He shook his head. "But you know, taking this crazy risk, it's almost like I've started over, like I'm somebody again."

I got that. What Peruggia had wanted too, to be somebody. What we all wanted, dreamed of as kids, before the world got too real and dreams got crushed.

We were quiet a minute, but I could see Smith was still caught up in something, his eyes unfocused as if he were looking inward.

"You know," he said, "I've had two *semi*-serious relationships in twenty years. Both ended badly. I blamed the women, but it was me. It was always about the job—*gotta get ahead*, you know—and where did it get me? Stuck behind a desk wanting to get out, same place I started."

"You've got plenty of time. How old are you anyway?"

"Forty-seven."

"Hell, you've got half your life ahead of you."

"Yeah, the old half."

I laughed, but it made me look at *my* life: a job back home in jeopardy, no gallery, all the women I'd pushed away—and now Alex.

"When you're young, you think you have all the time in the world," Smith said. "Then one day, you wake up and you're forty-seven and you think: how the hell did that happen? You know, I bumped into one of those women not long ago, the last one I was involved with—two years we were together. She's married now, couple of kids, showed me pictures on her phone. I congratulated her, but you know what, it made me sad and sorry for myself, all that wasted time."

"Threw yourself a real pity party, huh?"

"Fuck you," he said. "I regret it is all. She was a good woman. Sometimes you don't know how precious something is until you lose it."

I pictured Alex across from me in the café, then saw her leaving.

"I'm not blaming anybody but myself," Smith said, "but I gave up a lot for this damn job."

"You think I had it so easy? Oh, wait, you know my whole life story."

"Yeah, I do. And I know it wasn't served to you on a silver platter. *Boo-hoo.* You think Bayonne comes close to the projects?"

"So it's a contest—my lousy life versus your lousy life?"

"Fuck you," he said.

"Fuck you," I said.

A few seconds passed, then we both cracked up. Laughed for a full minute, stopped, then laughed again. Smith rolled his big shoulders as if shaking it all off, the laughs, the philosophy, the self-pity.

"Hang on a sec." He went to the closet, got a shopping bag, and handed it to me. "I thought you might want this back."

Inside was my great-grandfather's painting. I stared at it a moment, a rush of warmth spreading through me, then at Smith. "Thanks," I said and meant it.

"Let's get back to work," he said. "I'd like to finish so we can plan our strategy."

I asked what strategy, and Smith said to find the real *Mona Lisa*—or at least discredit any forgeries. He went back to his laptop, all business, read off the screen, identifying the three known copies of the *Mona Lisa*—one in Vienna, one in Dusseldorf, another in a small museum in Antwerp—all dating from around the time Chaudron would have been making his copies. "If we locate another," he said, "that would be four, and if Peruggia was right, Chaudron painted *six*." He said he'd email and print out the stats on the forgeries, and I asked why, but Smith had already hit Print, and his portable copier was spitting out the page.

I looked it over, noted the INTERPOL name and logo at the top of the page—a globe encircled by an olive branch, the scales of justice below. "What does INTERPOL mean, exactly?"

"It is a contraction of 'international' and 'police.'"

"I thought you guys weren't police."

"We're not. Like I said, INTERPOL does the research, then turns it over to the individual police in a particular country to make the arrest."

I looked at the page. "So these are the museums that have *Mona Lisa* copies?"

"Right."

"How about the list of names and addresses below?"

"Collectors INTERPOL has linked to possibly stolen artworks and forgeries. Beside their names are artworks we know they own legitimately, but they're suspected of having other major works in their possession that are not so legit. This is a short list I narrowed down from the annual database that INTERPOL compiles."

I scanned the names, the artworks listed beside them, along with addresses, phone numbers, capsule histories—Wall Street CEO, corporate lawyer, retired junk-bond trader. I asked why these people had not been arrested, and Smith said because INTERPOL didn't have any actual proof, just suspicion, something that tied each of them to a stolen artwork, an important one. "They're all rich," he said, "not the kind of men to dirty their own hands." He paused, exhaling smoke. "If you're working with me, you should know these things."

"*Working* with you? So we're like rogues together?"

"This is serious." He laid his hand on my shoulder, and I felt an unexpected camaraderie, the kind of thrill I used to get with my Kill Van Kull brothers: a rush of danger. "We're in this together now, Perrone."

"And after? Then what? I just go back to my normal life." *Which was what?* My normal life felt so far away, like someone else's life, and a dull one.

"Yeah. And I go back to my desk job," he said, though I knew he hoped for a better desk. "I'm going after these collectors," he said. "One of them might have a Chaudron copy or even the actual painting. Don't you want to find out?"

I told him I did, and he gave me a genuine smile, the first.

"I just emailed you the list too."

I nodded, went back to the journal, the pages after the missing one. Then I remembered, got my jacket, tugged the wad of pages out of the inside pocket, explained to Smith that they had been behind the Vermeer. The pages were written in sections, with a heavy line drawn under the last sentence of each, some dated, some not, but I could see from the first page that they had been written after Peruggia's release from prison. I took a few minutes to make sure they were in order, that sentences followed consecutively from one page to another.

Smith hovered over me, lighting a new cigarette.

I waved the smoke away. "You know smoking is going to kill you, right?"

"One day," he said, taking a puff, pacing, jumpy, "but not yet."

I told him to sit down, he was making me nervous.

"So what does it say? Translate as you read."

I skimmed the pages and had another idea. "Look, that'll take forever—and drive us both crazy." I told him to take a break, go for a walk, give me time to read the pages on my own, then I'd tell him what they said. Not only did that make sense, but frankly, I needed a break from him and his relentless cigarette smoke.

"You won't leave anything out," he said, not a question.

I said no, and after a moment, he nodded, then headed out.

For the next couple of hours, I read. Scribbled a few notes too, though I wouldn't need them, the pages galvanizing and unforgettable. When I finished, I called Smith's cell.

He came back into the room, the smell of cigarette smoke surrounding him like a toxic aura, but I didn't say anything this time. I told him to relax, that if he wanted to hear everything, all the details, it was going to take time.

Smith leaned back on the sofa and closed his eyes.

"Hoping for a bedtime story?"

"It's helps me to see it," he said.

"I'll tell you everything, do my best to paint a good picture," I said and began to describe all that Peruggia had written.

70

Vincent recalled the nights he had spent watching Chaudron's apartment just after Chaudron had made his forgeries. How he had observed the couriers coming and going, always late at night, always in a hurry.

One night, after one of these men had come out with a flat package under his arm, Vincent followed. The man walked a long way, not stopping or idling until he was in the seventh arrondissement, home to the richest Parisians, with its ornate buildings, foreign embassies, and that mammoth praying mantis, La Tour Eiffel. Here, the man slowed, checking one fine home after another until he finally entered a corner building overlooking the Champ de Mars, a luxurious private home with white columns and balcony windows, topped by a large silver dome.

The man was out fast, with nothing under his arm, and again Vincent followed. This time into a small bar where he chose the barstool just beside him. He waited until the man had a drink, then another, gleefully celebrating, peeling francs off a large roll of bills. Vincent leaned close and slid his knife under the man's coat. He ordered the man to get up, kept the knife at his heart, his other arm over the man's shoulder as if they were the best of friends who had had too much to drink. Then Vincent led him into the bathroom, where he got him against the wall, the knife at his throat. He asked about Chaudron and the painting and to whom he had just delivered it.

"I have no idea what you are talking about!"

"I will kill you," Vincent said, and he meant it, giving the courier a prick of the knife.

That was enough to get the man talking, to admit he had gotten the painting from Chaudron, though he said it was Valfiero who had enlisted him and paid his fee. He claimed never to have met Chaudron before that evening, that he had merely been hired for a delivery job and that was all he knew.

"I will let you go unharmed if you promise not to divulge a word of our meeting to Chaudron or Valfiero," Vincent said. "If you do, I swear to find you and kill you!" Then he walked the man home, noting his address with another threat to his life if he did not keep their meeting a secret.

Now that he was out of prison and free, the nights Vincent had spent watching Chaudron's apartment and following couriers paid off.

It was dawn when he found the silver-domed house in the seventh arrondissement, where he chose a park bench across from the house and waited. At eight in the morning, a man came out, tall and distinguished in a fine suit, carrying a smart leather briefcase. Vincent followed him for several blocks and into a bank, waited until the man went into an office, then he approached and read the brass plaque on the door: GEORGES FOURNIER, PRÉSIDENT.

A woman came up behind Vincent and said she was Monsieur Fournier's secretary and asked what he wanted. He told her nothing. He could not afford to cause a scene. No matter what he said, he knew he would be seen as the man in the wrong, the poor man versus the rich one.

He went back to the same park bench and waited until the end of the day. His stomach growled and his mouth was dry, but he dared not leave his post. Finally, he saw the bank president turn the corner. He rose quickly and made his way to the bottom of the staircase that led to Fournier's front door. He did not move as the banker came up the path.

Fournier regarded him as if he were nothing more than a beggar. He threatened to call a gendarme, his face filled with annoyance and disgust.

Vincent said only two words, the name "Yves Chaudron," and though Fournier's eyes widened, he claimed he had no idea who that was. Still, Vincent did not move.

Fournier threatened to call the police again, and Vincent said, "You should. It will give me an opportunity to tell them about the painting you recently purchased from Chaudron and Valfiero."

With that, Fournier ushered Vincent inside, past a surprised-looking maid, up a grand staircase and down a hallway into a small library—though he persisted in saying he knew no one named Chaudron or Valfiero.

"If that were true," Vincent said, "then why have you brought me into your home?" When Fournier did not answer, he said, "The painting you purchased is a forgery."

"What are you talking about?"

"The painting, the one in your possession, the *Mona Lisa*, is very likely a fake."

Fournier tried to maintain his composure, but a corner of his mouth had begun to twitch. "You must be mad!"

"My name is Vincenzo Peruggia, the man convicted of stealing the *Mona Lisa*, a crime for which I have gone to prison. I am certain you have read about me. I stole the painting for Valfiero, who promised me money. It is a long story and I will not bore you with details, but Valfiero and Chaudron have disappeared, and I must find them. That is why I am here."

"And what has this to do with me?" Fournier asked, intent upon keeping up his charade.

"Chaudron painted something into each of his forgeries," Vincent said, "and there are more than one. You are not the only person to have been cheated by this conniving duo. If you let me see the painting, I can prove it."

"What is this proof you have?"

"Chaudron has put identifying marks into his forgeries."

"Tell me what kind and I will look for them myself."

"So you admit to having the painting."

"I admit no such thing!"

"Monsieur, you would have thrown me out long ago if it were not true. Please, stop wasting my time—and yours—and show me the painting!"

"How do I know you will not simply steal it from me? You, a convicted thief."

"I have done my time as a thief. All I want now is revenge, and not against you."

Fournier made him empty his pockets, then searched him for a weapon. All he found was a small jar of turpentine and a swatch of cloth Vincent had brought with him. When he asked why, Vincent told him he would see.

Fournier hesitated a moment, then led him up another staircase and down a long hallway where he tugged an attic staircase from the ceiling. He told Vincent to follow him up the stairs.

Vincent expected the usual dust-filled attic. Instead, it was pristine, with whitewashed walls and a shiny wooden floor. There were four easels with a cloth-covered painting on each. A chair set up in front. Beside it, a small table. On it, a bottle of brandy, a crystal glass, and an ashtray with a half-smoked cigar. It was Fournier's private viewing room!

Fournier lifted the cloth off the center picture, and there she was, with her knowing eyes and enigmatic smile. For a moment, Vincent wondered if he had made a mistake, if it was indeed Leonardo's original. He went closer to the painting and took hold of it by its sides.

"What are you doing?" Fournier shouted.

"Turning it over," Vincent said, and he did, setting the painting back on the easel, upside down. Then he leaned in and squinted at the place just below Lisa del Giocondo's hands. "There," he said. "You see those two marks?"

Fournier came in close. "Yes. What are they?"

"Initials. Y and C. For Yves Chaudron. He has signed his painting!" Then he directed Fournier to sniff the painting. "Do you not find it strange that such an old painting still emanates the odor of linseed oil and varnish?" He did not wait for an answer but opened the jar of turpentine he had brought with him and shook a few drops onto the clean cloth. Before Fournier could stop him, he swiped it across a small swath of canvas, then turned the cloth around so Fournier could see it had come away stained with pigment. "Do you think five-hundred-year-old paint comes off so easily? No, monsieur, it does not."

Fournier was up now, unveiling a painting on another easel, a still life of fruit and flowers. "I know this painting is legitimate. I purchased it from the most reputable gallery. Its provenance is undeniable." He snatched the turpentine cloth from Vincent's hand and dragged it over a tiny corner of the still life. When he turned the cloth around, it was clean.

"At least you have one legitimate painting," Vincent said.

Fournier scowled as he unveiled the third painting, a Venetian scene. "Canaletto," he said. "Purchased at the same gallery. I have the provenance papers of authentication to prove it." He whisked the painting with the turpentine cloth. Here too, it came away clean. Then he unveiled the fourth and last painting, which Vincent recognized immediately.

"This one you also purchased from Monsieur Chaudron," he said.

"How do you know?"

"Because I saw it in his studio. It is called *Le Chemin de Sèvres*. The original hangs in the Louvre."

With his mouth set tight, Fournier dragged the damp cloth across the landscape. It came away stained with color. Now he turned back to his *Mona Lisa*, staring hard at the initials. He tested the surface again in another corner, and one more time, the cloth came away blemished by pigment.

"I thought she was mine," he said, his voice a mix of disgust and defeat. "What a fool I was."

Vincent would have agreed, for he felt no pity for him, but he needed his help. "We are both fools."

"I want them *dead*!" Fournier said.

"But first you want your money back, no?"

"Can you find them?" Fournier asked.

"I am determined to do just that. But I have no idea where they might be. I hoped you would know."

Fournier shook his head, then stopped. "Wait… I bought another painting from Valfiero just a few months ago."

Vincent asked to see it.

"I sold it," Fournier said. "It is probably another forgery, and if so, I am now implicated. But that is not the point. What matters is how I bought it and where—from Chaudron's studio in the south of France."

"And you have been there?"

"No," Fournier said. "I sent a courier. I had been given a daguerreotype of the painting. I paid half before, the other half when it was delivered."

"Whom did you pay?"

"Valfiero. He was always the intermediary, the businessman. I never met Chaudron."

"And this courier, you can reach him?"

"There is no need." Fournier turned to a small desk and slid open the drawer. "Here," he said and handed Vincent a small card. On it, the name *Café Bleu*. "It is in the town of Lacoste, in the Vaucluse region. That is all I know, all that Valfiero would tell me, and all that I was allowed to tell my courier."

"So your courier went?"

"Yes. He met Valfiero in the café, where money was exchanged for the painting."

"And you say this was only a few months ago?"

Fournier nodded.

Vincent took the card and slipped it into his pocket.

"So you will go?" Fournier asked.

"Yes. Right away."

"I will go with you. I want to confront those bastards!" Fournier shouted, fists clenched.

"Monsieur, you are the president of a bank. Are you willing to take such a risk with your reputation?"

Fournier drew in a long breath, looked at Vincent, then back at his counterfeit beauty. "No, I will have to trust you."

And so, they made a pact. If Vincent retrieved the money, he would return the bulk of it to Fournier and keep a third as his reward.

In truth, Vincent's plans did not include Fournier. If he found Valfiero and Chaudron and got the money, he had no intention of sharing it with anyone. That money represented the return of his son and that was all he cared about. Fournier could afford to lose the money. But Vincent could not.

The Café Bleu was in the center of the small medieval town of Lacoste. Vincent walked from the train station, the train a necessary expense though one he could hardly afford. It had been a long walk, though even in the cold and drizzle, the walled town appeared lovely and peaceful. The café was neat and simple, tables with blue-and-white-checkered tablecloths, matching curtains.

The waitress, a young woman, blond and pretty, greeted him with a smile, and for a moment, his eyes played a trick, transforming her into Simone. He tried and failed to stifle a loud sigh.

The waitress asked if he was all right.

"Yes, fine. Thank you. A brandy, please. It is so cold." He rubbed his hands together.

"Yes, it has been awful, raining for days. How I long for the sun."

It was the kind of thing Simone often said about the cold Parisian days, Vincent thought. "Do you live in town?"

"Yes. My entire life." She eyed him a moment, perhaps uneasy about giving such information to a stranger. Vincent smiled to put her at ease.

"Where are you from, monsieur?"

Vincent almost said *nowhere*. "Paris. Though not originally."

"Oh, Paris! I've never been but I long to go. Is it very beautiful?" Her face filled with longing.

"Yes, very beautiful." Vincent wanted to tell her everything, this girl who reminded him of Simone.

"One day, I must go."

"Yes, you must. Paris will embrace you. It is a city that admires beauty," Vincent said, unable to stop himself, a foolish man flirting with a young girl.

"Oh—" She blushed. "Your brandy." She scurried away, her wide skirt billowing above her ankles, evoking yet another vision of Simone.

Vincent stared after her, then forced himself to look away. He slid the journal out from under his jacket, opened it, and scrawled across a page, "Arrived," followed by "Café Bleu," then closed it. He would fill in the details later.

The girl returned and placed a glass of brandy in front of him. "Would you care for something to eat? We have a wonderful herb omelet or—"

"Perhaps in a moment. After this." He raised the brandy glass. "I wonder if you know a friend of mine, a fellow artist."

"You are an artist? How *merveilleux*! I thought perhaps you were a writer," she said, eyeing the blue-covered journal.

"Oh, this… It is just…a notepad, nothing special." He drew it closer. "My friend, the artist, Yves Chaudron, I believe he lives nearby."

"There are some artists living in town and just beyond."

"He is a small man with a mustache and—"

"May I help you?" A woman of fifty or so had come up behind the waitress, her tone unfriendly and suspicious.

"My *mère*," the girl said.

Vincent stood and bowed slightly. The woman did not smile, her eyes wary.

"Who is it you are looking for?" she asked.

Vincent described Chaudron again, and the woman shook her head no, very curt, very fast.

"Perhaps his friend then," Vincent said and, without naming

him, described Valfiero, from his pointy nose and sharp features to his limp and silver cane.

The woman's face opened, then closed. "Why do you ask?"

"Oh…" Vincent waved a hand, straining for nonchalance. "We had business in Paris once. I was passing through and remembered he had a house nearby."

He could see the woman taking stock of him, his dark, foreign looks, his worn jacket.

"I do not know such a man, monsieur." She turned to her daughter. "Brigitte, there are other customers."

Only two that Vincent could see, a couple at a table across the room.

"*Oui, maman,*" Brigitte said and turned away.

Vincent sipped his brandy, convinced the mother knew Valfiero; he'd seen it in her face. After a moment, he signaled Brigitte.

"Another brandy, monsieur? Perhaps something to eat now?"

"Yes. Another brandy, and that omelet you mentioned." He had little money left but he was hungry, and he needed to spend more time here, needed to get the answers he had come for. Valfiero and Chaudron were nearby; he could feel it.

By the time he'd finished a smoke, Brigitte had replaced his brandy with a new one and set the omelet just beside it, the eggs golden and sprinkled with green herbs, and Vincent scooped up a forkful. "This is delicious. Did you make it?"

"Oh, no. The cook—my mother—did."

"Please tell her it is excellent."

"I will," she said. "You must excuse my mother. She can be a little abrupt with strangers."

"It is perfectly understandable. I apologize if I was rude to her."

"Oh, no," Brigitte said, waiting as if wanting to say something more. She leaned down as if to arrange the salt and pepper shakers, though they did not need rearranging. "The man you speak of," she whispered, "the one with the cane and limp, an odd duck, who spends his money freely in town and often on dinner and drinks here. My mother would not like to lose his business."

"I only want to say hello to him. It has been some time since we last saw each other. When you live in a big city like Paris, you lose track of old friends. It is sad. We were once quite close, and I would like to see him again."

Brigitte took a moment to look behind her, then leaned down again, whispering. "He lives in an old stone house with blue shutters and tall evergreens on either side, about two miles south of town. It is the only house for miles. And the other man, the artist you described, he is there too."

Vincent thanked her, taking hold of her hand. He wanted to press it against his cheek, to call her Simone, if just for a minute.

She let him hold her hand a moment, then gently slid it out, and when he looked up, her face was flushed before she hurried away.

Outside, the damp and drizzle had not let up. Vincent tucked the journal into the waistband of his trousers and pulled his jacket over it. He peeked through the café's window for one last look at Brigitte. He felt embarrassed by his actions with such a young woman and walked quickly past the small shops that lined the town's main street until he came to the old stone wall and passed through the archway. Here, the sidewalks gave way to a dirt road.

He felt a combination of excitement and rage, which he had been tamping down for months. Now, as he walked, he let it fuel him. He only wanted what he was owed, but he was prepared to fight for it, the switchblade in his pocket hammering against his thigh with each step.

The clouds parted, and rays of sun illuminated the stone house with blue shutters. It stood alone on an incline, the tall evergreens the waitress, Brigitte, had described standing like sentries on either side.

Vincent tugged the journal out for one last entry. *"Trovati!"* he wrote. *I found them!*

71

"Holy shit!" Smith was up, lighting a cigarette. "So what's next? Did he go to Paris? Did he sell the painting?"

"I don't know," I said. "That's it, all he wrote."

"You kidding? *Fuck*. Well, at least we got the most important info, how to identify the forged *Mona Lisa* paintings."

It was true, and what I'd come here to find out. So why did I feel a hollowness in my gut and an overwhelming sense of loss?

Smith was already planted in front of his laptop, fingers on the keyboard. "I need to run a check on this Fournier," he said. "Maybe there's something in my INTERPOL databank."

"A hundred years later?"

"You never know." He typed for a minute. "Nope, nothing on the name Georges Fournier." A couple more minutes of typing, then he turned the laptop around.

"What am I looking at?"

"Google Maps, a street view."

A grand-looking house with a silver-domed roof filled most of the screen.

"The banker's house... It's still there?"

"Yeah," Smith said, "and tomorrow, we go check it out."

72

"I'll do the talking," Smith said, then raised the knocker, which was large and made of metal, possibly iron, the face of a horned creature with a heavy ring that hung from its mouth. It looked old, expensive, and a little intimidating, like everything about the domed house.

A woman in her sixties opened the door, elegant and crisp-looking in a beige straight skirt and blouse. Smith displayed his INTERPOL ID, introduced me as his "associate," and I felt it again, a thrill that went even further back than my posse, something primal: the little boy who loved playing with toy soldiers.

Smith told her we were there on old but official business and added *"rien de sérieux,"* his French pretty good to my ear, but the woman answered in English, the way the French always do, and she looked wary, eyeing Smith suspiciously. "Are you Madame Leblond, the present owner of this house?"

She nodded, and he asked if we could come in. She hesitated, opened the door, then led us through a foyer that opened into a large sitting room with modern furniture and abstract paintings on the walls, incongruous in such a stately old home. She indicated a sleek leather sofa for us and arranged herself on a stiff-backed chair tentatively, eyes narrowed, mistrustful.

Smith asked if she had lived there long, and she said, "Why?"

"It's a simple question, Madame."

"Yes," she said. "I've lived here much of my life. It was my grandfather's home, then my father's."

"Does anyone else live here with you?" Smith asked.

"No. I live alone. Is this really necessary?"

I wanted to tell Smith to take it easy, use a little finesse. It was clear he was a researcher, someone unused to questioning people, his technique, such as it was, a tad less than charming.

Smith told her it was just routine, asked again if she lived alone.

"Yes," she said, "I am divorced. I have a son, but he lives with his wife on the Île Saint-Louis. Now what is this about?"

"Your grandfather was Georges Fournier?"

"My mother's father. He died before I was born."

"May I ask how—"

"Monsieur." Madame Leblond cut Smith off and stood up. "You will have to explain why you are here and what this is about before I answer another question."

I tapped Smith's arm, but he ignored me.

"You're not in any trouble, Madame."

"I should hope not! I know nothing of my grandfather's affairs."

"But you live in his house."

"Is that a crime?"

"Of course not."

"I don't think I want to talk about this any further," she said.

"It's nothing to be alarmed about," Smith said, "just a few more questions. Please, sit."

Madame Leblond sat, though she did not look happy about it. She said she had inherited the house when her parents died. Smith asked how, and she hesitated, then said "In a car accident, a long time ago." He said he was sure her grandfather had been admirable and honest, just that he may have come in contact with a painting that had a dubious provenance, not that he would have known.

"It's only lately"—I made it up as I spoke—"that this painting has come to light. That's all we are checking."

She looked surprised but also, for the first time, interested. "I am afraid my grandfather's collection is long gone," she said, "except for the joke."

"The joke?" I said.

"Come have a look," she said.

The study was dark, totally unlike the bright, modern sitting room, bookcases sagging under the weight of overfilled shelves, an easy chair with stuffing dangling beneath its seat, wallpaper curling along the seams. But none of this mattered. What caught my eye was the painting.

"It is humorous, no?" Madame Leblond said. "The joke, as I have always called it."

Neither Smith nor I were smiling, the two of us mesmerized by the painting, which hung on a wire, unframed.

"I guess it is quite good," she said, "for a copy."

I came in closer to study the brushwork, the soft blurring *sfumato*. I saw the initials too, could even make them out upside down.

"And this belonged to your grandfather?" Smith kept his voice steady and calm.

"I believe so. It has been hanging in this spot since I was a little girl. This was my grandfather's study, then my father's. I did not want to change it. Not even to change the wallpaper or paint the walls. Sentimental of me, I suppose, but after my father died, I decided to leave everything as it was." She turned to face us. "This can't possibly be the painting you have come to see."

"It is," Smith said.

She asked why, and he said there were other such fakes and that INTERPOL was collecting and cataloging them so they could never be sold as originals.

Madame Leblond looked incredulous. "How could anyone believe this painting is real when everyone knows the original is in the Louvre Museum?"

"Some people are easily fooled," Smith said, trying to sound offhand.

"Goodness," she said, "if I thought that were possible, I would have sold it for a million euros years ago!" She laughed for the first time, then sobered. "I am kidding, of course. It was the only painting left in the house when I took possession. As far as I know, my mother had sold all of her father's collection after he died."

I couldn't help but ask *how* her grandfather had died.

"I believe it was a heart attack," she said, frowning, "on vacation in the south of France."

Smith asked to take a few pictures, cell phone already out, photographing the full painting several times and details, then asked if it was okay if we took the painting off the wall.

"*Mon dieu!*" she said when she saw the back, the faux stains and the Louvre seal, all perfectly replicated. "I never saw the back," she said. "How remarkable."

Smith said nothing, his cell phone camera clicking away. While he took pictures, I asked another question. "You say your grandfather died in the south of France. Do you happen to know the name of the town?"

"A small town in the Vaucluse region," she said. "I believe it was Lacoste."

Lacoste.

The medieval town Vincent had described was back in my mind, along with too many unanswered questions: Did he find Valfiero and Chaudron? Get what he was owed? Ever see his son again?

73

He sits on the park bench shifting his weight, pinches the side where he'd been shot to feel the pain again, a way to remind himself that he is alive and there are still things to be done. The rain has started up and he is cold, disgusted. He has called the middleman to let him know the two men have gone into the silver-domed house. He was told to wait, to find out who lived there.

He checks his watch; a half hour since they went in.

He recognized the man with the American as the one he had fought with, tall and definitely strong. Though he looks forward to a rematch. He does not like to lose a fight and rarely does. Where he comes from, losing a fight, losing *anything*, is inconceivable, even punishable.

An image blooms in his mind: his brother falling, blood spreading, soaking into the earth. Andrei, tall and towheaded at nineteen, older by one year, his best friend, his hero—and the promise they made to never be separated and how they had kept that promise, even as Andrei died in his arms. He sees men dying all around him—not men—boys, unprepared for combat. *And for what?* A war that even the former Soviet leader had referred to as a "disgraceful, bloody adventure."

Was it then—when his brother died—that he stopped caring? Or was it seeing the masses of dead children killed by cluster bombs set off by the separatists or his own men? Who could tell?

He squeezes his eyes shut, thinks that losing his brother has made it impossible for him to feel, when in fact what he has felt since that moment was that he too wanted to die.

The front door opens, and the image dissolves like a piece of old movie film caught in a projector, bubbling red and blistering.

The two men head down the steps. He tugs the hat lower on his face, but they are so deep in conversation they pass right in front without giving him a look. He hears the American say, "Lacoste," has no idea what that means but makes a note to find out.

When they are a block away, the Russian checks the tracking device, watches the red dot turn a corner, gets up, stretches, and yawns. He is tired of all the watching and waiting, his patience and restraint exhausted at forty-one, or is it forty-two, his falsified papers changed so often he can't remember. What he needs is *action*. *Fun*. He makes his way to the front door of the silver-domed house and raises the knocker.

74

"The Louvre called," Smith said as he came back into the room after his cigarette break.

"That was fast. Didn't you just send the pictures you took of Madame Leblond's *Mona Lisa*?"

"Wouldn't you call the person who sent you photos of *another Mona Lisa* if you were a curator at the Louvre?" Smith paused. "They're going to let me have a look at the *real* painting, I used my INTERPOL clout, but there's a hitch… I have to go alone."

"*What?* I thought we were in this together. All for one and one for all. You called me your *associate*. Did you sell me out, Smith?"

"No. It's just that they're insisting on credentials, and you don't have any."

"And you do? Maybe not for long." A low blow and I knew it, but I was pissed. I wanted to be there to see for myself, to be in on the discovery—whatever it was. I'd earned that much.

"That's the deal, like it or—"

"The deal *you* made."

"Look, I had enough to force their hand. I threatened to go public with what we had if they didn't agree to let me see the painting, but that was it. You know I can't back up my threat. I go to the Louvre tonight, after closing, a private viewing with the director. That's the deal, and it's *final*."

So this was what it had come to, after all that had happened, after all I had risked—to be excluded. I stared at him a long minute, then sagged into a chair. "I told you I needed something, that maybe I'd write about this, and you agreed to that."

"And perhaps you can, if that's what you want."

"It isn't a question of *want*. My job might depend on it." I stared out the window at the late-day sun, adrenaline and disappointment leaking out of me like air from a tire, along with all I had done, hoped for, and all I'd left behind. If I couldn't write about the discovery, what was I supposed to do?

"Listen, I promise to tell you anything I discover. We did good work, my friend, and it's not over yet."

"It's over for *me*."

"Not true, and don't whine, Perrone. It's unattractive."

"Oh really, *you're* going to give *me* charm lessons? Next, you'll be telling me to toughen up and be a man."

"Nah," Smith said, "I know that's hopeless." He smiled. I didn't. "No matter what, we still need to investigate that list of collectors I gave you."

"What makes you think I'm going to help you after this?"

"Because you want to know the truth as much as I do."

75

He stands across the street, staring up at the hotel's worn brick facade, shivering, Paris even colder than Florence. He promises himself a vacation, someplace warm, the Caribbean or, better yet, Miami Beach. He was there years ago and liked the pastel-colored hotels, the ocean waves, and the Cuban food, though he hadn't had time to enjoy any of them, the job too fast—one day to locate the subject, second day to take him out, third day already leaving. This time, he will get a suite in one of those peach-colored hotels, order room service and a hooker. He is imagining lying in the Florida sun, his pale skin going pink, when his cell phone vibrates. He holds it away from his ear though he can still hear the middleman's annoying nasal voice.

"We received your package."

"Good," he says, picturing himself taking the painting off the wall and placing it under his jacket, recalls the rich woman's expensive smell, how he had demanded that she tell him what the two men wanted and how she told him they had been there about a painting and showed it to him, a forgery, *a joke*, she said, adding that the men had photographed it and that they were INTERPOL agents. That surprised him. Maybe the other guy, but not the American, at least he doesn't think so.

"The boss was pleased," the middleman says.

"What did *you* think of it?"

"*Me?* I didn't open it. I just sent it."

He knows the middleman is lying. No question he opened the package and looked at the painting. In this business, everyone is a liar and a cheat, and knowledge is power.

"Are you watching them?"

"Yes," he says, still distracted by flickering images of the rich woman and the sound of her protests as he twisted her pearls until she was quiet. A shame. He didn't mean to. The moment got the better of him. Though he always needs to protect himself. Never leaves a witness, someone who can identify him. He does not tell the middleman any of this. Why should he? He has gotten them the information they want, plus the painting, a gift, free of charge. What do they care if he has a little fun, as long as the outcome is the same? They should thank him.

"Are you there? Did you hear me?"

"Yes," he says, glancing up at the hotel window, its incandescent glow pulsing against the Paris night.

"They have the diary," the middleman says. "The boss says it's time you retrieved it."

Finally, he thinks, though it doesn't feel like enough. What about the American and the other man, the one who may be working for INTERPOL? He cannot just let them walk away.

76

We walked a few blocks, Smith needing to clear his head before his appointment at the Louvre. I shivered, pointed out that it was snowing.

"It never snows in Paris," he said.

I turned my hands up toward the night sky, snowflakes melting in my palms. "This is called *snow*, Smith. And I'm freezing."

He told me to stop being a wuss, patted my head like a dog.

I shrugged his hand off, tugged my jacket tighter. All I wanted was to go with him to the Louvre. "Everything that's happened," I said, "it has to mean something."

"I don't know," Smith said. "Sometimes things just happen. We make our choices and have to live with them, but we can't control our destiny."

"Wow, that's deep," I said, mocking him, but it made me think about the choices and risks I'd taken and my uncertain future, my destiny, looming.

Smith asked if I thought I'd made a bad choice in pursuing my great-grandfather's story. I told him I didn't know—and that was the truth.

"I have no doubt you'll find a way to let this fuel you," he said, "to do some good with what you've learned."

I wasn't so sure. Right now, it felt like the end of something, not the beginning I'd hoped for. I dug my hands deeper into my pockets as Smith led the way into a small park, a bronze plaque indicating it was the Jardin Catherine Labouré and that it used to house a convent.

The park was mostly dark, trees and vines forming a canopy above our heads, small pinspots of lamplight illuminating patches of ground and empty benches.

"Are you ready to take on the world's most famous museum, maybe uncover a one hundred-and-eight-year-old secret?"

"Ready as I'll ever be." Smith tugged a pack of cigarettes from inside his coat. I told him he had to quit, and he promised he would, soon.

He had just flicked the lighter, his face lit up like a jack-o'-lantern, when I felt the kick, breath knocked out of me, and I went down. A dark silhouette of a man, club in one hand, something shiny and metallic in the other, slashing across Smith's face, the two of them struggling. I got back up, but the club caught me above the ear—a white flare of pain as I stumbled back, saw Smith swinging and punching and the club tumbling to the ground, but the man kept thrusting and jabbing, seconds seen in fragments like a stuttering film, Smith falling as I got back up, climbed onto the guy's back, tried to choke him, take him down, hearing voices from far away, "*Arrêt! Arrêt!*" growing louder and a whistle shrieking and the man breaking loose and running.

"Luke..." Smith whispered my name.

I leaned down, one of the overhead pinspots illuminating us dramatically as if we were on a stage, got my hand under his head, heard him suck in a breath. "Hang on," I said. "You've got a date with the most famous woman in the world, remember?"

Smith managed a smile, gripped my hand as the whistles and shouts grew louder and the shadows became real.

77

The police station of the seventh arrondissement had blinding fluorescent light. I squinted, my eyes burning. Touched an aching bruise above my ear, recalled the shriek of whistles, the shadows that morphed into uniforms, watching them load Smith into the back of an ambulance, riding in a police car, my head ringing the whole time.

I was shuttled into a white room, spotlights mixed with cold fluorescents, one of the spots trained on me.

The French cops were out of a hard-boiled detective novel. Two of them, one young and mean with bad skin that gave him the look of a reptile, the other middle-aged and rumpled, reminded me of Columbo, playing nice, but not really. Their questions had started out routine and repetitive, but I'd answered them a dozen times and was tired of it.

The Reptile leaned over me, asked again, *"Pourquois étiez-vous dans le parc?"*

I stared at him as if I hadn't understood.

Columbo said, "Give the man some space," and added a phony smile. I knew he was playing me. For the umpteenth time, I said Smith and I had been in the park taking a walk. I didn't say anything about the Louvre, figured that was none of their business.

The Reptile said, "In *la neige*—the snow?"

I told him, "Yeah, I wanted to make a snowman," and he

grabbed me by the shoulders and held me firm. The air in the room went thin and charged.

Columbo told him to take it easy, sat down opposite me, lighted a cigarette, offered me one. I shook my head. "We were taking a walk," I repeated. "Is that illegal in France, like ketchup? Why the hell aren't you looking for the guy who attacked us instead of wasting your time and mine?"

"Relax," Columbo said.

"I was just attacked by a knife-wielding, club-swinging thug, and you're telling me to relax? That the best you can do?"

"Where were you going?" the Reptile asked again.

"How about home?" I said. "Unless you're arresting me."

The Reptile put his face in mine, so close I could smell the garlic on his breath, and grabbed me by the shoulders again. One of us might have thrown a punch—I know I was ready—if just then, the door hadn't opened.

The inspector, fortysomething, cropped hennaed hair, gray suit tight across the bust, a badge pinned to her lapel: DANIELLE CABENAL, GENERAL ASSEMBLY, LYON, FRANCE. She dismissed the cops with a cool nod, sat down, and placed her hands on the table. Her nails were short, perfectly filed, free of polish.

"You came all the way from Lyon?" I asked.

"It is a very quick flight," she said, her English clipped.

"What time is it?" I'd lost track, had no idea what I'd done with my cell phone.

"Morning," she said, nearly 10:00 a.m. "I am sorry."

I told her I was okay, just a little bruised.

"I was referring to Analyst Smith."

"What about him?"

"His condition is critical. I am afraid he is not expected to live."

A rush of heat skittered through my body, followed by a chill. I stood up fast, blood rushing to my head, grabbed hold of the chair to steady myself. "That can't be... He had some cuts and bruises but—"

"I am afraid it was much worse than that," Cabenal said, her face sphinxlike. "Internal bleeding, blood loss—"

"But I was with him. He smiled, for Christ's sake. He's got to be okay."

"According to the doctors, no. I am sorry," she said again, but she didn't sound or look sorry.

"Where is he, which hospital? I want to see him."

"That is impossible. He is in critical care. In the unlikely event that he survives, there will be no communication between the two of you ever again."

"I can't even find out if he's okay?"

Cabenal pressed her lips together as if words were piling up behind them that she did not want to let out. Then she did. "*If* Analyst Smith survives, he will be fired—he is *already* fired, his actions indefensible—and you will have no further contact with him. Do you understand?" She stared at me, waiting for an answer.

"I'll make a deal. If you—"

"We are not making any *deals*, Mr. Perrone."

"Just let me know if he's okay, that's all I want. Otherwise"—I met her gaze—"I'll pursue it on my own, and I don't see how you can stop me."

Inspector Cabenal's eyes narrowed. "I *can* stop you, Mr. Perrone, and I will. But fine, if he lives, I will let you know. But you will not be in touch with him again. That's the *deal*. Are we clear?"

I gave her a barely discernible nod.

"All right then." Cabenal folded her hands on the table again, all business. She told me they had been through Smith's computer and notes. "I know you were helping him, a mistake to get a civilian involved—and that was the least of it. He had no authority to be doing any of this."

"Doing what?" I arranged my face into a mask of innocence.

The inspector raised an eyebrow, the only part of her face that moved. "There is no need to be coy, Mr. Perrone. We know what he was after, that he was on his way to the Louvre Museum. Did he tell you he was authorized to do such a job?"

"No. In fact, he let me know he *wasn't*, that he was acting on his own."

"That is not the way INTERPOL works," Cabenal snapped. She took a short breath, rearranged her features back into a cool mask, smoothed a hand over her tight-fitting jacket. "He would surely have been fired for that alone."

"I don't know anything about INTERPOL," I said, "but I can tell you Smith is a good man, a dedicated man."

"INTERPOL will take over the case now, working with the Paris police. That is the way it is done. We have a red notice out for the man who attacked you and Analyst Smith."

Cabenal asked what I could tell her about him. I started to describe him, and she stopped me, disappeared, and returned with a forensic artist, the old-fashioned kind, one who worked with charcoal and a sketch pad. He asked Cabenal to leave us alone.

"I find it works better if I'm alone with a witness," he said.

Cabenal hesitated, lips pursed, but she left.

I sat with the guy, an American named Nate Rodriguez, on loan to the Paris police for some big case he was not allowed to discuss. An intense though likable guy about my age, a New Yorker who made me miss home and also made me comfortable and got me talking. I gave the description, and Rodriguez stopped me several times to clarify—the shape of the man's face—"round...no, square and broad"—the man's nose—"flat, almost as if it had been squashed"—and his eyes—"deep set, pale, blue or gray, almost colorless."

I watched the sketch artist use an eraser to remove most of the tone from the man's eyes, the drawing taking shape. "You're good at this," I said.

"I've been doing it a while," he said.

"His teeth," I said, seeing the man's sneering smile. "They were short and discolored."

"You have a good visual memory," Rodriguez said, his hand and charcoal moving on the paper while I added details as they came to me. After a while, he turned the pad around so I could have a look.

"Almost," I said, directing him to expand the jaw, lower the brow, and make the mouth wider while keeping the lips thin. He erased and redrew according to my direction, the two of us in sync. After another fifteen, twenty minutes, he turned the pad around again.

"Jesus. That's him. How did you do that?"

"You did it," Rodriguez said. "I only followed your direction."

"I don't know about that," I said and stared at the sketch, a sense of accomplishment accompanied by a chill of recognition.

Inspector Cabenal studied the sketch, said INTERPOL would run it through their identification databanks and fax it out to all the Paris precincts.

"I think he may have killed several people," I said, the young monk and Quattrocchi in my mind.

"You need to write a statement, everything that occurred, everything you remember," Cabenal said.

I thought I had answered all her questions, more than once, and said so.

"Not all," she said. "Do you prefer a laptop or a pen and paper?"

I chose the laptop and typed for a long time. I described, in detail, how I'd received Quattrocchi's email and came to Florence, my first day in the library, the thrill of opening the journal and beginning to read. I wrote of Brother Francesco's warning—*Ha un amico a Firenze?*—and how I suspected it might have been the cause of his death. I wrote of my search for the booksellers in Florence and Paris and their suspicious deaths. I wrote about Étienne Chaudron and his girlfriend, their bloodied faces and dead bodies sparking in my mind as I did so. I saw the missing journal page behind the Vermeer painting and the initials in Chaudron's forgeries and wrote it all down, every detail, every event that had happened since I'd left home, thinking as I typed that this was what I had hoped to tell the world—not the deaths but the discovery. Instead, it was a police report that no one outside of a few INTERPOL officers would ever read.

The only thing—the only *person*—I left out was Alex. She was gone.

It was all gone, what I'd hoped to discover, what I'd hoped to do with the knowledge. It felt like a folly, and a deadly one.

I stopped typing and scrolled through the pages. It looked like a proposal for a book I would never write.

I glanced again at the forensic artist's sketch and saw the man who had attacked me in Étienne Chaudron's living room, on the drizzly Parisian street, and again in the park, his knife slashing at Smith—a juddering horror film, the images etched into my mind forever along with a thought: no question the man would be coming back for me.

Cabenal read my statement, occasionally stopping to glare at me. Afterward, when the statement was printed out and I signed it, she handed me my cell phone and said I was free to go.

I thought: free to go *where?* I wasn't ready to go home, to face my tenuous teaching job and no art gallery, to leave behind so many things unanswered, to leave Smith.

On my way out, I stopped at what appeared to be the sergeant's station, a uniformed gendarme manning a desk, constantly on and off the phone and looking harried. Clearly, it was a busy morning for crime in Paris. In between calls, I sympathized with him in my best French. I kept up the banter and false camaraderie, then very casually asked where they had taken my "partner" John Smith. I hoped he was too busy to ask for an ID, and he didn't. He took another call, skimmed through a mess of papers on his desk, and said, "Hospital Saint-Jacques," then went back to his call.

There were dark clouds over Paris as I hurried down the street, turned the corner, found a bench, and made the call. "I'm looking for a patient, an American, John Smith." I was put on hold for so long I was startled when a voice came back on the line. The woman asked if I was a relative and when I didn't think fast enough to say yes, she said she could not give me any information.

"I just want to know if he's okay?"

A gap of silence, then, "All I can tell you is that Mr. Smith is no longer in critical care."

"So he's doing better?"

"I'm sorry, that is all I can tell you," she said, then hung up.

I called Cabenal, and it went straight to voicemail. I left a message asking about Smith's condition. Reminded her we had a deal, that she'd agreed to let me know if Smith survived. I sat on the bench for maybe twenty minutes, waiting for her to call me back, then walked the Paris streets for a couple of hours, but my phone never rang, and I knew what that meant.

I wasn't sure where I would be sleeping that night, but I knew what I wanted, and it would not be hard to find.

78

How many bars had I hit?

I remembered the first, a hotel bar on Saint-Germain-des-Prés, and not five-star, where I picked up a woman or she picked me up, married she said, her husband "un bum." I told her I was a bum too, the two of us laughing like that was the funniest comment ever, making out in between shots of whiskey, not a pretty picture I'm sure. At some point, I obviously left, because I was in another bar, this one a couple of notches lower than the first, where the bartender cut me off after three, maybe four drinks. I left—actually I was led out by the bartender, swearing at him the whole time—*Connard!*—*T'es un salaud!*—*Va te faire foutre!*—not my finest performance, though I remember feeling proud that I knew all those French curse words. I realized too late that the third place was a gay bar and could have scored big—I had a vague memory of some guy in leather licking my face. After that, I couldn't remember much. It was clear I'd thrown up, though I had no memory of it, only the telltale reek of vomit.

I was awakened by a gendarme nudging me not so gently in the ribs with his boot. I managed to get to my feet, my head splitting, body leaden, still nauseated and surely disgusted—with myself.

For the life of me, I couldn't remember the name of the hotel I'd been staying in, and the anonymous key card was no help. I tried checking into a small boutique hotel, but the woman at the desk was not having it, and I couldn't blame her, not when I caught my reflection in a window and realized I smelled like a vomitorium.

I ended up in a third-rate motel that didn't care what I looked like, where I slept for a full day, awoke to drink maybe a gallon of water from the bathroom tap, went back to sleep for I'm not sure how long, finally got up, took a shower, and realized I had left my bag of clothes at one of the bars.

I dumped my shirt in the trash, washed the vomit from my jeans, cleaned off my leather jacket and wore it out, zipped up to hide the fact that I was shirtless. I was surprised that I still had my wallet and silently thanked the manufacturer of my jeans for the zippered inside pocket.

I found a vintage shop, rummaged through a rack of shirts, chose one that looked clean and not too hideous. I bought a pair of cheap sunglasses too, my eyes stinging, but it was more that I felt like hiding. After that, I found an internet café where I had several cups of black coffee and used one of their computers to do a search to find the nearest AA meeting, which I did in the American Church near Les Invalides. The church was for Americans abroad, the meeting held in English, maybe twenty people. I listened to a young woman testify about her husband getting custody of their two small kids. Then a man, a professor of English literature, wearing a suit and tie, talked about being drunk at work and having no memory of why he had three sexual harassment charges against him, though it no longer mattered, because he had already been fired from his university despite having tenure—a cautionary tale if I ever heard one.

After that, there was a lull, and it seemed as if no one else was going to talk. I hadn't planned to share or qualify, but then I was standing and introducing myself. "Hello. My name is Luke, and I'm an alcoholic."

I heard my name echoed back to me, both comforting and distressing: I couldn't believe I was here after a decade of sobriety.

I shut my eyes, didn't want to see the people in the room, though I knew they'd all been down this road and wouldn't judge me. I saw Quattrocchi and Brother Francesco in my mind but didn't know what to say about them. I saw Smith, my arm around him, the weak smile he had managed despite the fact that he was dying, and that was it, I couldn't stop the tears. I tried to sniff them back, kept blinking and swallowing, but it was no use.

A dozen voices told me it was okay, to let it out. I wiped my cheeks and tried hard to pull myself together. "I lost someone," I said. "A friend. Not my fault but—" I stopped. *It wasn't my fault, was it?* It had been Smith's idea to follow me, not mine. *But if I hadn't gone searching for the journal in the first place, he might still be...* I had to stop thinking like that. It was no use, no help, and too late.

It's a disease, like measles or chicken pox. Alex's words.

I was glad she wasn't around to see me like this, and though I wanted to see *her,* I doubted I ever would.

"I feel..." *What did I feel?* As if I'd lost everything, but all I said was, "I want to be clean and sober again," and everyone nodded. And later, when people came over to pat me on the back and congratulate me for being there, I felt the tears gathering and fought them so hard because I knew if I started crying again, I might never stop.

79

New York City

The painting sat on the vault's concrete floor, just below another version of itself. For over an hour, he had been looking from one to the other: two sets of eyes, lips, the same folded hands. The paintings appeared identical down to the cracks in the paint. But how to know if one was real—and which one—the question he had been obsessed with for so long?

He gazed at the portrait, whispered, "Tell me, Lisa." Of course he knew her story well, had read everything there was to know about Lisa del Giocondo, the silk merchant's wife: born in 1479 into a minor branch of the distinguished Gherardini family, married at fifteen, five children, outlived her husband, Francesco del Giocondo, who had commissioned the portrait when Leonardo was strapped for cash, a situation soon altered as commissions began to pour in, so that the painting was never finished, never delivered.

"Are you her?" he asked, looking from one set of eyes to the other.

He sat back, dropped heavily into his gold Platner chair.

When he had begun monitoring the American, all he wanted was information, something that would absolutely, finally, tell him whether or not his painting was the original or a forgery, something he had wanted, *needed* to know for so many years, that he alone owned the world's most famous painting. And his chances had just doubled. Of course no one could know, or he might lose them both—or worse, get caught—though he would never let that happen.

Another look from one *Mona Lisa* to the other, cell phone already to his ear.

"That man of yours, I need you to terminate his employment." Other than sending him this painting, which was, he had to admit, a great gift, the man's actions had been totally out of control, nothing he had instructed, and way too risky, inviting trouble he did not need.

"Okay, I'll let him go."

"I do not want him *going* anywhere."

"I see." A pause. "I'll have it taken care of."

"I want *you* to take care of it. No one else, understood?"

"But that's not my—" The middleman stopped. "Of course."

"And I will need verification, some documentation, photos. Find a way to get them to me. Safely, of course."

The collector hung up, took a step closer to the paintings, eyes flicking between them. "Oh, Lisa," he said. "What I do for you."

80

It had been a week since I'd gotten back to New York, the first few days spent getting over my bender, nursing my grief and exhaustion and shame. When not attending AA meetings, I had stayed home, moving from bed to couch, finally to the paint-stained chair in my Bowery studio where I'd stare, for hours, at the makeshift altar I'd created for my great-grandfather so many years ago. It appeared different now, laced with danger and tragedy. I considered dismantling it, had started twice, but a sense of hollow disappointment and unfinished business stopped me. Intersession would be over in a couple of days. I'd be back in the classroom, and I worried about facing my department chair and dealing with the tenure committee. What would I tell them? What did I have to show?

I wanted to forget everything that had happened, especially Smith's death, but his ghost would not give up. Most of all, I wanted to forget Alex. Impossible. I could not stop thinking about her—who she was and where she was. I had tried her cell phone twice, listened to a recording that told me it was no longer a working number, had searched Facebook, Twitter, and Instagram, had called Brooklyn Friends and was informed they'd never had a student named Alexandra Greene.

Had she lied about everything?

I had done my share of lying too, but not about my *name*.

Would I ever find her or hear from her? Did she even exist? I tried to pretend I didn't care, though I thought about her every day, dreamed of her most nights. I wondered if she ever thought of me, if she had ever cared for me at all.

When my mother called and asked me to visit, I said yes, mainly out of guilt—it had been six months since I'd seen her. I took the bus from Port Authority, brought my laptop along and tried to do some schoolwork, but there was so much on my mind that I couldn't.

Bayonne's West Sixth Street never changed, and the overcast day didn't help, gray sky, gray houses, gray leafless trees, gray siding of my old attached home in need of a touch-up. I was planning my escape before I reached the front door.

Inside, it seemed smaller than I remembered, the ceiling low, plastic-covered furniture crowded, fake flowers on the laminated-wood dining table, the air musty with melancholy. My mom had prepared dinner, and it wasn't bad, had even made those pop-up oven rolls I'd loved as a boy, and I still liked them. She had stopped drinking a few years ago and was the better for it, though she still looked a decade older than her fifty-eight years, and it made me sad. My dad, the same age, looked eighty, and not a good eighty, fleshy pouches under bloodshot eyes, splotches of red on his cheeks and nose. He was distant at dinner, where he sucked down a six-pack, then collapsed in front of the blue light of the TV.

My mom and I stayed at the kitchen table and talked, a rarity. The quiet woman I'd known all my life was unusually loquacious, and for the first time, I saw her as a separate person, not just my mother, and recognized that she was lonely. At one point, she said she was proud of me and all I had accomplished, and she brought out a scrapbook she kept with photos from my college graduations and my degrees, articles and pictures of exhibitions and reviews, a couple of interviews, all laminated, a total surprise. It made me feel really bad that I hardly saw her, and when she asked me to stay over so we could have breakfast together, I said yes.

My old room was preserved like a museum, but to *what* I wasn't sure. There were none of those sports banners or trophies that "good" high school boys had in their bedrooms. Mine still had posters for Judas Priest's *Painkiller* album, one for Iron Maiden, and the flyer I'd framed from GG Allin and the Murder Junkies' last performance. The lava lamp I had thought so cool at thirteen was still on my nightstand, along with three books, *European Artists*, *Fight Club*, and *Colleges in America*. I flipped through the college book, noted the pages I had turned down and the places I'd circled twenty years ago, all art schools.

I looked through *European Artists* for a while, then caught up on a few emails. I tried to sleep but couldn't, my old bed too narrow and too soft. I watched a YouTube video about a virtual reality project the Louvre was going to unveil with its upcoming Leonardo exhibition: a seven-minute ride *inside* the *Mona Lisa* where the viewer got a speedy art history lesson including highlights of Leonardo's methods and Lisa del Giocondo's life, ending with a virtual ride on one of Leonardo's flying machines, as if it had actually been built, the viewer soaring through the painting's dreamy landscape.

Part of me wanted to take that ride—mainly to see if I might catch a glimpse of Chaudron's initials, though if they existed, the Louvre would surely not reveal them. I was sure the experience would be fun and easy; sit back, do nothing, be entertained. Nothing wrong with that. Or was there? Did people really need to take an imaginary flight inside a painted landscape? Couldn't they just look at the artwork? Wasn't that enough? The thing that really got me was that you didn't have to be in the museum or anywhere near the painting, just get on a virtual reality platform and voilà! The only thing missing was the actual painting.

I switched off the YouTube video, thinking *always something new,* but the idea irritated me. Or did it threaten me—threaten the notion of old-fashioned painting? *Old-fashioned.* Was that what I'd become? I could hear Vincent sneering at the cubists, saw him fleeing Picasso's studio, running from the future into the safety of the past. I hated the idea of being conservative or nostalgic, something every artist had to face, how much of the past we wanted to preserve while moving forward.

It was late and I tried sleeping again but could not stop thinking, my mind stuck in the past, in Vincent's head, feeling angry and vulnerable and endangered. It was finally happening—no one needed the real thing, art and artists becoming obsolete.

But I knew something else: that there were people out there willing to kill for actual paintings and surely for the *Mona Lisa,* even a forgery.

That was it. I was up. No way I'd sleep now.

The attic looked worse than ever. Dust like tumbleweeds, spiderwebs like suspension bridges. I guessed the last person to clean the place was me, age fourteen, and I hadn't done a good job back then. The steamer trunk was still there, several new layers of dust on it since I'd last opened it. Now I opened it again. More dust, the smell of mildew. I expected to see the rifle, forgetting I'd not only taken it to show to my Kill Van Kull buddies but later sold it at an antique gun convention for thirty dollars.

I had never gone through the trunk—finding the rifle and mug shot had been enough—but now I did. Moth-eaten shirts and pants, a pair of brown boots, the leather desiccated and cracking, a wooden box. Inside, velvet-lined, but whatever jewelry it may have once contained was gone. A couple of rumpled cardboard cartons, one with old-fashioned long johns, the other with two pairs of delicate women's gloves and a small photo, sepia-toned, of a man and a woman in formal dress. My grandfather and his wife? The trunk's lining had split, coming away from one side, and something peeked out—an envelope, no stamp or postmark, just a name in now-familiar script: *Simon Peruggia*. Inside, folded pages, the paper thin and yellowed but otherwise in good shape. I started to read them, but the light was bad, the attic air suffocating.

My bedroom was better, no cobwebs, though my narrow bed was uncomfortable. I ended up stretched out on the floor, using the bed as a headboard.

Dear Simon,

I had written a journal in which I told of my crime. Why I did it. And how. That journal was lost a long time ago. I am writing some of it here again because I want you to know what happened. Because I want you to know the truth about your father.

There were a dozen pages. The first few things I knew and had previously read—Simone's death, meeting Valfiero, stealing the *Mona Lisa*, Chaudron's forgeries, and the bank president, Fournier—much of it abbreviated as if Vincent had been in a hurry to get it down. After that, Vincent wrote of his plans to go to the south of France, again something I knew, which I read quickly. But I slowed down as I started to read the remaining pages.

81

I had walked from the town of Lacoste determined to find Valfiero and Chaudron. And I did. The house with blue shutters sat on a small incline bordered by evergreens. Exactly as the waitress Brigitte had described. A Lorraine-Dietrich was parked in front. The fancy motorcar purchased no doubt with money from the sale of forgeries. I made my way toward the house through bushes and trees. I crouched low. Inched toward a window. Dared a peek. There was a large palette on a wooden table. Paint tubes and brushes. Paintings on the walls. Chaudron's studio! Two easels stood side by side. Both with Mona Lisa paintings on them! One perfectly painted and finished. Another only half-completed. They had told me all the copies had been made and sold. But they were making more to sell!

I crept along the house to another window. Peered into a room opulently furnished with velvet couches. Gilded mirrors. A Persian rug covering the floor. All obvious rewards of the duo's unscrupulous dealings. I heard the tinkling sound of a phonograph record. I saw Valfiero and Chaudron at a table across the room. Each with a glass of wine. Valfiero puffing on a cigar like some South American potentate. Chaudron was in a paint-stained smock and appeared to be singing along with the music.

I fumbled the knife from my pocket. I flicked the blade open. I allowed my rage to build. Then I sprinted to the front door. Threw it open! Burst into the room! Kicked the chair out from under Chaudron and watched him tumble to the floor! I got an arm around Valfiero. Put my knife against his throat. Chaudron tried getting to his feet but I leveled my boot into his gut.

Valfiero called me DEAR BOY. Claimed they had been planning to be in touch with me.

I called him a liar. And of course he was. He acted calm though I could feel his heart pounding. He continued his charade. It was DEAR BOY this and DEAR BOY that. He said they had money for me and asked Chaudron to fetch it.

I followed him into the bedroom. Held Valfiero close with the knife at this throat.

Chaudron started to open a large wooden chest. I shoved him out of the way. Moved closer. Tried to see into the chest.

Valfiero said it was all there. Hidden under the blankets.

I leaned over the chest. Chaudron leveled a kick. I began to topple and Valfiero summoned what was left of the South American shantytown boy he had once been. He elbowed me hard and broke free. Chaudron tried to get hold of my flailing arms while Valfiero rustled through the chest and came up with a gun. He aimed at me. Told me there was no money.

I screamed I would kill him. Kill both of them.

Valfiero laughed. Called me DEAR BOY again. Trained the gun on me while Chaudron peeled the knife from my hand.

I shouted they had stolen everything from me. That they owed me. But it was no use.

Chaudron tied my arms behind my back and bound them with rope. I struggled but Valfiero pressed the gun against my temple. He wanted to kill me then but Chaudron argued they needed to wait and kill me later. Behind the house. After dark. And Valfiero agreed. He taunted me. Laughed at me. Called me an immigrant and a thief. Said no one would miss me.

They searched me. Found my other knife. Tugged the journal from my waistband. Chaudron flipped through pages. Handed it to Valfiero and he did the same. They saw I had written about them. They were shocked and amused. Said they would keep it and read it later. Then Chaudron slid it into his jacket.

They forced me into a chair. Tied my wrists and ankles to it.

I told them I knew they had given me a forgery. Asked if the finished Mona Lisa in Chaudron's studio was the original. They refused to tell me.

Valfiero drew his spidery hand across my cheek and I spit in his face.

Chaudron tied an oily paint rag around the bottom of my face. Stuffed it into my mouth.

Then they drank wine and smoked cigars. They dared to raise their glasses of wine to me. And laughed.

I watched. Bound and gagged. Impotent rage burning in my gut like acid.

I tried to think clearly. My knives lay on the table just beside Valfiero's gun. Could I jerk the chair closer? But there was no way to reach them with my hands tied.

The two of them became quite drunk. Chaudron wound his phonograph and played the record. Did a drunken little dance while Valfiero applauded.

The windows grew dark. They were about to take me outside and kill me.

Then the front door flung open and Georges Fournier stood in the doorway. A pistol in his hand.

Chaudron made a grab for the gun on the table. Fournier knocked it to the floor. He trained his pistol on the two men. Ordered them to untie me.

I coughed and cursed as the gag came out of my mouth.

The bank president demanded that Valfiero and Chaudron return his money. Valfiero was all innocence. Asked Fournier if he was unhappy with his purchase.

Fournier said he knew it was a forgery.

Valfiero denied it. Said it was Leonardo's masterpiece.

I shouted he was a liar. But Fournier already knew that. He had seen the proof. He whipped his pistol across Valfiero's face and Valfiero stumbled and fell. Chaudron pressed a linen napkin to his friend's bloody lip. Then he sprang up. A wild man! Leaping at Fournier. Knocking the pistol from Fournier's hand. It skidded across the floor. I made a dash for it but Valfiero got there first. He waved the gun in the air ordering all of us to get back. But too late. I was already in motion and our bodies collided.

The shot reverberated throughout the stone house.

Chaudron fell.

Valfiero scampered on hands and knees to his friend. Chaudron stared down at the blood on his smock. It was a moment before Valfiero saw the wound. He assured Chaudron it was only his shoulder and not serious.

I raced to get the gun. So did Fournier. Then Valfiero. The three of us struggled over the weapon. One more time the gun fired.

Fournier stumbled back. Hands at his neck. Blood spurting. Then he fell to the floor. I tore the hem from my shirt and wrapped it around his neck. The blood seeped through quickly. Fournier got an arm around me and pulled me close. Whispered that no one must ever know what happened here. Then his arm dropped. His body went slack.

It was only then I realized that Valfiero and Chaudron had fled. I saw the trail of bloody footprints leading to the front door. I raced after them. But too late. The Lorraine-Dietrich was already disappearing down the road.

I came back to the house and looked at Fournier's lifeless body. I had never intended this. Never wanted it. But it was too late for regrets.

I headed outside behind the house. Found a shovel. Began to dig. I was thankful for the cloudy night. No moon or stars to illuminate my terrible work. I dug and dug. The thought of my son kept me going. When the hole was large enough I used the Persian rug to drag Fournier's body outside. I went through his pockets. There were over a hundred francs in his billfold.

Then I rolled his body into the grave. Used the rug to cover it. Shoveled dirt back in. Gathered rocks and pebbles and fallen branches and spread them across the new layer of dirt until it was hidden.

I went back inside the house. Cleaned blood from the floor and walls. Washed my hands and cleaned the sink. Then I went through the house searching for the money. I did not think they had time to take it. I searched every drawer in the wooden chest and the bedroom dresser. The closets and under the bed. I slit the mattress. Ransacked the kitchen cabinets. Knocked glasses and fine china to the floor. Moved the potbelly stove and icebox away from the walls. Stomped on the floorboards. But none gave way.

I went outside again. I thought perhaps they had buried the money. I raised the shovel. But where to start? I had no idea. I sagged onto the cold earth and covered my face with my hands. My body drained and exhausted. Simone's face appeared in my mind. I heard her call my name. But it sounded more pitying than soothing.

I searched Chaudron's studio. The drawer below the paint table. The one tiny closet. Tested the studio floorboards here as well. Nothing.

I examined his forgeries. A Dutch still life. An English landscape. A medieval Madonna and child. Chaudron had aged and cracked the paint brilliantly. In any other place I would have sworn it was real. I lifted the finished Mona Lisa off its easel. Studied the dreamy landscape. The subtle coloration of the flesh. Lisa del Giocondo's beautifully articulated hands. I searched the area below them for initials. There were none. Chaudron had not yet painted them in. Unless this was the original!

I turned the painting around. Noted the stains and marks and the Louvre stamp. But I had seen Chaudron ape these elements before and they proved nothing. I sniffed the surface. But the studio reeked of oil and turpentine and it overwhelmed all other odors. I could have tested the painting with turpentine but no longer cared if it was real or not. A thought had taken shape in my mind. A plan. A cultured man like

Fournier had fallen for a fake. There would be others. Perhaps this was the original Mona Lisa. Perhaps it was one of Chaudron's forgeries. It did not matter to me.

I wrapped the painting with cloth and tied it with twine. I turned the story over in my mind. I would say I had returned a forgery to the Louvre. Which I had! That I had hidden the original for after my release from prison. And now I wanted to sell it.

It sounded plausible. Possibly even true. A plan I knew I could carry out. I had followed couriers from Chaudron's studio to art collectors and dealers. I would go to these buyers now. Tell them the paintings they had purchased were forgeries. That the one I had was real. Perhaps I would not be lying. I had already accomplished the impossible task of stealing the world's most famous painting. From the world's most famous museum. Selling it would be easy.

I undressed. Found clothes in the bedroom closet that fit me well enough. I looked for my journal. Then remembered Valfiero and Chaudron had taken it.

I burned my bloodstained clothes. Spread the ashes. Prepared to leave. But Chaudron's forgeries flashed in my mind. Poisoned my gut. I wanted to rid the world of these fakes. These abominations. These counterfeit beauties!

I grabbed the half-finished Mona Lisa off the easel and put my foot through it! Gripped the Dutch still life and did the same. Tugged the English landscape off its nail. Studied the forger's masterful hand for a moment before using a palette knife to slit the canvas until it hung from the stretcher in shards. I threw the Madonna and child to the floor and stomped on it. Wood splintered beneath my feet. Then I stood back to survey the damage. I dug the tin of La Paz from my pocket. Rolled a cigarette. Lit it. Waved the match out. Dropped it to the floor. And turned to go.

It was then I noticed the small flicker of red. My match. Still alive.

On a tangle of oily rags. I stomped on it with my heavy boots. But the sparks spit and scattered. The flames curled in the direction of Chaudron's palette table. Toward bottles of oil. An open tin of turpentine. I tried to crush the flames with my hands. Singed my palms. Stumbled back. I watched the flames undulate and twirl. Hypnotized. How easy it would be to lie down and let them take me. To join Simone. I inhaled the smoke into my lungs. Felt it begin to constrict my breath.

Then an image of you Simon my newborn son flared in my mind brighter than any fire. I knew I had to live. I tore from the studio. Out the front door. Swallowed deep gulps of cold night air.

I had the cash I had taken off Fournier in my pocket. I put the painting in the back seat of the bank president's Berliet. And I was ready.

My hands were shaking but I started the motorcar. I had driven little in my life but had a feel for engines and driving came naturally. I maneuvered the Berliet onto the main road. The car's mirror reflected writhing flames of red. The crackling sound of burning wood competed with the sound of the motorcar's rumbling engine. But I did not look back.

I kept my eyes on the road. Headed north toward Paris. The thought of selling the painting and reclaiming you, my one thought. My only thought.

It was a few weeks before I had accomplished it. Sold the painting!

I never said it was the actual Mona Lisa. I did not have to. The fact that I was the thief who had stolen it from the great Louvre Museum was more than enough proof.

The sale was conducted by a fence. I never met the buyers. They had met my price of five hundred thousand francs and that was all I cared about.

I steered the Berliet along dirt roads once again. Your grandmother was now living in her small home in Toulouse. A place I had once visited with Simone, your mother. It took two days from Paris to reach the outskirts of the town and it was late when I arrived. I found a room at an inn. Ate and drank alone. Spoke to no one.

That night I dreamed Simone and I lived in a grand apartment with you our beloved son. We were renowned artists. Feted and critically acclaimed.

I awoke with tears in my eyes. But I was happy. I believed the dream was an omen that I would get you back.

In the morning I took my time getting ready. I scrubbed my face. Shaved carefully. Trimmed my mustache. Parted my hair neatly into place with pomade. Put on the new clothes and shoes I had purchased in Paris. I needed to look my best. Needed to look prosperous. I tore the lining from my old coat where I had hidden the francs. Carefully tucked them into a money belt. Tied it around my waist. Covered it with a bulky woolen vest and buttoned it to my collar.

I drove from the inn along narrow country roads. My thoughts of Simone. Of our one visit here years ago. A beautiful summer day. Simone radiant in a white dress. Her blond hair loose around her face.

The house was how I remembered it. A tiny stone cottage with weathered yellow shutters. I brought the Berliet to a stop.

Your grandmother came out and stood on the porch. An infant was in her arms wrapped in a blanket. She seemed not to know me. Perhaps blinded by the bright winter sun or the expensive car or my fancy new clothes. Then she recognized me. Her face went hard. She asked what I wanted. I told her just to talk. To come into the house. I was careful to keep my voice calm and gentle.

She assessed me for a long time. The fancy car. The expensive clothes. It felt like an eternity before she said yes.

The house was messy and crowded. The crib filled half the living room. Wet diapers were draped over the backs of chairs.

I asked if I might have a look at you.

Marguerite hesitated, then rolled the blanket down to reveal your fine gold hair and long lashes surrounding eyes the same color as your mother's. My heart swelled with so much love and sadness.

I told your grandmother I had made a lot of money. She said nothing. But I saw a slight softening of her face and a trace of curiosity.

I asked if I could hold you.

Another hesitation then she handed you to me. You nestled your head in the crook of my neck. I had never felt such joy. Tears sprang to my eyes.

Marguerite wilted into a chair beside the kitchen table. She looked old and weary.

I asked her what she had named you. She said Simon and I whispered it again and again as my lips brushed your cheek. Simon. Simon.

I asked Marguerite if she still hated me. She said she was too old for hate. And too tired.

Then we sat at the kitchen table and drank coffee and talked. I told her I had much success in Paris selling paintings. My own paintings. I was not sure Marguerite bought my lie. But she said nothing. I could see she needed my help. That she wanted to believe me.

I helped her straighten up. I added logs to the fire. Marguerite cooked and mashed peas and I fed them to you. When you cried I walked you until you fell asleep. Then I laid you into your crib.

I came back to the table where Marguerite was waiting. She asked how much money I had. I told her a lot. Enough for all of us. All of it made from the sale of my paintings. She said it did not matter how I had gotten the money. She was tired and alone and no longer young. That the baby was difficult. But she did not want to lose him. He was all she had left of her daughter.

I looked into her eyes. I said he was all I had left of Simone too.

She told me about a house for sale down the road. A simple stone house. Sturdy. Twice the size of her house.

I said I would buy it if all three of us could live there together. She said yes. And then she cried.

82

I awoke on the floor, curled in a ball and achy, morning sun streaking through my Bayonne bedroom window. My first thought: *I have to call Smith, have to tell him what happened to Peruggia.* Then reality set in, but I said it anyway. "We got it, Smith, the end of the story."

My dad was still sleeping, no doubt nursing a hangover, and I had breakfast with my mom. She asked if I'd slept well, and I told her I had, a lie, but a part of me felt good, satisfied in a way I hadn't felt since I'd come home, knowing that Vincent had been united with his son. My mom made scrambled eggs and strawberry pancakes and I ate everything, using half the bottle of Log Cabin while she interviewed me about teaching ("It's great") and my art career ("It's great") and her favorite topic, if I was seeing anyone ("no one special"), another lie, though it wasn't really, as I was no longer seeing Alex.

Back in the city, I called Inspector Cabenal and left my questions on her voicemail: had they had found Smith's attacker, and was anyone pursuing the Chaudron forgeries? I doubted I would hear back from her and didn't. I wondered how they could just let it go, not pursue the Louvre or Smith's list of suspicious art collectors. The thought had me going through my papers, but I couldn't find the list. Then I remembered Smith had emailed it to me, found it in my in-box, and printed it out.

There were four names with Manhattan addresses. I stared at them, questioning why I'd printed it and what I thought I could possibly do. Call them, say, *Hey, you don't know me, but do you happen to have a stolen artwork? Maybe a forgery of the* Mona Lisa? *Or maybe the original?*

A ludicrous idea.

Then I thought of Smith, felt as if I owed him something, that perhaps I could at least clear his name with INTERPOL, though it wasn't just about owing or obligation. It was about something a lot less noble: revenge. An image of myself: pack of Marlboros rolled into the sleeve of my tee above my tattoo, with my posse, on the hunt, getting even with someone we decided had wronged us. We were not always right, but that never stopped us. Funny, how far I thought I'd come. But did we ever really leave our former selves behind?

I didn't spend a lot of time pondering that philosophical question. Instead I checked out the first name on Smith's list, Jonathan Teivel, noting the artwork beside his name, and quickly formulated a plan. I told his secretary I was an art historian writing a piece on the artist, Titian, wondered if Mr. Teivel had such a painting, and if so, would he let me see it, all this made up on the spot and before rational thinking could stop me.

The secretary, officious but nice, said her boss was in a meeting, but she would relay the message. I hung up feeling both disappointment and relief, though it didn't stop me from making another call. Another secretary. The same story about the article I was writing. This time, the boss was traveling and would not be back for a month. I put a question mark beside his name and, still working off my small shot of adrenaline, called the next name on the list. This one, a lawyer who, according to his paralegal, was on a case in Los Angeles and not expected back for several weeks. Another question mark next to his name. One more name to call.

"Rembrandt?" the personal assistant, friendly and chatty, repeated the artist's name I had just given her. "Mr. Baine does collect art, some of it in our offices, but there's no Rembrandt here that I know of. Perhaps in one of his homes, though I'm not certain," she said. "Mr. Baine isn't in, but I will convey your message."

I had done it. Made the calls. It was enough. Smith would be proud of me. Now, I waited to see if they'd produce anything. I doubted they would.

83

The financial district is closed up, everything quiet at 2:00 a.m.

The Russian drags on a cigarette as he heads down Water Street to the arranged meeting.

The middleman has asked to see him. Why, after two jobs where they had never met? *A trap? Probably.* He had done his job and now they were finished with him. He has dealt with such men before and is ready, but he wants to see what he might get out of the middleman first, like who he is working for, thoughts of vengeance buzzing in his head like a hive of killer bees.

The neighborhood is practically deserted at this time of night, but the Russian's fine-tuned radar picks up the grinding sound of a garbage truck, a distant siren, a foghorn on the river. He angles furtive looks one way, then the other, his hand toying with the knife in his pocket.

At Broad Street, he turns east toward the river.

A bar, Street Angel, open all night, the only one in the neighborhood, you can't miss it.

And there it is, the bar's neon sign blinking like a warning in the dark.

The Russian is less than a half block away when two men come out of nowhere, one in front, one behind, and drag him into an alley. He is prepared for the attack but not for the buzz on his neck and his body going spastic, though he manages to knock the Taser from the guy's hand, then sees the other guy has a gun. Muscles convulsing, he grabs hold of the silencer's long barrel, but the man fires, the bullet grazing the fleshy edge of the Russian's palm, but he doesn't let go, gets the knife from his pocket, jabs the guy in the gut. But the other one, the one with the Taser, is up again. The Russian punches him, then charges, all two hundred and fifty pounds of him knocking the guy to the ground. Landing on top of his assailant, he gets hold of the gun and presses it to the guy's temple, says, "So…you…are…the man…I have been…taking orders from."

The guy beneath him groans, "Nooo…I was hired by *him*…" He angles his chin toward the other man, the one on the ground who's been stabbed. "I don't know shit! I'm no one!"

"Agreed," the Russian says, shoots him in the head, rolls off, gets to his feet and, despite still-twitching muscles, aims his gun at the man on the ground, the one trying to stanch the knife wound in his gut.

"Who do you work for? Who sent you to kill me?"

"I…just do as I'm told…like you. Follow orders."

The Russian grins, baring his short, discolored teeth. "You have a choice, my friend. In five seconds, I start shooting off fingers and toes, or you tell me what I want and I walk away."

The guy looks up, eyes blinking like a dying light bulb. "What… what do you want?"

"Your boss. His name."

"Don't…know it. Never did. Never met the guy. You know how it works." His hands are pressed against his belly, blood leaching between his fingers.

"A phone number then."

"He will have me killed."

The Russian leans over, fumbles a cell phone out of the

middleman's pocket. "Do not worry," he says and cocks his gun. "He will not have to." He shoots the guy twice, just to be sure. Then swipes his hat off the ground, turns his coat inside out to hide any blood, and steps out of the alley.

He scrolls through the middleman's cell as he makes his way down the deserted street with one thought in his mind: to find the man who ordered this hit and kill him.

84

It was only a day later that Jonathan Teivel's secretary called back to say her boss would see me. I was surprised, thought about not going, then I did.

Fiftysomething, hair combed back from a high forehead, Teivel looped his thumbs under striped suspenders. "Remind me again why you think I own this Titian painting?"

"A curator friend," I said, "in Europe gave me a list of paintings and collectors who he thought owned Titians."

"Your friend is mistaken. I own some art but no paintings by Titian." Teivel glanced at the wall of windows that flooded his office with bright morning light, a view of the Hudson River, the Statue of Liberty, the New Jersey coastline. "Your friend works at which museum did you say?"

I hadn't said, but I did now. "The Louvre."

"*Really?* What's his name?"

"Gingembre," I said, doubting he would check with the Louvre curator, particularly if he dabbled in stolen art.

"Well, I'm afraid your friend has wasted your time."

If so, I couldn't help but wonder why Teivel had bothered to meet me. I told him it was okay, that I had time.

He offered up a wolfish smile. "My secretary says you're an art historian, writing about Titian."

"About Renaissance art in general."

"I see. And for what publication did you say?"

Again, I hadn't. "An academic journal," I said. "If not Titian, who do you collect?"

"This and that, some Renaissance, some contemporary."

"Which Renaissance artists?"

"Raphael and Giorgione. Drawings only, of course. I'm afraid paintings are out of my league."

I looked over his grand corner office, the impressive view. I'd done a little homework, knew Teivel was a founding partner in the investment firm, one of the biggest and most prestigious in the city. I doubted there was much out of his league. The sun caught the gold on his wrist.

"I see you're admiring my watch. Vacheron Constantin... Traditionnelle...perpetual calendar...open-worked." He enunciated every word, pushed his cuff up to show it off. It looked like a sundial, actually four miniature sundials, all the inner mechanics on display.

"Rose-gold case and sapphire crystal glass," he said, raising his wrist to my face. "Two hundred and seventy-six parts. Thirty-six jewels. Days of the week, forty-eight-month calendar, including leap year, and of course phases of the moon."

"Of course," I said, catching a whiff of his citrusy cologne.

"I'd be lost without it. You should get one for yourself."

"Sure," I said, knowing he was playing with me. "I'll trade in my Timex."

He laughed too loud.

I asked if I could see the Raphael and Giorgione drawings he'd mentioned, and he said, "They're in my various homes—Park Avenue, Palm Beach, Aspen—not in the office. You're not an art thief, are you?" Another too-loud laugh.

I laughed too. "No. Just an associate professor of art history."

"And where would this *associate's* job be? Some community college?"

I was happy to drop the name of my respected university, the one I might soon be fired from, though I had a feeling Teivel already knew where I taught, knew everything about me.

"Good for you," he said. "Do you live in the city?"

"On the Bowery."

"The *Bowery*? Really? Hard to imagine the Bowery, formerly skid row, would be a desirable location, though apparently things have changed. Do you feel safe there?"

I told him it was perfectly safe nowadays.

"I suppose," Teivel said. "Though you never know, do you? I mean, anything can happen—anywhere."

Was he threatening me? "That's why I have dead bolts on my doors," I said.

"No bars on your windows?"

"I'm on an upper floor. So unless it's Spider-Man—"

"My favorite superhero," Teivel said.

"Really? I'd have guessed Wolverine."

Teivel barked a Wolverine-like laugh. "You flatter me."

Not a chance. We talked a few more minutes about the contemporary art he collected—Warhol, Basquiat, Koons—but Teivel seemed to grow bored. Perhaps he'd gotten what he wanted, did not feel sufficiently threatened by me. He ushered me toward his office door and offered a handshake.

"If I were you, I'd get bars on those Bowery windows," he said and squeezed my hand, hard. "You never know when Spider-Man might show up." He barked another laugh.

"Nah," I said and squeezed his hand back. "I was never afraid of little Peter Parker."

"What about Wolverine?" he said, letting go of my hand to usher me out the door, which closed in my face.

85

At home, I dug out Inspector Cabenal's card. I knew she wouldn't be happy to hear from me, but I wanted to tell her about Teivel, run his name past her and see if it meant anything.

I was surprised when she answered the phone, and I was right: she was not happy to hear from me. I asked about Jonathan Teivel. The name meant nothing to her.

"It was on Smith's list of collectors, ones he intended to investigate—"

"And you saw this man?"

I told her I had.

There was a pause, then her words came like gunfire. "Mis*ter* Perro*ne*! If you per*sist* in these *mat*ters, I will have no choice but to report you to your local authorities and have you *arrested*. Do... you...understand?"

I wanted to tell her to go fuck herself, but I said nothing.

"Are you there? Did you hear me?"

"I'm here."

"Anything Analyst Smith was investigating is no longer your concern. No longer his concern either. His work here is finished. Are we clear about that?"

"Perfectly," I said and hung up.

I went through the motions of cleaning my loft, a way to work off my anger. Was it that INTERPOL didn't care about these unscrupulous art collectors or that anything connected with Smith had been discredited, dismissed?

Anything Analyst Smith was investigating is no longer your concern. No longer his concern either.

Cabenal's words played in my mind as I made a show of organizing my desk, crumpling papers, jamming pens and pencils into a holder.

His work here is finished. Well sure, he was dead.

I stopped a moment, stared out the window at a neighboring building without seeing it, kept hearing Cabenal's words, something about them odd, the phrasing off—*no longer his concern*—*his work here is finished*. Did that imply it was not finished elsewhere? Was it possible she had just told me that Smith was *alive*?

I replayed the call I had made to the hospital in Paris.

Mr. Smith is no longer in critical care.

At the time, I had assumed that meant he'd died, reinforced by the fact that Cabenal had never let me know if Smith survived, which had been our deal. But what did she care about a deal with me? She was finished with me and with Smith—dead or alive.

I called her back, but this time, it went to voicemail. I didn't bother to leave a message. I got the international operator for Lyon, France, asked for John Washington Smith. No listing. But somewhere, I had Smith's number; I was sure of it, remembered him handing me his card. No, he hadn't handed it to me, he'd stuffed it into my shirt pocket. And after that? I thought for a moment, remembered calling him, scrolled through my call log but nothing looked familiar. So where had I called him from? The taxi—after I was attacked. Right.

I dug out my wallet, went through it, and there it was, the small white card jammed in between euros and dollars.

I listened to the phone ring three, four, five times. Maybe I was crazy; maybe Smith *was* dead. Then his voicemail kicked in. "Leave a message." That was it, no identification, but definitely his voice. An old message? Would his phone still be working if he were dead? Maybe.

"Smith," I said, "this is Luke Perrone. I have something to tell you. Call me back, uh, *if* you're alive—"

I hung up. A moment later, my phone rang.

"Perrone."

"Holy shit! You *are* alive!"

"How did you get this number?"

"You gave it to me, remember? Jesus, all this time, I thought you were dead."

"I may as well be."

"Self-pity never suited you, Smith."

"Fuck you, Perrone."

"Fuck you too. Just tell me, are you in one piece?"

"I've got more stitches than a football, but I'm fine."

"Cabenal told me you were dead. Not exactly. She said there was little chance you'd survive, internal organs punctured, shit like that."

"It was touch and go for a while, and I'm guessing Cabenal is sorry I *didn't* die—save her and INTERPOL a lot of embarrassment. I lost my job *and* my spleen, but apparently you don't need your spleen. Other than that, I'm pretty much in one piece."

"Jesus. I'm calling that bitch and letting her have it."

He asked me not to, said it would just cause trouble for both of us.

"She let me think you were *dead*, Smith. You know what that did to me?"

"Cried like a baby, huh?"

I heard the tease in his voice for the first time. "Worse," I said though didn't go into it. I told him about unearthing his list of collectors, making the calls, about Teivel's threats.

"Are you crazy?" he said.

"No crazier than you."

"Look, it's too late. I'm fired, erased. It's like I never existed."

"Where are you?"

"My shitty Lyon apartment, where else? But I'm getting out of here."

"Where to?"

"Don't know yet. Where does a forty-seven-year-old with no job and no prospects go?"

"The private sector?"

"And what, be a guard in some suburban bank?"

"Suppose I prove you were right?"

"What are you talking about?"

"Follow up with these collectors, see what I can find out. Something to show INTERPOL you were onto something big, a way to clear your name."

"My *name*? Jesus, Perrone, you're still a romantic. Nothing you say will sway INTERPOL. I told you it's too late—and too dangerous."

I wanted to say *You deserve better, all you did*, but I knew he was right. I couldn't save him, had just barely saved myself.

"Just stop what you're doing," he said. "I'm not asking. I'm *telling* you. Stop. You hear me?"

"I hear you."

His sigh through the phone sounded like a windstorm. "Look, I appreciate it, but it's no good, and you can't take the risk. You saw what can happen, remember?"

I remembered.

"Promise me you'll give it up."

I promised.

86

That night, I had trouble sleeping. When I did drift off, I had crazy dreams: Smith dying on a Paris street, Jonathan Teivel's fancy watch melting like a Dalí painting, the *Mona Lisa* floating upside down. In the morning, I had to remind myself that Smith was alive, and I was pissed I'd done my grieving with booze. I wanted to call Inspector Cabenal and give her hell, but I knew Smith was right, that it would just cause trouble. I thought about Teivel, his barking Wolverine laugh and threats. Smith was right about that too: looking into these guys was dangerous, and I had to stop. Give up the folly and concentrate on myself, my life and career, figure out what I was going to say to the tenure committee and get back to making art.

I opened my laptop, found Smith's list of art collectors, and deleted it. Then I crumpled the hard-copy list and tossed it into the trash.

Next, I dismantled the altarpiece and emptied the file cabinet—maps of the Louvre with Peruggia's route, my correspondence, the essays and theories about the theft I'd been collecting for over twenty years, all in the trash. The only thing I kept was the mug shot, though I decided I looked a lot less like him since shaving off the mustache and getting a shorter haircut.

It felt good to throw everything out, a new beginning, not just a new day.

I unwrapped the paintings I'd left unfinished weeks ago, leaned them against the wall, then arranged my brushes and tubes of paint. I took time organizing the colors in a spectrum around my palette, the way I had back in art school, earth tones next to yellows next to reds next to purples and blues, larger tubes of black and white on either side. I liked doing something orderly after so much of my life had felt out of control.

I took in the unfinished paintings.

Strong and colorful, filled with promise and an inner logic that helps lift them above ordinary abstractions, so said the *New York Times* four years ago, the time of my last exhibition. So what had happened to all that promise?

I glanced over at the small canvas I'd propped on the window ledge—Peruggia's still life of fruit arranged on a red cloth, everything outlined in dark blue-black.

Minutes later, I was hammering nails into the wall, hanging a new blank canvas—I never used an easel—then I squeezed paint onto the palette, filled jars with mineral spirits and medium.

It was hours before I stopped and stood back to see what I'd been doing.

The painting—based on a view of my studio window and beyond—had been created with slabs of heavy paint, an abstraction but also a cityscape if you looked long enough. Ugly and beautiful and unlike anything I had ever made, the paint so thick it would take weeks to dry, edges of forms cut into the pigment with the back of my brush or outlined in inky blue-black.

I stared at the canvas, evaluating it as if someone else had painted it. It was possibly the most honest and compelling artwork I had ever made, an image created entirely of feeling, of being in the moment. For the first time in years, I wanted to keep painting.

More nails in the wall, another blank canvas. This time, I drew directly with the paint, allowing the brush to do what it wanted, to guide my hand. An hour passed, the painting rough and not fully formed but buzzing with life: a nude without a face. I tried to paint the face in several times, each time wiping it out with a rag, leaving a mess of smudged paint above the breasts and neck, though I knew exactly who I had been trying to capture—a woman I'd been unable to capture in real life. A woman I had abandoned—or had she abandoned me?

I dumped my brushes in mineral spirits, changed out of my studio clothes, scrubbed the paint from my hands, the whole time with Alex on my mind. A minute later, I was on my cell phone. Spence. Dalton. Brearley. All upscale Manhattan private schools. None of them had ever heard of Alexandra Greene.

I glanced back at the unfinished nude, and I felt it, that Alex was here, somewhere in the city. I knew it.

87

He peers up and down the street, colorless eyes raking over new buildings and old ones, a metal structure identified only as the New Museum, the sidewalk teeming with people in motion. He looks for someone who is standing still, focuses first on a young man checking his cell phone, then a disheveled man on the corner—homeless or just playing the part? He can usually spot a professional, but it is more difficult here in Manhattan, on this odd and diverse street called the Bowery—so many different sorts of people: sophisticates and bums, Americans, Asians and Europeans, some decked out in furs, others in clothes so threadbare they have to be freezing, a damp wind blowing across the city from its two large rivers.

He checks his tracking device, the red dot hovering, the American at home, just five stories above him. He replays a few moments of their time together in Florence and Paris and considers their odd bond. He knows the American is his connection to the man he is after, the man who has tried to have him killed. He suspects this man wants the American dead too and likely has someone watching him. He scrolls through the American's calls and texts, not sure if they are important, but he will check them out.

The handheld device pings: a signal that the American is on the move. A few minutes later, the Russian glances up, and sure enough, there he is, exiting the building. The Russian turns away but keeps an eye on the device, on the red dot moving, then dares a peek over his shoulder and sees the American disappear into the subway.

In less than a minute, he has picked the front door lock and makes his way up the old metal staircase to the fifth floor.

The door to the American's loft is just as easily picked.

He steps in, surveys the uneven wooden floors and tin ceiling, the spare furnishings, a large wall crammed with books, more on a low wooden coffee table, one right on top about that artist he had seen in the Florence museum and liked, Caravaggio. He thumbs through it, stops on a full-page color reproduction of the Medusa head, and tears it out. Rolls it into a tight tube and slips it into his breast pocket.

He pads down the hallway into another, even larger room with canvases on the walls, splatters of paint on the floor, the smell of oil and turpentine heavy in the air. He goes up to a painting and touches it. His fingertips come away stained with pigment, the surface of the painting left with slight indentations. He picks up a brush, uses it to whisk his fingerprints away. Wipes the brush handle with a rag, uses the same rag to clean his fingers, turns it inside out, and stuffs it into his back pocket. He stops a moment to admire a painting of a nude without a face, has to stifle the urge to leave the American a note: *I like this one—finish it!*

A laptop sits on a long wooden worktable, beside it a stack of bills, a checkbook, several notes he cannot read, the American's handwriting an indecipherable scrawl. The trash basket beside the table is small, overflowing, and he stoops to pluck out a half-crumpled piece of paper, attracted by the blue globe insignia, and flattens it onto the table. Now he sees it is the INTERPOL logo and a list of typed names. He thinks of the elegant woman in the domed house and how she told him the men were from

INTERPOL. Could the American possibly be working for INTERPOL, or did this paper belong to the other one, the man he killed? Either way, names on an INTERPOL list are something he needs to check out. He wedges the paper into his pocket behind the tightly rolled Caravaggio picture. Then, he takes the neat stack of bills, envelopes, and checkbook and moves them from one side of the table to the other. No fun if the prey has no inkling that he is being stalked.

88

I started at Dalton. Another fabricated story. This one, that I was writing an article on New York's "best private schools." The headmistress was willing to cooperate. I had done my homework too, knew some of their famous alums, Claire Danes, Anderson Cooper, Chevy Chase, names I could drop along with Alexandra Greene's. "She's become a well-known art historian," I said, though the administrator had never heard of her. I showed her the cell phone picture, one I'd taken of Alex asleep in our hotel bed, cropped to a discreet headshot. The headmistress said she did not recognize her. I made her look again. She said she was absolutely certain, and I believed her. There'd been no telltale tic, no hesitation.

It was the same at Spence.

I was close to giving up by the time I got to Brearley, one of Manhattan's best "white glove" schools for girls.

"It would have been about a decade ago," I said to this headmistress, a woman out of central casting, tight bun and matronly figure.

She said she had been in her position for almost thirty years and did not recall any student named Alexandra Greene, "and I have an excellent memory for all my girls, not that I am at liberty to disclose such information."

I showed her the cell phone photo.

"Oh," she said. Then, "No. I have no idea who that is."

But I'd seen it, the flash of recognition in her eyes, the pause, the change in tone. I wanted to push further but knew it wouldn't help, the woman already saying goodbye, wishing me luck with the article, and leading me out of her office.

Back home, I felt it right away, a palpable sense of invasion, the same feeling I'd had in my Florence hotel room, as if the air had been disturbed, along with the same stale odor of tobacco. I went through the large front room, then into the bathroom, swiping the shower curtain aside, half expecting to find a shrieking Norman Bates. In the studio, I peered in between paint racks, on and under my long worktable. Nothing appeared to be missing. Still, something felt off, papers and envelopes on the left side of my laptop that I could have sworn I always kept on the right—or did I?

I kept looking, but nothing seemed out of place. Had the paranoia I'd felt in the past few weeks become a permanent part of my psyche? Or was it Jonathan Teivel's barely veiled threat: *You feel safe on the Bowery?*

I checked the windows and opened one, all sorts of odors wafting in: booze, garbage, gasoline.

One more tour through the loft produced nothing, so I shrugged it off as paranoia. What else could it be?

I finally sat down at my computer and did the Google search I'd intended to do when I'd first come in. I typed *Brearley yearbooks*, did the math, then typed *2008 and 2009*.

I skimmed the 2008 yearbook, then took my time with the seniors, each girl with her own yearbook page. But no Alex. I did the same for 2009. Again, nothing. I tried 2010, skimmed through alphabetically arranged photos, and stopped at the G's.

No Greene. I was disappointed but kept going, stopped dead at a page of photos. *Alexis Verde.*

Less than a minute to get the connection: *Alexandra Greene. Alexis Verde.*

Verde: the Italian word for *green*.

I went to Facebook, typed in Alexis Verde, and there she was, the small photo unmistakable. But the only way I could see more was to "friend" her, and though I considered it, I knew it was a bad idea.

A little more digging and the internet white pages produced a listing: Alexis Verde, New York City, age 24–30.

I thought about investing in the $9.99 Intelius search, but did I really want to find her when she so clearly did not want to be found?

Alex/Alexis. Who had lied to me about her name and where she had gone to school.

What else had she lied about? And why?

89

Richard Baine Jr. looked to be in his midsixties, about my height with a full head of pure white hair.

When his assistant had called to say she'd relayed my message and her boss would be happy to see me, I thought: *No, I promised Smith I'd give it up.* Then I did a quick Google search, found no background on Baine, other than the fact that he'd created one of Wall Street's most successful investment firms, and I was intrigued.

So much for promises and resolve.

Now I stood in his thirty-eighth-floor office, its cool white walls hung with old master prints, a view of the Chrysler and Empire State Buildings and a wide swath of the Hudson River.

Baine stood behind a marble-topped desk that had nothing on it but a computer, not a single paper, folder, pencil, or pen, everything about the office pristine. The large screen on the opposite wall, rolling market information, was silent.

"So you're a self-made man," I said.

"What makes you say that?" he asked with an affable smile.

"There was just so little background on you. It was as if you were born on Wall Street."

"Not quite." Baine laughed, exposing bright-white teeth. "So you've done some research."

"Doesn't everyone these days?"

"Not me," he said. "I'm from an era when you didn't know anything about a man until you met him, and I prefer that."

I apologized, but Baine waved it off, explained he was semi-retired, "only in the office a day or two a week, mainly to annoy my partners."

I studied one of his prints, an intricately detailed study of hands. "Is this a Dürer?"

"You know your artists."

"I teach art history, so..." I shrugged. "You collect old masters?"

"I used to, but no more. I've donated almost everything."

"And you've lost the desire to acquire more?"

"At a certain age, one no longer feels the need." Baine leaned closer to the print. "Beautiful, isn't it, all that delicate cross-hatching. I've had the Dürer print a long time, and a few others—that Rembrandt my secretary said you asked about. A personal favorite I did not want to give up for sentimental reasons, but my serious collecting days are over. I've come to think of collecting as a selfish man's game." He gave me an earnest look and asked if I collected art.

I told him I couldn't afford it, though I occasionally swapped a piece with an artist friend.

"So you're an artist."

"Well, sort of."

"Don't be modest, young man. I did not get to where I am by being modest." He patted me on the shoulder. "I love talking art with people who know something about it. I studied business, so I knew nothing about art until I started collecting."

"And you don't miss it?"

"Not really. I have a few pieces, and they're enough for me." He smiled again. "So you're writing about Rembrandt?"

"For an academic art journal—um, *Apollo*. It's based in London, very small. I don't suppose you've heard of it," I said and hoped he hadn't.

He said no and was surprised I was writing about Rembrandt, that most people didn't care about him anymore, no matter how synonymous his name was with art.

"I'm one of the people who still thinks Rembrandt is a great artist."

"Then you must have a look at my Rembrandt print. We'll have a drink, and you can tell me all about the piece you're writing—" He stopped, apologized, said he'd forgotten he was leaving for London the day after tomorrow.

I told him that was fine, I could wait until he came back, but he said no.

"I may be gone several weeks, possibly a month. Come by tomorrow evening, six thirty. I'm all set for my trip and will be home with nothing to do."

"I don't want to impose," I said.

"Don't be silly," Baine said and handed me a card with his address.

90

The American exits the building, and the Russian lags behind, shielded by a crowd of men and women, all so rich-looking he can't decide if wants to *be* them or *kill* them. He knows the American has just seen one of the people on the list he has taken from the loft—he's cross-checked the telephone number through a white pages app. Has done a Google search too, knows the man is a financial fat cat, just like the other one, Teivel—whom he followed home from his office after the American left the other day, watched him go into a Park Avenue building with several doormen, all of them nodding.

He knows where Teivel works and lives and now where this Baine guy works. It will not be difficult to find out where Baine lives too.

He watches the red dot move, allows the American a good head start, then follows him into the subway station and onto the subway, maintaining a safe distance, eyeing him through a dozen straphangers. He closes his eyes. Once again pictures the American's loft, the large airy studio and canvases slick with paint. A life so unlike his own, though he sometimes has trouble imagining that his own life is real. A young woman beside him, a girl really, kohl-lined eyes, hair streaked purple, a ring through her nose, keeps falling into him each time the train stops and lurches.

She reminds him of his first job after the war, the young girls he sold to traders, something he could not get away with nowadays with all the do-gooders and international agencies up in arms. What did they know? It was not as if those girls had anything better at home. He has to stop himself from looping a finger through the girl's nose ring and leading her off the train, making her his slave. He smiles at her, but she stares ahead, her earbuds obviously drowning out all surrounding noise, her look blank, transported no doubt by some idiotic tune, which sounds to him like insects chirping.

He looks past the girl and through the crowd to make sure the American is still there. He tugs his hat lower on his forehead, pats his breast pocket, feels the tube he made from the picture he ripped out of the book. He pictures the *Medusa* painting, the slithering snakes and severed neck, all that blood, the look of pure terror. Every job teaches him something. This one, about the artist Caravaggio. Obviously, a kindred spirit.

91

For eight dollars, Intelius, the online public-records search engine, had provided the address on East Thirty-Second Street. It was not at all what I'd expected. I had always pictured Alex in a plush Upper East Side apartment with river views and two or three doormen, not in Murray Hill, a neighborhood that drew students and young people looking for reasonable rents.

I checked the address again to be sure, then made my way to the redbrick midsize building. There was a doorman, but only one. I asked for Alexis Verde, and when he said she was out, I made a show of checking my cell phone and said something about possibly getting the time wrong, then turned and headed down the block, a part of me relieved. I hadn't planned what I would say if she'd been home. At the corner, I stopped and waited.

Ten minutes passed. Then twenty. A part of me wanted to run, but I had to see her, had to know who she was and why she had lied.

I started making a list in my head, why I loved her, or thought I did: her looks, her brains, her wit, her voice, her poise, her touch, the way she seemed to get me. Though it was possible everything had been a lie. The only thing I knew for sure was that I was in thrall to a woman I thought I had known but didn't.

I paced one way, then the other, rehearsing what I'd say, but couldn't concentrate, my emotions all over the place. I kept darting looks around the corner and down the block, hoping to see her, at the same time dreading it.

A half hour later, still trying out a variety of opening sentences, I spotted her coming down the street. I waited until she was a few feet away before I stepped out of the shadows.

"Luke—" She gasped my name, froze a minute, then maneuvered around me and practically ran toward her building, me beside her, talking the whole time.

"Why did you lie to me? I'm trying to understand... I thought... I don't know what I thought... Talk to me, *please*... Explain this—"

"You've got to go!" she said, then dashed into her building.

"I'm not going away," I called after her. "You owe me an explanation."

The doorman blocked my path, a young Latin guy, name tag *Edwin*, chest and arms straining against his tight uniform. He laid a hand against my chest. "Don't make me call the cops, sir."

"Edwin." I turned his name into a plea. "Have you ever been in love?"

He gave me a compassionate look, told me to go home and have a drink. Any other time, I'd have laughed at the irony. I shouted Alex's name one more time, then turned to go. I was a few feet from the entrance when I heard her voice softly call my name.

We were side by side in the elevator, not speaking, then in her apartment. I tried to think of something to say but couldn't. The apartment was not what I'd imagined either—large and airy but with old casement windows, a dining table with mismatched chairs, a slightly worn sofa, wooden floors in need of sanding—a stage set for two actors who had not learned their lines.

"Alex... Alexis... I don't know what to call you."

"This isn't a good idea, Luke."

"Which part? Me being here or all the lies you told?"

"What about *you*? What about *your* lies?"

"I was…trying to protect you."

"From *what*?"

"I didn't want you to get hurt."

"I don't understand…" she said, her face a diagram of confusion. "I was trying to protect *you*."

"Protect *me*?"

"I never meant it to be like this. I didn't think…" She closed her eyes, swallowed, tears on her cheeks, and I pulled her close, my lips on hers before she could protest, and she kissed me back, then pulled away, told me I had to go.

"Not until you tell me what's going on. I'll tell you anything you want to know about me, anything at all, if you will just tell me what's going on."

"It's too late," she said.

"For *what*?"

"For this. For us." She turned away, light from the windows bleaching her face of color. "It was a job—to find out what you were doing—in Florence."

I wasn't sure I'd heard her correctly. A *job*? Had she been spying on me? But why? "Is this about Peruggia's journal?"

She said yes so quietly I could barely hear her, clutched her by the shoulders, forced her to face me, asked *why* again, pleading, furious, my voice trembling.

"I can't tell you," she said, trying to pull out of my grip, but I wouldn't let go.

"You can't—or *won't*?"

"It doesn't matter. Not now. You have to forget this ever happened. Forget *me*."

I wanted to shake her. "It's not just about *you* and *me*, Alex. People *died*. Do you get that? I'd like to forget that, but I can't. I'm going to find out whether you tell me or not. I have a list of names, art collectors who—"

Alex stopped struggling, her face close to mine, prickly with expectation and dread. "Art collectors? What do you mean?"

I told her about Smith's list, the collectors of stolen art, and that I had started contacting them.

"You *what?* You have stop. *Now!*" Her voice pleading, a throb. "Listen to me, this journal—the people you're dealing with—are dangerous, more dangerous than you can imagine."

"And you're working for them, these dangerous people?"

"I... It doesn't matter anymore. Just *stop*."

"It's too late. I've already seen some of them."

"*Who?* What are their names? Tell me their *names*."

"Jonathan Teivel and Richard Baine. Those names mean anything to you?"

She took a quick breath. "No—" she said, the word bitten off.

"You're still lying, aren't you?"

She pulled out of my grip, opened her apartment door, her hand at my back. "Just go!" she said, her last words before she pressed me forward, shut the door, and turned the lock.

92

Down the street, half-hidden under the awning of a tall building, the Russian waits too. Having bought himself a topcoat of the softest wool, he feels like one of the many well-dressed New Yorkers he sees everywhere in the city. Never in his life has he spent so much money for an article of clothing, but the coat, purchased at a post-Christmas sale, was half-price and so soft he cannot stop petting it. "One hundred percent cashmere," the salesman had said. The hat had been on sale too, a gray felt fedora to replace the old one, which was spotted with blood. "Mud stains," he'd said. He bought a new pair of sunglasses too, metallic and reflective; he can see out, but no one could see in.

From behind the shades and under the brim of his new hat, he has been watching, has seen the American and the blond, the two of them going into the redbrick building.

He is getting close. He can feel it. His instincts are always good. Invaluable in his line of work, though he is tired. He needs a break: the beach, that pastel-colored hotel.

But first, he will find the man who tried to kill him and pay him back and, if possible, make him suffer.

93

Alex listened to Luke banging on the door and calling her name. Hands over her ears, she went into her bedroom, sat on the edge of the bed, and stared at the blur of sky outside the windows until he stopped.

She couldn't believe it. He'd found her. What she had hoped for. What she had dreaded. She felt like sobbing, screaming, flailing about her room, but she sat still and silent, wondering what to do.

When she realized she had no choice, that he would find out no matter what, she reached for her cell phone and punched in the number.

"Alexis, dear," the man said, "I have been waiting for your call."

94

I held up two shirts, one blue, one white, not that it mattered. I couldn't concentrate on anything since I'd left Alex, surely not what I should wear to see a Rembrandt print I hadn't cared about in the first place.

I'd found her. Alexandra Green. Alexis Verde.

And she had been spying on me.

The idea of it, that this woman I could not stop thinking about, this woman I thought I loved, even now, was someone hired to watch me.

I chose the blue shirt for no reason, my mind only on Alex—who she was and if she was still lying to me. Of course she was; I'd seen it on her face. But about *what*, exactly? And why hadn't I recognized the lies before? Because I'd been dazzled by her, blinded. Maybe that was all it was, dazzle, not love.

My mind was spinning, looking for an answer, an explanation. I had to know. I wasn't ready to give up or let her go.

I got dressed on autopilot, decided that after I saw the Rembrandt, I would go to her apartment, stand outside all day and all night if necessary. I didn't care how long. I had to convince her to tell me everything, to trust me, even if I could not trust her.

95

Riverview Terrace was a row of six elegant townhouses on a cul-de-sac at the end of East Fifty-Ninth Street, a private drive that ran north from Sutton Square, fronted by a plush, rectangular garden, locked and gated, with spectacular views of the East River and that sculpture in the sky, the Queenboro Bridge—a part of the city I had never seen before. It looked out of another century, and undoubtedly it was. No din of traffic, no cars or buses whizzing by, just the lapping of water and an occasional foghorn.

The iron gate buzzed open, and Baine's voice, hollow through the intercom, instructed me on how to find his house, describing an intricately carved wooden door.

I imagined a servant would answer, but it was Baine, looking a combination of elegant and relaxed in a navy sweater and slacks, Top-Siders on his feet.

I stepped into a foyer of dark wood and marble floors. "I had no idea this neighborhood even existed," I said.

"You can pass it a dozen times and not even know it's here," Baine said. "It's totally hidden from the world, which is why I like it."

Who wouldn't? I took in the wide curving staircase before me, the oak banister and richly carpeted stairs. "You have a beautiful place."

"Thanks," he said, leading me down a hallway lined with ornately painted pottery on pedestals.

"Greek?" I asked.

"You have a good eye. Mid-eighth century. Late Geometric."

"So you *do* still collect."

"Oh, I've had these for centuries. No pun intended." Baine smiled. "Come. This way to the Rembrandt."

He led me into a small study, more dark wood, upholstered chairs, a built-in bookcase, a rug the color of blood. "There," he said, pointing to a heavily framed print set atop an antique desk and leaning against the wall. "Have a look while I get you a drink." He turned to a bar cart with bottles of wine and liquors, crystal glasses in several shapes and sizes.

"You don't hang it?" I asked, moving closer to the print.

"It's been packed away. I brought it out for you."

I told him he shouldn't have bothered, and he said it was no bother at all.

"Wine?" he asked. "Or something more serious? I have a wonderful single-malt scotch."

"Sounds great," I said, "but I don't drink."

"You may want to change your mind." Baine raised the bottle. "Macallan 25, aged twenty-five years. You sure?"

"I'd love to, but no thanks. Water will be fine."

"A shame," Baine said, pouring scotch for himself, Perrier for me. "Here's to art," he said, clinking his glass against mine, then lifted a large bone-handled magnifying glass from the desk, handed it to me, and told me to check out the details.

I moved the glass over the print, the same as I had done with the *Mona Lisa*, with an eerie feeling of déjà vu. There were figures hidden in the trees and clouds, astonishing and beautiful. I told him it was so much better in person, as if I knew the piece.

"That's true of everything, isn't it? Nowadays, people think they know something because they can see it on a computer screen, but

that's no way to see art or the artist's hand, the texture, the paint…
Forgive me, I go on."

I told him I liked hearing someone who was passionate about
art. "I think some of my students prefer seeing a facsimile on their
laptop. It's easier and more convenient—no crowds, no noise."

"I'd have to agree about the crowds and noise. I've stopped
going to museums. I dislike peering over shoulders, hearing
everyone's opinion. That's no way to appreciate art," he said, just
beside me, both of us studying the Rembrandt. "This print is only
one of three that exist in the world today, though I didn't know
that when I bought it. I just admired all the work Rembrandt had
put into it." He faced me. "So tell me about this article of yours."

I started to explain a theory about Rembrandt's way of
working—something I'd lifted off the internet—when there was
the soft thud of a door closing.

"My wife," Baine said and excused himself.

I continued to look at the print but was distracted by voices.
I could make out two, Baine's and a woman's, their conversation
muffled by distance, thick walls, and carpet. It went on for five
minutes, then ten. After another five, I'd had enough and ventured
into the hallway.

Their voices were still indistinct but louder here, and I could
tell they were arguing.

"Leave him out of this," the woman said.

"Sorry," Baine said, "but I can't do that."

I didn't want to be in the middle of a marital spat, but something
in their voices drew me forward. I took a few more steps down the
hall and heard the woman say *"Please."* It was just one word, but
the imploring way she said it was enough to send a chill through
my body.

96

She looked up as I came into the room, lips parted in midsentence. "Oh my God—" Then she blinked slowly as if to make sure what she was seeing was real.

I was trying to take it in too, the unreality of the moment, the room blurring behind the two central characters. A minute to collect my thoughts, to find my voice. "Is this the guy you've been working for?"

"You don't understand," Alex said. "You think you do, but you don't."

"Well," said Baine, "now that we've got that out of the way, let's adjourn to a *less* comfortable setting." He opened a desk drawer and withdrew a small pistol.

Through a buzzing in my ears, I heard fragments of what he said: *Ed Brown Compact...no kickback...fits the hand...under $3,000.*

He aimed the gun at me.

"Let's get down to business, shall we? I need your help with something."

I was still trying to locate my feelings, everything in high relief, Baine's gun, Alex's face, my mind a kaleidoscope of half thoughts and images—torn journal pages, Brother Francesco on a stretcher, dead booksellers. Could Richard Baine possibly be responsible for all that?

"*Please,*" Alex said.

"Stop whimpering," Baine said. "It's beneath you, embarrassing."

"Go to hell!" she said.

"Alex," I said. "Tell me what's going on."

"You will get your answers when I get mine." Baine planted the pistol against my back, urging both Alex and me forward.

"You're insane," Alex said to him.

"Please. No need for name calling, my dear." Baine led us into the hallway, then down a staircase. At the bottom, into an office, telling me where to find the key, how to push the bookcase out of the way and open the vault. When it was open, he ordered us inside and flipped a switch. The room flooded with light. Alex beside me, the two of us gasping in unison. I looked from one artwork to the next, then two *Mona Lisa* paintings, one hanging on the wall, another just beneath it.

"Jesus," Alex said. "I never—"

"No, you never," Baine said. "These are for my eyes only."

It only took a second for me to see the initials in the *Mona Lisa* resting on the floor, a Chaudron forgery for sure.

"All of them stolen?" I asked.

"Not all," Baine said. "Some bartered, others paid for more dearly than you can imagine."

"Oh, I can imagine," I said, thinking again of Brother Francesco, Quattrocchi, and the booksellers. "Tell me, does all this make you happy?"

"You have no idea *how* happy," Baine said, a malevolent smile spreading across his face.

"You have a very good eye," I said. *Keep him talking and wait for the right moment.*

"True," he said. "But enough small talk. I need to know: the two *Mona Lisas*, which is the original?"

"If I knew the answer to that question," I said, "I'd be a rich man."

"But you *do* know. You have the pages from Peruggia's journal, the ones that contain Chaudron's secret."

"No," I said. "You're wrong. Those pages were torn out, but not by me. If you had me watched, you know that."

"Stop—lying!" Baine spit the words, his gun trained on me.

"Shoot," I said, "but you won't get your answer if you do."

"I'm waiting," he said, eyes narrowed, the gun aimed at my heart.

"Killing me won't make any difference," I said, trying to gauge the moment. Could I tackle him without killing myself?

Baine shifted the gun. "How about I kill her instead? Will *that* make a difference?"

"Don't tell him anything," Alex said. "He won't do it."

"Let's see how much he cares for you," Baine said. "Think of it as a test: he loves me, he loves me not."

"You're *sick*," Alex said.

"I'm not the one who slept with him," Baine said, "for *money*."

"Shut up!" she shouted, then quietly to me, "It wasn't like that—"

"So what was it?" I asked her, as if we were alone.

"You don't understand, Luke. I—"

"Please," Baine said, "enough daytime drama." He rolled the gun in a small arc from Alex's head to her heart. "He loves me, he loves me not. Which is it, Luke? I'm running out of patience."

"He *doesn't* love me," Alex said to Baine, as if trying to telegraph what she wanted me to hear—you do *not* love me!

"Beauty for beauty," Baine said, looking from Alex to the two *Mona Lisa* paintings. "A fair exchange."

"He won't do it," Alex said. "Believe me. He *won't*."

"We'll see about that," Baine said.

"Go ahead then," she said. "Do it."

Baine drew the gun closer to her breast, but I saw something in his face—doubt? fear?—and his hand was trembling.

A split second to make the decision, body coiled, ready to leap.

97

"Stay where you are!" Baine cocked the trigger. "Do not make me do this."

I froze; there wasn't enough time. I looked at Baine, then Alex, and caught a look between them, something fraught, but more than that.

"Go on," Alex said to Baine, chest out, challenging him.

"Oh, Alexis, what does it matter now? I lost you so long ago."

"Yes," she said. "You did."

"She still blames me for divorcing her crazy mother," Baine said. "It's absurd. The woman is mad as a hatter."

Alex's slap came fast and hard. Baine didn't flinch, but his cheek bloomed red.

"Your *father*?" I said.

"People find it so hard to understand." Baine shrugged. "But really, what is this parent-child thing, a mass of cells and genes? Any fool can procreate."

"Go on then!" Alex said. "Shoot me! Shoot us both!" She was practically shrieking now, her body trembling. "Is that what you want, the two of us rotting away in your little vault with your dead artists and your dead artworks! Go on then. *Shoot!*"

Baine just sighed and shook his head. "How little you understand about beauty and immortality, Alexis. It's hard to believe you really are my daughter. And such a sweet child you were, all smiles and golden ringlets, and so eager to please." He turned to mc. "Of course, she still is. Not with *me*, not unless it's about money, but *you* saw it, didn't you, Luke, her eagerness to please, to do whatever is *necessary*. Quite effective, isn't she?"

Alex turned to me, tears tracking down her cheeks, and I lunged, tried to wrest the gun from Baine's hand, but he swung it hard into my face and I staggered back, a hand to my cheek.

Alex screamed.

Baine cried, "Watch out! Do not get blood on my paintings!"

I stared at my fingertips, the red, the blood, and it came to me. All he cared about. His paintings. I swiped my bloody hand against an Edouard Manet seascape.

"*Stop!*" Baine shouted.

I yanked the painting off the wall and threw it to the floor, foot hovering inches above it. "The painting or Alex," I said, daring him. *Was he really willing to kill his own child for a roomful of art?* When he said nothing, I brought my foot down hard, grinding it into the canvas. Baine's face went from pain to stone, but he didn't lower the gun from Alex's heart.

"Plenty of Manets in the world," he said with a studied calm, though I could see his hand was shaking. "*Enough*. I want my answer *now*. Which *Mona Lisa* is the original?" He pressed the gun against Alex so hard she let out a cry.

"Wait—" I said. "I'll tell you." I moved quickly to the twin paintings, made a show of looking from one to the other.

Baine was waiting but impatient, the gun twitching in his hand.

"Give me a minute," I said. "I'm trying to find something here."

"Where?" Baine inched closer.

"Something the art forger, Yves Chaudron, put into his copies." I bent down to study the lower painting, peering closely at its surface. "Yes. It's here."

"What is…*where?*"

"Wait…" I glanced up, eyes on the painting above. "Damn. It's in this one too!"

Baine's eyes flicked between the two paintings.

"I hate to tell you," I said, "but you've got *two* fakes."

"No! How can you tell? *Show me.*"

"It's easier to see in this one," I said and bent down, pointing at the spot just below Lisa del Giocondo's hands. "Look for yourself."

Baine kept the gun trained on Alex and leaned over, trying to see what I had pointed out. And in that instant, I bolted up, the top of my head connecting with his jaw. Baine tumbled backward, and his gun fired just as a large silhouette filled the vault's entrance.

98

The intruder's silhouette had taken solid form, the man who had attacked Smith and me in the park. "The gate was easy to pick," he said, a gun in his hand. "You should warn your rich neighbors."

Baine had righted himself and was rubbing his jaw. The Ed Brown Compact had flown out of his hand after firing and lay in a corner of the vault like a small creature playing possum.

Alex, flattened against a wall, held the mangled Manet painting against her chest like a shield.

"Are you okay?" I asked, and she nodded, though she looked pale and unsteady.

The intruder glanced at the two *Mona Lisa* paintings, then at Baine. "I am the one who sent you the second painting. I work for you, or for your middleman, that fool you sent to kill me."

"I have no idea what you're talking about," Baine said.

The intruder smiled, lips pulled back to expose his small, stained teeth. "Your middleman is dead, but I have his cell phone, with your number on it. I do not think you want to play games with me."

Baine gave a bored shrug. "How much do you want?"

"Not money," he said.

"What else is there? Art?"

"I am here for your life." He took a step, thrust the gun into Baine's gut hard enough to make him double over.

As he did, I lunged for the Ed Brown, got it, and aimed it at the intruder.

"You shoot me and I shoot this pig," he said, his weapon still aimed at Baine. "But I am used to shooting and you are not. I will manage one more shot, and you will die too."

I cocked the gun.

Alex cried out, "Luke...no!"

The intruder aimed his gun.

Baine lunged, grabbing hold of the guy's arm. Baine lunged, grabbing hold of the guy's arm, but the guy fired, once, twice, and Baine fell. But the gun fell too, just enough time for me to fire, and I did, again and again, until the gun was out of bullets.

It was only then that time normalized and I could see what had happened: Baine in a corner gripping his shoulder, the intruder on the floor, blood leaching out of his head and chest, Alex against the wall, her eyes shut tight. A moment later, she dropped the Manet painting, toppled forward, and I raced to catch her.

I saw it now. A bullet had torn through her sweater, a spot of dark maroon spreading.

"Oh no! God no!" Baine cried, crawling toward her.

"It was...*your* bullet," she said. "You...who killed me, *Father*."

"No...no... I never would have done it... It was just a threat... a game."

"A *game*?" Alex laughed, a bubble of blood bursting at her lips. "Go to...hell."

Baine curled up in the corner, clutched his shoulder, and whimpered.

I got my arms around Alex, noticed for the first time that I'd been hit, a sleeve of my blue shirt streaked with blood, but I hardly felt it and didn't care. I held Alex, told her not to talk, that she'd be okay.

She whispered my name, "Luke," asked me to hold her, to talk to her. "Tell me anything," she said.

I held her tight and started talking. "Remember how the librarian was always telling us to be quiet, and the Duomo lit up at night, so beautiful and…" I stopped, choked up, couldn't think.

"Please…don't…stop…" She gripped my arm.

"Hang on," I said. "You're going to be fine."

"Please," she said, "keep…talking."

"Yes," I said and joked about the plague book she'd been reading and slid the cell phone from my pocket and dialed 911, told them where we were as another image slid across my brain: Vincent in the back of a taxi, holding Simone and singing while she coughed blood and begged him not to stop.

Alex's face had gone white, her lips purple. I kept talking—about the café where we'd first had coffee and the fancy hotel where we had spent our first night—but by then, Alex's grip had loosened, she'd gone slack in my arms, and I knew she could no longer hear me.

99

The day was chilly but there were hopeful signs of spring, trees starting to bloom, crocuses making their way up through patches of earth, the sky a sharp cerulean blue, the sun strong. I had over an hour and wanted to walk, to think. So much time had passed, and I was still trying to make sense of things and how I felt. I headed north up the Bowery past Cooper Union, its old buildings in sharp contrast to the new modern one, something I'd been thinking about a lot lately—the past and the present. There was construction on every other street, adding to the noise in my head as I made my way uptown, though I still arrived early.

It was just past lunchtime, the café half-empty. I chose a booth in the back, ordered coffee, and passed the time checking my phone, reading and rereading emails so that when Alex said, "Hi," I was startled to look up and see her.

She took a seat opposite, removed her silk scarf, and unbuttoned her jacket.

"You look well," I said, measuring my words. I wanted to say *You look so beautiful*, and she did. Though something had changed, something knowing and open in her expression, almost as if I were seeing the real Alex for the first time.

She ordered a cup of tea and waited until the waitress was gone. "You shaved," she said. "I can see your face."

"Is that a good thing?"

"Yes," she said, then looked down.

I hadn't seen her since that night she'd been shot almost four months ago, and though I had called the hospital every day, had gone there on three separate occasions, she had refused to see me, until now.

I asked how she was feeling.

"I'm fine now," she said. "The bullet grazed my lung, but you know that. It looked a lot worse than it was." She laid her hand over her breast as she spoke, then took it away as if the gesture was too intimate. "The surgeon told me I was lucky..." She paused, thanked me for coming to the hospital, asked about my arm, which had totally healed, then said, "I'm sorry that I didn't, couldn't see you, but—"

"I'm just glad you're okay," I said.

She thanked me again and let out a breath. "I want to say that I'm sorry, that I..." She shook her head and fell silent as if she'd run out of words or had reconsidered what she'd been about to say, then painted on a smile. "Enough about me. What have you been doing?"

"Oh, right," I said. "You don't know."

"Know what?"

"That I returned it—the *Mona Lisa*."

"*What?*" She leaned toward me.

I leaned forward too, wanted to touch her face, to kiss her, but held back, strained to keep my emotions in check while I told her what happened.

"You understand this is not for public consumption. None of this can be repeated," I said and asked for her word.

"Yes, I swear."

I decided to trust her, because in fact, I was bursting to tell her. "I went to Paris—to the Louvre—explained everything, showed them the evidence, and gave them back the original. That's the short version. It was a bit more complicated. I worked through INTERPOL, had an analyst and an inspector along with me. I'll tell you all about it another time." The words *another time* echoed in my head, and I kind of hoped there would be one. "But it worked out really well for my friend, Smith, the analyst. He was reinstated, even got a big promotion, but that's another story."

"You have *friends* at INTERPOL? I always knew you were a spy," she said and laughed, then stopped. "So you're telling me you found the original painting and returned it to the Louvre, that the *Mona Lisa* that has been in the museum all these years was a *fake?*"

I nodded.

"And the original was—*where?* How did you find it?"

"It was…" I paused, couldn't help dragging out the moment. "Hanging on the wall in your father's vault."

"*What?* Wait… So you lied to him that day?"

I nodded again.

"Wow," she said, was quiet a moment, then, "Promise me something."

"Anything."

"That my father will never find out he had the original. I don't want him to have the satisfaction of knowing that."

"He won't hear it from my lips."

"Nor mine," she said and sat back, shaking her head. "So you won't get any credit for this major discovery?"

"No," I said. "We made a promise to the museum. Only the Louvre and INTERPOL know the truth. All the documents, everything, are sealed. For all I know, shredded."

"Wow," she said again. "Well, I'll never breathe a word of it."

"You can't. Not even at your father's trial."

"I promise," she said. "But there won't be a trial."

"What do you mean? Why not?"

"He probably spent a day in jail, if that. I'm sure he's out on bail, though I don't really know. I haven't spoken to him, and I don't intend to, not ever." She sucked in a breath, let it out slowly.

I told her we didn't have to talk about it if it was too difficult, and she said it was okay, that she wanted to talk.

"So why no trial?" I asked.

"He'll be long gone before that ever happens."

"Isn't he wearing one of those ankle things?"

"Oh, I'm sure he's paid someone to wear it for him by now. He has money hidden in accounts all over the world. He'll simply disappear."

"At least all his stolen paintings were returned."

"Yes," she said, "that's something."

We were both quiet.

I wanted to tell her how much I cared for her, ask if she'd ever cared for me, but I didn't say either, afraid to hear her answer. Instead, I asked, "How's your mother doing?"

Alex took a moment. "She's why I did it... You know that?"

I nodded. I had figured that out.

"My fath—Baine, threatened to put her in a dreadful state facility, and..." She took a breath, held it a moment. "It doesn't excuse anything, I know that. But everything Baine paid me I put in an account for her care. I've prepaid the facility for the next two years, which is something. After that...well, I have time to figure it out."

"That's great," I said, and she nodded, running a finger under the chain that held her locket, a thin gold line against her cream-colored skin, like the painting I'd been making of her.

"So why Verde?" I asked.

"It's my mother's maiden name. My father left when I was a kid. There was no reason to use his—" She stopped, then softly,

"Look, I have to say it. I'm *sorry*, Luke. For everything. I never thought, never imagined—"

I was sorry too and said so. I had rehearsed this moment a dozen times, the things I wanted to say, but they no longer seemed to matter, and *sorry* was enough.

Alex nodded, brightened a bit, asked what else was going on with me, and though I was a lot less interested in talking about myself, I wanted to keep her there, so I told her I was painting again and how different the work was from what I'd been doing before. "I've even had a few dealers over, and one of them is interested in giving me a show when I get a body of work together, which may take a while but—"

"You see," she said. "I told you once that you had nothing to worry about, that you'd get another gallery, remember?"

I said I did and remembered thinking that even then, she seemed to believe in me and how much it had meant to me. "I think I asked if you were a witch."

"No comment," she said but smiled and said she was happy I was painting again.

I told her how I felt I was onto something new and how I just wanted to keep painting and see where it led. She leaned in, and I could see she was really listening. I wanted to tell her everything about my new paintings because I wanted her to respect me, to be proud of me, something I'd never had when I was young and had worked so hard to get and had almost lost. I thought of Peruggia, how Simone had believed in him and his art when no one else did, and how, when she died, she had taken that belief with her, and the loss had driven him to lie and steal.

"A friend told me that you never know what will get you working again, what will *fuel* you." What Smith had said to me, something I'd almost forgotten, and he was right.

"That's great to hear," Alex said. "Are you back to teaching?"

"Yes, and that feels better too." And it was true. I'd been enjoying it, feeling like I really knew my subject and wanted to be there. "It's sort of funny," I said. "I now see the mystery in art history and think I convey some of that to my students."

"Now there's a good course title, 'The *Mystery* in Art History.' It even rhymes."

I smiled then fell silent, and so did she. There were so many things I wanted to say that I could almost feel the words at the back of my throat, but I wasn't sure Alex would want to hear them.

"I'm glad you're doing well," she finally said.

"And what about you?"

"I have a lot to sort out."

"I'm sure you will," I said.

She thanked me, started to get up, and I said, "Stay, *please*," no longer caring if I sounded needy.

She sat, tentative. "I'm thinking about going away."

"Oh? For how long?"

"Until I'm…healed."

"I thought you were."

"I'm not talking about my lung. I just need…more time. I have to be here for my mother, so it won't be long."

I was happy to hear that much, though I wanted to say, *And what about me? What about us?*

Alex stood.

"Wait—" I couldn't control the urgency in my voice. "There are…things to say."

She sat again but perched as if ready to flee.

"Nothing bad," I said. "Just something I've been thinking about."

"Okay," she said, chewing her lower lip, like she was expecting me to say something accusatory or terrible.

For a moment, my mind went blank, all the thoughts, all the rehearsed sentences, gone. Instead, a question formed in my mind, something I had been thinking about since I'd come home. "Would you say the past influences the present, or the present influences the past? I mean, what we discover about the past, does that influence our present, who we are now, or is it the reverse?"

"Very philosophical," she said, and the worry on her face eased. She tapped a finger to her chin. "I'd guess I'd say it's a little of both." She was quiet a moment, looked away, then back at me. "There's something I've been thinking about too, something I want to ask *you*."

I waited, those few seconds some of the longest in my life.

"Can we ever *forget* the past? What was said and done. Get past it. Get *over* it?"

"Yes," I said, relieved, and reached for her hand. "I know I can."

Alex didn't say anything, just let out a breath as if she'd been holding it in for a very long time. Then she gently wrapped her fingers around mine.

THE SOUTH OF FRANCE

Summer had come early this year, the middle of May, the sky a hazy blue, the sun strong and hot. Simon crept through tall purple irises and grass so new and green it looked fake. Vincent watched, sweat on his face and arms, soaking the back of his shirt. He had finished clearing logs from the house into the small shed he'd built so that he and Marguerite and the boy would have more room. Now he watched the boy, just three months shy of his third birthday, make his way across the lawn with intent, then saw what it was that had captured the toddler's attention: a frog, leaping away each time the boy reached out to snatch it, each time failing and falling onto his side, laughing as if it tickled. Vincent laughed too.

Somehow, he had done it, gotten past the grief. He had not forgotten Simone—no way he ever would or could, nor did he want to—but he had moved forward.

He watched again as Simon lunged at the frog, missed again, tumbled and giggled, then another leap and grab, this time getting hold of the frog, which struggled in his hand. "Ooh!" Simon cried and looked back at Vincent, his arm outstretched to show off his prize. "Look!"

"Good catch," Vincent said.

Simon cooed, the sun dappling his cheeks and bringing out the gold in his hair. Then, very consciously and deliberately, he opened his hand and watched the frog leap away.

"Go, frog," he said. "Go!"

Vincent nodded and smiled. "Good boy," he said, thinking how it was all in the game, in the chase and the capture. He thought of his time in prison, a memory starting to fade, as if it had happened to someone else. He thought of the promises he had made too, especially the one to Simone, that he would bring her the painting, a foolish promise that no longer mattered. What mattered was his last promise—to be happy—and he had kept it.

He pictured Simone pirouetting, her wide skirt lifting above her ankles, her luminous smile.

Simon took his time getting to his feet, somewhat unsteady, arms reaching up, and Vincent lifted him from the grass and held him, Simon gazing up at him with *her* face, Simone's face. Then the boy threw his arms around Vincent's neck. "Papa," he said, and Vincent felt his heart opening so wide he thought it might burst. He hugged the boy, who nestled in the crook of his neck, looked past his golden curls to the stone house he had bought and refurbished, the bushes and shrubs he had planted, finally starting to bloom. He was no longer the immigrant, the drifter, the man without an identity. He was home now, a man with his son.

AUTHOR'S NOTE

What you have just read is based on a true story.

These are the facts:

Vincent Peruggia, a one-time Louvre employee, stole the *Mona Lisa* from the museum on August 21, 1911. The details of the theft have been reenacted in the opening scene—how Peruggia spent the night in a museum closet, removed the painting from the wall, and left the frame and box he himself had constructed in a hallway—all this based on reports of the crime.

The newspaper stories about the theft have been taken from actual articles.

It is also true that Peruggia hid the painting in a specially designed trunk in his apartment and that he attempted to ransom the painting to the Italian government at the Uffizi Museum, where he was arrested and sent to Murate Prison, in Florence, Italy.

After the theft, the Louvre Museum did close for a week and was searched by sixty policemen.

All the rewards mentioned in the novel are true: the Louvre posted a reward of 25,000 francs, as did the two newspapers, *Le Matin*, which offered 5,000 and *L'Illustration*, which offered 40,000.

The artist Pablo Picasso, along with the poet and art critic Guillaume Apollinaire, were suspected of the crime, brought in for questioning regarding the theft, interrogated, even tried, but eventually freed.

Both the Marquis Eduardo de Valficro and the art forger Yves Chaudron were real people, both suspected of playing a part in the crime, though this was never proved. Of their ending, little is known.

A vandal really did toss acid at the *Mona Lisa*, and another threw a rock; both incidents occurred in 1956 and caused some damage to the painting, though not serious.

Many forgeries (one might call them "variations") of Leonardo's *Mona Lisa* exist.

More than one art historian has speculated that Leonardo's *Mona Lisa* in the Louvre Museum could possibly be a forgery, switched at the time of the infamous theft (or even before, which would mean that Vincent Peruggia stole a forgery only to replace it with *another* forgery; see newspaper article on page 52). These bits of conjecture and doubt are what inspired my story.

READING GROUP GUIDE

1. How do you define art? What would you say makes a masterpiece?

2. Art theft and forgery are complicated and fascinating crimes. Why would someone prefer to own a masterpiece (which must be kept secret) rather than viewing it in a museum? Is forgery an art unto itself?

3. Had you heard of Vincent Perrugia's theft of the *Mona Lisa* before reading the book? What else did you learn while reading?

4. Early on, Luke seems to have a different sense of time than the Italians around him and is told to be more patient. How do American values contribute to impatience? How can we slow down in our daily lives?

5. John Washington Smith decides against using official INTERPOL channels when Luke's communications with Quattrocchi first catch his attention. Why did he want to pursue the matter personally? What were the consequences of his decision?

6. Describe Alex. What does she want? Do you think she is justi-
    fied in doing what she does?

7. While posing as an art dealer, Smith suggests that buying and
    selling art doesn't contribute to the betterment of mankind. Do
    you agree? How do monetary transactions shape our ideas of
    artistic and social value?

8. Vincent resists becoming involved in the theft for a long time.
    What finally convinces him to steal the *Mona Lisa*? How does
    economic inequality perpetuate crime?

9. Smith describes making and collecting art as an addiction. Do
    you think his viewpoint is supported by the events of the book?
    Can you think of any real-world examples that prove him right?

10. Chaudron is meticulous in his forgeries, but he can't resist sign-
    ing them. What do you think motivates him to endanger his
    work, even subtly? Would you take such a risk in his position?

11. What drives Luke to break his long record of sobriety? How
    does it compare to his temptation in Florence?

12. Why does Luke keep digging after he returns to New York?
    Would you have been so persistent in his place?

A CONVERSATION WITH THE AUTHOR

How did you first hear about Vincent Peruggia's theft of the *Mona Lisa*?

I was reading a pamphlet about the history of the Louvre museum, and it was mentioned in one sentence, but it stayed with me and captured my imagination: the idea that someone actually stole the *Mona Lisa* right out of the museum!

Do you think your interpretation of events could be the truth?

I based as much as I could on facts—newspaper articles about the theft and art historians who had various theories—but when it comes down to it, what I love most is to invent stories and scenarios that *might* have been.

Luke and Smith have an unusual partnership. Was there anything in particular that inspired their wary trust and reliance on each other?

At first, their relationship is based on need; they cannot get what they want or succeed alone. After a while, they start to respect each other's intelligence and dedication. I thought a lot about these two men, how they came from tough backgrounds and had to create themselves, become new people, something many of us do to move forward, sometimes to survive. I saw that as an eventual bond between them, seeing something of themselves in the other person. To me, that is one of the most important human qualities: the ability to empathize with others.

You're an artist and replicator yourself. How did your experiences in that realm shape the book?

Having gone to art school and being a painter helped me understand Luke and his desires as well as those of the art forger in the book, Yves Chaudron.

I have been painting replications of known artworks for art collectors for over two decades. Though I would never try to pass them off as forgeries, I do my best to make exact copies while abiding by the legal guidelines concerning art replication: I change the size or medium, I use contemporary art supplies that would be detected under scientific scrutiny, and I always sign MY name on the back. Making "fakes" has given me tremendous insight into the world of art forgery, how you sort of slip into the skin of the artist whose work you are replicating and how exciting it is to have this finished painting that looks exactly like that famous Picasso or Manet, but *you* made it.

When my daughter was about ten, she asked why I didn't just sell my reproductions as the originals. I explained why it was illegal to replicate other people's artwork and try to pass it off as your own. She understood but still thought I should try to sell my copy as the real thing!

What are the most common misconceptions about forgery and replication of famous masterpieces?

I think most people believe art forgeries are easily detected, but that's not true. Many forgers elude detection for decades, fooling museums, auction houses, and experts. Eventually, they make a mistake (like accidentally using a pigment that was not invented until a few years *after* the painting they are forging), and that's it—they get caught. There are many forgeries in well-known art collections and museums all over the world, awaiting detection.

How do you build your characters? Do any of your friends or acquaintances make their way onto the page?

For me, characters come to life on the page. I have an idea about a character, but I don't really know who they are until I start writing them. Then I have to think about how they look, how they talk, what motivates them. And they change all the time. I'm always rereading and thinking, *So and so would never say that*. Some of my friends and their attributes do sneak in, but for the most part, my characters become themselves, and I tend to think of them as real people who actually exist. If anyone, they might all have a little bit of me in them, as I am the one writing/creating them.

Which of the characters do you most relate to? Did you have a favorite to write?

In this book, I am closest to Luke. He's the younger, taller, handsomer, smarter, more talented me. Although whoever I am writing at the moment tends to be my favorite. And I love writing bad guys and psychopaths, because I'm always trying to see what makes them tick. Awful people are so much fun on the page and so awful in real life!

Smith describes private collectors as thieves keeping art away from the rest of the world. Do you agree with him?

No. It made sense for his INTERPOL character to think like that, but most art collectors I know are people who love art and want to fill their lives with it. If I could afford it, I'd do the same.

How can art be shared most equitably?

Museums are great equitable places, public warehouses that take care of masterpieces big and small. I was just in NYC's Metropolitan Museum of Art, and it's one of the best places in the world. You can spend the day imagining yourself in ancient armor or walk around the Egyptian Temple of Dendur or look at Impressionist paintings—any art you desire is there.

But there are many kinds of "art." You can frame a block of stamps (as I did with a recent Marvin Gaye stamp), put it on the wall, and it looks amazing and only cost the price of the stamps.

The layers of surveillance make the plot nerve-racking, even when Luke's research is taking its time to progress. How do you balance suspense and frustration in your pacing?

A character's frustration has nothing to do with a book's pacing, which is a separate thing that you, the author, control. The reader is thinking *Hurry up, Luke*, because they're ahead of him and worried, which is what you want because it ratchets up the suspense.

Do you have any advice for aspiring authors, especially those interested in history and thrillers?

I always say *read*. Things come to you when you're reading that might not otherwise. Plus, you learn from other writers. If you want to write thrillers, read a lot of them and dissect a couple to see how the author constructed the plot. The same with historical novels. My initial inspiration for writing this book came from two novels, *Possession* and *The French Lieutenant's Woman*. Of course I read so many crime novels that a part of my brain is always thinking *Where is the mystery?* And in any book, I need to know *What is the "engine" that is driving this story?*

ACKNOWLEDGMENTS

My thanks to Shana Drehs for her faith, astute editing, and ease, along with Molly Waxman, Kirsten Wenum, the talented art department, and the rest of the extraordinary Sourcebooks Landmark team. My friends SJ Rozan, Janice Deaner, Tolga Ornek, and Joyce Carol Oates for their feedback. For providing beautiful refuge when I needed it, Susan Crile, Jane Rivkin, and Margo Alexander. For encouraging me to take the trip back to Florence, my daughter, Doria, who encourages and inspires me every day. Judd Tully for introducing me to Lorenzo Pezzatini, who was not only great company but got me into Le Murate prison, and to Valentina Gensini, the director of *le Murate Progetti Arte Contemporanea Florence*. For being my personal Italian translator, Vito Racanelli. Parts of this book were written (and rewritten) at the Writers Room, NYC, and at Yaddo, the best place any artist could ever hope to be. And with special thanks and gratitude to my agent and tireless editor, Jane von Mehren.

ABOUT THE AUTHOR

Jonathan Santlofer is a writer and artist. His debut novel, *The Death Artist*, was an international bestseller, and his novel *Anatomy of Fear* won the Nero Award for best crime novel of 2009. Jonathan created the Crime Fiction Academy at the Center for Fiction. As an artist, he has been making replications of famous paintings for private collectors for more than twenty years.